Praise for Lori L. Lake's previous novels

Lavender Magazine:
"Considered one of the best authors of modern lesbian fiction, her work—part action, part drama, and part romance—gleefully defies categorization."

Jean Stewart, author of *Emerald City Blues* and the *ISIS* series:
"This is the best book about police officers I've ever read. Lori Lake takes us to a world where just doing your job requires putting your life on the line at a moment's notice. The brave, skilled women of *Under The Gun* are an inspiration and a revelation. And who would have thought that for tough, intimidating, super-cop Dez Reilly, opening her heart to Jaylynn Savage would be the most frightening experience of all?"

M.J. Lowe, reviewer for *Midwest Book Review:*
"Lake's *Gun Shy* is the story of two somewhat reluctant women who finally learn to believe in themselves and each other enough to commit to love. Covering just over a year in the lives of these women, the novel reads like a season's worth of episodes from a television show that lesbians might wish was on TV... *Gun Shy* is an engaging, readable book... The characters are interesting and the action drew this reader into the story. Amusingly, Lake seems to have created two lesbians that are the antithesis of the standard U-haul joke."

Marianne K. Martin, author of *Mirrors, Love in the Balance,* and *Legacy of Love:*
"I am thrilled to see a writer like Lake take the risk, leave formula and genre restrictions behind, and be willing to put in the hard work necessary to put forth a truly creative product. Lake continues to grow and mature in her craft and is poised to guide the characters she has sent out into the world through the grappling necessary for their own maturity."

Ronald L. Donaghe, reviewer for *Foreword Magazine* and author of *Common Sons* and *Cinátis:*

"As she did with *Ricochet in Time*, author Lori L. Lake writes with authority—this time about police training and procedures, the day-to-day rigors of being a St. Paul police officer, and the myriad human conditions police officers must cope with in the line of duty. That is the backdrop of this most absorbing story of two police-women... *Gun Shy* is a multilayered work, and just when you think you've got characters and situations figured out, the author throws you a curve. Be prepared for a nice ride, then look forward to *Under The Gun*, which will continue this story of these two fascinating women."

Lesbian Worlds:

"Complicated familial relationships, extended families, friends, legal rights of gay and lesbian couples, the court system, homophobia, and more are all dealt with deftly in this volume, in a manner so natural that at no time does it seem heavy-handed... *Ricochet In Time* is a story that both shares important wisdom, as well as provides some entertaining hours of reading."

Midwest Book Review:

"Lori Lake is one of the best novelists working in the field of lesbian fiction today."

Different Dress

Lori L. Lake

Regal Crest Enterprises, LLC

Nederland, Texas

ISBN 1-932300-08-2

First Printing 2003

9 8 7 6 5 4 3 2 1

Cover design by Talaran

Published by:

Regal Crest Enterprises, LLC
PMB 210, 8691 9th Avenue
Port Arthur, Texas 77642-8025

Find us on the World Wide Web at
http://www.regalcrest.biz

Printed in the United States of America

Musical Lyric Permissions

All song lyrics copyright to Lori L. Lake except:

Go by Kristen Schuldt from the CD "Glad Game"
© 2001 Hydraulic Woman Music
Used with Permission

Acknowledgments

Warmest thanks to my "First Editor," Day Petersen, for advice and encouragement, and to my official editor, Barb Coles, for all the hard work on this long manuscript. For insightful early critiques, credit goes to: Carrie Carr, Betty Crandall, Linda Daniel, Nann Dunne, Karen "Kas" King, Joyce McNeil, Kim Miller, Sulli Sullivan, Jan Trumbo, and everyone at Carrie's Crossing. Gratitude for proofing and galley reviews to: Ruth Boetzel, Carrie Carr, Betty Crandall, Linda Daniel, Nann Dunne, Betty Harmon, Reagan Hnetka, Marilyn Jacaway, Kim Miller, Maureen Shaffer, and my judicious buddy Norma.

I cannot thank Talaran enough for the gorgeous book cover—what a knockout! Special thanks to Kristen Schuldt for "Go" and for all the musical inspiration over the years. I am very grateful to Kim Miller for the New Mexico assistance (especially the lizards and hot sauce!), and *gracias* to Carmen "Packer" Rodriguez for sound advice regarding my rusty Spanish. Thanks to Lindsay Bullard for standing in the wings, always ready to give me helpful medical information and diagnoses. Best love and hugs to Angela Reese, my talented "Websister" who created and maintains my website.

I owe Sulli Sullivan big time for letting me watch her work backstage and for sharing details critical to the authenticity of my fictional tour. Hugs and lifelong appreciation to Emily Saliers and Amy Ray for allowing me a behind-the-scenes view of a real-life tour, and to the Indigo Girls' tour manager, Matt Miley, and his crew for all the technical information.

As always, Diane is last on the list, but first in my heart. Thanks for making it possible for us to achieve so many of our dreams.

Lori L. Lake
August, 2003

Dedicated to Kristen Schuldt
Who brought me back to the music
All those years ago

Chapter
One

KIP GALVIN PERCHED on a wooden bench in the dark in front of Professor Java's Coffeehouse. She tried to pretend she cared two cents about the chatter coming from the young men standing before her. *Why is it that I never really get a break from performing? Next time I'll camp out in the bathroom for the entire twenty minutes!*

She could tell the topic of conversation was about to change, so she held up a hand. "Uh, guys? Give me a few minutes here, will you? I need to get my head together to go back in and play."

"Oh, sure."

"Yeah, no sweat. We understand."

The two men backed away, leaving her to rub her aching temples. A headache had come and gone all day, and though it had lifted some since she'd started singing, a nagging rhythm still beat irregularly in her head.

She rose and looked through the open door into the shop. With the overhead lights off, the coffeehouse was dim in the back by the stage, illuminated only by a table lamp in the corner and a couple of wall lamps near the eight tables scattered around the room. The air smelled of cinnamon and sweet chocolate. Two dozen twenty-somethings sat drinking hot chai, coffees, and espresso as they waited for the evening's entertainment to return from intermission. Though it was mid-June, the Minnesota weather was not yet overly warm, and the patrons sat comfortably without air conditioning in the back of the shop.

When Kip returned to the stage and picked up her Gibson guitar, the small crowd gave her a hand. "Let 'er rip," someone called out. She grinned at the encouragement and plopped down on the tall stool to begin the second set.

"No time like the present to trot out a new song. Here's one called 'Upside Down.'" She settled the guitar, found her starting chord, and picked a brisk arpeggio, then sang:

The world is upside down, spinning 'round, spinning 'round
If you don't know where you're going, you never will arrive
When no one seems to care
If you live, if you die...

The folksinger sang in a rich and easy voice with her eyes closed. Dressed in brown sandals, blue jeans, and a white Math Masters t-shirt, she looked thirty, but lately had taken to saying she was "pushing forty." Her curly, light brown hair framed a pale face with high cheekbones and intelligent gray eyes. When the song finished, the crowd clapped enthusiastically and someone called out, "Play the Lacey Leigh Jaxon song."

Kip wouldn't admit it out loud, but she was getting tired of the song. For one thing, "Wyoming" was being overplayed on the radio. For another, everywhere she went, people wanted her to sing and play it, but they wanted to hear it how Lacey Leigh Jaxon did it, not the way Kip had originally written it. Lacey Leigh had kicked up the tempo and made it much peppier than Kip had intended. "Wyoming" was, after all, more of a lament than a pop tune.

"I wrote this song as a ballad," she said into the microphone. "The original version is a little different from what you hear on the radio. Still want to hear it?"

When the coffee-drinking crew clapped and yelled, "Yes!" she started picking the background melody.

To be honest, she liked it much better as a dirge, for that was what it was. She'd written the song last summer while driving home to Minnesota from Yellowstone National Park. She hadn't actually been driving when she wrote it, but the inspiration for the song came from the miles she covered when she left the East Entrance of the park and navigated the twists and turns of the many mountain passes. She was alone—though the vacation had originally been planned with her partner. She had no way of knowing that between April, when they made the arrangements, and the end of June, they would break up and Bren would leave her. Accommodations were already paid for, and her teaching job was done for the summer, so she took the trip anyway. But on the way home, there was a time when she'd actually considered just steering the old Chevy Silverado over the cliff and ending it all.

As she steered slowly from one switchback to another, tears coursing down her face, a refrain kept popping into her head. Pretty soon, she pulled over into a Scenic Overlook and wrote out the words on the back of the Triple A Trip-Tik. For good measure, she got out of the truck, opened up the back canopy, and took out her guitar. Sitting on the open tailgate, she worked out the chords and cemented the words and melody in her head. Later, halfway down one of the Big Horn Mountains, staring out across a canyon at a snow-covered peak, she decided that, with or without Bren, life was probably worth living.

She traveled the rest of the way home without incident and spent the remainder of the summer doing what she was doing right now—playing in coffee shops around the Twin Cities and Wisconsin border area. At the end of the summer, she and five other area musicians got together and laid down tracks for their favorite songs. She sang backup harmonies and played guitar for others' songs, and in return, she'd gotten bass, drums, piano, and some lead acoustic guitar on her tracks. Unbeknownst to her, Bill Brett, one of the biggest flakes of the group, had taken "Wyoming" and sent it off to a friend, who knew a friend, who knew a concert promoter. Next thing Kip knew, some guy was calling to ask if he could pay her five thousand dollars and royalties to let his singer record her song.

It came from out of the blue, but it seemed like a good idea at the time. She had an attorney look over the paperwork, and everything squared up, so she signed. The check came, and with money to spare, she'd bought a new amp, a portable soundboard, and two PA speakers. Now, wherever she played, she could adjust to the surroundings and make it sound quite good. Tonight, in Professor Java's, the tone and clarity of the performance were just right. That was probably one of the reasons her headache had gotten better.

She finished the song to hearty applause and went on to sing long past the contracted two hours. She didn't mind, though. There was little she enjoyed more than to entertain, to tell stories about the songs, to share her own special take on the craziness of the world. She had no one to go home to—not even a dog, since Bren had taken Ozzy with her when she left. Now, after a year, Kip was used to it. She had grown to enjoy the quiet time, the peace at her silent house. After a day of dealing with rowdy seventh graders, it was nice to come home to a place where everything was exactly as she had left it.

She finished her set, did two encores, and then said good night, much to the consternation of the coffeehouse audience. Some of them helped her pack up her gear and stow it in the back of the truck—another thing she appreciated at these informal gigs. She shook a few hands, sold and autographed six of her self-produced CDs, and then she was on the way home.

DURING THE SCHOOL year, Kip was in bed by nine and up at five a.m. Once summer arrived, she liked to sleep in, especially on nights she played a gig. Tonight, the ride home from Hastings, where Professor Java's was located, gave her thirty minutes to wind down. By the time she arrived at her house in St. Paul, she felt good and tired. She pressed the button for the automatic garage door, waited for it to open, then pulled in, careful to stay clear of the motorcycle leaning on its kickstand on the left side of the garage. Looking at her watch as she got out, Kip noted it was after midnight. She lifted the back hatch of the Silverado canopy and started to drop the tailgate, then decided to let it all go until morning. Once it was closed up, she went to the house entrance and shut the garage door. Wearily, Kip opened the door that led into her home, locked up, and went upstairs to get ready for bed.

It wasn't until mid-morning the next day that Kip checked her answering machine. She'd already had coffee, read the paper, and cleaned up the breakfast dishes before she thought to go into the den and look at the flashing red light. She pressed the recall button and recognized the voice of her good friend Mary.

"Kip! Kip, where are you? I've got exciting news. I just heard your song on MPR! Public Radio! Have you heard it yet? Did you know about this? Call me! Call me!"

What song? Lacey Leigh Jaxon's version? On Minnesota Public Radio? Well, that doesn't make any sense. Kip grabbed the phone and dialed Mary's number from memory, waiting with curiosity for her friend to pick up. Instead, she got an answering machine, but before she could leave a message, someone was beating on her front door and hollering, "Kip, Kip!"

The musician hung up. *No need to leave a message for a woman who is already here.* Puzzled, but laughing to herself, she hustled over to the door and opened it.

Mary tumbled in, speaking a hundred words a minute.

"Whoa! Whoa! Slow down, Mar. What's up?"

Mary's brown eyes were wide with excitement, and she spoke quickly as though she was out of breath. "I heard your song on the folk program on MPR last night, and then I tuned in to the local country station, and I heard it again—twice in four hours."

"Wait a minute. Here, come in the kitchen." Kip turned and Mary followed her. They went into the dining area next to the kitchen as Mary excitedly restated what she had already said, then lowered herself into a wooden chair at the table. Kip stepped over to the counter and took a mug down from the cupboard. "You want coffee, right?"

Mary nodded. "Love some. Lots of—"

"I know, I know. Lots of sugar." She poured a cup and took it over to her friend, along with the sugar bowl. "Which song are you talking about? The one Lacey Leigh Jaxon is doing?"

"No, of course not. I've heard that a million times. One of yours, off the CD you all did."

"Which one?"

"It's 'What I'm Looking For.'"

"You're pulling my leg, right?"

The brown-eyed woman shook her head solemnly. "I am *not* kidding, Kip. Why don't we turn on the radio? We'll probably hear it again. It's a great song, and I think you have a local hit on your hands."

The musician slid into a chair with a mug of coffee for herself and a plate full of sliced banana bread. Mary grinned and helped herself. Kip shook her head. "I don't understand. I haven't even had a chance to send my CD around to anyone yet. How did that song get out?"

"They didn't say it was on your CD, Kip. The DJ said it was from a compilation with several local artists."

"Oh." Kip sat thinking for a moment. "We did put together a batch of songs, and Bill Brett said he was going to try to squire them around to the radio stations."

"He must've been successful." She took a hearty swig of coffee. "Mmm, I love sweet coffee."

Kip looked at her friend's coffee cup, which was filled nearly to the brim now that Mary had added four spoonfuls of sugar. "I wonder what this all means?" She brought her hand up to her chin and tapped it with her fingers. "Might not mean anything at all."

Mary broke out in a wide grin. "It might mean you're going to be famous and hit the big time!"

"We'll see. I'm not so sure I want to be famous and hit the big time."

"Oh, that's nonsense, Kip. Of course you do."

Chapter
Two

THE LAST OF the setting sun slipped over the back of the huge amphitheater's band shell, and the woman out in the empty open air auditorium gave thanks that the painful glare was receding. Kneeling next to the sound station behind the last row of bleachers, she crawled under the big soundboard and checked the phone connection only to find the line partially severed. *Ah ha. There it is. A simple thing, after all.* She unplugged the phone jack and, on her knees, backed out from underneath. Using a wire stripper from her tool belt, she fixed the loose wire and covered it up with electrical tape, then crawled back under and plugged it in. She hoped that would fix the problem. It was handy to have a communication link from the back of the venue to the stage wings.

Jaime Esperanza, electrician, assistant production manager, sound tech, and occasional stage musician wormed her way backward and out from under the six-foot-wide "desk," also known as the front-of-house soundboard, FOH for short. Her boss, Eric O'Connell, who oversaw production and sound, would spend most of the next six hours standing behind the board during the concert set to begin at 8:00 p.m. Glancing at her wristwatch, she noted she had only forty-five more minutes before sound checks began.

She and Eric had been working with the tour techs, Tom and Lance, for the last four hours to set up the arena's stage, sound, and electrical systems. A few minutes earlier, the three guys went backstage to supervise the uncrating of the stage gear and musical instruments, and she was left to troubleshoot. Everything had seemed fine at first—except they couldn't get any power to the comm phone, and the house manager who was supposed to "know the arena like the back of his hand" hadn't been worth the air he breathed. She wondered how someone with so little knowledge of the venue could be put in charge. He was a real poseur and just stood around for the first hour watching Jaime, the crew, and the stagehands work. She had decided long ago that instead of the *Lacey Leigh Jaxon's Roamin' From Wyoming Tour*, they should have called this *The Girl Scout Tour* because her team always seemed to leave the arena in better shape than they'd found it. At the last concert, they'd left behind a multitude of new stage bulbs and some cable she'd spliced into various lines. At least the local light crew, a team of four technical guys who set up the lights for the show, seemed on the ball. They were on dinner break for another half hour, but the four men seemed competent. In addition to the venue's lifters and pushers, hired as stagehands by the house manager, the crew was rounded out by two local kids in their early twenties hired on for one night only. They were strong, strapping young men who wanted to make some quick bucks and have the chance to meet the performers

Jaime took a deep breath, arched her back and tightened the muscles, then bent forward and stretched them. She stopped to wipe the side of her face on the shoulder of her short-sleeved t-shirt. For now, it was warm and dry, but as the Nevada sun set, it would gradually grow cooler, and she'd be in a light jacket by the time the opening act was through. She scanned the knobs and controls on the console, flipped two switches, and picked up a mic. From the overhead speakers, her voice rumbled out. "Eric, pick up the stage phone." She waited a moment until the red light on the handset went on and picked it up. "It's fixed, boss. We're rockin' and rollin' now."

"Okay." He hung up, and she did the same. Now she just had to get every microphone, every sound monitor, and every speaker in perfect working order in—she looked at her watch again—forty-three minutes. She let out a sigh.

Jaime slid out from behind the mixing desk and hustled down toward the stage. Sweat caused her hot pink t-shirt to stick to her back. Five-foot-seven and broad-shouldered, she was lean and slim at the waist, with a flare of hips and long legs. She carried little fat on her frame, and the muscles in her arms and shoulders were tight and strong from the hours upon hours of hefting equipment, packing and unpacking gear, and working on wiring over her head. She wore high top tennis shoes and dark gray cargo shorts with pockets full of wires, black permanent markers, electrician's tape, and a pair of wire cutters. A well-worn leather tool belt hung low on her hips and contained all the gear she thought she would need: screwdrivers, wire snips, a small hammer, nails, screws, tacks, hooks, gaff tape, a slim Mag-lite flash, and various other useful items. Without this belt, she felt naked, and it never left her waist until show time—and only then if she had to play an instrument. On nights that her musical talents weren't needed, she usually wore it until she was done for the evening.

Jaime's black hair formed a cap close to her head. Her eyes were nearly black, and to anyone who asked, she tended to describe herself as a Mexican half-breed. She was proud of the Mexican half—Aztec Indian, in fact—and at least she knew what that half was. As far as the other half went, she had no idea. Her mother had gotten pregnant outside a bar one night after having far too much to drink and had only ever known the man's first name and certainly not his nationality. Jaime carried her mother's last name, her dark hair and eyes, and her memory. Magdalena Maria Esperanza had died three years earlier. The memory still hurt.

She reached the apron of the stage, planted her left hand on it, and with one smooth motion, vaulted up the four feet to the marred surface. When they first arrived, she'd spent several minutes striking raggedy old strips of masking tape from the floor, and now she stopped long enough to pull out a roll of one-inch reflective tape and spike new markers. Pacing off the area and gauging the dimensions by eye, she placed the sticky tape as she organized the layout of the stage in her imagination. She'd done it so many times in the past eight months that she thought she could accomplish it in her sleep. As she finished, a stagehand, followed by Eric, wheeled in the first of several giant speakers. With a smile on his face, he said, "You haven't had your union break yet, Jaime."

"Yeah, right." She scowled as more hands wheeled in the tech cases and giant work boxes, amps, monitors, and instrument cases. "Hey guys, listen up and follow Tom's lead on where to put everything. We've got limited time, and I want to see this stage set up in less than twenty minutes."

Tom, a tall skinny guy with a mass of black wavy hair, nodded. "We gotcha covered, Jaime." He gave a toss of his head. "Get a move on, guys."

"Thanks, Tom. I'll be back in a few minutes. I sure hope you'll all be ready because we're on a tighter timeline than usual."

Eric stepped around a monitor and grabbed his clipboard. "You better let Wes know we ran into trouble and may not nail the 8:00 start time."

She smiled. "Like that's a surprise."

"Yeah, well, better warn him in advance, just in case."

"Okay, boss. Be back in a bit."

"All right, kiddo." He disappeared into the wings as she turned and exited stage right.

She liked it when he called her kiddo. She felt a genuine fondness for Eric O'Connell. Fifteen years her senior, he wasn't quite old enough to be her father. She enjoyed working with him, though they had nothing in common. He was a fifty-three-year-old Irishman with gray-blue eyes and thin, graying hair that used to be blond, which he tied in a ponytail. He was short, for a man, with a portly physique. Toe to toe, they looked directly into one another's eyes.

The band shell was set up so that all the dressing rooms were down a flight of stairs from the wing at stage right, but you could reach the stairs via a corridor that ran behind the stage. A loading dock door also opened right into the corridor, which was unusually convenient. Many nights, Jaime remembered the hands carting load after load of equipment from the trucks across parking lots, down slopes, into dark and twisting hallways, up and down stairs before finally reaching the stage. They were behind schedule, but the ease of unloading was a real advantage.

She took the stairs down to the dressing rooms, meeting Wes Slater in the lower hall. As tour promoter, general manager, and production overseer, he was a powerful presence. He reeked of money. The gold rings on his fingers, the Rolex on his wrist, and the expensive suits he wore accentuated his forceful personality. He was also a good six-four and towered over most of the stagehands and techs.

"Jaime! What's the deal? I just looked at the stage, and you don't have *shit* set up." He pinned her with his dirty blue eyes, and she was struck once again at how much he looked like a mean-spirited John Wayne.

"Yup. We're behind schedule."

"Why the *hell* is that?" He had a way of putting emphasis on swear words that made his every statement sound threatening.

She calmly ticked the items off on three fingers. "Local lighting crew was late and it took longer to do the rigging than usual. Ignorant gonk who runs the place doesn't know his head from a hole in the ground. Eric and I had to troubleshoot the electrical system. One damn thing after another." She'd learned long ago that Wes Slater didn't respect—much less listen to—anyone who didn't curse like a longshoreman, and though that wasn't her usual mode of communication, she tended to throw in occasional swear words to soothe him.

He put his hand to his chin in a gesture he affected a lot, then tapped at the point of his chin with the nail of his thumb. "Why aren't you up there helping then?"

"Came down to tell you the bad news. Wanted to update

Nicky and Lacey, too."

He made a growling sound in the back of his throat. "You go talk to that fairy, and I'll speak to Lacey. No need upsetting her unnecessarily."

"Yes, sir." She spun around and went the opposite direction, toward the dressing room Nicky Kinnick was in. She didn't know why Wes kept calling the opening act a fairy. Nicky was anything but gay. He loved women, and there was no doubt that women loved him. His sweet, soft-pop/country songs went over big time with the ladies, and they came to shows in droves or dragged their boyfriends along with them. Every show, at least one woman threw her bra or panties up on the stage, and though Nicky acted like he was embarrassed, backstage he'd admitted after the first show that he loved it. She liked the fact that he had a sense of humor. His debut album was called "Uncle Knick Knack's Treasure Chest," after the tongue-in-cheek title song he'd written about a junk dealer from his hometown.

She knocked on his door and waited. When he opened it, he stood smiling at her, wearing shorts and a polo shirt and holding a *Popular Mechanics* magazine. He was tall, clean-cut, brown-haired and brown-eyed, with a great body tanned to perfection. He was just the type of man she'd go after—that is, if she liked men in that way. She grinned back at him. "Hey, how ya doing?"

"Couldn't be better." He gestured into the room. "Care to join me in non-air-conditioned splendor?"

She didn't move. "It is a little warm down here, but it's cooling off upstairs now that the sun is going down. Sorry, I can't come in, Nick. We are so far behind right now. I just wanted to let you know we're likely to start late tonight."

He nodded. "All right. Thanks for the news." He winked and waggled his eyebrows. "Any groupies up there you could send down to entertain me?"

"Yeah, right." She chuckled. "Wes wouldn't let anyone down here right now if you paid him."

"Oh, well. At least I tried." Gesturing at the magazine in his hand, he said, "At least I always have my trusty magazine. See you in a while."

She gave a curt nod and turned away, wondering how he always managed to be so relaxed and pleasant before his shows. Lacey Leigh Jaxon, the headliner, was never so calm. In fact, Jaime was glad Wes was telling Lacey about the delay. That way Jaime was assured of missing major histrionics and verbal attacks. As she hit the stairs to head back up to work, she was surprised she wasn't hearing screaming from the star's dressing room. She checked her watch again. *So much for my break. I didn't really need one anyway.*

She cut across the stage, weaving between stagehands, instruments, and equipment, and went down the hall to the green room. She passed a caterer setting up a warming tray and went to the cooler where she dug out a bottle of spring water, popped it open, and drained half of it. Carrying the bottle along with her, she hustled down the hall to rejoin the crew so they could finish the stage set up and start their line checks.

JAIME STOOD IN the wings and watched the end of Nicky Kinnick's act. He was supposed to have a forty-five-minute set, but the crowd was wild for him. Although the concert had started late, Wes Slater was grudgingly letting him have an encore. Nick waved off the band and went out onstage, grabbed one of four guitars off the toast rack, and pulled the strap over his head. The lighting director, who Jaime thought was doing a pretty nice job, dimmed the lights gradually as Nick pulled a pick out of his pocket and the audience sat back on the bleachers. Slater took the opportunity to signal one of the techs to let the curtain down, since Nicky was so far downstage, practically right at the edge. Once the curtain fell behind the performer, the hands swarmed the set and quietly started moving things around and setting up new mics.

"Well, folks, thanks for sticking with me through the set..."

"We love you, Nicky!" a high voice in the audience screamed, and there was more cheering and stomping.

Nicky grinned. "Have you all been burned by love?" A loud roar rose from the crowd, and he nodded as he plucked a few notes on the guitar. "Me, too. Here's a new one I wrote recently." He strummed a minor chord, then began picking a delicate melody. When he leaned into the mic, his voice was warm and rich, but when Jaime heard the words, she shivered and got goose bumps all down her back.

Should've known you were trouble before I let you in my bed
And now you up and left me, I can't get you out of my head...

She turned away, allowing the melody to wash over her, but refusing to let the lyrics register further. She went to the far corner of the wings, plugged in the lead guitar, and turned on a tiny Pignose amp. In minutes, Lance, the instrument tech, would have the rest of the instruments set up onstage, but Drew liked to get himself and his guitar all situated in the wings. He had some odd quirks, but he was a terrific lead guitarist, so Jaime did anything for him she could. Quickly she checked to see if his Fender was in tune and was satisfied to find that it was. She switched off the amp and replaced the guitar, which Drew would be coming for in about fifteen minutes.

Nicky's song ended to more wild applause, and he came off the stage excited and triumphant. The house sound came up, a tape of songs by various artists including Faith Hill, the Dixie Chicks, Trisha Yearwood, and Shania Twain—or The Big Four, as Lacey Leigh called them.

It was time for Jaime to change clothes. Tonight Lacey was adding a honky-tonk song to the play list that included some fiddle, and so when they segued into the sixth song, Jaime would sidle onstage and play. As usual, she'd wear black jeans, a t-shirt, black boots, and a black cowboy hat. She preferred to blend right into the background of the stage and always high-tailed it off stage as soon as she could. She was content working behind the scenes, but sometimes she was called upon if someone was sick or got fired. She was forced to play rhythm guitar for two dates before Wes hired the new guy, Gary Culhane. He'd been with them now for about two weeks and seemed to be working out fine, for which Jaime was thankful. She had a miserable time being onstage for two entire concerts. *Give me tech and sound work any day!*

Gary and Drew worked well together on guitars, and both could sing backup vocals as needed. The twins, Marcus and Davis, played keyboards and bass, respectively. Along with Drew and the big drummer, Buck, they had been with Lacey since her very first road show. As far as Jaime was concerned, Drew, Buck, and the twins were the heart of the band. Everyone else came and went. Wes Slater hadn't been able to keep a fiddler or someone who played mandolin, so she was stuck there at times. In fact, she couldn't help but think that this tour was on the order of bizarre. She'd never seen so few people have so many roles. Usually there were two or three techs to do the job she was doing. She was just glad she wasn't a regular backup singer. Lacey had two vocalists, Candy and Shelley, who doubled as Lacey's makeup and costume assistants. No way would Jaime want that job.

After dressing, she grabbed her tool belt and a lined windbreaker and made her way back into the band shell to find Slater just outside the stage door speaking to Gary. The rhythm guitarist looked like James Dean, with the same sort of swaggering attitude. His brown hair was wavy, and the black jeans were tight in all the right places. Slater lowered his voice when Jaime entered, but other than turning his back to her, he did little else to hide the fact that he was giving the younger man a serious chewing out. Gary stood listening, a toothpick poking out from between his white, even teeth. Jaime passed by, wondering what that was all about.

She was nearly to the curtain when Slater's voice hissed, "Jaime!" She wheeled around and raised her eyebrows. With a toss of his head, he said, "Check the time, and then you go get Lacey. And you better be goddamn good and ready."

She didn't ask what for. Lacey had only two moods before a show: charming—or pissed as hell. Jaime had no idea what to expect today, but she'd already seen it all and tried not to take any of it to heart. She peeked out into the wings and searched for Tom or Lance, then gestured their way. Tom, the stage sound tech, walked toward her. "Time?" she asked.

"Ready if you are."

"You sure everything's live?"

He nodded.

"Flash pots are a sure thing?"

"Yup. Ready to roll."

She leaned around the curtain and waited a few seconds until Eric looked her way from the console at the back. She held up her hand, five fingers spread, and he gave a nod, then she made her way around to the stairwell, headed down to the headliner's room with the big star on the door, and tapped on it. She was greeted with a peal of laughter as Candy opened it. She and Shelley wore identical skimpy outfits—bright blue sleeveless dresses with spangles running diagonally from the right shoulder to the left—and sparkly high heels. Their faces were covered with more makeup than she had worn all together in her entire life. In their scanty dresses, she never could understand how they avoided freezing their tushes onstage on a night like this.

She met Lacey Leigh Jaxon's eyes from across the small dressing room and said, "You're on."

Lacey took a long pull from a wine cooler and rose from the director's chair in which she sat. She, too, wore a considerable amount of makeup, and in this light, all three women's faces appeared garish and harsh. The tiny singer let out another laugh as she moved across the ratty pile rug. She wore pale pink slacks— size 2—white high heels, and a tight pink tube top with spaghetti straps barely holding it up. Under the bright lights onstage, she would appear to be wearing white. Her long blonde hair was wavy and laced with bits of glitter. Jaime could see the mood was light, and in a way, she was grateful, but that also meant Lacey may have already drunk too much. She gazed over the head of the advancing star and met Shelley's eyes. The backup singer shrugged her shoulders and shook her head. Jaime took that to mean Lacey was all right.

"Let's go, girls," the star said. "Can't keep our public waiting." She paused in the doorway and put her hand flat against the upper chest of Jaime's black t-shirt, then pointed her index finger and ran the tip of it from under her chin, down to the hollow in her throat. For a brief moment, Jaime gazed into the emerald green eyes, which were made unnaturally green by colored contact lenses. Lacey's actual eye color was a flat blue, her hair was light brown, and her original given name was Eustacia Lynn Jacks. But like a lot of things in show business, nobody was who they'd originally started out to be. With one final coy look, Lacey moved through the doorway and gracefully down the hall toward the stairs, with her two backup singers in tow.

The blushing electrician pulled the dressing room door shut and followed them, her windbreaker over her arm. Candy and Shelley never commented on all the teasing Lacey did, but Jaime figured they had to know that she and the singer had had a fling during the previous road trip. She tried to be philosophical about it, but no matter how she thought about those seven weeks, it hurt—and it solidified her belief that relationships were a waste. They never worked out, and she didn't know why she had ever tried to have one. She forced herself to stop thinking about Lacey Leigh and instead focused on the backup singers' legs. *How in the world do they walk in those high heels without wobbling?*

As she followed them, she composed herself so that by the time they were stage left in the wings, waiting, she wore her regular passive face. The house music faded out, cutting off Wynonna in mid-song, and a deep, rumbling drum roll sounded loudly throughout the amphitheater. The atmosphere around Jaime was tense as they all readied themselves. Drew picked up his guitar and monkeyed with the strap until he got it situated comfortably. Big Buck, almost six-six in his boots, nervously clicked his drumsticks together. With the curtain still down, the band walked out onto the stage. Slater gave them mere seconds to find their marks, then nodded to Lacey and the girls. He spoke into a walkie-talkie, and the stage curtain, illuminated by only the dimmest of floor lights, began to rise as the pre-recorded drum roll faded out.

From the viewpoint of the audience, all that could be seen was a dark stage with an occasional sparkle of light shining off guitars or mic stands. Furthest from the spectators, upstage where Buck sat in the dark at his drum set, there was a snap-snap-snap-

snap in 4/4 time, and a bass line started up. Then, without warning, flash pots on either side of the stage exploded with dazzling radiance. Far upstage, above and behind Buck and the drums, a blood-red neon light flashed across a backdrop. In cursive, it spelled the star's name, *Lacey Leigh Jaxon.* The lead guitar twanged, and then Gary's rhythm joined in. Before the spectators' eyes could adjust, a streak of white strolled onto the stage, and the gutsy voice started singing the uptempo song.

> *Memory is such a terrible thing*
> *Wish I could forget I used to wear your ring*
> *Once you shared my life, but now you're gone*
> *And me? Well, I have to carry on.*

The house went wild and those in the front rows were on their feet. The tiny singer already had them in the palm of her hand. It never ceased to amaze Jaime how something as simple as a coffee can, a thin wire, a battery ignition system, and some photographic flash powder could set off such a successful pyrotechnic, but the crowd always loved the flash pot effect. They also loved this song, Lacey's most recent country radio hit, *Mama Was Right (I Hate To Admit)*:

> *A box of letters, an old shirt,*
> *And three big debts are all you left*
> *My mother always said you were an SOB*
> *Oh, lord, it's hard to face her and admit,*
> *But mama was right*
> *She better not rub it in*
> *What she don't know is probably good*
> *'Cause leaving me wasn't your only sin...*

Jaime watched the house from the wings. Nicky Kinnick sure was a great warm-up act. He'd left these people totally wired. She looked at her watch: straight up ten p.m. The show was at least forty minutes later than usual, but the mob out on the bleachers behaved as though they were fresh as the first light of day. When Lacey wrapped up the first song, the whole place was on its feet again. She bowed and smiled, every bit the gracious hostess, and in a breathless voice said, "Hello, Reno!" The assemblage roared back, and she hit them again. "This one's for all of you, my favorite city, my favorite fans. Go ahead—y'all get comfy and have a seat." The band played the first bar of a slow ballad, and she sang:

What do you share when there's no one left in view
Not a word of comfort can you say
What do you do when it's over and done
And everyone you love has gone away?

Jaime hated this song. She turned and walked quickly to the narrow corridor that ran behind the stage. She knew she couldn't wander too far and opened the back door to peer out into the darkness. A twinkle of lights along the fence and a glow of yellow from the windows of the gatehouse shone her direction, but otherwise, it was pitch black outside. Jaime stepped out the door and looked upward at the stars and the moon. The lot was deserted, with no lights coming from the buses or trucks. She could hear the pounding pulse of the power ballad's bass and drums, but the words were distorted and unclear. A cheer went up—a rush of acclaim that came at a person onstage like a wave of air, which Jaime could feel even out here in the back. The band started up the next song, a twangy piece with a lot of "I love you's" in it.

She strolled across the lot, kicking large rocks and wondering if the Welling was ready. That was one thing she had to take on faith—that by the time she needed it, Lance would make sure the violin was properly tuned. They hadn't let her down yet, but there was always a first time. She didn't much like the Welling, but it could be plugged into an amp, whereas her J.B. Schweitzer needed a pickup mic and couldn't be relied upon for good sound balance and equalization in this kind of arena. She started keeping the Schweitzer under lock and key at the beginning of this latest tour after an instrument appraiser informed her it was worth over three thousand dollars. Jaime was fourteen when her grandfather gave her the Schweitzer, his prized old fiddle, and now she was sure her mother hadn't had any idea of its value, otherwise it would have gone to the pawnshop many years ago. It was the one thing Jaime had left from her mother's parents, and she treasured it. She wished she were playing it tonight instead of the Welling, which always felt so stiff and foreign. Finished with polyurethane, it had an uncomfortable chin rest. Her Schweitzer, burnished smooth from years of use, fit her, molding to her neck and shoulder the way a good fiddle should.

Though she could see a guard posted near the chain link fence, no one was in the dimly lit gatehouse. A tattered paperback book lay open, face down, on a shelf. She moved closer, almost to where her nose touched the window, and squinted to see the title, *Child of Silence* by Abigail Padgett. She had not heard of this author, but it looked like an interesting mystery, so she tucked the name away in the back of her head and turned to stroll toward the open stage door. Just as she reached it, a large form filled the entrance.

"Get the *hell* in here, Jaime! Jesus! That friggin' new song starts in probably less than a minute." Wes Slater held a handkerchief in one hand and twisted the end of it with the other. Stepping out of the way, he muttered, "Goddamn shows are going to be the death of me."

She gave a nod and slipped past him to head into the darkness of the wing. Slipping her laminated backstage pass from around her neck, she tucked it in her jacket pocket and draped the windbreaker over a chair next to her tool belt.

Lance gave a relieved sigh when she approached him. "Jaime," he whispered. "You're set. Just get out there and pick up the violin."

Taking a deep breath, she moved to a seam in the curtain far upstage, parallel with Buck's drums. She slid through, her black outfit blending in with the dark shadows in the corner. Lacey was doing a dance step at the final bridge before the chorus, and when this song ended, the new one would begin. Jaime picked up the violin and bow and got as comfortable as she could, then moved the instrument to rest position and stood absolutely still while the star finished the song to thunderous applause. Her cowboy hat was so low that she knew nobody would recognize her later when she took it off. That was just as well. It was better to blend in and then, after the song was over, fade away like a wraith in the night.

When the audience calmed down, Lacey let out a little sigh. The bass line kicked in for the next song, providing a steady, melodic rhythm in the background. The star said, "Hello, Reno!" The crowd cheered, waved, and generally went nuts with excitement. "I love Reno. You're always such good sports. We got started late, a few things went wrong, and yet, still you're hanging with me."

The crowd erupted, stamping and whistling. Jaime kept herself from shaking her head. Lacey was such a fake. That was one thing she knew for sure. The blonde star had little respect for the masses who came to see her, yet she worked them into a frenzy with this sort of homespun fakiness—perhaps just because she could.

"Folks, I wrote a new honky-tonk song—well, actually, it isn't your standard honky-tonk song 'cause the good beat doesn't much go with the sentiment." Buck started up a rhythm on drums, with Gary hitting some twangs on lead guitar. The chord progression Marcus played on keyboards was catchy, and the audience started to clap in cadence. "This one's for you all out there trying to deal with someone leaving." She took the mic off the stand and put one hand on her hip. Her voice was sassy, in contrast to the words.

Just today I read your letter
Saying it was all over
Between us
I realize that it would be better
Believing it was over
Between us...

Jaime rolled her eyes. It was times like this that she just wanted to quit and move on. Lacey wrote so convincingly about lost love, and yet, she had never been dumped. Instead, she seemed to wait until the object of her affections least expected it, and—wham!—upside the head with the proverbial two-by-four.

I know that you can't wait to leave
Get away from all the things there were
Between us
But late at night I have to grieve
For all the love I think there's lost
Between us...

Jaime took a deep breath and got ready. She touched the bow to the violin's strings and pulled a quiet wisp of a whine out of the fiddle. The part she was to play increased gradually in volume through the bridge, and then when Lacey finished singing the bridge, the violin solo took off into a raucous hoedown of a part.

She closed her eyes and let the beat of the drums, the throb of the bass, and the rhythmic keyboards roll through her. With one toe tapping, she swayed with the music, then moved the bow across the strings like lightning. She felt, almost more than she saw, when the spotlight hit her. It was odd how much heat they emitted, even from so far away. The solo was a frantic cacophony of music, surrounded by the blare of the rest of the band. Only eight bars long, it blew by, fast as the wind, with no errors, no stumbling, and then she was winding down, tapering off, one final high whine fading away, and Lacey finished the song.

The song ended in a crescendo of keyboards and drums. Again, the crowd went wild. Lacey bowed, then stood tall and waved a hand toward the band. The star never acknowledged her musicians more than this. Sometimes Jaime wondered if Lacey even remembered all their names when she was onstage. The blonde bowed again and turned to smile at Jaime, who gave her a quick nod. The singer turned back to the crowd as the spotlight on the fiddler faded.

Jaime glanced up to the sound console, and when she thought she had given the sound guys sufficient time to cut her line, she set the violin down, confident there would be no feedback to interrupt the story Lacey was now sharing with the audience. They hung on her every word, so much so that when Jaime backed up and slipped through the seam in the back curtain, nobody could have even noticed.

In the wings, she grabbed the lightweight jacket she had left lying over the back of a folding chair. She was covered in sweat, and as she cooled down, she'd be cold if she didn't have something to stay warm in. She picked up her tool belt and slung it around her waist, then threaded the belt.

"Good job on the solo, Jaime." Tom nodded with approval, his hands poised over the console that adjusted the side monitors blaring out the music that the band heard.

"Thanks." She moved next to him and watched as he brought the levels up a little when needed. She looked up at the tiny woman out under the spotlights, conscious of the ache she felt behind her breastbone. Seven weeks. That's all she'd had—seven weeks. It had been exactly forty-nine days, too, for Lacey had shut her out of her life on day fifty, three days before the last tour had ended, which, strangely enough, had been on April Fool's Day. There had been a one month break before this tour began, and Jaime was glad to have had it. For some time, she had considered not coming back and had, in fact, told Wes Slater she was through. Then the damn fool had offered to make her assistant production manager, double her salary, and triple her per diem...how could she resist?

Over the last three months, she had become more philosophical about what had happened. Sometimes she felt a certain triumph that none of the men who came after had lasted more than three or four weeks. Nicky Kinnick had been, apparently, only a one-night stand, though she had felt bad for him. She knew what it was like and how it continued to hurt, and she wondered when the emptiness and sadness would depart.

She and Tom stood, arms crossed, watching the last several numbers before intermission. She was lost in thought, when she felt something brush her shoulder, and the smell of aftershave came to her. She looked to her right to find Nicky Kinnick leaning into her, shoulder to shoulder, and smiling that drop-dead thousand-watt smile. Into her ear, he hollered, "She sure can be a bitch, but wow! Look how she can charm a crowd."

Jaime grinned, turning dark eyes to his. She shouted over the
music. "You're not so bad yourself, hot stuff."

He laughed out loud. "I'm gonna miss you, girl, when this
tour's over."

She felt the blush rise in her cheeks and was relieved that it
was so dark he wouldn't notice. She stood between the two men,
listening to the music and feeling fatigue seep into her bones. The
Indiglo light on her watch revealed it was only ten to eleven. They
had a long night still ahead of them.

Lacey wrapped up her final song, a rollicking number with a
hook in the chorus that just didn't quit. Even after the star was
taking her bows and the band finished the last notes, the tune ran
through a person's head. Jaime liked that song, though. It was
mindless, but for some reason it lifted her spirits.

The local security detail, big guys dressed in black t-shirts,
sauntered in front of the stage as Lacey Leigh turned stage left,
giving one final wave to the screaming, stomping audience. Jaime
watched the tiny blonde make her way to the stage wings followed
by her backup singers. The beaming smile turned quickly to a gri-
mace once the tiny woman was offstage. The house music went
up, and the curtain went down as the blonde stomped past Nicky,
Tom, and Jaime, and she was barely to the door to the back corridor before she exploded. Jaime turned to see Wes Slater towering
over the little blonde as she let loose.

"What's with the fucking Sparkle Fairy out there? He lit me
all wrong. I'm sure I looked yellow, goddammit! Yellow!"

Wes stammered, "Now, Lacey—"

"Don't you dare 'Now Lacey' me! Do you know how many
times I gestured to ask for more monitor and side fill?" Now she
was screaming. "How can I perform if I can't fucking hear myself
sing? Godammit, you people are useless idiots! The lighting
sucks, and the sound system is totally fucked!"

The guys from the band, hot and sweating, were clustered
around Nicky and Jaime, waiting to get past Lacey, but the star
and the promoter were blocking the doorway, and nobody wanted
to try to sneak past.

Nicky called out, in an affable voice, "Hey, Lace, you looked
gorgeous out there. You were dynamite."

The star turned to him, leaning forward at the waist, and spat
out, "Fuck you. What the hell do you know—you with your whining white boy songs of false hope and stupidity. You think I give a
flying shit what you think, you faggot!"

Jaime watched as Nicky literally took a step back. Wes

reached out and took Lacey's shoulder from behind, and she wheeled around, her hands in tight fists, looking like she was ready to hit him.

Wes leaned down low, speaking softly to the young woman, but Lacey kept interrupting him with curses and then threatened that she was not going back on after the intermission. At that point, the rhythm guitarist, Gary, stepped forward. He strutted over, and lightly touched her elbow. She spun on her heel, a snarl on her face, but when she saw it was Gary, she hesitated.

"Hey, baby. Let's you and me go get something cool to drink, something *chilly* to cool us down a bit." He gave a toss of his head as he reached for her hand. "Let these people go do their jobs. By the time you and I are done with our refreshments, the lights and sound will be fixed."

Jaime looked up at Wes, then down at Lacey. Wes was turning purple with rage, but Lacey's face had softened, and she leaned into Gary and let him put an arm around her and guide them past Slater and through the doorway.

A simultaneous exhalation came from most of the men. *Oh shit*, Jaime thought. Now she knew what Wes had been lecturing Gary about earlier. Didn't seem like Gary had taken it too much to heart though. Wes disappeared from the doorway, and then Nicky turned to her and said softly, "Jaime, I think you and the crew have been the one bright spot in this whole tour, but that's it. I'm outta here." He gave her a friendly pat on the shoulder as he moved past, then reached the door and called out after the promoter. Her eyes followed Nicky, and she frowned. *He doesn't really mean that...does he?*

She turned to find Tom shaking his head. He punched his right fist into his left hand repeatedly. "Do you know how tempted I am to hit the suck button on her sometime?"

Jaime could see he was holding back his temper, and that he was hurt. She also knew how easy it would be for any technician to make minor adjustments to the equipment, and the sound and quality of Lacey Leigh's voice would, indeed, suck. Tom may have been tempted but he had never done it. "Tom, you—"

"Jaime! She never *once* gave me the high sign! Not once! How dare she say the sound was bad? That was about as near perfect as it's ever been, Jaime. Jesus." He turned away, and for a moment she thought he looked like a small boy ready to cry.

She reached out and took a firm grasp on his forearm. "Tom! Tom, it's not about you. You're doing a great job. Eric and I appreciate you—even if she doesn't."

"That's right." Both of them were startled, but it was only

Eric coming up behind them. "It sounds great from the audience, and these fans are loving it." He stopped and ran his hands over his thinning hair. "She being a prima donna again?" Tom and Jaime both nodded. "God help us if we ever get famous, if that's what it turns a person into. Let's forget about that bullshit and make sure she doesn't have anything to complain about when she hits the stage again, okay?"

She looked at her watch. *Oh brother.* The second set was slightly longer than the first, but at the rate they were going, the show wasn't going to wrap until well after midnight. *Oh well. That's the way it always goes.*

The three of them joined the others in checking lines, resetting mic stands, and preparing the fog machine. The second act started in a rush of dry ice fog from which Lacey emerged, dressed in a floor-length satin dress. Jaime didn't look forward to some of the sappy ballads, but she figured she'd grit her teeth through them. She was going to make damn sure that nothing went wrong to give the star cause to berate any of them again.

Chapter
Three

THE NEXT FEW days whirled by so quickly that Kip had trouble remembering what happened when. Before Mary had left on Saturday, the phone rang, and there on the line was the concert promoter who previously bought the rights to "Wyoming." He asked her to join Lacey Leigh Jaxon's summer tour.

"We just lost our opening act," Wes Slater told her. "Our next date is a week off—actually, this coming Friday. Will you join us?"

She was so stunned by the request that she sank into the kitchen chair, breathing quickly, and Mary's eyes widened in alarm.

"Tell me more, Mr. Slater," she choked out.

"You get the stage for approximately forty minutes every night as the opening act. You can sing and play whatever you want. We pay you a flat fee for each performance, and you have to pay for any backup singers or instrumentation. We'll provide tech assistance, of course, and you can travel on the crew bus."

He went on to further discuss the payment, accommodations, and travel. Her head was spinning with all the information, but she made notes and told him she would call him back. She stood to hang up the phone, and then turned to look at her curious and concerned friend. "Mary, I may not see you much this summer."

"Huh?"

"You're not going to believe this, but I'm going on tour."

Mary leapt out of her chair, and the two women whooped and hollered and did a happy dance around the kitchen.

Even now it made her smile to think about how happy Mary—and her other friends—had been for her. She felt bad about canceling her coffeehouse gigs, but every shop owner assured her that he or she understood. She had no idea if she would ever again have the chance to see what a pro tour was like, so she jumped on board without further thought.

When she called him back later to settle up final details, Wes Slater instructed her to bring along any guitars or musical instruments she needed, but no other gear. All cords, lighting, amps, and the like would be provided. She had to do a marathon shopping trip to purchase stage clothes, twenty packs of spare guitar strings, and various odds and ends. *Somehow I don't think jeans and a Math Master's t-shirt will be sufficient.* She'd never worried about how she looked at a coffeehouse show, but she knew this was a whole new world.

Shopping at the Mall of America was excruciating, but she realized it wouldn't be practical to buy things while on the road, so she purchased a variety of comfortable slacks, shirts, and jackets. With two large suitcases, a garment bag, two guitars in ATA cases, and two carry-ons, she was also concerned that she'd need a sherpa and a pack mule to get by. But Wes Slater had assured her she would have a small, but functional, bunkroom on the tour bus, and that she could stay in hotels along the way, too, if she preferred. She decided to wait until she could check out the situation before she decided one way or the other. As a public school teacher, she was used to working in tight spaces with a horde of cranky youngsters. She had a hunch she'd choose to save money on hotels and stay on the tour bus, even if it was cramped, but she didn't know for sure yet.

On the day of departure, she dragged all her stuff out to the front porch and sat down on the front step to await the taxi. It was noon—and warming up considerably. Sometimes a Minnesota summer day in early June took a while to heat up, but today she sat on the concrete step and the warmth of the cement below her seeped through her jeans. She heard a vehicle come down the residential street, and leaned forward to rise, thinking it was the taxi. Instead, a brand new SUV—a Ford of some kind—pulled into the driveway. *No...it can't be...*

But it was. She stood up, bile rising in her throat. The short, stocky blonde hopped out of the driver's seat and swaggered toward her. Her legs were already starting to bronze from the sun, and she looked great, dressed in running shorts and a three-quarter-sleeved t-shirt. She looked every bit the part of the star catcher on her company's softball team.

"Hey, Kip," she said. "What's shaking?"

Kip shrugged. She wanted to say, *Who the hell are you to show up here, now?* She took a deep breath. "Why are you here, Bren?"

"There's some softball gear out in the garage that I forgot all about. Think I could pick it up?"

Wordlessly Kip leaned down to pull her keys from a carry-on bag, then unlocked the front door and pressed the automatic door opener switch just inside. The garage door lumbered upward, and her ex-lover strode over and disappeared into the opening.

Kip stood in the doorway of her front porch, her heart pounding almost painfully in her chest. It had been over a year since Bren left her for another woman, and she thought she had gotten past the pain, but obviously that was not the case. It wasn't that she wanted to reunite now, though. Kip just felt like such a failure. She'd devoted so much time and attention to this one impossible woman, and for weeks after Bren left, she'd tried so hard to get her back. After a while, the pain had coalesced into a kind of rage and helplessness that even now scared her. Apparently the anger had not yet burned out. Or the hurt.

Kip thought her ex was taking an awful long time in the garage. *She's probably coveting my motorcycle again.* When the blonde emerged from the garage, she carried a tattered yellow bag. She moved up the walk and smiled at Kip. "This stuff was all mine—couple of gloves and a bunch of balls. The bag might've been yours. Do you mind—"

"No, take it," Kip was quick to say.

"Thanks. So..." Bren looked at the bags and guitars stacked on the porch. "Going somewhere?"

Kip nodded. "A little trip. See some new friends." She had difficulty speaking. Her tongue felt thick in her mouth, and for one scary moment, she was afraid she was going to burst into tears, but then she ducked her head back into the house and punched the button to close up the garage.

"Well, have fun," Bren said. She stood there with a bland expression on her face, looking as though she hadn't a care in the world, and she seemed to be waiting for something. Fortunately, the taxi arrived. "Oops. I better get my truck out of the way. See ya."

Kip nodded. *With any luck, I'll never have to see you again.* She stood for a moment watching the back of the woman she used to love, the woman who had originally pledged to stick by her through thick and thin and then had betrayed her. She shook her head, wondering what the hell had happened, and whether there was anything she could have done to prevent the end of their relationship. Then she gave a little shiver and bent to pick up the first of the bags.

In short order, she was in the taxi on the way to the airport, and she was able to put the unexpected—and unpleasant—visit behind her. Before long, her stomach was doing flip-flops as she sat in the airport, awaiting arrival of the plane taking her to Great Falls, Montana. From there, she'd depart for Helena. She was good and early, and that gave her time to consider what a huge step she was taking. From coffeehouse chanteuse to big time opening act. Kip couldn't help but think it was a little overwhelming, and she had no idea what to expect. For a moment, she thought of the old story of the country mouse meeting up with the city mouse—though in this case, Lacey Leigh Jaxon, the country mouse, was probably going to be a whole lot more worldly and knowledgeable than little old city girl, Kip Galvin. She felt a thrill of anticipation thrum through her, and she could hear her heartbeat in her head, which made her feel light-headed as she sat watching all the activity around her. The high she was experiencing gave way to concern when she thought of her two guitars in the cargo hold of the plane. She'd never flown to a gig before, and she wasn't sure how safe her instruments were. She could only hope they wouldn't get tossed around and damaged.

The DC9 jet left on schedule, and in ninety minutes, Kip arrived with time to spare for her connection in Great Falls. The airport covered only a few acres, and she moved leisurely down the short corridor to the proper gate. She stopped along the way and purchased a mocha coffee and ate a banana from her carry-on bag. Arriving at the gate with twenty minutes left before boarding, she was surprised to see a very small plane out on the tarmac.

The musician approached the one clerk behind the tall counter near the entrance to the walkway that led to the plane. "Excuse me. Is this the right gate for the connecting flight to Helena?"

"Sure is." He nodded and hesitated a moment, looking her in the eye. "Is there a problem?"

She frowned. "Is that the plane out there?"

"Yes, ma'am."

"There must be some mistake." Cautious of her half-full container of coffee, she set down her carry-on bags and pulled the flyer out of the side pocket of one of them. The ticket showed that the first leg of her trip was to be on a McDonnell Douglas DC9 Jet, while the second leg was on a Dehavilland Dash 4 Prop. "That teeny little plane out there is my plane?"

"Yes, ma'am, and a reliable plane it is. It makes this flight twice a day—day in, day out—unless there's a blizzard, which there surely is not today."

She stood looking at him, unsure, then bent to tuck her ticket back in the bag. "Okay, thank you."

"We'll call you to board shortly, ma'am."

Picking up her bags, she thought about the plane crash that had occurred the day before. Of course, it had happened out east, and it had been a giant jet, but this miniscule little plane made her nervous. She shuffled over to a seat and settled into it, her back to the window. She pulled out the ticket and checked it. *Only thirty-one minutes. I just have to be on that dinky thing for about half an hour. I can do that. And look at the bright side—there are so few passengers that I probably won't have much wait for my luggage.* A voice came over the intercom, calling her flight, and with trepidation she headed to get in line behind the others.

MAD AS HELL, Jaime pulled the tour bus into the parking lot at the airport, steering the giant tank off to the side and coming to rest across eight parking slots. This was the downside to touring. Sometimes the transportation arrangements blew up in her face. The local limo company was supposed to send a car, but the driver had called at the last minute to report he'd been in an accident. She—and Eric, as well—did have motorcycles stowed in the semi, but she could hardly pick up the new opening act and all her gear while riding a Harley, so here she was, navigating the Queen Mary into the busy airport's satellite parking lot.

She let out a sigh and checked her watch to see that she had made it in time. Exiting the bus, Jaime pulled the door shut and then locked it. She made her way past other buses and RV's and walked a good quarter-mile across the lot to the entrance. When she looked back, the black bus didn't look so massive, but the bright red lettering on the side that proclaimed *Lacey Leigh Jaxon ~ Roamin' From Wyoming Tour* was plenty sizeable.

Strolling along with her hands in her jeans pockets, she felt comfortably warm in the June sunlight. Her red t-shirt was plenty warm enough. The night before, she listened to a copy of the demo CD Kip Galvin had sent to Wes by overnight mail. Jaime thought the guitar work was excellent and the voice as well. Many of the songs were a bit uneven and poorly mixed, but some of them were real gems. She listened through twice—once with the tunes playing as background music while she organized things in the tour bus cubbyhole assigned to her, and the second time while lying in the bus bunk as the behemoth meandered down the road toward Helena. They'd arrived in the capital city just a few hours before, and the rest of the crew were getting settled at a hotel near the venue for Friday night's show.

She wandered through the terminal, following the signs for the airline until she came to Gate 12. She checked her watch,

thinking that she was five minutes early, but even as the thought
crossed her mind, the plane taxied around the corner and slid into
the bay. Before too long, people trickled out, strolling through the
glass doorway. She watched closely. No one had any clue what
this Kip Galvin looked like. Jaime wasn't sure of her age. She
automatically ruled out the three businessmen and the tourist family who emerged down the ramp, as well as an elderly lady and a
solid-looking, light-brown-haired woman carrying two canvas
bags. Beyond them were two middle-aged, gray-haired women,
talking and laughing. Then came four more men single file, followed by two pilots.

Uh oh, I should have brought a sign. She re-evaluated the passengers. *Either she missed the plane or else...* Her eyes came to
rest on the brown-haired woman who was just now passing her.
Jaime cleared her throat. "Kip Galvin?" she asked softly. "Kip?"

It came out a little louder the second time, and the woman
with the two canvas bags stopped and turned to face her. "Hello?"

"Are you Kip Galvin?" The brown-haired woman nodded,
her gray eyes meeting Jaime's. "Glad to meet you. I'm Jaime
Esperanza. I was sent to pick you up." She stuck out a hand and
waited while Kip set down one bag and enclosed her hand in a
warm grip. "How was your trip?"

"Not too bad on the first leg. The second leg would have been
better in a plane larger than a go-cart with wings."

Jaime grinned as she released the other woman's hand.
"You'll be flying a lot closer to the ground now for a while. The
tour bus hardly ever takes flight. Let's go get your luggage—I
assume you've got several trunks?"

Kip shook her head and picked up her bag, then joined Jaime
in a casual stroll along the corridor to the baggage claim area.
"I've got a couple guitars, two suitcases, and a garment bag."

"I think we can handle that. Want me to take one of those?"
She gestured toward the carry-ons.

"Nah. I'll be fine. They aren't heavy."

Jaime surreptitiously examined the woman walking next to
her. She was light-skinned, with rosy cheeks, and the lightest dusting of freckles. Her face was rather heart-shaped with a high forehead and fine eyebrows, and she moved gracefully, as though she
could walk indefinitely. The hands carrying the two bags were
large and strong, and Jaime looked forward to hearing her play
guitar.

They stood next to the unmoving conveyor belt making small
talk about the weather and the success of the tour until the
machine clicked on, and with a groan, the belt began to move.

After a moment, baggage came wheeling out from the hole in the wall. The ATA cases arrived, and without bothering to grab any other bags, Kip hauled the big silver boxes off one at a time and knelt down to open each one and inspect the instruments.

Jaime watched Kip as she removed first one guitar and then the other. The musician was not quite the same height as Jaime and she was no skinny Minnie, as Grandma Esperanza used to say. She wasn't thin, and she wasn't exactly fat—simply short-waisted and compact. In jeans and a Henley top, she looked solid, and she also appeared comfortable in her body as she squatted next to the guitar cases. The electrician didn't think Lacey Leigh would feel like Kip was much competition, and for that, she was grateful. Obviously, pretty boy Nicky Kinnick had been far too great a threat to Lacey's towering ego. Jaime was still angry that Lacey had run him out. Of course, Nicky could have used thicker skin, too, but at the same time, Jaime understood why he'd thrown in the towel. It was a lot of stress being on tour with a raving bitch like Lacey Leigh Jaxon. She wondered how long it would be before Lacey showed her true colors and how this new woman would take it.

Apparently satisfied that her guitars were not damaged, Kip closed up the cases and carried them over to join Jaime.

"I didn't know which suitcases were yours," Jaime said, "though I am assuming they're the only ones left, huh?" She gestured toward the two black bags and the green garment bag that had just rumbled past. They disappeared through one hole in the wall, then reappeared seconds later from a different aperture.

"Yup, those are mine." When the bags reached the two women again, they snagged them off the belt, then set them down to take stock. Kip said, "This is a lot. I'll go get us a cart."

"That might be a good idea," Jaime said. "We've got a ways to go before we get to the bus."

Once they loaded everything onto the cart, they made their way to the parking lot. As they approached the bus, Jaime watched Kip out of the corner of her eye. The musician had an odd look on her face.

"Wow, when you mentioned a bus, Ms. Esperanza, somehow I had a van in mind, not a giant tour bus. The lettering on the side of this thing must be three feet tall."

"Sorry. We don't usually pick up the talent in the bus, but the limo guy got in an accident. And yeah, this thing is humongous, but you'll be calling it home for a while, too." She grinned as she unlocked the door and opened it. "Call me Jaime, will you?"

She opened the bay under the bus and stowed the ATA cases

there, then closed it and grabbed a suitcase. Kip reached for the remaining items and followed her up and in.

"I've seen pictures of these monstrosities before, but never been in one. It's big."

Kip looked around the interior of the front section of the vehicle. Behind the driver's seat was a good eight feet of comfortable-looking leather bench, parallel to the wall. The long bench hooked to the left into an L-shaped loveseat about a third of the way back. Next to the entrance, opposite the driver's seat, was a comfortable-looking leather seat that faced front. Behind that, a table was attached to the floor with a booth built around it. Four people could easily sit there. Beyond the table, built into the wall next to the loveseat, was an almond colored unit, about waist-high, that Kip pegged immediately as being a refrigerator. Past the open area was a narrow passageway on the left, and it was that direction to which Jaime was pointing.

"Let me show you around. Go ahead and leave your stuff right there, and we'll come back for it. This here's the lounge area. Your quarters are in the back, Kip—is it okay if I call you Kip?"

"Of course." She put down her suitcase and bags. "Why don't you lead on?" She followed Jaime to a corridor and stepped into a narrow passage about sixteen feet long. On the left side was a solid, wooden pocket door, and Jaime opened it. "Here's the bathroom. Even has a dinky little shower, though the hot water tank isn't all that huge and runs out pretty quick."

Kip poked here head in. "Well, it's bigger than an airplane bathroom."

Jaime laughed. "Not by much." She slid the door shut and turned to the other side of the hall. This little kitchenette has a microwave, mini-fridge, and storage space for snacks." She opened a cupboard. "Even has a coffeemaker."

"*That* will definitely come in handy."

Jaime took a couple more steps toward the back of the bus, and Kip saw tiers of bunks to the right and left. Jaime pulled aside the middle of three horizontal sets of curtains. "We've got three bunks here on each side. The two on the bottom are way beyond claustrophobic, but the top ones are big and have extra storage space. They're lighted and individually heated and air-conditioned."

Kip quickly noted that there was a recessed ladder in the middle as well as a metal grab bar about six feet above. "Oh, that's neat. Who sleeps in them?"

"The upper one here is mine, and Eric sometimes sleeps in the top one over there. The lower ones are open for anyone who needs them. Hardly anyone ever does use 'em, though, unless they're feeling really sick or exhausted. The guys are night owls."

Jaime dropped the curtain and strolled toward the rear. She pointed at the door of a tall, thin cupboard. "Once we get to the venue, you can borrow a regular case from the guitar tech if you want to keep a guitar on board here. We usually keep stuff in the bays under the bus or in a semi with the rest of the equipment, but there's a special storage space here for your musical gear—though if you want it in the stateroom, you can have it there, but it makes it pretty tight."

"All right."

"And here's the stateroom." She stepped toward a regular-sized door made of shiny wood with gold trim. Jaime reached for the gold doorknob, turned it, and entered the small space, leaving Kip standing in the doorway. Two wide, curtained windows, one on either side of the stateroom, allowed shafts of light to shine in. The right half of the room contained a full-size bed covered with a red and gold-colored coverlet tucked in so that the mattress corners were good and tight. The left side of the room contained a two-foot square table bolted to the floor with two chairs pushed up to it. A chest of drawers was built into the rear of the bus on the left, with a large mirror over it, and cupboards were recessed into the walls in various spots. To the right of where Kip stood, just inside the doorway, there was a large clothes closet. Jaime pointed things out, opened doors and drawers, and answered questions. "If you ever travel on another tour bus, you're unlikely to find it like this. The tour promoters own it, and they had it specially designed and decked out for Garth Brooks, and then the deal with him fell through."

"Oh. It's very nice." Kip took a deep breath, then let it out and sniffed. The stateroom smelled lemony and clean. "It sure is tidy in here. The last person must have been a real neat freak."

Jaime turned to face her. "Um hmm, that'd be me."

The musician looked past Jaime at the cozy room. She thought that having a place to go to, instead of a hotel, would save a lot of money. At the same time, she didn't want to have kicked someone out of their digs. Kip backed up, her face flushing. "This is your spot?"

"Nah. This is the opening act's spot. You're supposed to have these quarters. I was only using them temporarily because our last opener, Nicky Kinnick, didn't want to stay on the bus. He always got a hotel room, never rode the bus, and had a guy along who drove him in a nice sedan. Sleeping in here was fun while it lasted, but really, I'm used to the bunks. Let's get your stuff in here, and you can get settled before we get going, okay?"

"Sounds good. Where does Lacey Leigh hang out—at a hotel?"

"Most of the time, though she has a stateroom even bigger than this on the other bus. Her backup singers, Wes, and an occasional band member will usually ride in her bus. The band and crew almost always ride in this bus." She didn't have the heart to tell Kip that the band despised the way Lacey Leigh treated them, and they'd rather walk than travel in her bus.

The two women moved back out to the front and picked up bags and suitcases, transporting them down the tight hallway, and when everything had been carried in, most of it was on the bed. Jaime opened a door in the hallway right outside the stateroom. "Here is that storage area you can use for guitars, instruments, equipment. It has a good lock on it, too. There's already one guitar there—oh, and in the area up above, that's a mandolin and violin." Kip crowded past the other woman to look around the door. There were four long slots, one already occupied, where a guitar case fit perfectly, and then a thick elastic band could be strapped over the case to hold the guitar upright.

"Hey, that looks great."

"So, you want to use this—or do something else?"

"I think this would be fine."

"We trust one another on the tour. Everybody has access to the bus combination, but not this cabinet. I'll have a key; you'll have a key. We have to rely on each other to keep it locked, okay?" When Kip nodded, Jaime tucked the two cases in there and strapped them down, then stood up and shut the door. "I'll be up front. You let me know when you get settled."

Before Kip had a chance to say a word, Jaime wheeled around and disappeared. The singer looked at all the bags on the bed. *I'm supposed to get unpacked and settled now? Just get organized in five minutes so we can be on our way?* She stood for a moment in the middle of the tight space, then slid into the narrow spot at the foot of the bed and opened the closet there against the wall. The door had to be lifted up a little and out. It was designed well to keep it from rattling or opening when the bus hit bumps. She grabbed her garment bag, unzipped and unsnapped it so that it dangled at its full length, then hung it up, and slammed the door shut.

Opening a drawer built into the back of the bus, she found it to be solid, so she took all the contents from the canvas bags and arranged them in there: her journal, several books, a fat sheaf of musical notation paper, her cell phone, a plastic container holding office supplies, about fifteen CDs rubber-banded together, a couple of blank notebooks, and some bananas and snack items. She folded the canvas bags and stuffed them into the back of the drawer and shut it. She also noticed that there were two spacious drawers built into the base of the bed unit, but she wasn't ready to deal with the items in her suitcases, so she picked the bags up off the bed and set them, end up, at the foot of the bed. Finally the mattress was clear, and she dove onto it and rolled onto her back, pulling a pillow out from under the coverlet and tucking it behind her head. The mattress was comfortable. She thought it might take her some time to get used to the size of the bed, though. At home she had a king-sized bed—a lonely size, she thought—but this was small. Two people could sleep in it, but only if they were *very* good friends.

A rumbling sound caught her off guard, and the bed vibrated ever so slightly. She let out a startled squeak, then realized Jaime had started the bus's engine. She wondered what it would be like to lie here in the bed as the bus bumped along down the road. *Good grief! It must be noisy as hell in here! Guess I'll know soon enough.* She got off the bed and strolled down the narrow corridor and into the open lounge area. Jaime sat in the driver's seat with her back to Kip, but Kip met her eyes in the rearview mirror.

Jaime raised an eyebrow. "You have a question? You can't be ready so soon."

"I'll unpack the rest of the stuff later. I'm ready as I'll ever be." She came around to the front of the leather recliner and plopped down into it, giving the other woman a curious look.

Jaime put the bus into gear and navigated it through the parking lot. Kip waited until the bus was out on the street before she asked her first question. "What is your role on this tour, Jaime?"

"I do production mostly. I handle stuff on stage, do a little electrical work, help with sound. I make sure electrical, sound equipment, and the stage are set up for each concert."

"You don't usually drive the bus, though, right?"

"Actually, Eric and I do. We've both got CDLs—commercial licenses. The other bus is leased and comes with a driver, but this one is owned by Wes's company, and to cut costs, they haven't hired anybody for quite a while."

"I see. So how many people are involved in this tour?"

"My boss is Eric O'Connell who handles both production and sound. Wes Slater is the tour promoter and general manager. He also personally handles Lacey Leigh. The rest of us are band or crew, or in my case, both crew *and* band sometimes, too. We're running short on staff, so everybody's job seems to overlap."

"You sing?"

"Not much—not if I can help it, I mean." She pulled the bus up to a stoplight and threw a glance over her shoulder. "I play a little mandolin, fiddle, and guitar."

"Oh, that's cool. Is it fun?"

The light changed, and Jaime hit the gas. "Not really."

Kip wondered why it was no fun. She couldn't imagine playing music and not having a blast. Before she could ask another question, Jaime said, "Besides me, Wes, and Eric, there's two traveling crew techs, Tom and Lance. At each venue, the tour manager has already arranged for local stagehands and lighting companies to come in and set up the lighting system. Security, too. Then there are two backup singers and the five members of the band. Twelve total—most of the time, anyway. Thirteen now, with you."

"What about Lacey Leigh?"

Jaime felt the blush rise. "Oh, yeah. And Lacey." She glanced in the rearview mirror, but Kip wasn't looking her way, and for that she was grateful.

Kip looked out the window at the pleasant day. Thick stands of trees lined both sides of the road, and though they were on a main thoroughfare, everything looked a bit rustic. She'd checked up on Helena weather for mid-June and found it would be in the 70s for temperature whenever the sun was out, but if it was cloudy, it could get down into the 40s and 50s. Today was a lovely 73 degrees. She knew this because there was a display on the bus above Jaime's head that said so. *Bren would love this town.* A tiny, invisible stab of pain cut through her, and she closed her eyes. Seeing her ex earlier seemed to have made her more vulnerable than she would have liked. She was amazed that, even after a year, it could still hurt so much. Each time she thought she had gotten past the reality of the loss, some little thing popped up to remind her and bring her pain.

The bus slowed, and Kip opened her eyes. They were turning into the parking area of a two-story, log cabin-style motel. The lot was large and less than half full. Jaime brought the bus to a stop next to another black bus exactly like it, only the lettering on the *Lacey Leigh Jaxon ~ Roamin' From Wyoming Tour* written on that bus was hot pink instead of bright red. She looked to the black-haired driver, nervous and uncertain as to what would happen next. Jaime turned off the engine, then shifted a quarter turn in her seat, her jean-clad legs out in the aisle. She worked three keys off the key ring she removed from the ignition, and handed them to Kip. "Here. The silver one goes to the door here, and the gold one goes to your stateroom. That other one, the small one, locks the guitar closet. If I were you, I would go back there right now and lock up. Keep your valuables under lock and key. The gold key will also lock the clothes closet and all the drawers in there. Stan, the driver of the other bus tries to keep an eye on things, but you never know who might manage to get in here."

Kip nodded. "What's next?"

"I'm going to make sure this big boat gets hooked up to shore power so you have heat, lights, and A/C. And then—" she grinned, "you get to meet this weird bunch of people. For the most part, they're pretty nice. Then I think Wes wants to take you off for a burger or a snack or something and talk to you privately. He'll give you a precise schedule for Friday's concert—you'll get a written one the day before every gig. You come see me with any questions at all, okay?" She paused. "Oh, and one more thing..." She looked sheepish, but when her dark brown eyes met Kip's, the musician saw she was trying to be helpful. "Wes swears up a storm, and he can be a bit rude at times. Pay no attention to that."

"Okay. Thanks. I'll just go lock up and be right back." She rose and strode back toward the stateroom.

Jaime let out a sigh and shook her head slowly. *These people are going to eat that nice woman alive.*

Chapter
Four

KIP SAT IN her stateroom, trembling on the edge of her bed. She'd been offered a dressing room, but after checking out the small, sterile room, she decided she would rather hang out on the bus where it was quiet.

She'd made it through Wednesday's flight and had been confident later in the day when meeting the band, crew, Wes Slater, and the diminutive star, Lacey Leigh Jaxon. Everyone was very nice. Thursday she did fine at initial sound checks at the concert hall, though she was surprised that Lacey Leigh didn't do her own sound checks. Her backup singer, Shelley, did that task. Kip watched closely to get an idea of what she should do, and all went well. Eric O'Connell, the sound man, had encouraged her, saying she sounded great in the "small house." The hall seated four thousand, and every seat was sold. Kip didn't think it was a small house at all. She had never sung in such a large venue, and the idea of four thousand people was enough to make her worry she was going to faint. The last time someone asked her how she was feeling, she said, "Scared shitless." Now it was three hours later, Friday night at half past seven, and she was even more sick to her stomach.

With a mere half-hour until her first opening act on the Jaxon Tour, she was glad the bathroom was just outside her door. Right now she felt like she was going to vomit any minute. *What the hell was I thinking? Oh my God, what was I thinking?* She looked down at her black slacks, white shirt, and black vest and wondered whether anyone would notice if she slipped into more comfortable clothes and snuck out the back.

She opened the top drawer in the bureau next to her bed, pulled out her cell phone, pressed the *ON* button, and waited for the device to light up. It flashed *battery low* until she turned it off. *So much for the idea of calling up Mary or good old mom—or anybody else for that matter. I'll have to charge it later.*

She picked up the Gibson guitar from the open case on the floor, pulled it to her and strummed nervously. She was comforted that she hadn't let Lance, the guitar tech, take Isabelle away. Her spare guitar was out there with him in case of emergency, though. He said that he always kept the guitars maintained and tuned in the stage wings on the massive racks he worked from, but she wasn't having any of that. Kip needed Isabelle with her. She thought of her guitar as a feminine being—not human, but certainly divine in some way. And in fact, Isabelle was a calming feminine force. Her serial number, inside the body of the guitar, included the letters ISA, and right away, when Kip bought the guitar ten years earlier, she had known—felt—that the guitar's name was Isabelle. She and Isabelle had been a team for the last decade, and though she had another fancier and more expensive guitar, it was Isabelle she turned to for this, her first opening act on a major tour.

As she strummed and picked, she hummed a new tune, not something she had played before, and it amused her to think that if she were not going onstage in a short while, she could probably write a song since she liked the melody running through her head. She took a pad of paper out of her drawer and made some notes, writing down chords and quick musical notation, and left the pad of paper on top of the bed. No words came to mind, but she continued to monkey around with the melody and the pick pattern of this new song. So engrossed was she that she didn't hear any footsteps and was startled when there was a light tap on the door.

The folksinger rose, setting her guitar behind her on the bed, and opened the door. Jaime stood before her, all dressed in black. Kip looked down at her own outfit and said, "We're very nearly twins."

From behind her back, Jaime pulled a black cowboy hat. "But I bet you don't have one of these," she teased.

Kip shook her head, grinning back. "Nope. I look ridiculous in hats."

"Ah, but so do we all."

Kip smiled and shook her head. "No, that's not true. I bet you look fine in your hat."

Jaime changed the subject. "You're on in a few minutes." She consulted her watch. "Nine minutes, to be exact. You ready?"

Stepping back toward the bed, Kip pushed the drawer shut, palmed the stateroom keys, then snagged her guitar as she said, "Ready as I'll ever be."

"All right then. It's a very responsive crowd. Lots of kids, moms and cowboys. I think you'll do well tonight."

With a mouth gone dry, Kip croaked out, "I hope so." She stepped out of the stateroom, locked it, and slipped the keys into her pocket. She carried her guitar upright, in front of her, with the back of it pressed close to her body and the neck touching the side of her face, as they made their way out of the bus. Once out in the open air, Jaime walked beside her, one hand on Kip's left elbow. The musician, with heart beating wildly, found her escort's old-fashioned behavior somehow comforting.

Though the bus was very close to the stage door, she still had twenty paces to go, and there were people out and about. The low hum of their discussions ceased for a matter of seconds, and then someone said, "Hey, break a leg." Someone else said, "Knock 'em dead, kid." And then a security guard let them in, and she heard a new hum, the sound of four thousand people talking and laughing out front.

Jaime led her through a maze of passages to stage left, and when they stopped, Kip pulled her guitar strap over her head and got the instrument situated comfortably. She was used to plugging in onstage. It always gave her time to chat with the audience, but usually the audience was twenty or fifty or even a hundred—not four thousand. She peeked around the corner of the curtain and focused in on some of the faces in the front rows. Jaime was right. It looked like a lot of families and young people—cowboys and cowgirls. *I can do families and cow-people, right?* She snickered nervously to herself, and then Tom, wearing earphones, turned to her. He held up his hand, then counted back. "Five, four, three, two, one..." He made a fist. "We're ready when you are, Kip."

She took a deep breath, and then heard a low voice in her ear. "Sing just like you were in a coffee shop, Kip." The frightened woman swallowed and looked back into Jaime's dark eyes. "You've done it before—go do the same thing you always do. Concentrate on the front rows and just sing like it's a tiny little coffee shop."

Jaime smiled at her, and Kip smiled back, a blush rising from her neck to her scalp, then she walked onstage, plugged in her guitar, and said, "Hell-LOH, Helena!"

A smattering of applause began as the lights came up, and the restless crowd settled down, waiting impatiently to find out what kind of warm-up act this was. "I don't know about you all," Kip said in as strong a voice as she could muster, "but I can't get enough of Wynonna's music." A cheer came up from the audience. "I'm gonna open with a little tune of Wynonna's called 'A Little Bit of Love Goes A Long, Long Way.'"

She'd worked long and hard to put together the rhythm guitar for the strong 4/4 beat. Closing her eyes, she launched into the song and belted it out like it was the only song she'd sing all night. When she got to the end, the applause from the listeners was politely enthusiastic, so she moved right into another peppy song, this one called "Angelene" and originally sung by Jodee Messina. As she played and sang, she gradually became comfortable and opened her eyes to look out at the house. People were tapping their toes, and some of them—the ones she could see in the first four rows or so—knew the lyrics and were singing along. Her unease went away, and she realized Jaime was right. It was like singing in the coffee shop, except that the acoustics were so much better. The side fill and the monitors in front of her emitted such clear sound that it was easy to concentrate on singing and not worry about a thing, which was so very different from her stints in small shops where she was responsible for all the levels and sometimes couldn't hear her guitar properly. She gazed to her left and met Tom's eyes, giving him a little nod and smile, and suddenly, right in the middle of the song, she was filled up with a buoyancy of excitement that she hadn't felt in a long while. She felt like dancing.

From the wings, Jaime stood watching, her arms crossed over her black shirt. Tom elbowed her and gave her a nod, and she knew that he approved of the way the performance was going. She approved, too. She couldn't get over how much clearer and richer Kip's voice was live compared to the CD. The recording had obviously been a substandard mix because right now, Kip Galvin sounded like a million bucks.

The folksinger finished her song and thanked the audience, then said, "I'm gonna slow it down a notch now and play you something I wrote." She started picking a complicated and intricate intro, then hummed until she broke into the first verse:

I never did feel satisfied, I never did feel happy
Then again, at times I almost believed, what can I say?
You seemed to change the dark to light
And days were something special...

Kip's voice was still deep and lush, but the pain of the song was evident, and Jaime wondered whether the folksinger had actually experienced this—or was a big fake like Lacey Leigh.

I guess it wasn't enough just to have you for a time
And you're moving on again and I am left behind

To kid myself at how ironic it is that besides death
All the bad dreams I knew could really come true...

Jaime thought that if Kip had written the song and hadn't felt all those emotions, then she was a great actress. She didn't strike Jaime as being particularly false, so she found herself intrigued and wanting to know more about the singer.

She listened to as much of the act as she could, but at about the thirty-minute mark, Wes appeared at her elbow and poked her hard in the side. "Dammit! Go get Lacey. Tell her she's on in about fifteen minutes."

"Yeah, yeah." She scowled at him in the dark, knowing full well he couldn't see her, then she stomped off to the dressing rooms in the back to get the star. Lacey was in a foul mood, but Jaime didn't waste time taking any guff from her. As soon as the tiny blonde started in on her, Jaime turned and walked off. She could hear Candy and Shelley soothing the singer as the three of them followed her down the hallway. Then Jaime hustled back into the wings, to stand in her former spot, just in time to hear Kip strum the intro for her slow version of "Wyoming."

The sun is shining weakly
But a half sliver of moon is out
Why am I alone
In the pristine splendor of the Big Horn Forest
On an icy ribbon of highway
Roaming the snow-covered roads
Traveling alone, and scared
In Wyoming

She heard a gasp from behind her and turned to see Lacey Leigh stomping her foot and hissing at Wes Slater. A whole lot of commotion was going on in the dim area in back of her, and Jaime turned away to listen to the song, finding it strange to hear it sung slower, at a more mournful pace.

What a relief to make it to the bottom
Of Crazy Woman Creek
Off the mountains and away from the cliffs of destruction
I'll still be roaming
Miles and miles I'll be roaming
Alone for who knows how long
On this long highway through Wyoming

Now the bridge came, and in a full-toned voice, Kip sang:

The road is steep, switchbacks next to rocky hills
Climb up a mountain tall
Looking over the guardrail to the ravine below
It's a long, long fall

Jaime heard something said behind her, and it took a moment for the words to register. Before they did, however, Lacey Leigh was elbowing past her, and Jaime realized that what the star had said was, "Give me that fuckin' mic—and it better be live!" The blonde woman strolled out onstage, humming into a suddenly live wireless microphone. Jaime saw the look of surprise on Kip's face, but the guitarist didn't falter, instead, playing the melodic part perfectly. A huge roar came up as the audience saw that it was their Lacey Leigh Jaxon out onstage. They rose to their feet, too, as Kip segued right on cue into the chorus. She sang the words in her deep, clear voice, and Lacey Leigh hit the harmony part, a third above.

Been a rough trip, any way you look at it
Never knew how long I'd roam
Lost and alone and scared of what I might do on
The snow-capped peaks of Wyoming

Lacey Leigh moved over to stand next to Kip and reached up to put her hand on the taller woman's shoulder. Then they sang the last verse:

Hope this old truck will make it to the foothills of the
Bighorn Forest where Sitting Bull has sat so long
It's lonely here this winter day but I don't belong
Roaming lost and alone
On the snow-capped peaks of Wyoming
I'll still be roaming
Miles and miles I'm roaming
Alone for who knows how long
On this long highway through Wyoming.

Before the final guitar notes faded away, the audience was on their feet, clapping, stomping, and whistling. Lacey, dressed in her off-white, pinkish pant suit gave a deep bow, then stood and gestured toward Kip, who gave a nod and then waved, still holding her pick between thumb and forefinger. Lacey hollered into her mic, "Let's hear it for Kit Garvin!"

Jaime frowned. *Kit Garvin? Did Lacey just fumble on that one—or did she mangle Kip's name on purpose?* She had no way of knowing, but it didn't matter anyway, because what she and the technicians could hear clearly in the wings was mostly drowned out by the cheering crowd. The two women started to walk off the stage. Everyone standing stage left, including Candy, Shelley, the band, and crew, scattered to one side or the other, making a path from the side curtain to the back door for the smiling blonde and the still stunned-looking guitarist to pass. As soon as the two women cleared the curtains and were off the stage, the house music came up, and it was much louder than usual. Eric, out on the front-of-house console, was planning ahead, and Jaime couldn't help but laugh—not humorously, but with a feeling of absurdity—for she knew what was about to happen. She had barely reached Kip and taken hold of the neck of her guitar before Lacey Leigh turned and shrieked. Jaime flicked the end of the strap off the guitar and took it from the guitarist just in time.

"You goddamn stupid bitch! That's *my* song—do you hear me? My song! Where do you get off singing *my* song?" Lacey Leigh was a good six inches shorter than Kip, but she was like a wildcat, sneering up at the taller woman, cursing at her, and shaking her finger in Kip's startled face.

Jaime winced. *Oh, God. Only one night, and this poor woman is going to quit just like Nicky Kinnick did.* She took a deep breath and prepared to step in if Lacey got physical, but before she could do that, Kip spoke up.

"That's *enough.*" Her voice was strong and firm. "Your behavior is *despicable*, and you need to spend some time thinking about it!" She moved toward the smaller woman, and Lacey Leigh stepped back, momentarily cowed. "Go on now—off the stage. You go pull yourself together," and to Lacey's retreating back she shouted, "and don't come back 'til you've got yourself under control!"

Wes Slater let out a growl, then turned on his heel to follow his prima donna.

Kip stood breathing deeply for a moment, then became aware of everyone standing around staring at her. "What?"

"How the hell did you do that?" Tom asked. He set his earphones on top of the monitor and craned his neck down closer to her to hear what she had to say.

Kip shrugged. "Guess it pays to be a public school teacher. I just treated her like any of the mouthy seventh grade witches I have to deal with."

Everyone in the area broke into laughter. Lance was the first to come to his senses. "We have to get set, people. Tom!" The sound tech scurried forward. "Let's get the flash pots set up. We haven't got all that much time."

Jaime stood off to the side, holding the guitar, which was still warm from Kip having held it tight to her. Her eyes, merry and amused, met Kip's, and she thought, *Lacey Leigh, you have just met your match.*

KIP WAITED PATIENTLY for the throngs of people to file out of the arena, and then she rose from the side chair at the FOH desk. She thanked Eric for letting her watch Lacey Leigh's part of the concert with him from his soundboard area, and then she meandered down the main aisle. The two security guys still stood guard in front of the stage, and one put up a hand and started to say something.

"Chill, guys." She dug into her pants pocket and pulled out her laminated tour pass. "I'll have to forgive you for not recognizing me as the opening act since you had your backs to me through the whole performance."

"Uh, sorry about that. Can't be too careful," one said.

"No problem." She went around the side, up the narrow stairs, and across the stage toward the wings. She wasn't exactly sure of the quickest route to the dressing rooms, but she intended to find them. As she descended the first steps she found, she heard raised voices. Letting out a sigh, she headed toward the argument. The closer she got, the more she was sure that Wes Slater and Lacey Leigh were about ready to come to blows.

"I don't give a great goddamn, Lacey!" he roared.

She shrieked back at him. "You should. *I'm* the headliner! *I'm* the star! *I'm* the one all those people are paying the big bucks to see, and fuck you if you think I'm putting up with this!"

A deep voice pleaded with her. "You're *not* running this act out. Shit! We can't afford it. Lacey, this one's a nice woman with talent. Now—"

"I don't give a shit! Same whore, different dress. Every one of those bitches and bastards want to ride my coattails to fame. I won't have it!" Lacey let out another shriek, like a cat that's been stepped on.

"Cut it out, Lacey," he panted.

By then, Kip had reached the open door. She stepped into the brightly lit doorway, and because of the dimness of the hall, for a moment she wasn't sure what she was seeing. Slater stood in pro-

file, facing the right wall. The big man had hold of Lacey around
the waist from behind, pinning her hands to her sides, with her
feet up off the ground. His legs were spread wide to avoid all the
kicking she was doing.

"Let me go," she snarled.

"Gosh," Kip said, "I hope only headliners have to go through
this part of the after-show celebration." She stood in the doorway,
her arms crossed, fighting back a grin. Slater abruptly released the
kicking star, and she landed on her feet, tipped forward and nearly
fell, then caught herself.

"You get your ass out of here," Lacey Leigh yelled, both
hands up in the air and waving at her. "Who told you this was any
of your business?"

Kip turned her attention away from the screaming woman. In
a quiet voice, she said, "Mr. Slater, if you don't mind, I'd like a
word in private with Ms. Jaxon."

His face took on a look of astonishment, but he nodded and
brushed his hands together as though he had just finished a tough
job. "I need a smoke anyhow."

Kip moved further into the dressing room as he squeezed past
her and disappeared down the hall, his cowboy boots making a
receding thump into the distance. She took a deep breath and narrowed her eyes as she looked at Lacey. She unfolded her arms. "I
think you and I had better come to an understanding."

All the wind seemed to go out of the diva. She spun on her
heel and reached for a half-empty bottle of Chivas Regal sitting on
her makeup table. When she turned back, Kip thought she looked
awfully tired and old for only 28. In a resigned voice, the blonde
asked, "Why don't you come sit down?"

Kip scooted left and sat gingerly on the edge of a tattered
loveseat.

Lacey unscrewed the cap from the Scotch whiskey. "You want
a drink?" She gestured with the bottle. "I'm pretty sure I have
some cups in the bag." She sat in an overstuffed chair across from
Kip, reached down into a leather Coach bag, and rooted around
until she came up with several plastic cups nested into one
another. She set the bottle in her lap, separated two of the small
cups from the stack, and put the others back in the bag. Pouring
into the top cup, she said, "You want a full cup?"

"Oh, no. Just a shot would be fine."

Lacey giggled. "Guess this one's for me then." She set the
bottle on the floor and carefully slid the empty cup out from under
the full one, placed her drink next to her feet, and poured a couple
ounces into the remaining container, which she held out for Kip.

The folksinger rose and accepted the offered cup, then returned to the edge of the loveseat and waited.

The woman sitting in the chair before Kip had very clearly shifted from one personality to something completely different in a matter of two minutes. She was peaceful as she gripped the neck of the bottle in her left hand and the pale green cup in her right. Kip watched as the diva took a long pull, then raised tired green eyes. She was tempted to launch right into her demands and find out what Lacey might have to say, but Kip suddenly felt a wave of fatigue. She raised the drink to her lips and took a sip. "Whew. This stuff is strong."

"Mmm...but good." The blonde star's voice was low and throaty. She closed her eyes and took another swig. Kip could see Lacey's neck muscles ripple as she swallowed. When the star opened her eyes, she trained a hard gaze Kip's way, suddenly all business. "So? You've got the floor."

Oh, I do, huh? A hint of a smile came to the folksinger's lips. Kip drained the second and final swig of the Scotch and felt it burn all the way down. "'Wyoming' is my song." She dropped the empty cup into the wastebasket on the other side of her chair and watched as the pop star's eyes narrowed as her face took on a look that Kip would describe as feral.

"I paid goddamn good money for that song."

"You don't own my song. I wrote it. I own it. It's my song."

"I made it famous. I hit number one with it. It's *my* song."

"Your version is yours—but the song is mine." Kip could see the white of Lacey's knuckles on the neck of the bottle, and she realized she was enjoying baiting the woman far more than she should. Lacey tipped her head back and dumped the last of her drink in her mouth, then poured some more. When she raised her head again, the scowl on her face made her look twisted and ugly. Kip had a sudden vision of the young woman twenty years older, and she didn't think it would be pretty. *Drawstring bag with teeth* was the phrase that came to mind, and Kip actually felt sorry for her. "Listen, I'll make a deal with you. I won't sing 'Wyoming' on this tour. Nobody wants to hear the slow version anyway."

"No shittin'! They want to hear *my* version!" Lacey set the liquor bottle down on the floor so hard that Kip wondered why it didn't break.

Kip ran her tongue over her teeth, still tasting the Scotch and wishing she hadn't accepted it. "You know what your problem is, Ms. Jaxon?" Kip rose and the blonde's eyes opened wide. "You don't know when to quit—not even when you're ahead. I just gave you what you wanted, and instead of graciously accepting, you throw it back in my face." She took a step toward the door.

"Wait! Wait, you're right. You are so totally right. Goddamn totally right. Right, right, right. Okay." She nodded and pursed her lips. "Okay, forget I said that." She took a deep breath and looked around the room. Her eyes slid back to Kip's, then away. She held her manicured hand out in front of her and looked at her nails. "So, what do you really think? Can we make this work?"

Kip laughed out loud. "Well, I don't think we'll be exchanging clothes or favorite recipes, but there's no reason we can't get along."

"Hmmph." The diva drained the plastic cup she held, set it on the floor, then stood up and looked around. "Where did that—oh, here it is." She reached over to the makeup table and picked up the metal cap and bent over to screw it on the liquor bottle, then tucked the bottle into the leather bag. When she turned back to the folksinger, she looked tired again. "Walk me out to the bus?"

Kip looked at her a long moment, then shrugged. "Sure."

The tiny woman picked up her bag and followed the folksinger out into the hall where she reached up and hooked her arm through Kip's. "Well, honey, we're about to be mobbed at the stage door."

"Think so?"

Lacey nodded. "Oh, yeah, I know so." She sighed. "Always the same old thing."

"Same whore, different dress?"

"Something like that."

KIP HAD A good laugh the next morning. She sat reading the Helena newspaper in a diner a block down from the hotel where the buses were parked. In the Entertainment section, she found a review of the previous night's concert. The headline read *Lacey Leigh—Definitely!* and the article was accompanied by a great photo of the diminutive singer, which took up one-sixth of the page. The part that made her laugh was written late in the article: "Opening act Kip Galvin was no doubt thrilled when Jaxon came onstage to sing backup for the final song of Galvin's warm-up set. This reporter later learned that it was Galvin's first show with the tour. Isn't it just like Lacey Leigh Jaxon to come out and give a hand to a new friend?"

If she hadn't had her mouth full of scrambled eggs when she read that, Kip might have laughed out loud.

Chapter
Five

THE FOLKSINGER STOOD in the wings and watched as
Eric, Jaime, and the stagehands swarmed the stage area at the
North Dakota concert hall. She wasn't sure how they managed
such organization in so short a time, but this was the third venue
in a row where they had loaded in and completely outfitted a stage
and auditorium in a mere afternoon. She thought back to her simple PA sound system and shook her head in wonder. This was a lot
more complex than she'd ever imagined.

She hung back, slightly behind the thick, blood-red curtain,
but after a few moments, Jaime glanced up and caught sight of
her. She tilted her head to the side and met Kip's eyes, then rose
and strode in her direction. She moved like an athlete, smooth and
graceful, her shapely legs clad in mid-thigh-length Lycra shorts.
When Jaime was a couple strides away, Kip asked, "Did you play
sports in school?"

Jaime squinted and gave a funny half smile. "Sports? Why
are you asking about sports?"

"Oh. You look like an athlete. I just wondered if you were
athletic in high school."

"High school was a very long time ago for me. More than half
a lifetime. I don't think about it all that much. But no, I didn't
play sports. We weren't encouraged in my hometown. You?"

"I wasn't much interested. Spent all my time in the band and
music rooms, and didn't have any time left over."

Jaime gave a nod. "Do you need anything, Kip?"

The folksinger raised an eyebrow. "I'm sorry?"

"You need something? Is something wrong? Why are you
out here?"

"Nothing's wrong, Jaime. I'm just watching. It's interesting."

Jaime grinned, but she was looking at Kip as though she
didn't believe her. "Interesting? In what way?"

Kip shrugged. "I'm used to coffee shops, Jaime. It takes me, at most, maybe forty-five minutes to drag everything in by myself, set up, and then do sound checks. Everything I have for a show fits in the back of my pickup. This," she gave a wave of her hand out toward the stage, "is all amazing. Two semi's and two buses of people and gear. It's a lot, that's all."

Jaime brushed her hair out of her eyes. "When you put it that way, yeah, I suppose this does seem like quite the production."

Kip nodded. "What exactly are you doing out there with that gizmo anyway?"

Jaime turned and pointed. "That's a Genie Tower. The lighting guys raise it up to get the racks of lights to the right height. It works on compressed air, and this one's a real bitch to work with, but a lot easier than twenty ladders." She chuckled. "Not every venue has one, and believe me, ladders are a pain in the butt for some of the riggers."

"I bet."

One of the hands stood up and called for Jaime. "What?" she hollered back.

"You got some dykes in that tool belt of yours?" he yelled.

Kip was taken aback. She watched as Jaime reached into a pocket and pulled something out. It flashed silver as Jaime bent and slid it rocket-fast across the floor to the stagehand. "Thanks," he called out. Jaime turned back to Kip, and the musician's face must have revealed her confusion. Jaime frowned. "What now?"

"Ahh, well, what just happened there?"

"That guy asked for my d—." She paused. "Oh. Dykes. Diagonal wire cutters. They're called dykes."

"I see." Kip couldn't hold back the grin that came to her face, nor could she prevent the blush that started at her neck and suffused her face. "I was wondering how you could fit a little silver lesbian in that tiny pocket of your tool belt."

Before Jaime could answer, Wes Slater was shouting from the wings on the other side. "Why in the *hell* isn't the lighting complete? *Jee*-zus!"

"Gotta run," Jaime said under her breath. She spun on her heel and dodged around equipment and boxes, but as she moved swiftly away, it hit her that Kip Galvin had just made a joke about lesbians—and comfortably, too. That gave her pause, but she didn't have any time to stop and think about it because Wes Slater was yowling at her.

VERY QUICKLY, KIP fell into a rhythm. Wes Slater's bookings required them to play every two to four nights with an occasional double-header. She liked it best when they did a show and then the band spent the night at the local hotel and traveled the following day to the next venue where they had a day or more to get acclimated. It was subtle, but she could tell a difference when she was performing in the plains versus up in the mountains of Colorado or Wyoming. A few thousand feet made a lot of difference in her lung power, something she never expected.

The last day of June, they finished a show in Flagstaff, Arizona, and were scheduled to take off that same night for New Mexico. As usual, the semi's had already gone on ahead, leaving right after load out from the show was complete, but Lacey spent an extra hour doing press interviews and a local TV appearance, so the two buses didn't depart right away.

When they finally departed, Eric drove the crew bus. Gary and Lacey Leigh were still an item, so he rode with the backup singers on her bus, but Jaime, Drew, Buck, and the twins hung around in the crew bus playing cards at the table or jamming. Kip had been spending the late nights back in her noisy stateroom, trying to relax and unwind, but the engine was so noisy and the ride so bumpy that she never slept. She always came out at least once during the ride to stand in the narrow hallway and chat, though. She was shy around all the guys, but that night she resolved to go out and join them.

When she appeared, Buck, the big drummer, said, "Hey, Kip. Wanna get your ass kicked at poker?" He grinned up at her, his dark eyes mischievous. He sat with Marcus, Davis, and Jaime at the little table, and the four of them overflowed the small table setup. It had taken her a while to get it fixed in her mind which twin was which. Both had thinning hair on top, but Davis had a full beard, which he kept trimmed close to his face. Once she got used to telling them apart that way, she began to notice other things about the shapes of their faces or the way they grinned, and now she had no trouble discerning who was who.

The four of them looked her over, waiting for her response, and she blushed. She met Jaime's eyes, and then, debating for a moment, she shook her head. "I never was much for poker. You *would* kick my butt."

Skinny Drew sat on the long, leather side bench playing quiet riffs on an acoustic guitar. He cleared his throat and caught her eye. In his slow Texas drawl, he said, "Why don't you get your guitar, then, and come jam with me. They can kill each other at cards, and we'll write us the great American song."

She didn't need to be asked twice. She wheeled around and went to the back closet to get Isabelle, then went out to sit near

Drew. She did a quick string check and had him play his low E to
see if they were in tune. After some adjustments, she leaned back.
"What do you want to play, Drew?"

He shrugged. "Don't much matter to me. I can play along
with anything." She liked his deep voice. He had a twang, like
he'd grown up down south.

"Where are you from, Drew?" she asked.

"Texas born and bred, ma'am. San Antonio, home of the
Alamo and the Spurs."

She nodded and smiled. "That's one place I've not been. You
get back there much?"

"Yeah," he sighed. "I'm on the road some, but I do get back
when I can. My parents and little brothers still live there. And hey,
you'll be able to check out the countryside in short order, ma'am.
Only a few weeks 'til San Antonio comes up on the schedule."

"Yeah, that's true." She strummed a barred C chord. "How
about this?" She played a chord progression, and before she got
through the six chords, he was already strumming and picking and
bending notes. It gave her the shivers. A good lead guitar always
gave her goose bumps. She closed her eyes, smiling with glee.
After another run-through, she opened her mouth to sing.

> *Right now, you're holding my heart in your hands*
> *And though this is not how it was planned*
> *That's how it is, like it or not*
> *Things have to change and so do we*
> *No matter what I thought*

She didn't open her eyes when she heard somebody move
from the table, instead focusing on the intricate picking she was
doing and letting the wonderful notes Drew was playing reverber-
ate through her. Then as she started to sing the next verse, she
heard a gentle hum, like wind over water, and she opened her
eyes. Jaime stood leaning against the back wall, swaying a bit as
the bus rumbled down the road, and the mournful sound of the
bow on her violin strings sent a chill through Kip. It was time for
the next verse.

> *I could not imagine that you'd ever go*
> *And deep inside I wish you could know*
> *That people change*
> *They rearrange their lives and loves and living*
> *That someday soon you will, too*
> *I can't just go on giving*

She met the big drummer's eyes. He had a sweet smile on his face, and he set his arms on the table to keep time, making a *shooshing* noise on the tabletop with one palm while tapping with the other hand.

But why do people change?
The thought just breaks my heart
You can't belong to me, I know
We both knew it from the start

So right now you're holding my heart in your hands
It is not the way I planned
But things will change – like it or not
It's sad to say in old clichés
But soon we'll have to part

The song drew to a close, and there was silence for a brief moment—and then from the very front of the bus, Eric let loose a raucous whistle. "Whoowee!" he hollered. "Don't let Lacey hear that one, or she'll snap it up." He looked in the rearview mirror and grinned at Kip. "*That* is a rare and beautiful thing, girl. Do it again."

She blushed from the bottom of her neck, up into her face, all the way into the roots of her hair. Looking around at the crew surrounding her, she saw they were all smiling and nodding, but Jaime was frowning at her. "What?" Kip asked.

Jaime scowled and shook her head. "I sort of messed that up. Sorry."

Kip's eyes widened. "Messed it up? I thought that sounded great!"

Now it was Jaime's turn to blush. "Nah...I sort of took a wrong turn there when you switched into the bridge."

"I liked it how it was, Jaime. It sounded gorgeous." She turned away and looked at Drew. "You are the best, Drew. Damn, you're good. If I could play lead like you—wow!"

"Wasn't nothin', ma'am."

She laughed. "What the hell is this 'ma'am' business? You have to cut it out, my good man, or I'm going to start calling you 'sir.'"

He said, "You can put a boot in the oven, but that don't make it a biscuit." She let out a guffaw, then sat giggling, completely unable to speak. He laughed, too. "I'm no sir, but my mama taught me to treat a lady with respect."

"Let's get one thing straight, Drew..." She leaned toward

him. "I ain't no lady." Everybody laughed, and Buck made a ba-
boom sound on the table with his hands. Kip reached over and
touched Drew's forearm, which was resting on the top of his guitar. "Just call me Kip."

Marcus slid over in the booth and rose, saying, "People, I do
believe we should have a drink."

"You bet," said his brother, Davis. He got up, too, and went
to the little refrigerator. Marcus got out beer, and Davis asked if
anyone wanted Scotch.

Eric called out, "I'd love to join you..."

"Hey," Jaime said. "You focus on the road. I'll spell you in a
while, and you can drink all you want."

He gave a nod and hollered over his shoulder, "Can you turn
the lights to a lower setting, people? The glare is bugging me up
here."

For a few minutes, people scuttled around, mixing drinks and
opening snack bags, and then when they finally settled, Jaime was
sitting to Kip's left, holding her violin in her lap, and Drew was
on the other side. Marcus sat in the recliner sideways, facing
them, with his long legs lapped over one arm while he cradled a
bottle of Michelob. Davis had gotten another guitar and sat cross-
legged below Buck, who was still cheerfully ensconced at the
table. They looked to Kip, waiting, and she realized they were
ready to follow her lead. "Well," she said. "Any requests?"

"Your wish is our command," Drew said.

"Okay, how about a little Patsy Cline?"

Drew picked an intro, and she strummed a chord, then
stopped. "Hey, Mr. Guitar Man, how in the heck did you know I
wanted to do 'I Fall To Pieces'?"

He grinned. "Dunno. You just seemed in that kind of mood,
Kip."

Exasperated, she asked, "Well, how did you know what key
I'd be in?"

He made a little *heh-heh-heh* sound, then said, "I got your
whole range figured out, little lady."

Kip sat back, amazed. She looked to her left at Jaime. "I suppose you knew that, too."

Jaime let out a snort of laughter, her dark eyes shadowed in
the dim light. "Yeah, right. I don't even read music. *He's* the consummate musician. I'm just a hack."

"Now, now," Buck said. "Let's not be so hard on yourself."

Drew played the melodic intro again, and Davis thumped
through the bass line on the acoustic guitar. Kip played rhythm
guitar and sang. After that, they did a little Elvis, and then Dixie

Chicks, Cheryl Wheeler, James Taylor, Lucy Kaplansky, Tracy Chapman, Rosanne Cash, and three Indigo Girls songs. After a while, all the guys were singing along, and Kip was pleased to discover that everyone in the room could carry a tune quite nicely. She fell into the music, one song after another, and sang until her throat was dry, then asked for water and sang some more.

Jaime sat next to her, listening to the glorious voice. Relaxed and away from the concert hall, Kip's voice was even more wonderful than Jaime had first believed. She watched the gray-eyed woman, played a little fiddle here and there, and lost herself in the music so much that she forgot all about taking a turn driving, and they were at their next hotel destination after three a.m. before she realized how late it was.

Chapter Six

IT HAD BEEN over two weeks since Kip had joined the tour, and they were now on a break in New Mexico, pending their next show, which was to be a Fourth of July extravaganza in two days' time. Much of the town was revved up for the celebration with U.S. flags, taco stands, and fry bread fires and chili roasters going everywhere. The crew had been relieved to see that the outdoor pavilion was fitted with a great sound system. Jaime anticipated no major difficulties for tomorrow when they did sound checks. In the meantime, she had some time to herself.

Jaime lay on her side in the top bunk in the bus. Everything was dark and silent around her, and for the first time in over a week, she'd gotten a very good night's sleep. She pushed the button on her Indiglo watch: 10:40 a.m. She sat up and reached for the string for the side light. It clicked on, illuminating the cubbyhole she was in. From her seated position, she had a good foot of clearance over her head, which was much better than the two bunks below. The mattress was as wide as a twin bed, with a rounded wood railing that ran along the hallway opening. Once, when she'd felt ill, she slept in the bunk while Eric drove, and he had hit a bump that sent her flying. It was lucky the edge had been there to catch her, or she'd have been tossed right out of the bunk.

At the head of the bed was a mirror, which was very nearly useless. If she turned around and sat cross-legged, she could probably put on makeup—that is, if she wore any—but the mirror wasn't much good for anything else. Above the opening to the bunk, there was a narrow rack just wide enough for paperback books. The shelf, which ran the length of the bunk, was currently full of books, and she thought that she would need to give some of them up at the next secondhand bookstore they came across. At the foot of the bed, beyond the mattress, there was a deep alcove where she kept her two duffel bags; above that, built into the wall was a small TV set that she rarely watched. On the right was a lockable cupboard where she kept her valuables. Her violin, mandolin, and guitar she stored in the same walkway closet that Kip's guitars were in, while the concert Welling violin and several other guitars traveled in the semi with the rest of the stage gear. She didn't have a lot of room, but then again, she traveled light. She reached up to the climate control buttons near the light and turned off the one labeled A/C. Within seconds, she could feel warmth seeping in.

Everyone was off somewhere. Kip and Lacey were scheduled to go with Wes to the local radio station to be interviewed at ten, and nobody went to bed before two a.m., so she knew the guys were all probably sleeping in over at the hotel. She pulled some clothes out of her duffel, grabbed a pair of tennis shoes, and got out of the bunk. After tapping on the bathroom door, just in case, she slid open the pocket door, stepped in, and shut the door behind her. She stripped out of the sleep shorts and t-shirt she'd been in, then stepped into the stall, feeling a bit like Clark Kent in a phone booth. The tepid water felt good on her skin, and she soaped up and rinsed off in a matter of minutes, then emerged from the dinky shower stall, dried off, and dressed quickly in thigh-length tan shorts and a light blue t-shirt. Already perspiring, she went out into the lounge area to slip on her socks and Nikes, then crawled back up into the bunk and got a waist pack, sunglasses, and her keys. She locked things up, set her sunglasses out of the way on top of her head, and strolled through the heat over to the hotel coffee shop where she had pancakes and eggs.

After breakfast, she paid, left a good tip, and headed out of the restaurant. Both buses were in the parking lot, near the trucks, so she figured someone must have picked up Wes and the singers to take them to the interview. She made her way across the parking lot to the semi, unlocked the back, and threw open the double doors. It took a little work, but she got the ramps pulled out, then scooted up into the cavernous opening. They kept the things they needed least often toward the back, with the PA system, gear, and equipment toward the front. She and Eric had also built a special wooden storage spot on the left for their motorcycles. He hadn't ridden his for a while, so it was pushed to the back. Her Harley was easy to get to, right by the door opening and on the left. She grabbed the handlebars and pulled at it. The tricky part was getting it out far enough to grab the brakes, but not so far that it started off down the ramp and crashed at the bottom, taking her with it.

She managed to get it out, down the ramp, and to flip out the kickstand. She wished she were wearing boots, but it was way too

warm and, as the day went on, soon to be hot as hell. Tennis shoes
would have to do.

She shoved the ramps in, locked up the truck, and got on her
bike to kick-start it. The motor roared to life, sounding fine, and
she saw she had a nearly full gas tank. She revved the engine, put
it in gear, and wheeled toward the lot exit, but before she got
there, a late model Chrysler Concorde turned in, and she pulled to
the side to give it clearance. As it passed, she saw the driver was a
young man she didn't know, but then she caught sight of Wes
Slater in the front passenger seat and Lacey and Kip in the back.
She did a slow turn and followed the sedan to the front of the
hotel. The driver did not get out. He waited for them to exit, then
gave a wave through the open window and drove off.

"*Jee-zus* H. Christ!" Wes said. "Nothing like shit service!"

"Hey, Jaime," Kip said.

They were all dressed in jeans and flashy shirts, but Lacey
and Wes wore cowboy boots, while Kip wore tennis shoes. Jaime
thought the three of them all looked over-warm and irritated. She
turned the key off, and the engine on the motorcycle died. "How'd
the interview go?"

"Fine," Lacey said. "Just lovely. Have you seen Gary?"
When Jaime shook her head, the tiny woman turned and swayed
off toward the hotel entrance.

She turned her attention to the remaining two. "No problems,
then?"

Wes ran his hand through his silvery hair. "Nope. She was a
perfect angel. And Kip here did a nice job, too."

"But I'm starving now," Kip said. "Want to join me for a coffee break?"

She looked hopefully toward Jaime who shook her head
slowly. "Thanks for the offer, but I'm heading out now. Maybe
later."

Kip gave a nod and a smile, then turned and went toward the
coffee shop. Wes frowned. He pulled cigarettes from his pocket
and tapped one out, then stuck it in his mouth. Through clenched
teeth, he said, "Jaime, what the hell we gonna do 'bout that *sum-
bitch* Gary?" He pulled a gold lighter out of his pants pocket and
lit the cigarette.

"What do you mean?"

"I told the little asshole not to fuck with the talent—*dammit!*" He flipped his lighter shut and shoved it in his pocket. With
a squint in his eyes, he said, "You better start boning up on
Lacey's set again. He's gonna be history soon."

"What! Wes, you're not going to fire him, are you? He's a

really good rhythm guitarist."

The big man took a deep drag. As he answered her, smoke puffed out of his mouth and nose. "He's gonna fire his own ass. They've been all lovey-dovey for a month, but now they're starting to get on each other's nerves. It's just a matter of time." He took another long drag.

She sat on her bike, sweating into the leather seat, and wondered why Lacey had to go through people like they were disposable tissues. In a voice showing more pique than she meant to reveal, she said, "Can you tell me why we can't keep any of these guys once she dumps 'em?"

Slater dropped his half-smoked cigarette to the pavement and ground it in with his boot. He looked up and said, "Not everyone is like you, Jaime. Most guys won't take that kind of crap from a woman, so of course they blow off the tour. You better start practicing."

He turned on his heel and stomped toward the hotel entrance, leaving her stunned. In slow motion, she stood and leaned forward, preparing to kick-start the motorcycle. *Did everyone know? Were they all aware of what had gone on?* With a quick punch of her foot, the engine caught, and she hit the gas and peeled forward, spewing small rocks and sand behind her. She turned to the right out of the parking lot and into the bright sun. Fumbling for sunglasses tangled in her dark hair, she felt tears of shame spring to her eyes. Once she got the glasses situated, she looked about to get her bearings.

Then she settled in to the rhythm of the engine and the feel of the wind blowing in her face. She got out of the busier town area and onto a highway that stretched straight out in front of her, clear and dry. *Well, why wouldn't the whole crew know? I'd be stupid to think that they wouldn't have noticed—even though they are a bunch of unobservant men.* She chuckled and shook her head. *Guess they're not so dense after all.* She let out a sigh and increased her speed, and the hot wind rushing past her felt good on her skin and in her short hair.

She didn't need to look at a map to know where she was going. Four-lane highway 666 was the major thoroughfare in Gallup and consisted mostly of strip malls, fast food restaurants, and gas stations. Jaime always wondered who in their right mind would label a major road with numbers associated with the devil, but everyone around the area was used to it. If she were to head south on 666 for about an hour, she'd reach Zuni. If she headed north for a longer ride, Shiprock would be the destination. Turning west would take her to Window Rock, Arizona, capital of the

Navajo Nation, and then on to Hubbell's Trading Post, a National Historic Landmark and a place she loved going to when she was a kid. It made her smile to think of it, as it was everyone's ideal of what an Old West trading post should look like.

But she was going to none of those places. Once she passed through town, she would continue to travel east. At the north edge of town, she passed the local flea market that had been set up there every weekend for as long as she could remember. Jaime would have recognized it from afar, even if she were blind, because of the scent of chili roasting. With her mouth watering, she roared past the brightly dressed merchants and the acres and acres of small, white, tent-topped stands set up off the road. Little children chased one another in one area, and she saw a man leading a pair of sheep. The tourists were just beginning to arrive, ready to shop and haggle in the early morning sun.

She rocketed through time and space, and the further away she got from the bus, the crew, the tour, and Lacey, the better she felt. A couple miles from town, she turned onto a dirt road, conscious of the fact that she was going to pick up more road dust than she could possibly remove without a shower. She didn't care.

Jaime putt-putted along, passing homes in various stages of disrepair. She knew this road, its every dip and wide spot. She pulled the bike into a short driveway and came to a stop next to a faded tan house, then turned the ignition key and got off the bike. A giant hay-bale-sized clump of tumbleweed rested against the side of the house, and she wondered if a high wind came up whether it would tumble toward her motorcycle and break up all over it. Before she could debate that further, the front screen door slapped open, and a pack of kids spilled out, followed by a tall, regal looking woman.

"Jaime!" one of the boys called out. He skidded to a stop, along with his little brother and two other kids she had never seen before.

She reached out and poked him in the arm. "What are you little lizards up to, Jimmy?"

He gave her a sly look. "About five-three."

She laughed. "Pretty good for a ten-year old."

Jimmy drew himself up tall and said, "I'm almost eleven."

Jaime glanced up at the woman who came to stand behind her son. In a smooth, vibrant voice, his mother said, "In about seven months you'll be eleven."

He turned back, frowning. "Yeah? So what?"

The two women locked eyes and simultaneously shook their heads, rolled their eyes, then pushed through the dark-haired boys to wrap one another in a fierce hug. Jaime loosened her grip, still holding the woman lightly with one arm and said, "Emma, I've really missed you."

The black-haired woman grinned back at her equally dark-haired friend. "Likewise, my friend. Come on in. I've got the air conditioning cranked, and you can cool off."

Jaime reached down and dusted her tan shorts. "I sure got dirty."

"Not to worry. This pack of wild animals drags in more dirt in a day than you could in a month." She looked down at the four boys. "Go off and play. *Tia* Jaime and I need some time to ourselves."

For a moment Jimmy looked like he was going to argue, but he gave a sigh and darted out into the yard. Over his shoulder he shouted, "Last one to the big rock is a rotten egg!" Without another word, the three boys surrounding the two women struck out after him. A puff of dust rose up as they departed, mostly sticking to the moisture on Jaime's legs. She let out a sigh.

"Come on, girl. Let's go inside." They headed toward the door of the low-slung, hacienda style house.

The women weren't actually related, though upon casual glance, they looked enough alike to be sisters. Closer inspection revealed some differences. Where Jaime was angular and lean, Emma Little Whirlwind was softer, rounder in the face. Her heritage was mostly Navajo with a little Hopi thrown in from her grandfather's side. The two women had met in high school at a dance during their freshman year. They grew up on opposite sides of town and had never met until then. Jaime still remembered the dark school hall and the old Aerosmith song, "Walk This Way," that had been playing. Along one wall, single guys leaned, trying to look tough or cool. Across the wide gulf, on the opposite wall, twice as many girls stood around, mostly in clusters. Jaime hung out among them, but not a part of any group. She stood alone, her hands in her jeans pockets, the sole of one foot up against the wall and her knee bent out. A few feet away, a couple of other girls stood, uncertainly. Jaime watched as they inched their way toward her, and Emma had haltingly started a conversation, then introduced her other friend, Luz, whose mother was white and whose father was half Mexican, half Cuban. It didn't take too long for the three to become fast friends. They called themselves the Half-breed Wall-Nuts, and for most of their four years at Gallup High, that's exactly where they stayed at school dances: lounging against the wall and talking with one another.

Many years had passed. Luz moved away to California and

ran a dry cleaning business with her husband. Jaime hadn't lived in Gallup for years. Only Emma stayed behind in the area with her husband, Simon, and their two sons and daughter, and they now lived less than a mile from the house where Jaime had grown up. When not attending to her family, Emma's whole world was wrapped up in art. She painted, ran a gallery, coordinated seminars at an art studio for tourists, and arranged for native artists to work with local potters, jewelers, painters, and textile weavers.

The house was blessedly cool. They stepped inside, and Emma picked up a remote and turned off the cartoons playing on the TV in the living room. Jaime pulled a light blue bandana out of her back pocket and wiped her forehead. "I'll duck into your bathroom..."

"Sure, sure. And I'll get us something to drink. Pepsi, okay?"

"That's great," Jaime called back over her shoulder. She washed her face, arms, and hands, and returned to the living room area. "Hey." She let out a low whistle as she took in the large oil painting hanging over the sofa. A beautiful and proud Native American woman stood, looking off to the right, with the sun setting in the background. "That's new," she said, as she rounded the corner and found her friend sitting at the table in the combination kitchen/dining room.

"Yes. I painted it to sell, and Simon went out and bought it. He said it reminded him too much of me to grace someone else's living room." With chin in hand, she smiled. "I'm not sure I'll ever be that thin again, but otherwise, it is a little like me, though, truly, it isn't a self-portrait at all."

"It's gorgeous. You've really become quite the artist. I am so impressed." Jaime pulled out a chair and sat. With one hand wrapped around the fizzing glass of soda, she raised her eyes and met her friend's gaze. Neither spoke for a moment. Jaime looked away. "Yeah, yeah, you were right." She let out a sigh and slumped back a little.

Emma reached out and lightly gripped her friend's forearm. "I didn't want to be right."

"I know." She looked down, her face suffused with heat. It was such a relief to be with someone who understood her. "I wanted so much for things to work with Lacey Leigh." She shook her head just a little. "You're so lucky you found Simon. You sure he doesn't have a sister somewhere?"

"Nope. Same old boring brothers. Sorry." Emma pulled her hand away and picked up her glass to take a sip. "Don't give up. You *will* find the woman of your dreams. Just be patient."

Jaime let out a sputtering sound and rolled her eyes. "I'm tell-

ing you, I give up. I am *never* going through anything like that
again. Never. It's not worth the heartache. And it irritates me to
no end that you had her pegged the minute you saw her. How did
you know that?"

The artist shrugged. "She wasn't good enough for you—didn't
look into your soul. She hasn't enough of her own soul to appreciate the depth of another's."

Jaime thought about Emma's assessment, and she wondered
if it were true. She picked up her glass and took a big swig, then
wiped her mouth off with the back of her hand. "Well, it doesn't
take a medicine man to see that I'm bitter. She fooled me, Em,
totally fooled me."

"I know." The artist said the words softly, a gentle look in her
eyes. "Truth told, her spirit reminded me of your mother's."

"What?" The one word burst from Jaime much more loudly
than she intended.

Emma let out a chuckle. "No need to shout. Yes, she
reminded me, somehow, of your mother."

"Why the hell is that?"

"She was just so...so—I don't know—needy. Like she couldn't
stand on her own two feet."

Jaime crossed her arms and looked away. She didn't think
Lacey Leigh was anything like her mother. Her mother had
accomplished little in her life and had been a falling down
drunk—a happy drunk, but a drunk, nonetheless. Lacey was a vet-
eran stage performer. She was talented, beautiful, and sought after
by men—and women—far and wide. She didn't believe there was
any comparison. "You only met her once, and only for a few minutes. I don't think you saw her better qualities."

"Maybe so," Emma said, "maybe so. You hungry? Want
some tacos?"

"Store-bought? Or yours?"

"Oh, mine, of course. I made some for lunch, which we had
just finished when you rode up."

"That would be great, Em. I'd love that."

The artist rose, and they continued to talk as she busied herself in the kitchen preparing a piece of fry bread and lamb with
whole beans, lettuce, and cheese. "You want salsa?"

"Sure."

"Red or green?"

She grinned. "Christmas, of course." When Emma presented
the brightly colored blue pottery plate covered with the heated
Navajo taco, Jaime leaned forward and took a deep breath.
"Mmm, smells even better than the chili I smelled when I went by

the flea market."

"You know, we should go over there, Jaime—check out the booths. There's a man and his wife who moved to town recently, and they're doing some beautiful things with sterling and gemstones. You'd like their jewelry."

Jaime took another bite. "This is so good. Thanks. I've been away so long, and I don't get this kind of treat very often." She took a drink of Pepsi. "I don't have to be back 'til late this afternoon. I'll go shopping with you."

"Good. But we're taking the station wagon...and we'll be stuck with the four boys on the ride over."

"I don't care about that. Who are those other two kids anyway? They sure weren't a bit shy."

"I've been watching them for several hours every Saturday for a woman named Anna Herrera. She's the one renting your place."

"Oh."

"She's behind in the rent, Jaime, but I know she'll get caught up in time. She's a wonderfully kind woman."

Jaime waved a hand. "It's okay. I don't need the rent at the moment, and it's not much anyway."

"Let me tell you, she's an incredible potter."

"If I ever settle down, maybe she could make me some dishes—you know, barter."

Emma nodded. "I'll ask her. She makes the most beautiful and colorful bowls, and she badly needs time to herself to work. I told her I would watch the kids during the summer for her. Then when the boys go back to school in the fall, she'll pick mine up, since she has to get hers, too. It's a fair trade. Her boys are well-behaved, and they keep Jimmy and Justin busy. They all get along pretty well, despite the fact that none of them are in the same grade." She rose and scooped up the empty plate.

"I'm telling you, that was excellent. You ought to run a restaurant."

Emma laughed. "Fat chance of that. I'd get so fed up with the customers that I'd want to poison them." She rinsed the plate and put it with the fork in the sink, then wiped her hands on a dishtowel. "Let's get going and make the most of our time. You pulling out tonight after the concert?"

"Yes. We head to Albuquerque for a show Monday night, but then we don't have another until Saturday in Amarillo."

"A week break?"

"Yup." She rose and followed Emma into the living room. "Lacey is off to Nashville to cut a couple new tracks and do a video for the new album. It'll be nice to have a break from her."

Emma leaned out the front door and beat on a cowbell hanging on a metal post, then pulled the door shut. She grabbed up a black purse from a table near the door and rooted around in it until she came up with some car keys. "Kids'll show up shortly."

"You coming to the concert tonight?

"Nah."

"I'll get you all comp tickets—good seats, too."

"I don't think so. I don't like Lacey Leigh's music enough."

"Hey, Em, we have a great warm-up act now. This woman, Kip Galvin—she's got a wonderful voice, and she's really good. In fact, we're planning something totally sneaky for tonight."

Emma let out a sigh. "What happened to Nicky Kinnick? Did that little witch run him off, too? Now I might have come to the concert to see *him*." She put her index finger in her mouth and pulled it away, making a sizzling sound between her teeth.

"Yeah...I was sorry to see Nick go. He was a fine man." She nodded. "Well, tell you what. I'll leave you and Simon comp tickets and backstage passes at the box office 'Will Call.' Just come for Kip's set, or come for the whole concert if you want. If you show, don't leave without saying goodbye, okay?"

Jaime heard a squeaking noise, and then the front door burst open, and four black-haired boys, all dusty and sweaty, fell into the house. Emma said, "You can all turn right back around and go get in the car. We're going to the flea market." The cheers and jumping up and down were so loud that Emma had to shout over them. "Out! Now." They turned around and piled out the front door, leaving the two women laughing.

"Oh, to be that young again," Jaime said.

"No shit. I'd be a millionaire if I could bottle that."

JAIME PACED IN the wings, sweating in her black jeans and shirt. New Mexico in July was not a pleasant temperature for long pants and dark clothes. She was happy that the sun had gone down, and the outdoor arena was starting to cool. Despite the sand-colored curtain and stage, heat emanated from the very floorboards. She wiped sweat from her forehead with her shirtsleeve, then turned to Tom. Over the house music, she asked, "You're sure everything's live?"

"Yes," Tom said, sighing and rolling his eyes. "You're on, and Drew's guitar is all hooked up and ready to play, on a stand right behind the curtain."

"And you're sure it'll be her third song?"

"Yes, yes, yes. Eric made up some story about how he needed

to know so he could keep a close check on levels. She agreed, so don't worry. She's true to her word."

Drew stood on the other side of Tom, his arms crossed over his black button-up shirt. "Quit worrying, girl. It'll go fine." She didn't know why he was always so calm.

Adjusting the black cowboy hat she wore, Jaime debated whether to wear it onstage or not. She took it off and set it on a folding chair, then hesitated. Reaching down, she almost picked it up, then thought better of it and left it there. She didn't know why she was so nervous. The house music segued from "I.O.U." to Billy Ray Cyrus's "Achy Breaky Heart," and she wanted to scream at someone to turn it off. *Gawd, I hate that song!*

She and Drew had practiced Kip's song and she knew everything should go fine, but still, she worried. What if they crept out onstage and then flubbed things up? She knew Kip was kind and forgiving, but still, she wanted it to go perfectly.

Wes Slater materialized next to her. "*Dammit* all, you gotta go get the warm-up act, Jaime." He looked toward Tom. "We're ready, right?" When Tom nodded, Wes rubbed his hands together. "Let's get this friggin' thing going."

Jaime stalked out of the area, her heart pumping, and headed out across the parking lot to the bus. A security guard in a white t-shirt and jeans stood next to the bus door, and he didn't know her from Adam, so she dug out her backstage pass so that he would let her by.

Once inside the air-conditioned bus, she realized she was warmer than she thought and sweating profusely. She stood for a moment and took deep breaths, then headed toward the stateroom and knocked on the door.

"Come in," a muffled voice said, so she pushed the door open to find Kip down on her knees, digging through one of the built-in drawers under the bed unit. Her guitar lay on the red and gold coverlet. The gray-eyed woman looked toward the door. "I thought I had a bandana in here. Can't seem to find it."

"I can loan you one." Jaime stepped back and went to her bunk, hoisted herself up, and rooted around until she found a pale blue and white bandana. She jumped down and went back to the doorway. "Will this work?"

"Oh, yes. That'd be great. Thanks. I'll get it back to you once I do laundry."

"No hurry, Kip. I've got three or four." She watched as the singer shoved the drawer shut and rose, dusting invisible dirt off the knees of her pants. She accepted the blue and white cloth, folded it into a small square, and tucked it in her pants pocket.

"It's time, huh?" She grabbed up her guitar and turned to face the other woman.

Jaime nodded. "Looks like a good crowd, too."

Kip grinned. "You always say that." With her free hand she reached over and squeezed the tech's upper arm.

Jaime blushed. "But it *is* a good crowd—they seem real responsive."

Kip let her hand drop and shifted the guitar in front of her. "It's always nice to hear that." She squinted a little, with a perplexed look on her face. "You okay, Jaime?"

"Sure. I'm fine—just great. Why?"

"I don't know. You seem, hmmm...out-of-sorts or something."

"Nope. Nothing like that. C'mon, let's go." She spun around quickly and led her off the bus and across the lot to the stage door, where another security guy checked their IDs before letting them pass. They hovered in the wings while a fly buzzed around, and the heat pressed in on them. Kip took the bandana out of her pocket and wiped her forehead, then tucked the cloth back into her slacks.

Tom gave her the high sign and counted down, and Jaime watched the singer take a deep breath and stroll on to the stage. Eric cut the house sound and lights, and when Kip made it to the mic, she shouted out, "Hell-LOH, Gallup!" The audience gave her a quiet round of applause as the guitarist plugged in her guitar and strummed it once. "Good evening, ladies and gentlemen, and welcome to the Lacey Leigh Jaxon pre-game show. I'm Kip Galvin, and I'll be your play-by-play announcer for just a little bit."

A little hum of approval came from the crowd, and Kip went on. "Lacey Leigh is off getting ready to show you folks a wonderful evening, but first, I'm going to try to keep you entertained for a few minutes. Here's a little number you probably all know—feel free to sing along..."

From the wings, Jaime listened. In only a few concert dates, Kip seemed to have settled into a comfortable ease onstage. They had a crowd of about 2,600, but it didn't seem to be bothering the folksinger at all. The singer turned toward Tom and gave a little toss of her head, and Jaime watched Tom adjust the side fill to a higher volume. Kip glanced back and nodded slowly, and Tom gave her the OK sign.

Kip finished the song to polite applause and started in on another peppy one. Jaime gave Drew the eye, and the lead guitarist uncrossed his arms and followed her around the outside of the curtain until they were at the center seam. Jaime bent low and separated the cloth of the sand-colored curtains just an inch to peek out. The lights were directed downstage, where Kip stood, but upstage where she and Drew were, was all shrouded in shadows. Lacey Leigh's band set-up was completely arranged behind Kip, and all Jaime could see of the musician was her head poking up over Buck's giant assortment of drums.

"Jaime." Drew's voice was low and slow. "Quit frettin' and just relax."

She stood and scowled at him in the semi-darkness. He already had his strap over his shoulder and was getting the acoustic guitar adjusted. "How the hell do you always stay so calm?"

He gave her a lackadaisical shrug. "It ain't no big deal. We go out there and play. One song. You talked me into one song, and that isn't any big whoopee. It'll go fine."

"Uh huh. Right."

Kip was winding down on her second song, and when the applause was over, she said, "Here's a song I wrote. It's called 'Right Now.'"

As soon as she hit the first notes, Jaime slipped through the curtain, feeling Drew behind her. She went stage left, and he went right. She found the Welling on its stand and tucked it in under her chin, then picked up the bow. When Kip finished singing the first verse, Jaime touched the bow to the strings, and simultaneously, Drew stepped forward, playing the melodic lead guitar part. Their strings came in right on time, sounding clear and in tune. Jaime saw Kip's shoulders hunch in surprise, but the woman was a consummate showman. She stayed right with the song.

> *I could not imagine that you'd ever go*
> *And deep inside I wish you could know*
> *That people change,*
> *They rearrange their lives and loves and living*
> *That someday soon you will, too*
> *I can't just go on giving...*

Jaime concentrated on the mournful, low notes, using all her skill to blend with the guitars she heard coming from the side fill. As she played, she crept forward until both she and Drew were about ten feet to the side of the singer and behind her. Despite the heat onstage, the words and melody of the bridge and the final verse gave her the shivers. She and Drew both watched Kip closely, and when the gray-eyed woman gave a bob of her head, they held the final harmonic notes and ended together when Kip gave a final nod. Only one single beat of silence occurred in the arena, and then enthusiastic applause.

"Thank you!" Kip shouted. "Thanks. To my left, I have Jaime Esperanza, a gifted fiddler, guitarist, and mandolin player. She hails from right here, calling Gallup, New Mexico, her hometown. Let's have a round of applause."

Jaime held her violin out to the side and gave a bow, her face flaming red. She met Kip's eyes and shook her head a little, grinning, as the audience roared for their hometown girl.

Kip pulled the bandana out of her pocket and wiped her forehead as she said, "And on my right is one truly incredible fellow, Drew Michael Donovan, from San Antonio, Texas. Drew's been a guitar virtuoso since he was about eight, and he can pretty much play anything. I've never had the honor of playing with such a fine musician, and Lacey Leigh can count herself lucky to have him supplying all the really cool riffs and licks for both concerts and recordings. I bow to you, Drew." The crowd whistled and clapped, and Kip dropped down on one knee and leaned over her guitar, then popped back up to her feet, laughing and gesturing his way.

The lead guitarist's face flushed so red, Jaime thought that the usually calm, cool, collected Drew was going to burst an artery. A bubble of laughter rose up, and she pointed toward the man. When he met her eyes, there was a challenge in them. He sashayed over toward Kip, put an arm around her, and spoke loud enough for the audience to hear. "That was a mighty nice thing to say, Kip. And now Jaime over there is hoping you'll do 'The Devil Went Down to Georgia,' so she can have a nice, lil ol' fiddle part to play."

Kip laughed out loud. "You probably could easily pull that off, Drew, but I can't. And people," she looked out at the house, "I just want you to know that these two miscreants snuck up on me. I thought I was playing solo tonight, like usual, and I did *not* know they were going to come out here and accompany me."

A wave of laughter tumbled from out in the arena and up onto the stage. Kip looked to the right, then to the left. "What do you think, Jaime? How 'bout a turn at "Goodbye, Earl," by the Dixie Chicks instead? You two going to step up and help me here on the 'Nah nah nah's'?"

With her heart in her throat, Jaime tried to swallow. She saw Drew give a nod and take one step back, and then the folksinger played the intro and Drew joined her as Kip opened her mouth to sing. Jaime and the lead guitarist played their hearts out, and when the chorus came, they both moved forward and sang the background parts while Kip carried the song.

When that song was over, they did another and another and another, and then Tom was signaling from the side that their time was nearly up. Kip said a few final words to the Gallup crowd, and they exited the stage, laughing, as the house sound came up, playing Shawn Colvin's "Sunny Came Home." The whole troupe cut through the wings and into the anteroom beyond.

Backstage, Kip slipped Isabelle off and handed the guitar to Lance. She threw her arms around Drew, trapping his skinny arms against his sides, and gave him a peck on the cheek. She released the surprised man so quickly that he stumbled. "Don't take that wrong, now, Drew, but hey! You are *the* greatest!" She stepped away from him and grabbed Jaime's hand. Before Jaime knew what was happening, Kip put strong arms around her, and lifted her a couple inches up off the ground. The folksinger set her down and looked into her eyes, still embracing her.

Jaime relaxed against the other woman and wrapped her in long arms. She squeezed her in return. "You were great tonight, Kip."

Kip grinned into her face, her gray eyes so close that Jaime could see blue and white flecks in them. "I can't believe you did that, you sneaky little shit. It was your idea, wasn't it?"

"Hey, I'm not little."

"You're avoiding the question. It was your idea, wasn't it? Drew isn't that sneaky—right, Drew?" She stepped back and shifted a half-turn to find the guitarist standing with a quirky grin on his face.

"Not usually," he said, "but you seem to have had a bad affect upon me."

"C'mon, you two, I'll buy you a drink." She strode over to a sizable plastic cooler provided by the caterer, flipped the lid up, and dug around in the ice. "Water? Soda?" She went down on one knee and looked over her shoulder.

Drew said, "I'll take a water. I go back on in a couple minutes, and I'll take it with me."

"Nothing for me," Jaime said. "That bottled water tastes like mud. You know, the craft service here really stinks. Some of these venues have excellent food, but this is definitely not one of those places."

Just then, a white-shirted security man came up escorting two people. Kip rose, holding a dripping ginger ale and a spring water. The man was tall, over six feet. He had shoulder-length black hair, a rugged tanned face, and kindly brown eyes. He wore cowboy boots and a multi-colored shirt tucked into jeans and held the hand of a black-haired woman who closely resembled Jaime. The woman pulled away from the tall man and wrapped her arms around Jaime, then stood back beaming at her friend. "I see what you meant. What a great set. It was wonderful."

Kip handed the damp water bottle to Drew as Jaime turned to her and said, "Kip, these are my friends Emma and Simon Little Whirlwind."

"Glad to meet you," Kip said, as she wiped water off her palm on the leg of her pants and reached out to shake their hands.

Simon smiled. "Nice songs. Good music, Ms. Galvin."

"Oh, please. Call me Kip."

Smiling, he gave a nod, and his wife said, "Jaime told me she was going to sneak up on you, Kip, so it was amusing to be in the third row and see the look on your face when the additional instruments started playing." She grinned and shook her head. "Very nice concert. You have a lovely voice."

Kip blushed and said, "Thanks. That's nice to hear."

"Excuse me, folks," Drew said. "I best be getting out there. Nice to see you two again."

He stuck his hand out and shook with Simon, then nodded toward Emma and was gone.

Kip said, "If you want to see the rest of the concert, then you'll have to hurry to get your seats again."

"Oh, no," Emma said. "That was just the perfect amount. Now we'll get home right on time for our favorite TV program."

"And," Simon said, "before the kids kill each other."

Kip unscrewed the lid from her ginger ale and took a drink, feeling the fizzy liquid burn down her throat. She listened as Jaime and her friends spoke for a minute longer, then Emma reached out and hugged her. Kip watched as the dark-haired woman pulled back and put her hand at Jaime's collarbone, touching a silver and purple pendant hanging around her friend's neck. "This looks good on you." Jaime merely grinned. Simon slung an arm across her shoulders and wished her well.

"Bye, Kip," Emma said as she shook her hand. "It's very nice to meet you. Keep up the good work. You're gonna be big, I can tell."

"Thanks." Kip raised the green bottle into the air and smiled as they moved past and headed for the back entrance. She looked over at Jaime and saw that the black-haired woman was watching her departing visitors with a smile on her face. "Nice people."

Jaime nodded. "The nicest."

Chapter
Seven

THE NEXT DAY, in Albuquerque, Kip wasn't sure what to expect. The band had been in high spirits on the bus the night before. For the two-plus hours that it took to get from Gallup to Albuquerque, they all played songs, laughed, and drank a lot of beer. The normally taciturn twins had been wild with jokes and energy. Even Jaime, usually so reserved, let her guard down. She got out both her mandolin and the decrepit-looking violin and had coaxed out the most beautiful melodies. Kip found that she was enjoying everyone immensely. In fact, if she could fall in love with a group—and a group of mostly men—then she had done it. She failed to understand how Lacey Leigh could ignore such a talented group of fun-loving guys.

Once they reached the hotel, the others went off and checked in, and she settled down for a good night's sleep in her stateroom. She awoke the next day at eleven a.m. feeling refreshed, and at a quarter to twelve, when she went to the restaurant attached to the hotel, she found Jaime sitting in a booth with a giant mug of coffee and an oversized menu on the table in front of her.

"Hey, you!" Kip sauntered toward the table as Jaime looked up. "I never heard you get up this morning. Mind if I join you?"

"No, not at all. I tried to be quiet. Figured you could use the rest since we were such wild animals last night."

Kip slid into the booth. "What time did you rise and shine?"

"Couple of hours ago. Eric and I cased the joint and made sure the hall is set up."

The folksinger glanced around the restaurant and caught the waitress's eye, mouthing the word "coffee."

The woman hustled over with the coffeepot and a huge mug, which matched Jaime's. "Welcome to the Coffee Cup Café, ma'am. I assume you want a large coffee, caffeinated?"

"Large as you've got, with as much caffeine as you can get away with." She watched hungrily as the waitress filled the gargantuan mug. "I don't think I've ever had such a humongous coffee cup. How much liquid is this anyway?"

The woman put a hand on her hip and frowned. "Oh, 'bout twenty ounces, I'd say. I don't usually quite fill 'er to the brim 'cause that's a hell of a lotta coffee, and it's not like we're in Texas, ya know."

The musician leaned over the mug and took in a deep breath. "Smells great. Thanks."

"You want a menu?"

Jaime grabbed hers up off the table. "She can have mine. I know what I want." She closed the laminated menu and passed it over.

The waitress said, "Gimme the high sign when y'all are ready to order," and she whirled away to pour pints of coffee for another table.

Kip reached for the coffee creamer and systematically opened three packs, then dumped them in and added three packs of sugar for good measure. Picking up her spoon, she lifted her eyes and found Jaime scowling her way. "What?"

"You want a little coffee with all that milk and sugar?"

Kip let out a giggle. "What can I say? Black coffee gives me heartburn, not to mention a headache. I love it with milk or creamer. In fact—Miss?" She caught the waitress as she went by. "May I get some milk or cream?"

"Which?"

"Milk would be fine."

She took a sip of her coffee. "Oh yeah, that's strong." She opened the menu and took several more sips of the hot liquid. "So tell me, how are you this morning?"

"Not bad." Jaime leaned forward with her elbows on the table and chin resting in her palms. "You?"

"I feel great today. That was a lot of fun last night."

"Yeah, it was."

The waitress zoomed by, leaving a metal container of milk on the table without even pausing. Kip scooped it up and poured half of it into her mug until it was nearly full, then stirred it carefully. She looked across the table into the dark eyes and smiled. "You play a mean mandolin, girl."

"We aim to please."

"Want to learn the mandolin part for a song I wrote called 'What I'm Looking For'?"

Jaime smoothed her hair back and smiled. "Already know it."

"What do you mean—you already know it?"

"It's on that demo Wes got. He let me have the CD, and I

monkeyed around with it a bit. Learned it days ago."

"You're kidding!"

"Nope." She crossed her arms and sat back against the booth with a smug look on her face.

"So did you have yet another little surprise planned for me, Jaime Esperanza?"

With a snicker, Jaime gave a nod. "I just might."

"You going to let me in on it?"

"Nope."

Kip chuckled and shook her head. "You're having fun with this, huh?"

"Yes, I believe we are."

"*We?* There's a *we* involved? More than Drew?"

"I plead the fifth."

The singer picked up her coffee mug with both hands and guided it to her mouth. "Good grief, this thing's heavy."

"You've got a quart of liquid in there—probably weighs two pounds."

"I'll say." She took another big slurp, then set the mug down as the waitress came their way, flipping through her pad of paper. The folksinger shot a startled look at Jaime. "You go first—let me look for just a sec." Jaime asked for huevos rancheros, and Kip ordered French toast with a side of sausage, then closed the menu and handed it to the waitress, who spun around and headed for the kitchen. "I know I shouldn't have the sausage, but the hell with it."

"Why not?"

"I'm constantly watching my weight. Last thing I need is a bunch of fatty pork, but I guess I just don't care today. Next to Lacey Leigh, supermodels look fat."

Jaime snorted out a laugh. "Yeah, she's petite, but you look fine."

"Not if I eat three or four sausages a day."

"I won't tell anyone if you don't."

"Deal." She looked out the window at the dry, desert surroundings, then turned back to Jaime. "So how long have you been traveling on this tour?"

"This tour started in May. I had a break for all of April. I was part of the previous tour, too."

"How was that different?"

Jaime sat back, considering the question. She wanted to say, *by different, do you mean as regards my love life—the one normal week, the six months of flirting Ms. Jaxon did, and the seven weeks when we had a physical relationship? Or the fact that she dumped me and I can't even believe that I re-joined this crazy tour?* Upon reflection, she didn't think Kip needed to know all that. "The last tour was pretty much the same as this one. In eight months, we went through five opening acts, two mandolin players, and five rhythm guitarists."

"Went through? What does that mean?"

"Let's just say that Lacey isn't easy on the hired help."

A tapping noise drew nearer, and Jaime looked up, startled. A honey-soft voice asked, "Lacey isn't easy on what?" She placed a hand on the edge of the table, leaned forward, and grinned at Jaime, batting her eyes. Her pink bodice blouse was snug, as were her skin-tight black pants. Even though her stiletto heels were a good three inches, she was still not much taller than either of the seated women. "You're not telling tales out of school now, are you?"

The folksinger watched as Jaime sat up straight and met Lacey Leigh's eyes. For a moment, Kip saw a look of pain slash across Jaime's face. Then the light disappeared from her eyes, and she looked every bit the descendant of haughty Aztec warriors. She lifted one eyebrow and stared daggers. "Of course, I'm telling tales, Lacey. What else is left?"

Kip looked from her breakfast companion to the blonde and back. *Ah, so that's how it is. I see.* She cleared her throat. "You want to join us, Ms. Jaxon?"

Lacey Leigh turned her attention to Kip, her unnaturally green eyes amused. "Despite the fact that we have had our differences, there is no need for formality, *Kip.* I expect you to call me Lacey Leigh—or Lacey. And no, I won't join you. Candy and Shelley are on their way down, and if Gary ever gets his ass out of the shower, then we'll have quite a crew. We'll sit over there." She gave a wave toward the bigger booths on the other side of the restaurant, and it was then that Kip became aware that the entire café was almost silent, except for a hissing sound coming from a griddle in the back. She looked past the small woman to see that pretty much everyone in the place was watching with surprised looks on their faces.

"Well, looky here!" An excited manager dressed in too-tight polyester pants and a yellow dress shirt with a tie hustled their way. "Miss Lacey Leigh Jaxon. Oh, my goodness! We are so honored!"

Kip expected the star to be irritated, but the star stepped away from the table wearing a genuine smile as the din in the restaurant rose. Two waitresses and the manager fussed over her, and she allowed herself to be escorted to a large corner booth whose occu-

pants were now being rushed away. The folksinger didn't think she
had ever seen a busboy work so fast to clear a table and wipe the
seats. All the while, the manager was jabbering away, the waitresses gazed in awe, and the other diners watched with obvious
glee.

The folksinger tore her eyes away from the commotion to find
Jaime looking at her, a guarded expression on her face. Kip
frowned. "Is it like this everywhere you go?"

Jaime nodded, her arms crossed tightly in front of her.
"Pretty much."

"Thank God, then, that I'm not famous."

The tech's face showed surprise. "It won't be long, Kip. You
probably will be famous."

She slowly shook her head. "I wouldn't want that—not all the
adulation and fakiness. No way."

"You're kidding, right? You don't want men—and women—
falling at your feet, promising you their first born, offering you
sex and money and drugs? C'mon now." She rolled her eyes.
"That's un-American."

"Nuh-uh...I don't want that at all. I am dead serious. I'm
starting to think that I'm about as famous as I can stand." Just
then, Gary came strolling into the restaurant, his alligator skin
boots clomping on the floor. He wore tight black jeans and an
electric blue shirt, unbuttoned halfway. He was freshly shaved,
and both women reeled back and their eyes widened as he swept
by.

"Whoa!" Kip said. "That's some kind of aftershave."

Jaime uncrossed her arms, leaned her elbows on the table,
and curled a finger into the handle of her mug. "He's toast, you
know."

"What?" Kip picked up her mammoth mug, too, and took a
slurp.

"Mark my words: after tonight, he's out of here. I can tell you
for a fact that Lacey is fixing to dump him, and he's likely to get
fired."

"But why?" The folksinger set her mug down and stared at
Jaime, then glanced across the restaurant. "I don't get it. He's a
very good guitarist."

"She's tired of him. The romance has run its course, and she's
fed up. If he's like most of the others, his ego won't take it and
he'll either quit or be so insistent and annoying that he'll provoke
her until she asks Wes to fire him."

The waitress slid up, smacked their plates on the table, and
turned and sped off. A busboy came by to drop off a bottle of

maple syrup, and the container skidded from one side of the table to the other. Jaime stuck her hand out and stopped it before it fell off the side as the young man wheeled around and raced toward the other side of the café.

Kip laughed out loud. "Guess the service goes out the window when someone so famous shows up." Candy and Shelley strolled in, wearing high heels, short skirts, and a lot of makeup. "Here comes the rest of the wrecking crew." They sashayed by and made for the table where Lacey and Gary sat.

"Didn't you know, Kip? When you're famous, you require a minimum of two servers per person." Both of them laughed as they dug into their meals.

Kip speared a sausage and took a bite. "This is pretty good, considering the cooks probably have other things on their minds."

They watched all the ruckus going on across the room as various patrons got up and either passed Lacey Leigh's table to stare as they headed to the bathroom or stopped to ask for autographs. After the first brave soul, most everyone decided autographs were a good idea, and there was a steady stream of fawning fans.

Jaime focused on her meal, and the folksinger kept an eye on things out of the corner of her eye. Kip was halfway through her meal before either of them said anything. She took a swig of coffee from the half empty mug, wiped her mouth with her napkin, and said, "So, Jaime, do you want to talk about when she threw you over?" The black-haired woman stopped in mid-chew, her eyes wide, then choked and coughed. "Hey, hey..." Kip said. She was on her feet in an instant and around the other side of the booth. With one knee on the seat next to the wide-eyed woman, she beat on her back. "C'mon, Jaime. Don't make me have to do the Heimlich maneuver. C'mon now...come on...good girl." Jaime reached for her water glass as Kip straightened up, one hand rubbing the choking woman's back and her knee still on the vinyl seat. "You going to be okay?" Jaime nodded and set the water down, so Kip moved back around to the other side and slid in. "Sure you're okay?"

Jaime didn't answer. She cleared her throat once, then again. With hard eyes, she asked, "Why did you ask that?" Her tone was angry and accusatory.

Kip shrugged. "Inveterate nosiness, I guess."

"Why did you assume that?"

Kip shrugged again, tilting her head to the side. "I could just tell." She watched as Jaime seemed to deflate.

"It's that obvious?"

"No. Not at all. Don't worry."

"Well, then how the hell did you find out? Somebody say something?"

In a quiet voice, Kip said, "Nobody has said anything to me at all. Not one word. I just see my very same reaction in you when you are around her, and I noticed it quite clearly this morning."

Jaime pushed away her half-eaten breakfast. Her normally tanned face was red, and to Kip, she looked like she might cry. "You want to clarify what you mean by that?"

Kip picked up her fork and cut a wedge off a piece of French toast, then swirled it around in syrup. She kept her eyes on the plate and in a soft voice said, "Just before the school year ended last year—not this year, I mean last summer—Brenna, my partner of nine years, dumped me. Totally unexpected. Left me completely in shock. I've only recently begun to get a handle on it. The look on your face when Lacey was here was sort of this hopeless resignation, much like I imagine my face must appear when I see Bren." She hesitated, looking up at Jaime with worry etched on her face. "I'm sorry for making you uncomfortable. I—I shouldn't have been so intrusive. Will you accept my apology? It's none of my business, I know."

Jaime let out a long sigh. "Don't worry about it. You just shook me up is all. I didn't expect that." She reached over and pulled her huevos rancheros toward her and picked up her fork. "For that, you owe me a sausage." Without waiting for permission, her silver fork flashed across the table and stabbed into a little smokey. She was taking a bite of it before Kip could even react.

In a dry voice, Kip said, "Well, hey, take two—they're small." Jaime laughed. "And don't go choking on it, Miss Esperanza. Everybody knows that little circlets of hotdogs and sausage are what cause choking the most often."

"Oh, that's it, huh—not to be confused with invasive interrogations?"

"Hmph...I'm sure hotdogs are number one on the Surgeon General's list, not innocent little questions."

Jaime, holding her fork in the air, waved the other half of the sausage. "The last tour ended on April Fool's Day. She dumped me three days before it ended." When Kip didn't say anything, she went on. "I'll tell you the rest of the story some other time. Okay?"

The waitress appeared at their table, a frantic look on her face. The words came tumbling out of her mouth. "Y'all want anything else?"

The two women shook their heads. She pulled her pad out of her smock pocket, ripped a page off, slapped it on the table, and was gone.

Kip said, "I feel like Dorothy in the Wizard of Oz where she says, 'My! People sure come and go quickly around here!'"

Jaime nodded her head slowly, with a quizzical look on her face. "If I remember correctly, Dorothy had a lot of nosy questions, too."

"Yeah? And your point is?"

Jaime grinned, her teeth even and white in the bright sunlight that was now shining in through the window. "No point. Just making a comment."

"You want to learn a new card game?"

Jaime looked around the restaurant. "Business is picking up here. I think the other diners are calling their friends and relatives. I am pretty sure they'll frown on you getting out your Old Maid cards and us shuffling up for a game."

"That's not what I meant, you fool." Kip gave a toss of her head toward the black bus angled up to the electrical outlet in the lot. "I've got this new game called Phase 10, and I'll teach it to you if you want to come hang out for a while."

Jaime pressed her lips together and squinted her eyes to make a goofy face. "Okay. We playing for money?"

"Sure. I wasn't planning on that, but yeah, we can. You want that last sausage? I think two were enough for me."

"Yes." She picked her fork up again and speared the last sausage. "But I'm not paying for it."

"Yeah, yeah, yeah. I've emotionally upset you, so in fact, I'll pop for it all." She rose and reached into her back pocket for her wallet. "Of course, if you lose at Phase 10, you're buying the next meal."

"Ha. I'll see you and raise you five bucks."

"You wish," she scoffed.

THE TWO WOMEN sat in the booth at the table in the black bus with the air conditioning on high. They'd been chatting and playing Phase 10 all afternoon, not even stopping when Eric came out to move the bus from outside the hotel to the concert venue. Now they sat on a side street, next to the stage door, smacking cards down on the table.

"Damn!" Jaime said. "You *have* to be cheating. How'd you get that run so fast?"

Kip looked at her, triumphantly. "Got dealt most of the cards. You really ought to work on your shuffling, Esperanza. Or should I be calling you Esperanza-*less*?"

"What?"

"Get it? *Hope*-less." She batted her eyes, and in her best Southern accent said, "'Cause you ain't never gonna beat me at cards."

"Oh, we'll see about that. How 'bout I get a few of the guys and take you on at poker?"

"If you need reinforcements..."

In a mocking voice, Jaime said, "Well, we can't very well play poker with two."

Kip tipped her head to the side and surveyed the other woman with a slight smile on her face. "I have a hunch you might be very good at bluffing."

"Could be." Her eyes narrowed, and they glared at one another as though they were sixth graders having a stare down.

They both jumped at a heavy thumping sound. The front door of the bus slid open and Wes Slater's head and shoulders rose up on the other side of the recliner. He growled, "What in the *hell* are you two doing? Kip, you need to get your ass ready for the show. And Jaime, you need to get your ass out here and help Eric, Tom, and Lance. Whaddya think you are—on a fuckin' vacation?"

Kip was glad her back was to the door so she could keep Slater from knowing she was laughing. She watched Jaime glance at her watch. "I'll be out shortly, Wes. Thanks for the reminder." He slammed the door shut, causing the whole bus to shake, and Kip met her friend's eyes, her amusement apparent.

"Geez!" Jaime said. "It's three hours 'til show time and there is absolutely nothing to do. Is the guy paranoid, or what?"

Kip laughed out loud. "He's just used to you hanging out, keeping an eye on things, that's all."

Jaime rose. "Eric and I set things up this morning. It's a great little concert hall—didn't need a single amp or tower. Didn't need to run any lines or fix a single thing. Not one solitary bulb is out. I could walk in there two hours from now and have everything checked, double-checked, and totally ready in twenty minutes." She let out a sigh. "No big deal. I'll go check on things and come back later and change."

"Change?"

"Yeah, Galvin. You know—put on clean clothes?"

"You mean performing clothes?"

"What's it to you?" she said in a jeering voice.

The folksinger could see Jaime was enjoying teasing her. In a sweet voice, Kip asked, "You playing back up for Lacey Leigh tonight?"

"Ah ah ah...you're not getting anything out of me—not one

damn word. You'll have to wait and see." She stood in the narrow aisle with a smirk on her face, arms crossed, and her hip leaning against the side of the bench.

Kip sprang up and slid out of the booth. She grabbed Jaime by the arm and pulled. "Oh, please, please, please," she begged. "Don't leave me hanging. Come on, Jaime. Pretty please?" She grinned at the tanned woman, batting her eyes and smiling hopefully. "Is this working?"

"Not a bit." Jaime leaned forward and pointed a forefinger close to her face. "You just be ready for anything, all right?"

"For cripesake, woman, I'm going to be a wreck." She let go of the other woman's arm.

"I'll give you one hint—just one— but only if you tell me your play list."

"I'll have the hint first—and then I'll tell."

"You don't trust me, huh?"

"Absolutely, totally, completely—not. What's the hint?"

Jaime debated for a moment. "There's more than me and Drew."

"You're kidding!"

"No. Now, play list please."

"I'm being honest now. I hadn't exactly decided. I know I'm opening with that Wynonna song, but usually I sort of play it by ear."

"No fair!" Jaime stomped her foot. "I gave you a perfectly acceptable hint, and you've just cheated me!"

"All right, all right. I give in. I'll write down the ten or eleven songs I'm most likely to play and bring them out to you. You better get going or Wes will be all over you."

Jaime slid past her in the tight aisle. With mock seriousness, she said, "You better not be saying that to get rid of me."

"Oh, I would *never!*" Then the gray-eyed woman grinned wickedly as she watched Jaime amble toward the door. "I'll be out in a while. Trust me." When the bus door shut, Kip made her way back to her stateroom. She checked her watch to see that it was two hours, forty-eight minutes, until show time. She opened the door to her room and sat on the edge of the bed thinking about how much she had enjoyed the afternoon. Until just now, she hadn't realized how lonely she'd been.

JAIME MADE HER rounds of the hall, checking the equipment, making sure wires were properly tacked down. Tom and Lance had everything in order, just as she expected, but if she were asked, she could tell Wes things were under control. She heard footsteps behind her and turned to find Eric strolling her way.

"Hey, girl, how's your day?"

"Not bad."

"Here—Kip told me to give this to you."

He held out a scrap of paper and she took it, a frown on her face. "Oh. It's the play list. Thanks, Eric."

"No problem."

She reviewed the list for a moment, then tucked it in her shorts pocket.

"I'm telling you, Jaime, this is just about the most perfect setup I've seen."

"Yup. It does seem that way."

"Some of the security guys said they had a reggae concert here the night before last, and they were able to record an almost flawless live concert."

"Really?" She reached a hand out and put it on her friend's shoulder. "Want to see what we can come up with tonight?"

He ran his hand through his graying hair. "For Lacey—or Kip?"

"I was thinking of Kip."

"That's what I thought you meant. If you help me set it up, I'd be happy to do that. They've got a brand new 16-track in the booth."

With Eric doing checks from the booth, she spent half an hour stringing extra cords, setting up lines, and checking the equipment. Once she had everything arranged, she found the back stairs and made her way up to where Eric was. They both agreed that the booth was ideal for this sort of a concert hall. Instead of having the front-of-house soundboard behind the audience, it was above the crowd and below the balcony in a flat little room not even tall enough for Jaime to stand in. She ducked into the five-foot-tall doorway, took off her tool belt and dropped it on the floor, and settled herself into one of two rolling chairs. She scooted over next to Eric, who sat at the mixing board, a tiny side-light cutting through the dimness.

She said, "I feel like I'm in the nose of a jet airliner."

"Huh, true. They put some money into this theater. It's a real musician's hall. Look at the layout, the tiles, everything. It's just beautiful."

She looked through the clean glass toward the stage. If they were to film a performance, this was a perfect vantage point. An idea occurred to her. "Hey, when the guys and I are onstage, will you try to catch a couple photos?"

"Sure. Bring me a camera with your tripod. When are you on? You want shots during Lacey's sixth song?"

"No, no. No fiddle tonight. I mean while Kip is playing."

He nodded. "Okay. Can do. You and Drew sneaking up on her again?"

"No. Most *all* of us are sneaking up on her."

He chuckled. "It'll piss off Lacey, you know."

"So what! What's she going to do? Fire us?"

"She can't afford that." He turned his rolling chair and faced her with his hands on the knees of his jeans. "Jaime, there's a chance this tour could go bust."

Examining his worried face, she wondered what he meant, but she didn't ask. She waited a moment, and he went on, sounding reluctant. "I'm telling you something I don't want to tell the guys, and I shouldn't tell you. You have to keep it under your hat. Wes confided in me, and I'm telling you because I know you'll keep your yap shut. The night Nicky Kinnick left, he threatened to sue. Sure enough, he hired an attorney, and they're going to file a lawsuit unless Wes pays him the rest of the money he would have made if he'd stayed."

Jaime couldn't help it. She grinned. "Let me guess. Sexual harassment?"

Eric nodded and squinted at her with a surprised look on his face. "How'd you know?"

"Because she was merciless. Absolutely cruel. And you know what, Eric? Nick is a wonderful man. That guy has class. I think she knew it, too, and she was trying to bring him down. Just watch—she won't pay a lick of attention to Gary when she dumps him. He's a bit of a sleaze-ball, but Nicky was a class act. You wait and see. That guy Nicky is going places."

"Yeah, I agree, and I'm telling you right now, we can't afford to lose anybody, especially Kip. We can't afford a spendy opening act, and she came cheap. One woman and a guitar is about all Wes can swing. So if the guys want to get paid for doing two acts in one night, they can just forget it."

Jaime sat back in the chair and crossed one sandaled foot over her other knee. "None of us are doing it for money. It's fun. You should have heard what Drew said the other night."

"I did."

"Well, then you understand. That's why the other guys want in. Kip's made Drew feel good about playing again. He's been burning out on the same old sets over and over for Lacey."

"Yeah, I know. He hasn't been himself. Just promise me this,

Jaime—keep an eye on things. Don't let them get out of hand. If you and the guys want to play, fine. But make sure the guys know it's only for fun."

"Done." She rose, hunched over so her head didn't touch the ceiling. "Man, I'd get claustrophobia in here in *Das Booth*."

He chuckled. "We're ready for sound checks, kiddo, and—" he checked his watch, "it's seventy-three minutes 'til show time."

"I'll let Wes know things are fine and then go round everyone up. Lance's got instruments to tune. I'll see if he needs help, then go change. Oh, and I'll get that camera up to you in a bit."

With a nod, he turned back to the board, and Jaime picked up her tool belt and ducked to make her way out and over to the narrow stairwell. She spent the next three-quarters of an hour going over details that were already perfect, and then she hustled back to the bus. At least twenty fans and groupies hung out at the stage door and surveyed her closely, then turned away, uninterested. As she made her way to the bus, she thought about what Kip had said earlier in the day. Was the folksinger serious about not wanting to be famous? Jaime knew that she, herself, never wanted that kind of life. It was bad enough being on the periphery of Lacey Leigh's mad spin.

She unlocked the bus door, entered, and closed it behind her, pausing on the stairs to listen. All she could hear was the grind and whir of the bus's generator. The door to Kip's stateroom was closed. She stepped up, then headed for the refrigerator and took out a bottle of root beer, slouched down in the loveseat, and wrenched off the twist-top. She drank deeply and let herself relax, trying not to think of anything but the stringent taste of the fizzy soft drink. When the bottle was empty, she tossed it in the garbage and went to her bunk and crawled up into it.

She fumbled around in the dark until she found the metal switch on the wall and clicked on the light, then sat cross-legged in the middle of the bunk. Sorting through her clothes, she selected what was left that was cleanest: black jeans, a black t-shirt, and fresh socks and underwear. She would have rather worn a dark polo shirt, but settled for a plain t-shirt. Everything was dirty now, and she needed to make a run to a laundromat. She picked up a smooth wooden box with a piñon tree engraved on the front. The slim box was the only thing she owned that connected her to her father, and she had always been surprised that her mother kept it. Sometimes when she was very drunk, Jaime's mother spoke lovingly about the white man named Paul who, all those years ago, had come to the bar where Magdalena worked. He gave her mother the velvet-lined box, and she had made love with him in a car in the parking lot. A few days later, he left town. Jaime often wondered what would have happened if he had stayed—or if he'd even left a last name.

She opened the box. The hinges had been top-of-the-line, and even after over nearly four decades, they were still sturdy. A jumble of shiny necklaces and earrings twinkled up at her, but she had eyes for only one piece of jewelry. She picked up an amethyst pendant encircled in fine silver. When visiting her friend's booth at the flea market yesterday, Emma had pointed it out. "Look," she'd said. "It's half a double helix." Jaime raised an eyebrow, and her friend giggled. "Oh, yeah, that's right. You never were good at biology. Remember DNA and double helixes?"

"Not really—and wouldn't it be helices?"

"Hell if I can say. All I know is this is one beautiful pendant. Do you like it?"

Jaime had looked at it—at the shiny silver, the sturdy silver chain, the perfectly cut planes of the amethyst, which was about an inch-long and dappled different colors of purple and lavender. "Yes. It's lovely."

"I'm buying this, Noni," she called out to the jeweler. "For my best friend."

Jaime smiled, remembering the pride she'd felt at the designation of best friend. Emma Little Whirlwind was the best thing from her past and a link from it to the current time. She couldn't imagine how she would have made the passage through adolescence without her. She opened the clasp and slipped the chain around her neck as she hooked it. The pendant lay just below the hollow of her throat, a solid reminder of her friend's caring. Besides, it had been good luck when she had worn it the night before, and she decided she just might wear it every night they had a show.

She closed the wooden box and set it in the cupboard at the foot of her bed, gathered up her clothes, and got down from the bunk area. Her watch revealed that she had sixteen minutes, and she knew she'd better get moving or Wes would have a coronary. She stepped into the bathroom and slid the pocket door shut, ready to change her clothes.

KIP STOOD IN the wings holding Isabelle close. She was calmed to feel cool air and know that the concert hall was air-conditioned and comfortable. And Jaime had been right; the acoustics were great, and the house was packed full. An air of excited expectation electrified everything, and she was sure it wasn't all

from the audience. She was dying to know what Jaime had
planned. *There's more than Drew and Jaime. Who else? Would
Buck play some drums? Oh! That would be so cool! Or maybe I
could get some keyboards from Marcus. Even a little bass would
be welcome. I just wish I knew.* An exhilarated thrill went through
her, as though she were ten again and waiting by the Christmas
tree for her mom and dad and brothers to wake up.

Her stomach did flips, partly from nervousness and partly
from anticipation. She glanced at her watch, then over at Tom. He
gave her a nod and a smile, then something caught his eye behind
her, and she looked over her shoulder to see Buck grinning behind
her. "Gawd, you're tall, Buck."

"Easier to reach the drums that way." His shaggy black hair
was in disarray, and as usual, he was wearing baggy black jeans,
black boots, and a black t-shirt. She thought that of all the members of the band, he always looked the most like he had just rolled
out of bed—in ninja pajamas.

"You're helping me out a bit, huh?"

"Yup."

"Did Jaime mention I'm opening with—"

"Yup—Wynonna's song. Gotcha covered there."

"Where is Jaime?"

"She'll be along presently." Sure enough, he hardly had the
words out of his mouth before Jaime, Drew, and Davis glided into
the area, all in black and moving like wraiths. Everybody was
grinning, and the excitement level went up another notch.

Nervously, Kip said, "People, we haven't done this before—"

Buck interrupted. "We'll follow along, Kip. Don't sweat it."

Drew nodded, "Regular key, right?" She nodded. "You greet
the audience, we'll all get situated, and then Buck, give me a
count, and I'll do that twangy intro. One bar is me. Buck and
Davis, you come in on the second bar, and then on the fourth or
sixth, whenever, let 'er rip, Kip."

The house music stopped. Tom looked her way and started
the five count.

Frantically, Kip whispered, "So how do I tell you when to
stop?"

Buck laughed. "We'll figure it out when the time comes."

More than a little unnerved, Kip walked out onstage and
plugged in Isabelle. For just a brief moment, she blanked on where
they were, and then in a rush, she remembered. "Hel-LOH, Albuquerque!" The place was packed, with standing room only, and
they were an enthusiastic crowd, too. "My name's Kip Galvin,
and I hail from Minnesota where it is *never* this hot and dry. Glad

to see all of you came out here tonight—into air-conditioned splendor."

She heard a smattering of applause and grinned. She glanced over her shoulder, and everyone seemed ready, so she said, "I'm gonna open with a little tune of Wynonna's called 'A Little Bit of Love Goes A Long, Long Way.'"

"On four," Buck hollered, and his sticks went click-click-click-click. Drew hit the lead guitar intro, and true to his word, Buck came in on the second bar with a driving beat. Kip strummed a rhythm and she heard Davis's bass thumping. She opened her mouth to sing and felt like laughing with glee. To her left, Jaime stood playing a bright blue electric guitar Kip had never seen before. Tanned, confident fingers played a series of riffs in counterpoint to the overarching lead Drew was hammering out, and Kip sang the song all out, knowing for sure that it sounded great.

They got to a bridge in the song, and she turned to her right and pointed to Drew. "Ladies and gentlemen, Drew Michael Donovan!" He stepped forward and played the lead part. Over the side fill and monitors, she could hear the crowd hollering and screaming, and she knew Drew would be blushing. She finished singing the last verse and instinctively listened for the end of Drew's guitar part, then pointed her finger in the air and gave the "wrap it up" signal. They played two more bars, and then Buck gave a roll of the drums. She raised one hand and waited two more beats, then dropped her arm, and everyone ended on cue.

They got a thunderous round of applause. Over it, she shouted, "Thank you! Let's stay upbeat. Anybody like Mary Chapin Carpenter?" Plenty of voices screamed back that they did. "Here's one of my favorites of hers, 'Tender As I Want To Be.'" Buck hit the drums, and she heard Drew's lead bubble out, sounding at times like a popcorn machine. The bass filled in, and she sang the first words. At each of the two bridges, she heard the wah-wah, and both times she turned and looked over her left shoulder to locate Jaime and the electric blue guitar. The black-haired woman was so intent on her guitar and the wah-wah pedal that she paid no attention to Kip, much less the audience.

They finished that song, and Kip, slightly out-of-breath, waited for the house to calm down. "Isn't this a great band?" she asked. "I have to thank Lacey Leigh for loaning them to me. We haven't played together onstage before, but they're an amazing group of musicians, folks. This next song really showcases the talent of Davis Archambault, the best bass player I've ever had the pleasure to be onstage with. Davis hails from Gallatin, a town outside Nashville. He and his brother, Marcus, also a gifted musician, have been with Lacey's band since the beginning of her tours. I've got a special treat for Davis..." She grinned out toward the audience, and in a conspiratorial tone said, "Though he doesn't know it." She turned and looked over her shoulder. "Davis, do you know a bass line for my song, 'What I'm Looking For'?"

"Yes, ma'am."

"Okay, then. Go ahead and hit it."

Without a pause, Davis played the bass line, and one-by-one, everyone except Jaime joined in. Jaime slipped the strap off her shoulder and racked the electric guitar, exchanging it for her mandolin. She cradled the instrument in her hands and looked around the stage, listening to the song as Kip sang.

> *I'm not looking for one night stands*
> *Take it off and have at it*
> *I'm not looking for a classic wedding band*
> *Put it on, take it off, give it back*
> *I'm not looking for a faithful standby*
> *Run out of things to do – call you*
> *I'm not looking for a cheap high*
> *To me there's just got to be more to do*

At the chorus, Jaime began plucking the delicate background melody. She'd already played it so many times that her fingers knew it by heart, and she looked upstage at Kip's back, feeling a little bit in awe about this experience. The band was playing together as though they'd practiced for months, and Kip was obviously reveling in it.

> *But I have had a lot of life*
> *Yet not enough to quit living*
> *I'm just looking for a fifty-fifty chance*
> *To do some real taking and giving*

Jaime finished her part and let the last notes ring, then after they faded out, she put her hand over the strings to ensure that no errant notes got hit by accident. She listened in admiration to the full, melodious voice singing the song. In her own head, she could hear harmony parts, a third above, and a third below, winding in and around the folksinger's strong voice. Too bad they didn't have the backup vocalists to help. Even without added voices, it sounded wonderful.

I don't think I'm looking for a full time lover
That can be a big responsibility
But I can't look for a new beginning when this is over
Because a life of heartache just can't be
I'm not looking forward to a lonely time
Though I'm looking back on some already
I'm not looking forward to leaving you behind
But what I give doesn't measure up to what I'm getting

Jaime got ready to play her part again, and this time she listened closely to the chorus.

But I have had a lot of life
Yet not enough to quit living
I'm just looking for a fifty-fifty chance
To do some real taking and giving

She played her part again, hearing the melodic whining of Drew's lead, Kip's acoustic picking, and the drums and bass. She wondered if Eric was getting this on tape because from the stage, it sounded terrific. She couldn't wait to find out whether it was as unbelievable as she thought it was. As they played, she heard Kip singing a background part: *Pick up... shack up... break up... crack up...* and then the folksinger sang the chorus loud and clear.

I have had a great deal of life already
But I want to feel much, much more
Maybe I'm not looking hard enough
Or don't know what I'm looking for

The ovation was spirited, and Kip hardly waited for it to die down before she started playing a fast picking pattern. Jaime hustled to re-rack the mandolin and grab up her guitar. She wasn't sure what song this was.

Kip said, "Here's an oldie, but a real goodie, from one of my favorite gals, Dolly Parton," and she launched into the beginning of "Jolene." Quickly the band fell in, and by the end, it was a rollicking version during which Drew and Kip somehow managed to work in an extended guitar solo.

They got in four more songs, and the folksinger managed to introduce every single member of the band, and then the set was over. The excited group exited stage left.

"Oh my, oh my, oh my!" Kip said. "That was—simply fabulous!" She hugged people right and left.

"Geez, Kip," Jaime laughed. "You're bouncing off the ceiling."

"You would, too, if you were me. You guys were awesome.
That was just an incredible amount of fun."

Drew threw an arm across her shoulders. "It sure as hell was.
I thought Davis was going to fall on the floor when you called out
for him to have a solo."

Drew let out a guffaw, and Davis, usually so serious, cracked
a smile. "Damn, I need a drink," the bass player said.

Jaime said, "I'll get you some spring water?"

"No, I need a beer—and a water, too."

They were moving as a group, laughing and talking, and
emerged from the wings into the backstage area to find Lacey in
the anteroom arguing with Wes. Candy and Shelley stood off to
the side, looking uncomfortable.

"Goddammit, Wes, that's my band. *Mine!* Now they're all
worn out."

"Now, Lacey—"

"How many times have I told you not to 'Now, Lacey' me?"
The small woman, dressed in her pale pink slacks, pink tube top,
and white high heels, shook her finger up toward his face.

"Don't change the subject. Let me ask you once again, Lacey,
where is Gary?"

The little star settled back on her heels and let out a huff. "He
won't be playing with us tonight."

Jaime let out a sigh of her own. *Oh, shit. I'll have to play this
gig. Crap!*

Wes stood still, and for a moment Jaime thought that she
could almost see him counting to ten. In a patient voice, as though
speaking to a child, he said, "Will he be playing at the next gig
this coming weekend?"

Lacey Leigh crossed her arms. "No. I think not."

The big man put his hands on his hips. "Son of a *bitch!* What
are we gonna do for a rhythm guitarist?"

She shrugged. "Jaime, again, I guess."

"Excuse me," Jaime said, "I'm on tonight? What about the
fiddle part on 'Between Us'?"

"Yeah," Wes said. "What about that?" He crossed his arms
across his broad chest and stared daggers at Lacey.

Jaime was surprised to hear Kip speak up. "Say, I could probably fumble my way through rhythm on one song."

The diva turned with a startled look on her face. "Seriously?"

"Sure. How much time do I have?"

Wes looked at his watch. "In a perfect world," he growled,

"the whole *goddamn* bunch of you'd be pretty well ready right now. Now we'll be late."

Drew stepped forward. "Good crowd tonight. They'll wait. C'mon, Kip. Let me do a little run-through with you." He grabbed her arm, and they headed off.

Davis said, "Where's Marcus?"

Wes hollered, "Marcus! Somebody please tell me we haven't lost another miserable morphodite motherfuckin'—"

"No, sir! I'm here!" Marcus yelled out as he slipped into the room.

Wes pulled a white handkerchief out of his jacket pocket and mopped his brow, and Lacey turned to go. To the diva's retreating back, he shouted, "You're gonna be the death of me, Lacey Leigh Jaxon."

She whirled around, gave him a sweet smile, and strode back over to put her hand on his forearm. "You worry too much, Wes, honey. You're going to stroke out." With a toss of her head, she summoned her backup singers. "We'll be in the dressing room if anyone needs us."

The three women trooped off, leaving Jaime, Buck, and the twins. Jaime said, "Still want that drink, Davis?"

"Make it a double."

Chapter Eight

KIP HAD THE lounge area of the bus to herself. She sat in the booth, barefoot and dressed in cotton pajama bottoms and a t-shirt. The early morning sun slanted through the window on the opposite side of the bus, and she looked out to see the remnants of red, orange, and neon pink splashed across the sky. It had been a beautiful sunrise to watch and very fitting for a quiet Sunday in Albuquerque. For the entire tour, she hadn't been awake once at this ungodly hour—until today. The night before, she'd gone to bed, for the first time in weeks, at ten p.m. She was so glad she had a couple more days ahead of her to rest up. Lacey Leigh and Wes Slater had flown out to Nashville the day before to work on a video. Kip wasn't sure for which song either. All she knew was that they wouldn't be back until Tuesday night, and there wasn't another concert until Wednesday night.

Kip turned her attention back to the papers spread out in front of her. From an inch-thick stack off to the side, she took a blank page of musical notation paper and set to work putting down quarter notes with a thick-leaded pencil. She paused, pencil poised, her brow crinkled in thought. She turned the pencil over and erased one quarter note, then stopped to think again.

A thud sounded behind her, and she shifted and looked over her shoulder to see Jaime emerging from the upper bunk. The other woman dropped to the floor, wearing a tight sleeveless shirt and panties. Her thighs were well muscled, and the tan arms and shoulders were tight with sinew.

"Oh, good," Jaime said. "I'm glad it's just you."

She disappeared into the bathroom, and Kip set her pencil down, her heart beating fast. *Whew. Nice legs.* It's not that she hadn't noticed Jaime's attractive physique in the past, but she hadn't seen quite so much skin before. *She's pretty much a goddess compared to me. She probably even has abs that show.* Kip looked down at her thighs. They were solid—but with no visible muscle. She knew that somewhere under the padding around her legs and waist and arms there were some good strong muscles, but she was pretty sure no one had ever seen them, at least not since about the age of eight. She chuckled to herself. *Oh well. At least I'm healthy.*

The pocket door slid open, and Kip forced herself not to look, to stay focused on her music instead. She heard noises behind her for a minute, and then footsteps. "How are you this morning, Kip—and what in the hell are you up so early for?" Jaime slipped past her and slid into the booth seat across from the folksinger. Kip was relieved to see that she was now dressed in shorts and a red t-shirt.

"I felt rested, so I got up. I take it you didn't get enough rest?"

Jaime yawned and rubbed her eyes. "I'll probably take a nap later." She looked at the papers spread out on the table. "What are you working on?"

"A new song."

"Have I heard it?"

"No. I'm writing the music now."

"Writing the music?"

Kip smiled and raised her eyebrows. "Yeah, you know—putting down the music so I don't forget?"

"Oh."

"Do you write music?"

"Nope, not really." Jaime looked out the window and puckered up her lips like she was going to whistle. Instead she said, "I don't write music, and I think I told you before that I don't exactly read it either."

"Oh, wow. I have a minor in music, so I forget that other people are clever enough to just hear music and be able to play it. I have to work at it a bit harder, I think."

"I doubt it."

"Trust me, I could never step in and do what Drew does. I don't know how he manages. I either need the music, or I have to hear the song a number of times."

"You did pretty good on rhythm on that one song of Lacey's the other night."

"To be honest? That is such a simple song—three major chords, typical progression. I'd heard it enough, too, so it was easy."

"Lucky for her, I'd say." Jaime shook her head and crossed her arms. "I hope Wes brings back a new guitarist. I don't want to be stuck there again. And he'd better find someone completely dense and ugly."

Kip giggled. "You did a good job the other night, too. I was impressed. You're pretty phenomenal if you play everything by ear. How'd you learn?"

"My grandfather taught me to play the fiddle when I was very young. I don't even remember the first time he let me play. They said I was three. I took up guitar in junior high, and I picked up the mandolin in my late twenties. Actually, I'm not real good at mandolin. I'm still learning."

Kip nodded. "You might still be learning, but the pieces you've played have been damn good."

Jaime blushed. "Thanks."

"So how come you don't sing more? You have a nice voice."

The flush on Jaime's face deepened. "I've got an okay backup voice, but I'm no lead vocalist. I'm a decent enough rhythm guitarist, but I'm no lead. I can play a little backup mandolin or fiddle, but I'm no concert strings expert. My job is backup, and I try to do it the best I can, whether I'm stringing wire, setting up the sound system, or stepping in when we lose a musician."

"You're probably underrating yourself."

"Not really." She put her elbows on the table and looked out the window. "So, what are you doing today?"

Kip pointed out the window. "I have a date, right there."

Jaime narrowed her eyes and tried to follow where Kip was pointing. "A date?"

"Yeah, me and a hundred articles of dirty clothing. Everything I own stinks."

"Tell me about it!" She laughed. "Can I double date with you?"

"Sure. I've got Buck's laundry, too."

"What!" Jaime's smiling countenance quickly changed to a scowl. "Who the hell does he think he is—dumping his shit job on you?"

"Chill, baby, chill. I offered. He said he'd buy pizza at noon."

"Oh." Jaime raised an eyebrow. "Well, then I think I should help, and he can buy for me, too. He owes me plenty of favors anyway." With a smirk on her face, she crossed her arms and nodded. "Wouldn't you think that would be fair?"

THE TWO WOMEN sat sweating in the overly warm laundromat at a two-by-three-foot table as close to the doorway as they could get. Every once in a while there was a wisp of a breeze, but still, it was very hot and dry, and the bright orange paint on the adobe-style walls didn't help the room seem any cooler. There was barely enough room at the table for each of them to lay out their cards as they played them, which meant that they sat almost knee to knee. With no one else in the place, they had four loads going simultaneously. All the clothes had already been run through the industrial-sized washers, and now they were waiting for them to finish drying.

"Hey!" Kip said. "You can't play those cards yet!"

"Sure I can," Jaime said. "You gonna stop me?" She arched an eyebrow and gave the folksinger a proud glare.

Kip rose to the challenge, narrowing her eyes and grinning mischievously. "Um hmm, that's exactly what I'll do."

"Oh, yeah? Think you're mighty enough to take me on?"

"Yup. I may be old, but I'm pretty sure I can whip your butt."

"Ha! Right. We'll see who kicks whose butt."

"Just try it," Kip said. "You may be all of half-an-inch taller, but I've got you in the weight category. Boxing, wrestling, rugby, sumo—I've got you beat in all of them."

A laugh exploded from the black-haired woman. "You can't be serious?"

Kip gave a triumphant smile. "I fight dirty, too. When you get as old as me, you resort to whatever measures are necessary."

"Oooh, now I'm *really* scared. And you're not old. I've got you beat by centuries."

"I don't think so."

"Pullease! What are you 32? 33?"

Kip gave a great guffaw. "Man, are you ever off, but thanks for sucking up. It won't distract me from noticing that you're try-ing to cheat."

Jaime looked surprised. "How the heck old are you then?"

"Nuh uh...a lady never tells her age."

"Sure—*now* you're a lady. Well, you sure weren't one a cou-ple weeks ago when Drew was calling you ma'am."

"How old are you?"

"I'm not saying 'til you admit *your* advanced age."

"Okay, fine, but I'm telling you that you can't play those cards." She rose and walked across the cement floor to check on the clothes in the dryer.

Jaime picked up the three cards and sat back in her chair, a wry smile on her face. She knew she couldn't play the run, but she was enjoying all the teasing. Kip didn't miss much at cards—that was for sure. In fact, Jaime thought the two of them ought to con-sider taking on some of the guys in Hearts or Pinochle. She was pretty sure they could make some good money, especially off

Buck, who thought he was such a hotshot strategist.

Kip strolled back toward the little table. She wiped off her forehead with the sleeve of her t-shirt. "You know, we Minnesota girls aren't fond of heat. After all this, I think Buck owes us a pizza *and* ice cream."

"No shit." Jaime put down one card and discarded another. "So how old are you anyway? And how old do you think I am?"

Kip sat back down in the rickety folding chair. "Hmm, that's tough to tell with your heritage."

"Why do you say that?"

"Oh, I've got parents of my indigenous students who hardly look old enough to be a mother or father. Half the time I wonder if I should check their IDs just to make sure the kids aren't running some sort of scam on me with an older brother or sister." She crinkled up her nose and squinted across the table. "I think I'll be conservative and guess thirty."

Jaime gave her a broad smile. "Close. Oh-so-close. But no. You're off."

"High? Or low?"

She ignored the question and instead asked, "How about my estimate? Was I high? Or low when I guessed you at 32 or 33?"

"Low."

"You, too."

Kip nodded. "So we're both older than we look. I guess that's good news. I'm 37. Just turned before I came on this trip."

Jaime raised her chin into the air and took on a snooty look. "Well. I do believe that makes me your senior. I'm 38."

"For real?" She said it with a note of wonder in her voice, then reached up and touched Jaime's cheek. "You are *very* well preserved in your old age." She jerked her hand back, laughing maniacally.

"All right, that's it! You're pushing your luck, woman!" She rose, snickering, and walked over to the first dryer in the row and pulled it open. "These clothes are hotter than hell. Good enough for me." She rolled a basket over and pulled all the clothes out, then pushed it toward the waist-high table halfway across the room.

Kip joined her at the tall table, and they made quick work with the folding. Jaime went back for the second dryer's contents, and they systematically worked their way through folding that load, too.

"Jaime?"

"Hmm?"

"What did you do before this—or have you always been a tour

worker?"

"Actually, I've only done this for the last three years, since my mom died. I didn't work full-time for about a year while she was sick and dying." When Kip didn't say anything, she went on. "After high school, I did a little clerk work at a hardware store and an auto parts shop, then after a couple of years, I went to electrician school. I've worked construction on new home starts, done repairs at an electrician's shop, and I worked for the county for a while, too. I have to admit, though, I didn't like it. Pay was good, but the men were assholes."

Kip reached for one of Buck's shirts, and as she pulled it toward her, she saw a four-inch long, rubbery-looking critter drop to the table. It was sandy brown with a double row of dark spots on its back and down to the tail. She reached for it, thinking it was some sort of kid's toy, but when her fingers came in contact, it moved and then skittered wildly across the table.

"Aaaaaaah!" She jumped back, her hands above her shoulders with palms open. "Oh, my God! What in the hell is that?" Laughing hard, Jaime leaned over the table, trying to catch her breath. Still standing three steps away from all the clothes tangled up on the table, Kip put her hands on her hips. In an accusatory voice, she said, "What kind of tricks are you playing, Jaime Esperanza?"

Jaime turned, leaning back against the table and still giggling uncontrollably. Her words came out in gasps. "No tricks. *Dios mio*, that was funny." She laughed some more, and Kip could see tears in her eyes. "You should've seen the look on your face."

Kip checked around, but the little critter was gone. She stepped forward and grabbed the front of Jaime's t-shirt. "You didn't set that up?"

"Hell, no." Jaime straightened up and pushed Kip's hand away from the center of her shirt, then made a big show of smoothing out the wrinkles.

"What was that thing?"

"Just a little lizard—a side-blotched lizard."

"Side-blotched? What's that supposed to mean?"

"I don't know. That's just what type they are. They're all over the place, wherever it's warm and sunny.

"What was it doing in here? There's no sun in here," Kip said indignantly.

"Probably just enjoying the warmth, maybe finding something to snack on."

"Like what—laundry soap?"

"Maybe. I can't believe you've never seen a lizard."

"I've seen plenty of lizards."

Jaime crossed her arms. "Yeah, right. Where? At the zoo?"

Kip raised her voice. "I'll have you know we have a couple of green lizards in cages at school."

"In a classroom?"

"Yeah."

"I am sure Minnesota is known far and wide as the Lizard Kingdom of the North Woods, huh?"

Kip sputtered. "No, but it's not like I've seen this kind—this side-botched kind."

"Side-*blotched*. And they're all over the place." The folksinger glanced around the room, which caused another snort of laughter from Jaime. "Not all over the laundromat, Kip. All over the southwest. There are a million of 'em everywhere, and thank God for them, too, because they eat bugs."

"When they're not biting humans, you mean?" She moved over and gingerly picked up a blue t-shirt and shook it out before folding it.

"I don't know if you noticed, but that lizard's mouth was tiny." She reached over and took the folksinger's hand, then pointed at Kip's pinkie with her free hand. "Poor little guy couldn't possibly have gotten his mouth around your littlest finger." She grinned widely, her nearly black eyes dancing with amusement. With a squeeze, she let go of the hand she held and went back to the folding.

Despite the sweltering heat, Kip felt a shiver run down her back, and she was acutely aware of the warm, lean body inches from her own. She canted her head slightly to the side and looked out of the corner of her eye to see that Jaime was grinning as she bundled together pairs of socks. A feeling of elation thrummed through Kip's body, and she couldn't help but think that she liked this new friend a lot. She grabbed the last two socks on the table and found they didn't match. "Hey, you've been remiss in your duties."

Jaime met her eyes. "Hmm?"

Kip held up one sock, a rather large white one obviously belonging to Buck. She picked up another smaller sock. "This one's mine. This one's not. Wonder where their mates are?"

Jaime peeled apart a pair of socks. "Not these." She twisted them back together into a ball and tried two more of the five pair on the table before she found the mismatched ones.

"Remind me in the future to supervise all folding tasks you do."

"Remind me to bring weapons next time, so I can protect you

from big, scary monster lizards during all laundry tasks."

Kip elbowed her. "Ha ha. Very funny." She leaned into Jaime and gave her a soft, playful shove. Jaime narrowed her eyes and grabbed the folksinger at the ribs and pressed her thumbs into a suddenly convulsing diaphragm. Kip backed up wildly, trying to avoid the strong hands and shrieking with laughter, until she came into contact with the burnt orange wall. "Stop, stop!"

"Thought you said you could whip my butt."

"Not when I'm laughing!" Her hands darted out, and she grabbed the lean waist and squeezed, but the other woman didn't budge.

"Hate to tell you, but I'm not ticklish." The look on her face was triumphant.

"That's just—just—inhuman."

Jaime nodded as she grinned from ear to ear. For a moment longer they stood inches apart, hands on one another's middles, and then Jaime released her. "Guess I win that round, then, huh?"

"Sure, and that means you are awarded the full and glorious right to carry *all* the laundry." She hustled over and stacked their clothes into the bottom of the plastic laundry basket, filled Buck's paper box with his clean clothes, and stacked his box on top of the basket. "There ya go."

Jaime bent and picked it all up. "It's not like it's that heavy."

Kip moved over to the small table and quickly rounded up the scattered Phase 10 cards, then tucked them into the box, which she slipped into her back pocket. "To the bus or the hotel first?"

"Doesn't matter. Hotel is closer. We can drop off Buck's stuff, remove about twenty bucks from his wallet, and then take our things back to the bus."

They left the laundromat, and as they emerged into the dry air, Kip thought, *It's ten degrees cooler out here*. Within a few strides, it no longer felt cooler, and another bead of sweat dripped from her neck and down her back. As she walked, she glanced around and discovered Jaime was right. She saw a tiny movement on the ground, and a brown critter disappeared under a flat rock. A block further, she saw another lizard on the wall of an adobe structure. She wondered what else she wasn't seeing.

They entered the hotel into blessed coolness, and within a minute, Kip was shivering from the frigid air against the moisture on her skin. "Whew! Feels chilly in here."

"Yeah, no kidding. Brrr..."

They took the stairs up one level and walked down the carpeted hall to room 214. Kip reached up and knocked. She heard no sound from within. She went to knock again, as she said,

"Maybe he's gone—" and the door pulled back abruptly. With her hair tousled and a lacy wraparound robe barely covering her, Candy, one of the backup singers, stood in the doorway.

"Oh, sorry," Kip said. "We have the wrong room."

Candy said, "No, you don't." She stepped back and held the door open.

Kip heard Buck's voice. "I owe Kip some pizza dough, honey. Ha, that's funny, pizza dough." One bare arm, up to the shoulder, and his dark head popped around the corner. "Oh, hey, Jaime. How ya doing?"

"Not bad," she answered. "Seems like you're doing all right yourself." She rested the laundry basket against her thigh, and juggled the box holding Buck's clean clothes. Kip grabbed it from her and set it on the floor in front of Candy.

Kip glanced quickly toward Jaime and saw that she was trying to hold back a grin. Candy took the money from Buck's out-stretched hand, and he disappeared around the corner. As the backup singer handed over the bills, she met Kip's eyes with an odd look on her face, and it occurred to the folksinger that the other woman was embarrassed. "Do you want us to pick up any-thing for you guys?" Kip asked kindly as she stuffed the bills in her shorts pocket.

"No," Candy said. "We're fine." She pulled the satiny wrap-per tight around her and crossed her arms over the front of it.

"Okay, then, we're off. Oh, and Buck?" Kip called out.

She couldn't see him but she could hear him clearly. "Yeah?"

"I confiscated all the change in your pockets."

"Like I care?"

"That's pretty much what I thought you'd say." She turned to the backup singer. "Hey, take care, Candy, and maybe we'll catch a bite to eat with you down in the café."

For the first time, Candy seemed to relax a little. She smiled, her face now a little pink. "Thanks, Kip. See you two later."

The two women turned and reversed course down the hall-way. After they got a dozen steps away, Kip looked over at Jaime to find her staring her way. As soon as their eyes met, they burst into giggles. They got to the landing at the top of the stairwell, and Jaime dropped the laundry basket, took hold of the railing, and doubled over laughing.

Kip put her hand on Jaime's back and tried to stifle her own giggles. "Stop. Stop. Don't make me laugh."

"Damn," Jaime said. She straightened up and threw her arm across Kip's shoulder. "That was too funny for words."

"Is Buck known to be a big horndog or what?"

"No, not really." She paused a moment, then let her arm drop away. She bent to pick up the blue basket.

"What about Candy?"

Jaime shook her head. "Not that I know of. I know Shelley's had some flings—not this tour so far, though. I'm not positive about Candy."

"I wonder what the deal with the two of them is." They hit the bottom of the stairs and headed for the hotel entrance.

"Don't ask me, but I'll be teasing Buck later."

They reached the front door, and Jaime spun around and backed out, holding the plastic basket at waist level, then held the door open for Kip. The folksinger moved through the entrance and out into the hot sun. It hit her like a wave of fire, and her skin instantly went from cool to overheated. "I sure hope the A/C on the bus is working."

"Me, too."

She unlocked the bus and pushed the door open, then waited for Jaime to pass through with the laundry. As she followed her up the stairs, she said, "Do you want to eat something now—or wait until later?"

Jaime put the basket up on the table. "Doesn't matter to me. I can eat snacks here now or eat pizza. Either way. Was he cheap? How much did he give you?"

Kip dug into her shorts pocket and pulled out the three bills. "Three tens."

She whistled. "That was right generous of old Buck." She chuckled and held up her hand for Kip to give her a high five. "You hungry now?"

"Yeah." The folksinger dug into the laundry basket and pulled out one stack of her clothes, then went back to her stateroom, unlocked the door, and set everything on the bed. She returned to the lounge area and got the other stack.

Jaime squatted down and rooted around in the small refrigerator. She looked up at Kip as she went by and said, "We've got a brand new container of picante sauce and about three kinds of chips. You want to have chips and salsa and wait until later in the afternoon to go out for dinner?"

Kip paused in the narrow passageway in front of the door to her room. "Don't you have other things you'd rather be doing today?"

"Not really. And by the way, I am interested in a rematch at that damn card game. I'm sure it was only a fluke you won the other day."

A laugh bubbled up from Kip. *We'll see about that.*

KIP LOOKED AT her watch and was surprised to find it was four p.m. They had been talking and playing cards for over three hours, but now Jaime looked like she was fading. Kip won another hand and tossed the cards into the middle of the table as Jaime let out a yawn. "What time did you hit the hay last night?"

Jaime yawned again. "About two a.m."

"You going to take a little nap?"

The other woman hesitated, as though she were going to deny feeling tired, then said, "Yes. That would be a good idea."

Kip gathered the cards and squared them up so they'd fit in the box. Jaime rose and moved slowly toward the tiny hallway with Kip behind her. "Will you feel invaded if I see what this bunk of yours looks like?"

Jaime shook her head. The folksinger waited as she went up the recessed ladder and disappeared through the drape, then slid the curtains aside. Kip stepped up, grabbed the overhead bar, and ducked in. Jaime sat cross-legged at what must be the head of the bed because that was where a couple of pillows were stacked. The folksinger left one leg dangling over the side for a moment, but there was a wooden ridge there that dug into her thigh, so she pulled her leg in and sat cross-legged, facing Jaime. She looked around the bunk, noting clothes and duffel bags stacked neatly behind her. She saw the TV, a number of cupboard doors and drawers, and noted that there was plenty of overhead space. She extended her arm over her head and touched the ceiling with her palm. "You've got lots of storage in here, but don't you get claustrophobic?"

"Nah, I don't spend much time in here—except to sleep." She raised a hand and pulled a string, and a pleasant light illuminated the compartment.

"Too bad there's no window in here."

"You'd probably feel like you were falling out all the time. It's bad enough having the opening to the hallway."

"At least it's cool."

Jaime pointed to a vent behind Kip's left shoulder, then to a panel on the aisle side of the wall. "I've got controls for the A/C here, and actually, I can get it pretty cold." She yawned again.

"Feels just perfect right now." Kip scooted toward the side. "I better go and let you get your nap. Will it bug you if I jump in the shower?"

"No, don't worry about it."

"Okay." She slung a leg over the side and felt around with her foot until she discovered the recessed step. "Hey, what time are we pulling out tomorrow?"

"We're only going to Amarillo. I don't suppose we need more than about six hours at the most, so I figure Eric will shoot to leave around ten or eleven—whenever checkout time is."

"Okay, that'll work." As Kip lowered herself, Jaime stretched her legs out, right in front of the descending woman. On impulse, Kip reached up with one hand and gave the muscle right above the bare knee a squeeze.

Jaime jumped and said, "Whoa."

"Oh, ho ho," Kip said with an evil grin on her face. "You *are* ticklish somewhere, after all."

In a grumpy voice, Jaime said, "No one's supposed to know that." She turned on her side, facing the folksinger. "If you tell anyone, I'll have to kill ya."

"Yeah, right." She gave the extended leg a final pat and finished her descent, then went into her stateroom and gathered up a change of clothes. She had perspired so much earlier in the afternoon that the back of her shirt felt funny, and she would be happy to change into clean clothes. Feeling much better after a quick shower, she crept quietly down the narrow hallway and into her stateroom, leaving the door open. First she put away her laundry, and then for nearly half an hour, she sat scrunched up at the tiny little table and wrote in her journal. After a while, she put it away. She went over to the bed, arranged the pillows so she could sit up and lean against them, then sat on the edge of the bed and opened up the drawer in the built-in bureau. Rummaging through one of her canvas bags, she pulled out her CD player and headphones, got out an old Indigo Girls disc, and popped it in. She settled back against the pillows with a new paperback and opened the book to read.

Kip didn't remember falling asleep, but when she woke, the CD had finished playing, and the only sound she heard was the whir of the air conditioner. With her eyes shut, she moved the lightweight book off her chest and onto the bed beside her, then lay there thinking about the last wisps of a dream. She had been crying—walking through a desolate landscape, no shoes, lost, and with no help in sight. It was unsettling because she didn't know what she was mourning. All she knew was that she was filled with sorrow, and she didn't know where to go with it. There was more to the dream, a great many more details, but they slipped away before she could capture them, leaving her feeling disoriented. Sitting up, she reminded herself that she'd had some version of this type of dream ever since Brenna left her—but not lately, not for the last few months. It troubled her to have the same theme pop up again.

Pushing the dream images out of her mind, she reached into the open drawer next to the bed and removed a different CD, this time by Cheryl Wheeler. Exchanging Indigo Girls for Cheryl, she sat back again and adjusted the headphones. The guitar and smooth singing voice soon soothed her. She turned up the music, closed her eyes, and lay there thinking. The face that swam into her mind's eye was that of Jaime—the black hair, the dark brows, the intense, nearly black eyes, and the high cheekbones. In conversation earlier today she learned that Jaime was all alone in the world, with the exception of some distant cousins whom she rarely saw. Her mother had been a barmaid until she died at age 53 from alcohol abuse. Jaime hadn't gone into detail about that, but from watching her, Kip's intuition told her it was still a painful loss. Her other close relatives, the maternal grandparents, died when Jaime was in her mid-twenties. Kip had shared sketchy information about her own family. She thought it better to save the details for later, if they should happen to discuss such things again.

Looking at her watch, she was surprised to see it was past six p.m. From the angle of light slanting in the side windows, the sun was certainly lower in the sky. She picked up the CD player and shifted over onto her left hip, then rolled up on her knees and scooted across the bed so she could lean against the side of the bus and look out the window. She put the CD player on the bed and raised her fingers up to the metal edge of the windows, peering out as though she were Kilroy gazing over a wall. The sun sat low in the sky, and though it was a couple of hours until sunset, already the heavens were laced with the beginnings of the pink and blue and orange she had seen at sunrise. She leaned her forehead against the window and enjoyed the easygoing voice that sang about wanting to be in love, of wanting to give of herself and be as true as an arrow flying in windless skies. The song made her smile. In some ways the tone was sad, but then again, the singer still harbored hope in her heart—hope that she might yet find love again.

Kip felt the bus suddenly dip, and before she realized that it was merely her bed's mattress moving, Jaime was next to her, shoulder to shoulder, smiling warmly as she knelt beside her with her fingers gripping the metal ledge. The folksinger slipped the headphones off and dropped them onto the bed next to the CD player. "Why is everybody always sneaking up on me?"

Jaime smiled. "Dunno. I did knock, but if you're deaf from headphones or off in a reverie, you're going to get startled, and that's all there is to it."

"How'd you sleep?"

"Good. I feel a lot better."

"In my family, when someone wakes up with pillow hair, we always say, 'You must have slept *real* well.'"

"Yeah, yeah. My hair's so thick that once it gets bent like that, it won't straighten out unless I wet it."

"I'd be glad to go get a bucket."

"Very funny."

Kip smiled, then reached up and brushed Jaime's cheek lightly with her fingers. "You also have marks from something on your cheek."

Jaime frowned and brought her own hand up to her face. "Like chocolate or ink or what?"

The folksinger dropped her hand. "No, red streaks like you slept on a couple of pokey wrinkles in the pillow. The marks will disappear after a while. Just be glad you didn't fall asleep on candy. I did that once at Halloween, and it took four washings to get the marshmallow out of my hair."

"I thought marshmallows were made out of water-soluble stuff like eggs and sugar."

"These had red dye number 6 or 8 or whatever in them. Turned my hair an odd shade of pink. My hair was a lot lighter brown back then, too."

Jaime chuckled. "Hope your parents got pictures of that."

Kip rolled her eyes. "If you ever have occasion to meet them, I'm sure they'd love to show you. They've enjoyed torturing me many times over the years, and believe me, that's not even the worst picture from my childhood." She turned back to the scene outside the window.

Jaime followed Kip's gaze. "It's going to be a pretty sunset."

"I think so."

"Want to go get something to eat, then watch the sun go down?"

"Will it be hot?"

"The sunset? Or the meal?" Jaime grinned devilishly.

"Oh, geez. Sometimes you have a very quick wit, Ms. Esperanza."

"We aim to please."

"I was talking weather, not food." Kip slid down onto her left hip and sat back, swinging her legs away and over to the side. In one smooth movement, she was on her feet next to the bed. "Do we have to go to the crappy café here at the hotel?"

Jaime stuck one long leg past the foot of the bed and levered herself up. "I thought you had your heart set on pizza."

"We're in New Mexico. Shouldn't we have Mexican?"

"Well, I can sure say I would enjoy that."

"Okay, let's walk down a couple blocks. I saw a cantina down past the laundromat that had a horde of people sitting there at lunchtime. If that many were there for lunch, I'll bet their food is good for dinner, too."

"Sounds logical. Let me do a quick rinse in the shower and change, then I'll get my wallet, and we can go."

"Okay. That'll work. Maybe you'll get a chance to unbend your hair."

Jaime gave her the evil eye and disappeared down the hall.

Kip lowered one knee to the edge of the bed and reached near the wall for the CD player and headphones. She dropped them into the open drawer next to her bed and closed the drawer, then stood up, looked around, and thought for a moment. She decided to change out of her t-shirt. The pale blue polo shirt she took from the drawer under the bed smelled fresh and clean. She took off her t-shirt and pulled on the clean top and tucked it into her cargo shorts. When she looked down, she smiled to see the little alligator over the breast. She thought of the tiny brown lizard in the laundromat and hoped she didn't see any more tonight.

Chapter
Nine

KIP WOKE THE next morning to an odd sound. She could swear that over the whir of the air conditioner, she could hear the pitter-patter of rain. With her eyes still closed, she lay under the red and gold coverlet and listened. The sound of water spraying came again, and she opened her eyes and focused on the window up to the left. Beads of water dripped down the windowpane. *It's raining? Raining in Albuquerque?* She slipped out of bed and crossed the room to look out the window by her table. She could see that this side of the bus had been wet, but most of the water had dried off leaving spots here and there on the glass. She turned back to the other window, which was now receiving a hard spray of water, and came to the conclusion that someone was washing the bus.

Stepping out of the stateroom, she called out, "Jaime?"

The curtain to Jaime's empty bunk was opened partially, so Kip assumed she was the one outside spraying down the bus. She slipped into the bathroom, and when she was finished and slid open the pocket door, she heard the door at the front of the bus open and Jaime came bounding up the stairs.

"*Hola, mi amiga. ¿Como esta?*" Jaime asked.

"*Estoy* a lot less awake than you seem to be." Kip grinned, then yawned. "What are you doing?"

"I just finished up the wash jobs on both buses." She strolled through the lounge area and came to the mouth of the passageway where Kip stood. Her hair was damp, but her face was warm and relaxed.

"You should have waited for me, and I would've helped."

Jaime shook her head and rolled her eyes. "It's part of my job, Kip. You're the opening act. You don't do that kind of dirty work."

"I wouldn't have minded. Too bad we're traveling today. It's going to get dirty all over again."

"It's supposed to start out clean and be good advertisement for Lacey Leigh."

"Oh. Guess I can't argue with that. So, did you already have breakfast?"

"I had a doughnut and coffee hours ago. I am now ready for a real breakfast. Can I go with you?"

"Absolutely, but I'm jumping in the shower first."

"Me second. I got wet and pretty much filthy."

Kip took a quick shower, washed her hair, and in less than half an hour, she was ready. While Jaime cleaned up in the tiny bathroom, Kip took her hairbrush and moved out into the common area, sat at the dinette booth, and looked out the window. For some reason she was feeling a little blue today. As she worked the brush through her hair, she thought about that. *Maybe I just didn't get enough sleep*. She got her damp hair into reasonable order, then pulled it back into a ponytail and rubber-banded it securely. She had just enough length now that she could get it up off her neck, but it felt odd, especially because it had been years since she had put her curly hair in a ponytail.

She sat quietly for a bit longer, listening to the shower run. After a while, she heard Jaime thumping around in the small bathroom, and when she finally burst out into the lounge area, Kip felt like an electrical switch had been flipped. She took a deep breath and soaked in an energy that was not there a moment earlier.

"You ready, Kip?"

The folksinger slid out of the booth as Jaime reached it, and Jaime nearly knocked her over. "Hey, you pushy thing!"

Jaime stopped in the narrow aisle and put her hands on either side of the folksinger's hips from behind and burst out laughing. "Sorry, sorry. Who would think that such a sleepyhead would suddenly move so fast?" She slipped past the folksinger.

Kip took a deep breath, her heart beating fast. She didn't feel one bit sleepy all of a sudden. She followed in Jaime's footsteps as they headed up the aisle toward the front of the bus. Jaime's black hair was still wet, and her eyes were bright and clear, full of merriment. She wore a sleeveless white tank top, pearl gray shorts, and Teva sandals. Kip hesitated.

"Yes?" Jaime waited. "You have something to say?" She raised her eyebrows and put one hand on her hip. "You've decided you're not hungry any more?"

"No, it's nothing. Whatever it was just flew out of my head." She swallowed and watched Jaime open the door, suddenly realizing that she was more than hungry...she was starved, and not just for food. She was hungry for love and connection and affection.

Hungrier—she realized—than she had been for a long while. As they walked across the parking lot, something directly behind her breastbone dropped down into the pit of her stomach. *Oh my, I'm not so sure this is good. I could fall right into love, headfirst over a cliff. Oh my.* The thought came to her with a tune attached, and she faltered a bit when she stepped on an oddly-shaped rock. She caught herself, but at the same time, Jaime reached out and grabbed her at the elbow.

"You okay, Kip?" she asked, with concern in her voice.

"Oh, sure. Fine. Thanks."

"You don't seem yourself."

"I'm just hungry." *That's an understatement.* She carried on a little conversation with herself in her head, and there she was glib and clear, but every time she opened her mouth to speak to Jaime, she felt like someone had thrown a blanket over her head and tossed her in a trunk. They reached the hotel café, and Kip pulled the door open.

Jaime reached past and held the door wide. "Too bad last night's cantina isn't open for breakfast."

"No kidding. That was great food." She'd had a wonderful time with Jaime the night before at Rosario's Cantina. She wasn't sure why she didn't figure things out then, but obviously, overnight, her brain had kicked into the realization that she was in trouble here. She went into the restaurant and saw the sign inviting them to seat themselves, so she selected a large, circular booth away from the windows and out of the bright, early morning sunlight. They both got settled into the booth, a good four feet apart, and the waitress came over to serve coffee. Kip took a sip, and again, the little tune ran through her head, along with words now:

Falling in love with you,
Falling in love, it's true,
There's no when, it's really if
I'm going head first over a cliff

For a brief moment she considered asking the waitress for a piece of paper, but then she decided that if the song fragment and tune were meant to be, they'd stay in her brain long enough for her to get them down on paper—later. She gripped the coffee mug tightly and closed her eyes to visualize a sheet of lined paper with her own hand entering the musical notes needed.

When she opened her eyes, Jaime was staring, her head tilted to the side and a look of concern on her face. The black-haired woman leaned far forward, reached across the wide expanse of the table with both hands, and grasped Kip's wrists. "I mean it, are you all right?"

Kip smiled. "Yes. To be honest, the song goddess is trying to get me to hear a song. That's all."

Jaime let out a sigh, released her hands, and sat back. "That's good. I was starting to worry you were about to have a seizure or faint or something."

The touch of warm hands further solidified Kip's emotions. She had no idea what Jaime was feeling—perhaps merely friendship—but she was very clear that she, herself, was on dangerous terrain, and she wasn't sure how to go about finding out where Jaime stood. *Perhaps the electrician was put in charge of looking after me while Wes and Lacey Leigh are gone. Perhaps she's just killing time. Perhaps she—oh, hell! I don't know what to think!* Kip didn't feel she could—or should—ask anything along those lines, and she felt a little panicky about sitting here in the restaurant facing those piercing black eyes.

The waitress appeared and delivered menus, and as she stepped away, Kip was happy to see Drew and Eric come strolling in. She put an arm in the air, and both men saw her wave and headed their way. She scooted to the left of the booth as Jaime scooted right. They ended up sitting next to one another, but not too close, and the relief that flooded through the folksinger was like a shot of warm brandy. Drew sat to her right, Eric sat to Jaime's left, and they all had plenty of room.

"How are you guys doing?" Kip asked brightly.

"Oh, man," Drew said. "I'm so dang hungry, I could eat a rattlesnake." He accepted a menu from Jaime. "You already know what you're getting?"

"Yeah," Jaime said. She put her elbows on the table. "Need any help rousting the rest of the boys?"

Kip looked sidelong and saw Jaime had a mischievous look on her face.

Eric narrowed his eyes. "Who'd you have in mind, Miss Nosy-Butt?"

"Just thought maybe Buck—and *Candy*—might need a little wake-up call."

Drew closed the menu and slid it across the table to Eric. "They've always had a thing for each other, Jaime, since they first met. Haven't you ever noticed?"

She frowned. "No, I had not. How do you know?"

He gave a shrug, and his black t-shirt bunched up across the chest, then flattened out again. "Just knew, that's all." Leaning his elbows on the table, he signaled to the waitress and pointed to his coffee cup, then turned back to Jaime with a challenge on his face. "How do you know they haven't found the real thing?"

Jaime shrugged as Kip looked back and forth between her and Drew. She finally asked, "How come you continue to believe there's such a thing as the *real* thing anyway?"

"Just do. Seen it before in others, and I hope to see it myself personally."

"You always say that," Jaime said, "but how long have I known you—three years? You've never found it so far, right?"

Drew sat back and crossed his arms. He gave her a smug look. "I'm a patient man. If you know what you're looking for, little lady, sooner or later it will pop up." He glanced to his left. "Right, Kip?"

She sputtered as she looked up. "Wuh—well—I don't know that I'm a very good person to ask, you know. I mean, for sure, it's not like I found the real thing forever or anything like that. Not yet anyway."

"Ah," he said, his eyes twinkling, "but you're still looking, ain'tcha?"

She looked into his blue eyes and saw only kindness. "Yes," she said firmly. "Yes, I am."

"Oh, come on," Jaime protested. "There's no such thing as the real thing. Unless you're talking Coca-Cola. Nobody ever stays together forever, and nobody ever maintains a love that lasts. Everything dies off. Everything changes. Nothing stays the same."

"Geez, Jaime," Eric said with a laugh. "Who are you—the nihilistic Buddha?" He smacked the menu shut, and when he met Kip's gaze, he rolled his eyes. They grinned at each other like old friends.

"Jaime," the lead guitarist said, "I gotta go on record that I disagree with you completely. My parents have been together nigh on forty years, and the love between them is still there."

Something clicked for Kip then. She turned to Drew and said, "Your parents love you very much, don't they?" He nodded, though his face took on a slight pinkish color. "You know what, Drew? I can tell. You must have grown up feeling loved and cared for. It shows in the way you treat people."

Now the guitarist's face was scarlet, but he choked out a thank you. Jaime spoke quickly. "Maybe there are exceptions to the rule, but I don't see any of us on this tour with the real thing."

"Ah, ah, ah," Drew said, one finger in the air, "you can't say that about Buck and Candy. It might be the real thing, and only time will tell."

Kip nodded. *Only time will tell. That sure is true. Everything in life is that way.*

The waitress appeared and took their orders, and for the rest of their time at the table, they talked, shared food and joked about less serious matters. When it was time to leave, Drew insisted on picking up the check.

Eric slid out of the booth and stood over the table looking at the three of them. "It's almost ten-thirty. Everyone ready by eleven?"

"We're all ready now," Jaime said. "Right?"

Both Kip and Drew nodded as the guitarist slipped out of the booth, followed by the two women.

"Okay," Eric said. "I'll make sure that everybody else is ready. Meet you out at the buses in a bit."

He headed off, and Drew put a hand on Kip's forearm. "Could I have a word with you privately, Kip?"

Jaime looked at him oddly, then said, "I'll head out to the bus." She strode off, and Kip gazed briefly at the long legs, then turned her attention to Drew. He gestured toward the booth and returned to his seat. She sat across from him, curious.

"I tend to be a rather direct dude, Kip. I like you a lot, and I wonder if there's any chance of a fella like me asking you out."

She didn't say anything for a few seconds as the words sank in. She looked into his kind blue eyes and spoke the truth from her heart. "No, Drew. I could never be anything more than a very, very good friend. I'm gay."

He leaned back and took a deep breath, then nodded slowly. "I see. I'm surely glad I asked you this right up front. I feel a kinship to you, girl, but guess it's not from that real thing, huh?" He smiled, and the crow's feet in the corners of his eyes crinkled.

"I'm sorry."

"No need to apologize. But a guy can always hope, right?"

He grinned and she found herself smiling back. "How old are you?" she asked.

"Thirty-three."

"Ah, well, then I am way too old for you anyway." She gave him a sly grin. "I was out of high school before you were even a freshman."

He rose. "Age don't matter. Heart matters. That was a kind thing you said to me earlier about my parents and me. Helps me know you're a real fine woman, Kip. You deserve the real thing."

"And so do you, my friend."

THE BUS RUMBLED along down Interstate 40 with Jaime at the wheel. Traffic was light. With less than three hundred miles to travel, and with any luck, they'd arrive by half past four. Jaime had managed to keep the speed over sixty miles per hour for most of the last two hours, and wished she could go faster. The speed limit was 75, but the bus was like a big tank and maneuvered poorly. She didn't want to lose control, and since the semi's and other bus were behind her, she didn't make any fast moves.

Checking her watch, she saw it was after one. Pushing her sunglasses up on her nose, she adjusted them, then looked into the rearview mirror and wondered why the manufacturer bothered to put it in the bus. It wasn't like she could use it for driving, since no driver could ever see the tail end of the bus at all unless she looked outside at those side view mirrors. It was, however, handy for checking out the action behind her.

Right now, there was a break in the music. Until just a minute earlier, Kip, Drew, Marcus, and Davis had been jamming non-stop since they'd pulled out of the parking lot. Buck was noticeably absent. He was so big that he usually took up a lot of the booth, but today he decided to ride in the other bus with Wes, Candy, and Shelley.

Instrument cases and sheets of music littered the floor, with various people's arms and legs sprawled out all over the lounge area. Eric sat in the recliner, regularly making comments and giving good-natured critiques of the various songs they sang. Jaime longed to turn the wheel over and get out her own instruments. She was itching to get her hands on her violin. That hadn't happened to her for a while, the absolute need to get out the fiddle and play, so as she gripped the heavy-duty wheel, she was wishing she were anywhere but driving.

In the mirror, she watched as Kip, holding her guitar tight, took a long pull from a bottle of ginger ale, then set it in a cup holder and turned to Drew. A grin came to the folksinger's face, and Jaime saw her reach over and grab the guitarist's arm. She heard her say, "Don't you *ever* screw up, Drew?"

He said, "With music? Or life in general?"

"I was referring to music," Kip said with a smile as she let go of him, "but you can illuminate us all on the other topic, too, if you like."

"I do make mistakes, but I've been playing guitar so long that I can feel the music shoot right through me, and so long as I'm feeling it, shucks, it just comes out right."

Jaime knew exactly what he meant. Sometimes when she played the fiddle, she closed her eyes and just let herself feel her

way through a song. Even if something was off, somehow it all
came together—as long as she didn't fight it. The group behind
her launched into a new song, something she hadn't heard before
that Kip said was on Mary Chapin Carpenter's new CD. Jaime
could immediately hear a part for the fiddle, and her yearning to
join the jam intensified. Instead, she was stuck looking ahead
through the four-foot tall, extra-wide windshield. Everything she
saw was in washed out shades of tan and brown, white and gray.
She'd covered 126 miles of desert and seen only a few birds and
one roadrunner. Even the prairie dogs were in hiding. *No wonder
people occasionally fall asleep and run off the road out here. The
view is monotonous.*

She hung on for twenty more miles, and when they reached
the halfway point in distance, she caught Eric's eye in the rearview mirror and offered him a hopeful look. He gave a curt nod
and rose. "Ready to switch, are you?"

"Please," she said.

"Let me get a drink." He threaded his way back, stepping over
and around people, and went to the fridge to pick out a Coke, then
reversed his steps. When he was standing next to her, she leaned
forward over the wheel and stood, her foot still on the accelerator
and her hands gripping the steering wheel. He slipped under her,
and she slid out to the side. The bus lost speed when she removed
her foot from the accelerator, but he quickly got his foot on the
pedal and took over.

She let out a huff of air and grabbed the metal bar over her
head. Standing still, she took in the wreckage of the room. Kip
looked up at her, and Jaime couldn't help but think that the
folksinger was having the time of her life. Her eyes shone, her face
was full of color, and she looked—happy. Jaime was surprised to
identify the emotion she herself was feeling as jealousy: she was
jealous of the way the folksinger and Drew were getting along,
envious of Kip's rapport with all the guys in the band, and resent-
ful that Kip, Drew and Eric all seemed to believe that love and
contentment for each of them was just around the corner.

She picked her way through the group, and as they began to
sing another song, she ducked into the compact bathroom and
stood looking in the mirror. *What do you want, Ms. Esperanza?*
She realized she didn't know. Everybody out there seemed to
know what they wanted. Did they really? She couldn't say. She
washed her hands and dried them off, then slid wide the pocket
door and slipped around the wall to open the hallway side cabinet
which housed her instruments. She moved the Welling to the side
and reached for her Schweitzer. The case was new and clean and

such a contrast to the ancient violin, which she lifted out carefully. She needed a case that would protect the instrument, and the hundred-plus dollars she'd paid was well worth it. Moving the case aside, she took the old violin out to the lounge area where the crew was currently playing an old Jim Croce song, "You Don't Mess Around With Jim." Drew and Kip sat together on the long bench, and the lead guitarist was having a lot of fun with the solo part. Davis sat in the back corner love seat playing a bass, which was plugged into a small practice amp, and Marcus sat at the table with a miniature keyboard in front of him. As Jaime leaned against the wall, Drew and Kip finished singing the peppy song, and the whole crew ended it hooting and shouting at one another because nobody finished on the same chord, much less the same beat.

Once they stopped laughing, Kip said, "All right, Jaime's ready. Now we have some professionalism to rely on."

"Oh, get real," Davis said, his voice teasing. "I suppose *you* get to set the standard we're supposed to go by?"

"Yes," the folksinger said as she extended her neck and stuck her nose in the air. "Who could ask for anything more?" Davis wadded up a piece of paper and threw it her way. Kip picked it up where it fell. "Listen, Mr. Bass Man, just keep doing what you do best—thump, thump, thump."

Davis said, "Oh, no. Not me. I do believe you have me confused with Buck."

Jaime glanced at Kip as the folksinger's brows crinkled up, and then her face took on a look of surprise. She tossed the paper wad, rocket-fast, toward the bass player. "Oooh, Davis, you are so evil!"

Drew grinned, then stamped his foot. "I'm thinking they might be damn serious. Seems like they're hitched but not churched."

"Only a matter of time," Davis said.

Kip looked around the room. "Good gawd, you're like a bunch of old biddies the way you gossip."

From the front of the bus, Eric called back, "What else have we got to do?"

Marcus played an arpeggio on the keyboard, then in a deep voice said, "Ladies and gentleman, today on 'As the Lacey Leigh Jaxon Tour Turns' we have the story of true love. Will Bernard and Candace find their own true love?" He hit a sour note. "Or will unseen forces drive them apart? Stay tuned for the gripping story of passion and intrigue." He hit a button on top of the keyboard, and the final notes sounded like a cheesy organ.

Kip said, "You guys are so bad. Remind me *never* to tell you when I fall in love."

Drew strummed an open chord. "You won't have to tell us. We'll be able to tell, Kip."

Jaime thought the look on the other woman's face was one of surprise. The folksinger turned pink and said, "Not if I have any choice in the matter." She picked a pattern along with the chord Drew was playing. "Bernard, huh? Buck's given name is Bernard?"

"That's right," Eric called out.

Kip gave a little nod and frowned. She looked down at her fingers plucking the guitar, and when she looked up, she opened her mouth, and started in on Bonnie Tyler's old song, "It's A Heartache."

Jaime felt her face turn hot, and she was relieved no one was paying the slightest attention. She knew now that these men, whom she had always assumed were lost in their own private musical worlds, paid a lot closer attention to things than she had ever realized. She wouldn't be surprised to learn that they had talked just like this back when she and Lacey Leigh had been an item. The thought that they all probably knew exactly what was going on embarrassed her completely and made her stomach hurt.

She continued to lean against the back wall, one ankle crossed over the other, as she raised her fiddle and touched her bow to the strings. As she played a smooth background hum, she thought, *Uh huh, that's more like it. Nothing but a heartache. That's what the real thing is—a big old, unavoidable heartache. They can have it. The whole bunch of them can just have it.*

JAIME'S BAD MOOD extended into the late afternoon. They arrived in Amarillo and got the buses and semi's situated at the Lost Spur Motel & Boot Emporium. From the window, it looked well kept, though any claim to class was somewhat diminished by the slowly revolving white and silver cowboy boot up on a pole above the front entrance. She watched it glinting in the sunlight as it slowly went 'round and 'round.

Once the guys vacated the bus, Kip disappeared into her stateroom with Isabelle while Jaime tidied up the lounge area. She had just finished tossing two soda cans and some crumpled up papers into the garbage when Kip's door opened, and the gray-eyed woman came out into the narrow hall wearing the same cargo shorts, but she had changed into tennis shoes and a pale green tank top. She held a thin wallet in one hand and her bus keys in the other.

Kip paused and leaned against the corner piece in the hall-way. "Did you have any plans for dinner, Jaime?" The black-haired woman shook her head. "I'm going to go over and check out the Boot Emporium and then take a walk in the delightful heat until I find a place to eat. Want to come with me?"

Jaime bent and grabbed the plastic bag in the garbage can and pulled it out, then twisted it closed with the built-in red plastic strip at the top. "May as well. I need to toss the trash anyway."

Kip giggled, and Jaime gave her a serious look. "Geez, Jaime, you make it sound like such a treat, equating dumping the garbage with a walk with me."

Jaime felt herself blush. "I didn't mean it that way."

The folksinger moved toward her, and as she slipped past, she said, "I know. I'm giving you a bad time. I'll go over to the Empo-rium and check out the wares. When you're ready, come on over. If you change your mind, let me know."

Jaime made a sound, which Kip took to mean assent, so she stepped around the instrument cases lying in the lounge area and exited from the cool bus into the arid dryness of Texas. The hotel ahead of her was a split-level stone structure, with some sort of flagstone walkway. Kip wasn't sure what kind of paving stone it was, but she watched her step closely as the surface beneath her feet was rough and a little uneven. She reached the door and entered to find a vast lobby, half of which was obviously the boot emporium. On the left was the check-in counter, and to the right was the store as well as stairs leading up to the second-story hotel rooms. She saw a hallway to the left of the stairwell that she assumed led to other rooms. Past the hotel counter, on the left, was an open area that angled around to the left, but she couldn't see all of it. Solid-looking wooden tables and chairs were scattered around the section that she could see ahead of her. To her right, the boot merchant's counter ran perpendicular to the stairwell. No one was behind the cash register.

She turned to her left when the man behind the registration counter greeted her and asked if she needed help. "I'm going to look at the boots." He nodded and returned to the paperwork before him. She headed off to the right side to examine the leather goods.

Four tall, double-sided racks, which could be rolled aside and secured from theft, were stuffed full of leather footwear. For now, they were open and accessible. In addition to finely tooled leather boots in a variety of styles, she also found leather wallets, purses, and beaded bags on a display table. She picked up a pale tan purse, about five inches wide by four inches with a thin leather strap. The beadwork on the front of it wasn't like what she so often saw in the tourist shops. These beads were tiny, and she could see through the multi-colored pellets. The pattern, so tightly planned, showed a swash of various-colored blues across the top, a round orange sun in the middle of it, and what looked like a field of tan and white and brown wheat below. Moving the purse in her hands, the wheat almost seemed to shift, as though wind were blowing across it, and the beaded sky looked alive.

"That was one of the very last my son made before he died."

Kip turned to find a tiny, black-haired woman with dark, sad eyes. She was Native American, though Kip had no idea to which tribe she belonged. The woman was petite—barely five-feet tall— and dressed in huarache sandals, a tie-dyed t-shirt, and shorts. It was impossible to tell how old she was, but Kip thought some-where between thirty and fifty. "Your son made this?"

"Yes."

"It's beautiful."

"It's one of a kind." She reached out to take the purse from Kip, then opened it and pulled the front away from the back and pointed with one elfin hand. "He was good at this. See the stitch-ing?"

"Um hmm."

"All done by hand."

Kip waited while the lady folded the purse closed and handed it back to her, then she said, "I am impressed with the beadwork. It's beautiful."

"Not traditional Indian style."

"No, it's not. I've never seen anything quite like it." The sad-looking woman met her eyes, then looked away, and Kip could not keep herself from asking, from finding out more about the woman. "How old is—was—your son?"

"He was about fifteen when he made that." She paused and the folksinger waited, feeling the soft leather, knowing if she held her breath long enough, the rest would come. In a quiet voice, the small woman said, "He was sixteen when he died."

"I'm very sorry. Sixteen is far too young." She wanted to ask what had happened to such a young man, but didn't feel it her place to pry. She looked over the woman's head and across the quiet lobby.

"I suppose you think it odd that the proprietor of a place would come up and tell you that."

When Kip met the hollow-looking eyes again, she saw them brimming with tears. "The wound must be recent—and deep."

"Yes, just last year at this time. He was hit by a car crossing the busy street down the way. Be careful of that highway. It's dangerous and has claimed the lives of many." The wind went right out of Kip, and her own tears welled up into her eyes. The tiny woman frowned. "Miss? Miss, are you all right?"

Kip set the purse down on the display table and reached out with her free hand to steady herself on the boot rack she stood next to. "Yes, yes, I'm fine." A tear trickled down her face and she felt embarrassed. "I'm sorry. What you said just—it just struck— oh, that's a terrible choice of words!" She took a deep breath. "When I was sixteen, my eleven-year-old brother cut out into traffic and was hit by a car. He died—like your son."

"Oh, my! Oh, my, this is dreadful. Come with me." Kip felt the warm hand on her forearm, and she let herself be pulled over toward the stairwell, around the back of the sales counter, and through a door that led to a small room under the stairs. The ceiling slanted low on the left and higher to the right, and the space was deeper than it looked from the outside. To the left were short storage racks and shelves filled with boxes and boots. To the right was a miniature kitchenette with a sink, a microwave, and a counter no more than two feet wide. A two-person table sat in the middle of the cubbyhole, and it was there that Kip was led. She sank onto one of the wooden chairs while the tiny woman went to a mug rack next to the sink and took two cups, filled them with water, put them in the microwave, and flipped it on. Turning and leaning back against the counter, she said, "My name is Minnie Logan. I have lived here in Amarillo most of my adult life, though I was born and raised in Ohio." She reached out her tiny hand and Kip shook it.

"I'm Kip Galvin, and I've never been to Amarillo before. I was born and raised in Minnesota, and that's where I live now. I'm here with the Lacey Leigh Jaxon tour." She set her wallet on the small table and laced her fingers together in her lap.

A frown creased the tanned face. "You are musical?"

Kip nodded. "I play guitar and sing."

The timer dinged, and Minnie turned to take the mugs out of the microwave. Over her shoulder she asked, "You like mint or apple better?"

Kip chose mint, and in short order, she had a hot cup of tea in front of her, the tea bag steeping in steaming water. "Thank you. It's very kind of you."

Minnie sat across from her, gently dunking her own teabag into the hot water. "It's pure selfishness on my part. It gets lonely here. People come, people go. It is not I, but you, who seemed kind."

"I'm not sure what came over me, Minnie. What you said about your son, well, it took me right back in time to being six-teen-years-old and seeing my brother get hit by the car."

The dark-eyed woman nodded. "Though I didn't feel this way at the time, I am now glad I was not there when Eli died. I want to remember him whole. Besides, I could not have comforted him. He died instantly."

"My brother was not so lucky." Her eyes filled with tears. "Even after more than two decades, I still miss him."

"Yes, that is the way it is. I still miss my mother, and she died when I was nineteen. I am almost fifty now, and I think of her just as much as I ever did."

The two women sat quietly, sipping tea, and Kip thought about her little brother. In truth, she did not think of him often, though when she did, she felt something expand painfully in her chest. Even after all these years, she still felt sad. "Do you have other children, Minnie?"

The tiny woman shook her head. "Do you?"

"No, not yet. I'm not sure if I ever will. I'm 37 now, so the clock is ticking."

"It's never too late to mother a child. Just remember that. I have taken in foster children from the Mingo tribe upon occasion. My father and brothers still live in Ohio, and every so often they send a boy here for me to teach how to work leather—and how to behave. It was much easier when Eli was alive to be a foster brother to them. Since his death, they haven't sent any youths to me, I think, out of respect. But you have reminded me that per-haps it is time."

Just then, a clear bell sounded and Minnie popped up out of her chair to peek out into the shop. Kip heard a familiar voice. "I am looking for my friend?"

"Yes," Minnie said. "She is right here."

She turned to face Kip as the folksinger took one last gulp of her tea. She set it down hastily and picked up her wallet. "I would like to buy that purse, Minnie."

"Yes, I thought you would."

Kip followed her from the tiny room and out past the sales counter. "Hiya, Jaime," she said as she cut around one long boot rack on the way to the purse display. Jaime looked at her with a quizzical frown on her face, then tagged along behind. Kip said, "Minnie, I believe I will come back tomorrow and buy some boots, too. I didn't get a chance today to look at them, but tomor-row I'll have more time to try them on."

The native woman stopped at the display, picked up the purse they had been discussing earlier, and held it out to her. "Please accept this from me—in memory of my son and your brother."

Kip's eyes filled with tears again. "Oh, I couldn't...it's too much."

"No, Kip. I want you to take it and keep it to remember how precious love is. Please."

Minnie handed it to her, and the folksinger took it. "Thank you. That is very kind of you. I will treasure it."

"Yes. I know you will." She gave a full smile for the first time, and her face lit up.

Impulsively, Kip reached out and gave her an awkward hug. "Thank you, Minnie. I'll see you tomorrow."

"I open at ten." She gave a brief wave and nodded at Jaime, then turned and moved toward the cash register.

Clutching the beaded purse, Kip headed for the front door in a hurry. She sensed Jaime at her heels, and felt a touch on her shoulder as she reached the door.

"Kip? Are you okay?"

It was the second time she'd been asked that question in less than twenty minutes. She didn't answer, but burst from the cool, air-conditioned hotel out into the heat. The moisture in her eyes dried up almost instantly, which was lucky because the flagstones beneath her feet made her feel unsteady, and clearer eyesight was welcome. "I'm okay." She marched forward, across the hot cement, her wallet in one hand and the beaded purse in the other.

When she reached the bus, she tucked her wallet under one arm and fumbled in her shorts pocket for her keys, but before she could get them out, Jaime came around, stuck a key in the door and unlocked it. Kip stepped up onto the first stair of the bus, stretched her arm up to the left, and set the beaded purse on the leather chair. She turned to find Jaime staring up at her with a frown on her face.

"What happened in there?"

Kip hesitated, then descended. "Let's go get something to eat, and I'll tell you on the way." She pushed the door shut and locked it, handed the key to Jaime, and the two women fell into step next to one another.

As they strolled out to the sidewalk and along the busy street, the folksinger recounted some of what had happened. Before they traveled very far, though, they came to a steak house. Kip interrupted her story and stopped to examine the neat looking hacienda-style place, then looked at Jaime. "Want to go here?"

"Sure. At least it's close. Let's check the menu."

They approached the door and spent a minute looking through dusty glass at the restaurant's specialties. The entrees were moderately priced, and they had a wide variety of steaks, chicken, and lamb. "Works for me. What about you?"

Jaime raised her eyebrows and shrugged. "I'm willing to give it a try."

They entered a dark vestibule and Kip shivered. "Geez! It's cold in here. I hope it isn't this arctic in the dining area."

"I wouldn't worry about it. We're two women, and we sure aren't dressed too nicely. Of course they'll seat us by the kitchen door, and for once I won't protest. It's always twenty degrees warmer there." She grinned and reached over to touch Kip's arm in a way that the folksinger found comforting.

A man came to seat them. It was still early, so the steak house wasn't busy, but Kip had to smile when the young man led them straight back to the rear of the restaurant. The further back they went, the less frigid the air was, and the booth he led them to was perfect for two. They scooted into the tight, little booth, and he left them with menus, a wine list, and the promise of a waiter.

They opened their menus, but they didn't pay any attention to them, waiting instead for the bus boy to pour ice water. When he left, Jaime said, "So you went in there and she told you about her son who had died, and then what happened? How'd you make instant friends and end up drinking tea in her storeroom?"

Putting it that way made Kip laugh. "I suppose it does sound a little odd, but it was the most natural thing I've done lately. I felt like I knew her, Jaime. Like we knew each other in another life or something. She was easy to talk with, and it was so terribly sad that her son was hit by a car at such a young age. It made me remember my brother, Spencer."

"Why?"

The waiter appeared. "Something to drink, ladies? Wine or spirits?"

"You like wine?" Kip asked. Jaime nodded. "Do you prefer red or white?"

"Doesn't matter to me. Pick what you like."

She picked up the wine list and looked at it as she asked, "Have you got a good Merlot?"

"Sure. We have a nice house bottle."

"I'd like a *good* bottle. How about this one?" She pointed to something on the wine list, and the waiter craned his head.

"Oh, yes, all the California wines are excellent, and that Clos du Bois is excellent."

"Perfect. We'll have that." She set the wine list aside and

returned to her menu as he departed. When she looked over, she found Jaime sporting an amused expression. "What?"

"I suppose you're a wine expert, huh?"

"Not really. My dad is, though. He and my mom are university professors and have traveled a lot. He taught me a few things." When Jaime continued to grin at her, Kip said, "What? I know a couple kinds I tend to like."

"And you usually order a bottle?"

"Well, we'll get four or five glasses out of the bottle, and buying it by the glass we would have paid about the same amount for half as much wine. Even if we don't drink it all, it's still a better deal."

"I see." Jaime still looked amused. "Planning to get drunk then?"

"On two or three glasses of wine? With dinner? I don't think so."

The waiter hustled up and fussed around the table getting the wine situated and poured. Once that was done, he asked, "Would you like to order appetizers?"

Kip met Jaime's eyes. "It's up to you. Want to be slow and leisurely or more workman-like and get out of here quickly?"

"You kiddin'? I always want to take my time when I eat."

"Okay then, how about we try some stuffed mushrooms?"

"Sure. Never had 'em before, but I'll try 'em."

"Do you eat mushrooms? Do you usually like them cooked?" When Jaime nodded, Kip looked up at the waiter. "We'll have an order of the stuffed mushrooms."

"Yes, ma'am. And I'll be back shortly with a loaf of bread." He whisked off.

Jaime put an elbow up on the table and leaned her chin in her hand. "Considering that we're planted in the worst seat in the house, we seem to be getting good service."

"That's always nice." Kip looked down at her menu and her eye first found the barbecued chicken. She looked at all the other entrees, but she kept coming back to that one. Closing her menu, she said, "What are you thinking of having?"

"Steak sounds good."

"If I order this giant whole barbecued chicken, will you eat some of it?"

"Sure. You can have some of my steak, too."

"Deal." The waiter came with the stuffed mushrooms and bread, and took their order. When he left, Kip slid an appetizer plate in front of her as Jaime did the same, and each helped herself to a stuffed mushroom. Kip took a big bite. "Mmm. This is pretty tasty."

"Yeah, not bad. I don't know why I've never ordered them before."

"The bread looks great." Kip pulled a serrated knife out of the loaf, which sat on an inch-thick cutting board, and cut a slice. "Want a piece?"

"Sure." The folksinger cut another, and Jaime picked it up and took a bite. "Mmm...still warm."

Kip finished buttering her piece and took a bite. "As far as I'm concerned, bread is just a holder for butter, but you're right. This is really tasty." She set it down on her plate and swallowed the bite in her mouth, then put her forearms on the table, one on top of the other. "When I was sixteen years old, I headed off to school right on time every morning. I liked to get there with plenty of time to get my books in my locker and maybe chat with my friends. I went to a high school that was kitty-corner from the grade school. My younger brother was in fifth grade and was always running late. He usually walked with me. But he dragged along that day, so I left on time, telling him he'd better get his act together and run to catch up with me. Instead, I guess he took his time, then got on his bike and rode like a bat out of hell." She picked up her water glass and took a sip. She knew Jaime was watching her closely, and she was afraid she might burst into tears, but she went on. "After all these years, I'm not sure why I continue to feel emotional about this, but I do. He came tearing up the street and jumped the curb. I can still see it in my head, his front tire up in the air, spinning, and he had this big smile of glee on his face and then—wham!—a car hit him."

A look of horror crossed Jaime's face. "That's awful. He didn't...didn't die—"

Kip nodded. "Yes, he did. Not right away, but the internal injuries were too much, and even though they did surgery and everything that they could, he died two days later."

Jaime dropped her bread on her plate. "Kip, I'm so sorry. That's...that's just horrible."

"It really was. I was so traumatized. Thought it was my fault for not watching him closer, for leaving before him, for not being there when he decided to take the bike. Words can't even begin to express my horror. Keith—he's my other brother—and I were heartbroken. My parents were smart, though. They sent me right off to counseling, and that helped me a lot." She sat for a moment, looking down at the table, then looked up and met Jaime's eyes. "I wrote my first song for Spencer—both the words and the tune. I hadn't been able to put both together before that, but while I was trying to deal with his death, it all came together. I always thought it was strange that my music moved to the forefront then. Maybe it was a gift from God—or hey, who knows? Maybe my song god is now Spencer. Who can tell?"

"That's a nice way of looking at it," Jaime said softly. "Your other brother's name is Keith?"

"Yes."

"He's younger than you?" Kip nodded. "Tell me one more thing. Why are you called Kip? That's not your given name, is it?"

Kip smiled. "Funny you should ask. I guess you could say my name was a gift from Spencer. When he was about two, he had a speech impediment and couldn't say my name, which is Elizabeth. What came out of his little mouth was 'Kip,' and I answered to it." She shrugged. "It stuck." She looked off into the distance, remembering his soft, brown hair and the gray eyes so very like her own. "I'll always miss him. He was a rascal."

"I can see why talking to this Minnie brought all that up again. That's happened to me before about my mother." The words spilled out of her mouth, unplanned, and if her stomach had been roiling to hear Kip's story about her brother's death, it was really churning now after making that comment.

Kip frowned. "What happened to your mom? You said before that she died from alcohol abuse."

"That's true—kind of." Jaime crossed her arms in front of her and sat back.

"I think it's time to break out more of the fortifications," Kip said as she reached for the bottle of wine. "Ready for some more?" Jaime nodded, so Kip filled their glasses, and both of them drank deeply.

Jaime set her glass down, feeling the wine warm in her stomach. She leaned back against the booth's soft cushion. "I don't often drink, and I try not to get too tipsy. My mother drank far too much. Worked in a bar all her life until she had cirrhosis of the liver."

"She died from that?"

"No, actually, she was very ill and at home, and I was doing my best to take care of her. If she could have just laid off the alcohol, she probably would have lived a lot longer."

"She went out drinking anyway?"

Jaime shook her head. "She was so ill for nearly a year, and in so much pain that she couldn't drive or walk far. But all her old buddies from the bar came by with plenty of booze for her. She could always get it somehow, and I wasn't able to be there every minute of every day to prevent it." She rearranged the bread on her plate, then tore a piece in half and set both pieces down. She pushed the bread plate to the side and leaned her forearms against the table edge. "Somebody—I never found out who—brought her a bottle of whiskey, and she hid it from me. She got up in the middle of the night and drank damn near the whole bottle. I went out into the living room the next morning and found her lying on the floor. She'd gotten so drunk that she fell, hit her head on the edge of the fireplace, and bled to death."

"That must have been terrible, Jaime."

"It was. And the worst of it is that I remember I woke up in the middle of the night. I heard a noise...but I fell back to sleep. I've always wondered if I had found her in time if maybe...maybe she could have lived longer." She felt tears in her eyes, but blinked them back.

Kip reached across the narrow table and grabbed her hand. "It probably saved her from a lot of pain. Cirrhosis is a terrible way to die. Our neighbor had it, and his wife nearly went out of her mind because he cried off and on all day. They can only give you so much morphine without killing a person. It's an awful disease." She let go of Jaime's hand, picked up her wineglass and looked at it, then gazed over with a sad look on her face. "I'm sorry about your mother, Jaime. She did a good job raising you, though."

"Yeah? I bet you say that to all your friends."

"No," she said indignantly. "I do not."

"That's what you told Drew."

"What? No, no, no, oh You-of-Little-Memory. I think what I said was that he had been loved well by his parents. That's not the same. It sounds like your mom did the best she could with you, but by the grace of God and your grandparents, you turned out to be a good person."

Jaime sat up closer to the table, her elbows near the edge. "For all you know, I could be an ax murderer."

"Ha! Right. You've got way too soft a heart for that."

They bantered back and forth for a couple minutes, and Jaime's distressed stomach gradually calmed down. She took a bite of the bread on her plate and relished the nutty tasting, yeasty loaf. She listened to Kip tell a story about her first screw-ups onstage, and then the waiter brought their meals.

"Oh, wow, this looks wonderful," Kip said.

"No kidding." Suddenly Jaime was terribly hungry, and she cut into her steak and savored the first bite.

KIP DRANK THREE glasses of wine, and Jaime had two, so each of them was feeling warm and relaxed. The dishes were cleared, and Kip had a Styrofoam container filled with leftover chicken. Kip looked around at all the people in the now jam-packed restaurant. As a light-skinned Northerner, she was definitely in the minority. All of the restaurant occupants, including the wait staff, were dark-haired, brown-skinned people, Mexicans and Native Americans—some young, others older, and a number obviously on dates. Across from them at a table sat four businessmen, and Kip periodically caught bits of conversation about livestock. Despite the fact that she was different from every other person she could see in the restaurant, including her dinner companion, she didn't feel anyone had even noticed, much less cared. The soft music and golden-lit ambience of the restaurant was soothing, and when she examined the other patrons, she thought they looked happy.

She turned back to find Jaime studying her. Perhaps it was the wine, perhaps something else, but she let herself meet the dark eyes, and every bit of the hunger she felt rose to the surface. She couldn't deny it to herself any longer: *how easy it is to fall in love with this woman. Oh, no.* She had been avoiding the thought as much as she could, but it was clear now. A heavy feeling settled somewhere in the vicinity of her heart when she thought about the short weeks left on the tour. It wouldn't be good to act on the feelings she had—not good at all. She looked away from Jaime, her face flooding red, feeling relieved it wouldn't be very noticeable in the low lighting.

Jaime said, "You look pensive all of a sudden."

Kip smiled brightly and nodded. "Probably the fine food and the wine." She scanned the restaurant and caught the eye of the waiter. He gave her a nod and headed their way. She looked back at Jaime. "You ready to stagger back to the bus?"

"Is that a requirement? Staggering, I mean?"

The waiter reached their table. "Yes, ma'am?"

All business, Kip said, "We're ready for our check."

"Right away." He turned and left.

"We've had great service," Jaime said.

"Yes, we have, and the tip is going to reflect that." She picked up her wallet from the side of the table and rifled through it. Jaime reached for her back pocket, but Kip shook her head. "No, I'll get this. I dragged you in, and I'll buy."

"No, Kip. That's not necessary. It was a great meal—*excellente*—and I'll pay my share."

"Nope. I've got it."

Jaime reached across the table and gripped Kip's arm, and when their eyes met, the folksinger felt that sinking sensation again. Jaime said, "If you pick up tonight's meal, then you have to promise to let me pick up tomorrow night's."

The warm grip on her forearm, the black eyes, the sincere smile—all of these added up for Kip, and suddenly, she knew she would do nearly anything to spend more time with this woman. "It's a deal." Jaime let go of her arm. "It'll be your turn to dazzle me with your handling of the wait staff."

"Maybe I'll take you to a buffet—what'll you think of that?"

Kip laughed as she watched the waiter threading his way across the restaurant. At this point, she didn't care if they went to a fast food joint. She just wanted to spend more time with Jaime. "How would you feel about playing some music now—or do you have other plans?"

Jaime glanced at her watch. "No other plans—not a one. Let's do that."

JAIME AND KIP had been sitting in the bus playing guitars for about an hour. Enough time had passed that the effects of the alcohol lessened, and her emotions were more under control now. Kip was feeling more clear-headed than she had when they left the restaurant. She reminded herself that no matter where they went tomorrow night, she would not let herself drink thirty-five dollar bottles of wine. *Too hard to keep my feelings in check.*

She hadn't heard Jaime play an acoustic guitar before, and in fact, hadn't known she owned one. "I saw that pretty blue Fender you played at the last concert, but I didn't know you had this Yamaha."

Jaime nodded. "It's old—kind of a good campfire guitar. Still has decent action after all these years, though." She barred a chord and strummed her way up the fret board.

"Nice sound, too."

Jaime nodded. She set the guitar aside, leaning the neck up against the edge of the booth. She rose and went to the refrigerator. "Want something to drink?"

"Yes, I'd love that. Wine always makes me thirsty later. If there's some ginger ale in there, I'd like to have it."

"There is. Looks like I better do a hospitality run tomorrow, though. We're running low on everything here." She popped the cap off Kip's green bottle and then off the brown bottle of root beer she chose for herself. Kip set her guitar on its back on the long bench seat and rose, heading for the loveseat in the corner.

At the same time, Jaime followed her, carrying the two bottles. Kip sat and Jaime handed her the green bottle, then surprised the folksinger by settling in on the stubby couch right next to her. They looked out the window at the last vestiges of orange in the sky.

"You sure do have beautiful sunsets in the Southwest," Kip said. She took a swig of the bubbly ginger ale and turned to look at Jaime.

"I've been here so long that sometimes I don't notice." Jaime looked past Kip and out the window.

She was so close that Kip realized she could lean over and kiss her, if she were so inclined. *Lucky the wine has worn off*, she thought, then smiled.

"What? What's funny?"

"Nothing."

"Oh, come on. Tell me."

"Really—it's nothing." Just then, they heard a knock on the bus door, which made Kip laugh. *Saved by the bell...or a knock, anyway.*

Jaime rose, a frown creasing her forehead. "Hey, it's Drew." She went to the door and opened it, and the guitarist stepped up one stair.

"Hey. Y'all interested in coming over to the hotel and jamming with us?"

Jaime asked, "In your room?"

"You kidding? I think I got the smallest crib in the place."

Kip asked, "In the lobby then?"

"Yes, ma'am. They've got a decent PA there. Nothing great, but it'll work"

"Where?" Kip asked. "I never noticed it."

"If you walk past the counter there's that open space there with the tables. 'Round the corner they've got it set up where a band can plug in. I guess they have weddings and parties there."

Jaime shrugged. "I'll come. Kip?" She gave the folksinger a questioning look.

"Sure."

Drew said, "Great! Now we have someone who can sing. Will you bring your fiddle, Jaime?"

"Okay. We'll be over shortly."

He hesitated for a moment and reached down for something on the leather chair. "Hey, this is sure pretty."

Kip watched him as he turned an item over in his hands, then realized it was the beaded purse. "Oh, I forgot about that. I got it today in the Boot Emporium. It's just perfect, isn't it?"

"Yup." He held it out, and she strode over and took it from him. He looked up at her and smiled. "Put it in a safe place. It's real precious." He stepped down out of the bus. "See ya whenever you get over there."

Jaime closed the door behind him as Kip asked, "You just can't help but love that guy, can you? He's one of the nicest men I've ever met."

"He is." Her eyes settled on the folksinger. "You sure you want to do this?"

"For a while. I don't suppose we can be rowdy for too long, anyhow. It's a hotel, and people will be trying to sleep."

Jaime picked up her guitar and took it off down the hall to put it away in the closet. "Don't count on that. It's not even ten yet."

WORD MUST HAVE spread, somehow, because within half an hour of Kip's arrival, the number of people had doubled, then shortly after, tripled. Her guitar, as well as Drew's and Davis's bass, were plugged in to the PA. Marcus played his portable keyboard using its amplifier. Buck had dragged out his basic drum kit, a cymbal, and the snare. With Jaime's fiddle, Kip's vocals, and Candy singing background vocals, things were set up nicely. Eric showed up in the middle of the first song and started making adjustments to the dinky house soundboard. He also set up another mic for Candy so she and Kip didn't have to share. They were in the middle of Mary Chapin Carpenter's "Down at the Twist 'n' Shout" when he wheeled in a guitar amp, and when they finished that song, he quickly switched Davis to it, which greatly improved the balance.

Drew leaned away from the microphone toward Jaime. "Good job on the fiddle, kid."

She laughed. "You can't call me kid! I'm way older than you."

He grinned and looked around. Five new arrivals had waltzed in to join the crew of people sitting at the tables or lounging on the floor against the walls. "There's more people here than you can shake a stick at."

Kip laughed. "Where do you come up with these lines?"

"Dunno. Must just be a natural born poet. What next?"

"I don't know. You pick."

"You're the one who has to belt 'em out. So you pick."

Just then someone from the audience hollered. "Do you know any Johnny Cash?"

Kip spoke into the microphone. "We revere Mr. Cash." She turned and looked at Drew. "Folsom?"

He gave her a smug nod.

"'Folsom Prison Blues' it is." She and Drew hit the guitar parts, Buck smacked the drums, and over the next few beats, all the instruments joined in and found their place. With gusto, she sang the words to the song about a man behind bars hearing the sound of a train in the distance and mourning his lack of freedom. Their rendition of the song was peppy, and the people out in the audience whistled and clapped, obviously loving it. Looking toward Candy, she saw the blonde woman gazing at Buck while she sang the harmony line above Kip's part. The look the backup singer wore on her face was one of pure love. Buck was concentrating on rhythm so much that he didn't notice. As Kip sang the words, she wondered if Buck had also been hit with the Love Stick—or was he just playing around? She looked back at Candy. Though she didn't know Lacey's backup singer very well, she hoped it was the real deal for both of them.

They finished the song to rousing applause. Drew started in on the guitar riff for a new song, and Jaime's violin filled right in. Kip didn't recognize the Dixie Chicks tune right away, but as soon as she did, she fumbled for the right chord and joined. Into the mic she said, "It's like playing *Name That Tune*, guys." Drew laughed with glee, and she sang the first line of "There's Your Trouble." Candy's backup vocals sounded great, and Kip looked over and winked at the younger woman.

They played non-stop for another hour with the crowd growing larger and larger, until Kip could see that the clerk at the desk looked alarmed. Eric caught her eye at the tail end of the song they were doing, and he drew a finger across his throat. She gave a nod, and when the song ended, she said, "We're going to leave you with this one last song. It's an oldie but a goodie, so old, I don't even know if Candy knows it." She started playing the chords, picking a nice pattern, to John Denver's song, "Goodbye Again." She hadn't played it before with the band, but before she got two lines into it, Drew was on it. Then she heard the bass line, a keyboard melody complemented her picking, and Buck was keeping rhythm. At the chorus, Jaime contributed quiet strings, and Candy sang the descant. It was the perfect song to calm down the crowd and leave them in a contemplative and not rowdy mood.

When they finished, the couple hundred people burst into applause. She said, "Now don't forget to turn out for the Lacey Leigh Jaxon concert Saturday night. These are the talented members of her band, and you can hear some great tunes. Oh, and by the way, show your receipt for any purchase you make at the Boot Emporium between now and the concert, and you'll get a dollar off admission at the door on the night of the concert. Good night."

Eric flipped off the electrical to the soundboard circuit as Drew turned to her and said, "I never heard about that special deal."

"How could you? I just thought it up."

He laughed heartily, but suddenly they were interrupted by people coming up to talk to them, and it took Kip a good half hour to make it out of the place to the door. Jaime slipped away long before Kip did, and when she finally dragged Isabelle back to the bus, she felt plenty fatigued. Jaime sat at the booth, facing front, looking tired. Kip shut and locked the bus door, then placed her guitar carefully on the bench. She slid into the booth across from Jaime. "That was fun, but man, I'm tired."

"Yeah, me too." She yawned. "Thanks for the good dinner tonight, Kip. I've really enjoyed hanging out with you."

"You're welcome." She rose and reached for Isabelle, then shuffled down the narrow aisle. As she rounded the booth, she paused and impulsively threw her free arm around her dinner companion from behind and gave her an awkward hug. "Good night, Jaime. Sleep well."

She let go as Jaime replied, "You, too, Kip. See you in the morning."

Chapter
Ten

WHEN KIP AWAKENED, she lay in her bed looking up at the insulated ceiling of the bus. She was surprised at how fast the days and nights were going. The difference between her current surroundings and her regular life back home were striking. She thought wistfully of her house and wondered if Mary was remembering to look after her plants.

She had no idea what time it was, but blinding bright sunlight shone in through the bus windows, so it had to be past nine a.m. People in Minnesota, also on Central Standard Time, must be up and about. She rolled over and opened the drawer next to her bed and fumbled around until she found her cell phone. Checking the charge, she saw it was fine, so she plugged in the numbers for Mary's work and pressed SEND.

Her friend picked up the phone on the second ring. "Egret Pond Art Gallery, this is Mary."

"Hey, girl."

"Kip! I was just thinking about you." In an excited voice, her words tumbled out. "How is the tour? Are you getting along with the witch yet? Is it still lonely? How is it going?"

Kip waited for her friend to wind down. Mary could always be counted upon to spread around a generous dose of energy and excitement. "Things are going pretty decent now. Lacey and Wes have been gone since Saturday morning, and we've been on a short break since Friday's concert. We don't have another show until tomorrow night."

"What! Why don't you come home?"

"We played late Friday night in Albuquerque, then bused it over to Amarillo on Monday. I wanted to see the sights, hang out, take it easy. I didn't think it would work to make a rushed trip home, then have to turn around and come right back here."

"But everyone is missing you. Sam and Rubee were over the other night, and Joyce and I gave them the latest update, but we all miss you."

"Thanks, Mar, but we're traveling north soon enough. You're coming to the show, right?"

"Wouldn't miss it for the world!"

They spent ten minutes talking about what was happening back home, and Kip gave her the highlights of some of the performances. She also gave a few examples of how she was getting along fine with headliner and crew, but she didn't mention Jaime specifically. A part of her wanted to confide in her friend, but she didn't feel quite ready. By the time they rang off, Kip was caught up on all the Minnesota news, and she felt warmed and pleased by her best friend's encouragement and support. She put the cell phone back in the drawer and got out of bed to get ready for the day.

Forty-five minutes later, she'd showered and dressed, finished off a cup of instant coffee, eaten an orange and some coffeecake from the refrigerator, and was ready to shop. She checked her watch to find it was close to eleven. She didn't know where Jaime was, but the curtains to her bunk were parted, and it was clear she wasn't in the bus. After brushing her teeth, Kip snagged a pair of heavy socks, tracked down her wallet, locked up the bus, and headed toward the Boot Emporium. She got halfway across the parking lot before hearing a distant noise that sounded like her name. She turned, scanning the half-full parking lot, and didn't see anything. She had almost given up looking when an arm emerged from the back of the tour semi, followed by the rest of one lanky body which dropped four feet through the air and thudded to the ground into a half-squat.

Jaime came out of the squat to her full height and gave her a wave, which the folksinger returned. "Hey, Kip," she called out. "I was just coming to wake you up." She strolled toward Kip with a smile on her face. As she drew near, she said, "What do you have planned for the day?"

The warm sun shone brightly on Jaime's black hair. She looked relaxed in her tan cargo shorts and white t-shirt. Kip looked down at her own outfit—sandals, tan cargo shorts, and a white Math Masters t-shirt. "First, I think one of us has to change clothes. We're dressed like twins." She grinned, and Jaime reached out and whapped her on the shoulder with the back of her hand.

"My shirt is plain, and I have tennis shoes on. I think we can get by."

"I suppose it would be a little like confusing Arnold Schwarzenegger and Danny DeVito."

"I don't *think* so."

Kip looked down at her sandals, feeling her feet heating up as she stood on the cement in the lot. "I'm going in to buy a pair of leather boots. You can help me pick 'em out, if you like." Jaime fell in stride with her as she headed for the hotel again. "Then I thought I'd go back to the air-conditioned bus and wear them the rest of the day. I love new shoes and boots and sandals, don't you?"

Jaime grabbed the door handle and let Kip enter before her. "I guess it's a good idea to wear them where it's cool, but no, I must admit I've never been all that excited about footwear."

The folksinger moved toward the racks of boots. "You would be if you lived in Minnesota. We've got shoes for every occasion and for twelve different kinds of weather. Coats, too."

They hadn't even examined a boot before Minnie Logan appeared. "Good morning, Kip."

The folksinger turned to the small woman, smiling from ear to ear. "Good morning, Minnie. I don't think I had a chance yesterday to introduce you to Jaime Esperanza."

Jaime held out her hand. "Nice to meet you, Minnie. Kip told me about your conversation yesterday, and I have to say I admired the beaded purse you gave her. It's beautiful."

"Thank you," Minnie said warmly, then released the other woman's hand and focused her attention on Kip. "You're not really back for boots, are you?"

"Yes, I am. I'd like a pair something like this." She held up a medium brown boot with a rounded toe and a good hiking tread.

"All right then. Let's get you sized."

Jaime browsed through the shelves as Minnie helped Kip try on various boots. She came upon several pairs of leather moccasin-style slippers, she picked one up, and examined it. The inside lining looked soft, and the rusty red-brown exterior was sturdy and well-sewn. She slipped off her tennis shoe and slid her stocking foot into it. The moccasin formed around her arch, heel, and toes like it was made for her foot. Off went her left shoe to be replaced with the other moccasin which was just as comfortable. She bent and picked up her shoes, then walked over to sit next to Kip. Minnie was nowhere to be seen. "Hey, check these out."

"Slippers?"

"Yeah, and they feel great. I think I'm buying them."

"Thought you didn't care about footwear."

Jaime shrugged. "These are nice and comfortable." She looked up to see Minnie come out of the storeroom behind the counter with two boxes in her hands.

Kip smiled. "Save your receipt. You can get into tomorrow's concert for a dollar off."

"Very funny."

Minnie stopped in front of the folksinger and knelt down. "What was that all about? I've already had two guys in here trying on boots, and both of them insisted on having a receipt so they'd get a dollar off a concert."

Kip said, "Seemed like a good idea last night. We came in here and had a little jam session. We set up the band over there." She pointed toward the alcove around the corner from the hotel's front desk. "At the end, we had probably two hundred people here, and I had that bright idea, spur-of-the-moment. I hoped it would bring you some extra business, and I would gladly cover the few dollars that the box office gives credit for."

"That was kind of you, but won't you get in trouble with the concert hall?"

"No, I'll tell the promoter, and we'll make sure it works out." The native woman sat back on her heels while Kip leaned over and tied the boots. "Minnie, these feel good."

"Get up and walk around for a while to make sure." Kip rose and walked toward the front door.

The bootmaker fixed her dark eyes on Jaime. "What do you think of those moccasins?"

"I like 'em a lot. I'm buying them."

Minnie nodded, looking pleased. "You're my kind of customer. You have tried on one item, decided you like it, and now you are ready for the purchase. Makes it easy for the merchant, that's for sure."

"Normally I dislike shopping, but it was like these sort of jumped off the shelf at me." Jaime slipped out of the moccasins and set to work putting her tennis shoes back on.

Kip walked back their way. "Minnie, these are perfect. I'll take them. They'll be great for walking around the woods back home."

"They aren't particularly good for rocky up-and-down trails."

"Don't worry. It's Minnesota. A lot of the places I go are flat as flat can be."

"Do you want a box for them?"

"No, I'll wear them, and I don't think either of us needs a box." She looked Jaime's way, and the other woman nodded in agreement. "We're squished enough in that tour bus, so the less stuff the better."

Kip picked up her shoes and followed the bootmaker. Minnie took a key from her pocket and unlocked the cash register, then rang up the purchases. She gave them each ten percent off, despite protests, took their money, and presented them with their receipts.

Kip tucked her receipt in her pocket. "Will you come to the concert tomorrow night, Minnie?"

"Sure. I'll bring a receipt and get a dollar off." The tiny woman shook her head. "I don't think I had better."

Kip leaned her elbows on the counter. "Oh, yes, you should. And no receipt is necessary. You just show up at Will Call and pick up comp tickets. Our treat. Right, Jaime?" They both stood smiling at her and nodding. Minnie looked conflicted, so Kip went on. "At every venue, we are allowed a reasonable number of comp tickets. I don't have anyone using mine—and I haven't for the entire tour. Jaime, how about you?"

She crossed her arms and leaned on the counter next to Kip. "Nope. I don't know anyone here."

"So please come, Minnie, and use our tickets. I'll sing a special song just for you. How many people will you bring with you?"

Minnie looked surprised. "I don't know if I would feel comfortable bringing others and infringing upon your hospitality."

Kip nodded. "Okay, that settles it. We'll leave four tickets—no, maybe six? Would eight be enough?" The folksinger grinned as she saw how nervous Minnie suddenly looked. "Tell you what. Call around to your friends and relatives. Find out how many are coming, and I'll check back with you later in the day. How's that sound?" She reached across the counter and patted the thin, brown forearm. "You'll enjoy it, I think. Lacey Leigh Jaxon puts on a great show, and I have to say that my warm-up act is a lot of fun. Please come—will you?"

With a smile, Minnie nodded. "All right. You talked me into it."

"Great! I'll check back later."

"If I am gone to dinner or you miss me, I'll leave word with the front desk," Minnie said.

Kip nodded. "Okay, then, we're all set. We'll see you later on." She turned and headed for the front door, a smile on her face.

Jaime ambled along beside her. "You aren't seriously going to sit in the bus all day, are you?"

The folksinger paused at the front door, one hand on the metal bar across the middle of it. "You got a better idea?"

"Maybe. Do you know how to ride a motorcycle?"

"Heck, yes. I own one."

Jaime was surprised. "You do?"

"I'm the original motorcycle mama—ever since my brother Keith went nuts for cycles at fifteen. I think I've owned a bike non-stop for about half my life."

"*Excellente.* You want to take off on a tour of the country-side?"

"You mean rent a cycle for me?"

Jaime shook her head. "Wait a second." She spun around and strode over to the front desk to pick up the courtesy phone. Kip waited, leaning against the smooth glass of the front door. In short order, Jaime hung up the phone and sauntered back, a satisfied grin on her face. "C'mon."

Kip didn't ask questions, but followed her out into the heat. They walked across the hot cement of the parking lot, and by the time they were at the back of the tour semi, Kip's feet were warm in the boots. The leather already felt like it was molding to her ankles and feet.

Jaime took a ring of keys from her shorts pocket, unlocked the semi, and set her pair of slippers on the bumper. She rolled the door upwards, and pulled ramps out from underneath the floor. The inside was stuffed full. Kip saw cases for speaker towers, amps, and other gear. A metal rack, attached to the wall on the right side, was surrounded with tie-down straps and overflowed with gear and equipment she couldn't identify. On the left side she saw the handlebars of a motorcycle sticking out of a boxy wooden structure that had cartons stacked on top of it. "Can I help here?"

"No, that's okay. Hang tight." Jaime walked up the ramp and into the back of the jam-packed semi, and Kip watched her grab handlebars and pull a Harley cycle out. She maneuvered it down the ramp and put the kickstand down.

"Nice bike."

"Thanks. Now for the fun part." Jaime scurried back up the ramp and squatted down to enter the wooden chute. Kip heard a curse and scuffling, and Jaime gradually backed out of the four-foot-tall aperture pulling another bike.

"You've got two cycles?"

"This one's Eric's." She rolled the second bike down the ramp, then stopped at the bottom with it resting against her, and made a hissing noise. She shook her right hand and looked at it. Through clenched teeth she hissed, "*Aiyeee,* it hurts!"

Kip set her sandals and wallet on the bumper of the semi. "What did you do? You hurt yourself? Let me see." She stepped over and took Jaime's hand into her own.

"It's just a scratch," Jaime said.

"Yowch. Looks painful." Beads of blood welled up on the palm of the injured hand from an uneven scrape that ran from her wrist toward her thumb.

"There's definitely some sharp spots on the edges of that crappy, makeshift box Eric and I built."

"I guess! You should get the wound washed and bandaged." She let go of the wounded hand, far too conscious of how standing so close to Jaime made her feel.

Jaime put down the kickstand on the bike and turned to go up the ramp again. She reached for two sets of keys hanging from hooks that Kip hadn't noticed before on the side of the rattletrap rack. Still frowning, Jaime came down the ramps once more and bent to pick the left one up, push it over her head, and shove it back under the semi.

"Let me help," Kip said. She got on the end and helped push it in, then lifted the second one and assisted with it, too. Jaime locked the back. By this point, Kip was sweating and thirsty and her ankles felt like they were swelling in the boots. The thought of staying outside one more minute was terribly unappealing. "So will Eric be all right with me riding his motorcycle?"

"*Si, señorita*. I called him from the lobby."

Kip picked up her sandals and wallet and Jaime's slippers as well, then followed the bleeding woman over to the bus. They let themselves into the cool vehicle, and Kip set the handful of things she carried onto one of the seats of the booth. She followed Jaime into the tiny bathroom and watched her turn on the water and stick her hand under it. "Whoa! That hurts!" Jaime glanced over her shoulder. "It's going to be kind of tight in here, Kip."

The folksinger smacked her on the butt with the flat of her hand. "You're skinny enough. Get over it." Chuckling, Kip opened the linen cabinet to the side of the small sink and pulled out an orange washcloth, which she laid over her shoulder. She reached for the first aid kit crammed in between stacks of towels, then set the kit on the back of the toilet tank behind Jaime. Almost as an afterthought, she put the commode lid down, then opened up the kit and rummaged around. When she found a package containing gauze pads, she tore it open. A tune came into her head, and she hummed it as she stood waiting for Jaime to finish at the sink. When the other woman turned off the water, she let her hand drip over the sink for a moment, then turned to face Kip who took the washcloth off her shoulder and held it open in her two hands.

"What if I get blood on it?" Jaime asked.

"So what. It's orange. And it can be laundered." Jaime stuck her hand out, palm down, and Kip wrapped the washcloth around it and very gently dried the fingers and palm first. She tried to skirt the scrape, which had stopped bleeding, though some blood still oozed in the middle. She set the cloth down on the edge of the

sink, unscrewed the lid from a tube of antiseptic crème, and
handed it over. "Put a little of that on." She waited for the tube to
be returned to her, then capped it and stuck it back in the bag with
the other supplies. She picked up the gauze square and positioned
it over the scrape.

"I need my thumb to be free."

"I know. Sit down." Jaime didn't have much choice. Kip
placed a hand on one lean shoulder and nudged her back, so she
lowered herself to sit on the one seat in the room. Kip shifted
around in front of her so that she was leaning back against the
sink, between Jaime's knees, and she squatted down to put two
pieces of adhesive tape across the wounded hand. She wrapped
one strip partly around the brown wrist and attached the other
over the top of her hand, but avoided the thumb. "There. That
ought to work," she said as she stood.

Jaime flexed her hand. "I guess it'll do."

"You can take the bandage off in a couple of hours once it
gets dried out and scabbed over enough."

Jaime rose, and suddenly Kip thought the room was much
smaller than it had been a moment earlier. Jaime raised her unin-
jured, left hand and placed it on the folksinger's upper arm. In a
soft voice, she said, "Thanks, Kip. It feels better already."

Face aflame, Kip looked down. She shifted aside and reached
around the solid presence in front of her to stick the roll of adhesive tape back in the bag. Acutely aware of the warm body inches
away, she picked up the first aid kit and inched back and over to
the linen cupboard. Once she turned away, Jaime slipped past, her
skin and shirt so close that she brushed Kip's arm, back, and hip
when squeezing by. The folksinger trembled and felt her mouth go
dry. *Stop it!* she thought to herself. *Just cut that out.* She smacked
the closet door shut and went through the pocket door and to the
left to her stateroom. Taking a deep breath, she looked around the
tiny room and made herself forget about her physical response,
thinking instead about what she would need on a motorcycle ride.
It was so hot out that she knew she wouldn't want boots on, so she
sat on the bed and started unlacing. She pulled off the first boot
and dropped it to the floor, and then a thought occurred to her.
"Jaime?" she called out. "What about helmets?"

The dark head poked out from between the curtains in the top
bunk. "What about 'em?"

"I'm not riding without a helmet." She heard some grumbling, but after a few moments, Jaime climbed down from the
bunk, holding a compact canvas backpack. "I'll get you one out of
the semi. It's so hot out, I never wear one."

Kip frowned. "But if you wipe out, it's too dangerous."

"I know, but I'm careful."

She sighed. "Oh, boy. You know what? I'm not going unless we're both wearing helmets."

Jaime leaned against the outer frame of the bunk. "C'mon, *mi amiga*," she pleaded. "Don't feel that way."

Kip shook her head. "I just—I can't, Jaime. No way. I don't want to be out on the road somewhere and have something happen...not like, not like with my little brother."

The dark eyes in front of her went wide, and Jaime looked stricken. "I didn't think of it that way, Kip." She looked away. When she met her gaze again, Kip thought Jaime looked very sad. "All right."

KIP TORE ALONG down highway 136, the wind blowing down her shirt and into her face. The motorcycle's roar was muffled through her helmet. Hot sun beat down on the back of her neck and her arms, and she was grateful she had applied a liberal amount of sunblock. Still, she knew she would get a little burned. She didn't care. She felt too exhilarated to worry about it.

They had been riding for over an hour, first through the heavily populated city of Amarillo, and then northward. She didn't care where they went, but Jaime had told her they were headed for a quarry. In the last mile, the terrain had changed somewhat, and she thought she smelled water. Kip didn't know how to explain that, except that suddenly, a breath of hot air seemed slightly more humid, and she found herself thinking of the Mississippi River back home. She did a double take upon seeing a sign ahead: *Canadian River ~ 1 mile*.

Jaime exited from the highway and went another couple hundred yards, then pulled off into the sandy dirt on the side of the road. Like Kip, she wore a helmet and dark sunglasses. Kip pulled up next to her and watched her remove a water bottle from the backpack she wore. She took a long pull from the bottle, and offered it to Kip who took it gratefully. "You hungry for snacks yet?" Jaime asked.

"No, I'm good, but you go ahead." She took another drink from the bottle.

"I'm fine for now, too. Just checking."

Kip handed the water back. "What is this place?"

"We're near the red bluffs of the Canadian River."

"It's funny that it's called the Canadian River. We aren't anywhere near Canada."

"And it runs east-west, so it never reaches Canada either. I don't know where the name came from. Want to go further?"

"Oh, yeah."

"Good. There's an old flint quarry ahead—went there as a kid." She took another swig of water, returned the bottle to the backpack, re-situated the canvas bag on her shoulders, and pointed forward. "Let's go." She gave the bike some gas and rolled forward, and Kip followed her.

They made their way down the road to a dirt lot, parked the motorcycles, and Kip gratefully removed the hot helmet. Jaime wore the backpack, and they hiked off to explore the Alibates Flint Quarry National Park. Kip had never heard of this national monument, but she quickly found out from Jaime that the cotton-wood-shaded area on the river had been a place where prehistoric people dug up flint for tools and weapons. She learned that hunting and gathering tribes had lived in the area for six thousand years before the birth of Christ, and that stone and adobe villages had once populated the area. The farmers who had settled there used the rainbow-colored flint to make tools and traded it for goods with other wandering tribes.   Archeologists had found Pacific Coast seashells, pottery from New Mexico tribes, and even Minnesota pipestone. Kip wondered how people on foot and horseback managed to travel all the miles between the Mississippi and the Canadian River. Here she was, on a bus tour, and it seemed a slow and antiquated way to travel. What must it have been like to roam the Texas Panhandle, across the plains, over the prairies, and up to the cooler climes of Minnesota?

She followed Jaime as they made their way up a steep trail covered in loose gravel. She slipped a bit in her tennis shoes, but they took their time and had soon covered quite a distance. Though it was cooler here near the river than it had been back in Amarillo, she was still sweating. Stopping at the top of the trail, she pulled a bandana from her back pocket and wiped her face and neck.

"You doing okay?" Jaime asked.

"You bet."

"Good. The quarries are ahead."

They moved forward to find scores of shallow pits scattered along the edge of the bluffs. Kip worked her way around the first hole, a narrow pit about five feet across. She estimated that it was only two-feet deep. She continued forward until she reached the edge of the bluff and looked out across to where the river wound through the plains. "Wow! This is beautiful."

Jaime came to stand next to her, shoulders nearly touching.

They gazed out upon a verdant area speckled with trees and brush. In the distance, the water sparkled blue and glinted with silver and white as it moved slowly on its winding way. From their vantage point above it all, Kip could see across the plains, and she was struck by how desolate it looked out in the distance. "This is really something." She couldn't stop thinking, *Wow!* It was such different terrain, such a different expanse than she was used to, but still, she was awed by it. Less than a hundred years earlier, Apaches and other nomadic tribes had made this area their home, free of the interference of white culture. Now, however, she knew the Apache were an endangered group, decimated by the ravages of illness brought by Europeans and by decades of conflict with the technologically advanced white culture.

Jaime said, "My grandparents brought me and a school friend here when I was ten. We ran up and down all the trails, dug around in the quarries, and had a great time. My grandfather even found me a flint arrowhead." She paused, a wistful look on her face. "Those were happy times."

"Do you still have the arrowhead?"

"No. I don't know what happened to it. Guess I lost it somewhere along the way. But I'll always have the memory of the fun time here."

"I know what you mean. My family went to the border of Minnesota and South Dakota once for vacation, and we visited the Indian Burial Mounds there. It was so eye-opening for me to learn about the Native American culture. My brother and I just soaked it in. That's probably part of the reason he became a national parks ranger. He was totally fascinated. You'd be surprised at all the native culture throughout Minnesota."

"I have never been there, Kip. I'd like to visit someday."

Grinning, Kip leaned into her. "Since I live there, you'd *better* come visit."

Jaime gave a nod and pointed out toward the plains. "That's Lake Meredith—it's kind of a wide spot in the Canadian River."

"Isn't it weird how that gets done with rivers? Wherever there is a spreading out of the river, seems like someone decides to call it a lake. Same thing is true of the Mississippi around Lake City, Minnesota, where it widens into what gets called Lake Pepin. I wonder who thought up doing that?"

Jaime shrugged. "Beats me. You want to look around some more?"

"Sure." She got out her bandana again. "It's awful warm. I'll be glad to dry off on the motorcycle in a while."

"Me, too." Jaime turned and made her way over to the quarry

pits. "I swear these were deeper when I was here." She crouched down and peered into a hole.

"Well, they've done the reverse of erosion and filled in some. After all, it was practically three decades ago when you last saw them, right?" She strode toward the quarry hole.

Surprised, Jaime said, "No! Three decades isn't—well, okay, I guess it *was* a while back. But it wasn't thirty years ago."

Kip stopped next to her, where Jaime still squatted, a handful of dirt running through her fingers. "Twenty-eight, twenty-nine, thirty...seems to me that's pretty close to three decades, old woman."

Jaime rose, stifling a grin. She leaned close. "Watch out, *old woman*, or I'll toss you in the pit."

Kip looked down into the hole they stood next to. When she spoke, her voice held a challenge. "Better pick a deeper one than that one, Esperanza. Even I could pull myself up three feet."

She smoothed the bandage on her palm, then put a hand on Kip's bare arm. "Don't tempt me."

Kip reached over and grasped the backpack straps Jaime wore down her chest. "Go ahead. You'll be going with me." The taunt in her voice was unmistakable. She pressed her fists against the flat surface below the other woman's collarbones, and hung on to the straps with all the grip she could muster.

Jaime moved her hands up and grabbed Kip's shoulders, all the while grinning. "I feel like we're two sumo wrestlers."

Breathlessly, Kip said, "I think we have to bend over more for proper form." Jaime released her and threw her head back to laugh. Kip let go of the straps and looked at her own left shoulder. "Thanks for the mud." She pointed at her upper arm where the dust on Jaime's hand had adhered to the moisture there, leaving a dirty smudge on her skin. This caused more laughter. "You know what, Jaime? I should be the one throwing *you* into these pits."

"Just try." Jaime darted away, threading her way between the holes. Kip watched the long, smooth brown legs, admiring everything about the graceful way the other woman moved.

A COUPLE HOURS later, the two women were back on the road. They'd eaten a bag of peanuts each and split an orange before they took off, but Kip knew she would be starving by the time they reached Amarillo. She wasn't sure where they were going next, but she hoped wherever it was, good food would be involved.

It felt so good to have wind blowing in her face and cooling her overly-warm body. She looked down at her shirt, which was now plenty dusty, and was glad they had earlier, at Jaime's urging, each included a clean t-shirt in the canvas backpack.

After a quick stop to gas up the cycles, they arrived in the Old San Jacinto area of Amarillo, which was the city's original downtown area along the route of old U.S. 66. The locus of downtown had moved away over the years, and the area was now dedicated to a variety of art stores, craft and antique shops, restaurants, and boutiques. She was relieved when Jaime bypassed all of them and steered her motorcycle right into the parking lot of a Mexican cantina. Only a few cars dotted the lot, so they got front row spaces. Kip angled in next to her and turned off her engine. Instantly, the stifling, dry air pressed in around her.

Jaime took off her helmet and hung it from the back of her seat. She ran her hands through her hair and shook her head. "I *hate* helmets. I probably look scary."

Kip laughed. "You always look scary. Don't worry about it."

Jaime gave her a withering stare. "Don't make me hurt you." She slipped the backpack off.

"Ha! Like you would."

Jaime gave her a funny look. "What would you think of eating here?"

"This is fine. Anywhere is fine. Let's just make it soon." She got off the bike and made sure the kickstand was steady, then moved away from the cycle and fell in step next to Jaime. They got to the door of the restaurant, but found it locked. "Uh oh. No wonder the parking lot is so empty." Before she said anything more, the bright red door popped open a couple inches and banged shut. She looked at her watch. "It's 4:01. They must open at 4:00."

"Lucky for us." Jaime grabbed the door handle and pulled it open just in time for them to see the retreating back of the man who had unlocked the door. He didn't look back.

Kip followed Jaime into the cantina, caught sight of the *Restroom* sign, and tapped her friend's arm. "I'm cutting in here."

"Me, too."

When they emerged, both had washed up, combed their hair, and changed into fresh shirts. Kip said, "I feel positively human now."

They were ushered to a booth, and Kip sank down happily and accepted a menu. She looked at the relaxed face sitting across from her and watched Jaime open the menu. *I've enjoyed every bit of today. I could go off exploring with her every day and be fine with it.* Jaime's head jerked up suddenly and caught her staring.

Kip was sure she must be wearing some sort of daft look on her face, so of course her face flooded with heat.

"What? What are you thinking?"

Kip shook her head. *Time for the waiter to show up*, but there wasn't a soul in sight. Jaime surveyed her, dark eyes probing. "It's nothing. I was just thinking how much I enjoyed the day."

Jaime gave a slow nod. "Me, too. And don't forget, dinner's on me. You bought last night. I'll get tonight's."

"No spendy wines for this meal, though." Jaime raised an eyebrow and waited for more. "I'm not riding a motorcycle half in the bag." *Besides, I got a little too loopy last night for my own good, and I'm not taking any chances tonight.*

A young woman appeared at their table and greeted them in Spanish. Jaime had a spirited conversation with her, most of which Kip didn't comprehend. Then the two women were looking at her, and Kip waited for her dinner companion to translate.

Jaime said, "I asked her what's fun to do around here at night, and she said there's a play at the little theater down the street, but also that the planetarium has star shows and a night sky program tonight."

In an accent thick to Kip's ear, the waitress said, "I take my children and see star show. Is really cool."

Kip hadn't thought past the meal. Her stomach was growling so insistently that she would have consented to any show, any play, and realizing that, she grinned. "I'm game for pretty much anything."

The waitress nodded and said, "I bring guidebook. First, drinks for you?"

They ordered soda and assented to chips and salsa. When the waitress brought it all over a minute later, she set a thick booklet on the table. Kip ate several chips in a row while they gave their orders. When the waitress left, the folksinger picked up the booklet and thumbed through it, then handed it to Jaime. "Looks like tons of things to do here."

Kip ate another chip, this one dunked in salsa, and watched as Jaime opened up the first page of the guidebook and read for a few moments. "Hey, check this out," Jaime said. "Amarillo has the world's greatest quantity of the natural element of helium."

Kip laughed. "No wonder I have the urge to go buy mouse ears."

"Now what do mouse ears have to do with helium?"

"You know, you breathe in helium, and it makes you talk really high like Minnie Mouse."

"Oh, I see." She turned the page. "Well, helium is such a hot property here that they have a six-story stainless steel column dedicated to it."

Kip frowned. "I *wondered* what that thing was. You can see it off in the distance. It looks too short to be a radio tower, so that must be what it is." She sat back and forced herself to quit bolting tortilla chips, though her stomach was still telling her how hungry it was. She let her hands relax in her lap. "I take it you don't have anything planned tonight."

"Nope." Jaime dipped a large chip into the salsa and moved it around until she got some big chunks of tomato, raised it slowly, tipped her head a little to the side, and tried to get it all into her mouth.

Kip was laughing even before the inevitable occurred and half the chip—sauce and all—plopped down onto the table top. With napkin in hand, she leaned across the table and dabbed at Jaime's chin. "Can't take you out anywhere, can I?"

Jaime was so embarrassed, she stammered. "I...it...I usually don't..."

Kip rolled her eyes. "I can't believe that rattles you. Who cares? It's not like we're dressed nice."

"True enough." She looked down at the dripping half-chip in her hand, then popped it into her mouth. "You have to admit, these are good."

"And if we run out, we can always eat all the detritus on the table."

"Detritus?"

"You know—litter. Left over rubble and silt and trash after the stream dries up." She grinned. "I'm a school teacher. What can I say? My room is next to the language arts teacher's, and that was one of the words up on her board at the end of the school year." She smiled. "First time I've been able to use it since then though."

Before long, the waitress came back, and they got fresh napkins. They ordered Spanish rice and different kinds of tasty burritos, which they shared, along with many laughs before the check was finally presented to them. "I've got this," Jaime said, pulling out her wallet.

"Sounds good to me." As Jaime counted out money, Kip put her elbow on the table and her chin in her hand. "You know what?"

Jaime set a couple of bills on the table atop the dinner check. "What?"

"I think I'll get a room in the hotel tonight." She looked down at the front of her shirt. "This shirt may be clean, but I feel thoroughly grungy. I *could* shower in the phone booth in the bus..." She laughed and went on, "I think I'd like to take a nice long bath instead."

Jaime slid out of the booth and stood. "I take it that means no theater, no planetarium?"

Kip rose and stood facing her. "It's still early. I'll get cleaned up, and if you still want to do something later, why don't you come get me."

They headed toward the door. Kip caught sight of the waitress on the way out and waved. The small woman waved back and smiled, and then the folksinger was passing through the entryway and out into the glaring sun. She pinched her eyes shut and slowed her steps. The sun was so bright that tears came to her eyes, and it was a good half-minute before her vision adjusted.

"Hey, slowpoke!" Jaime stood next to her cycle, helmet in one hand and the other hand above her brow to block the sun. She looked like she was saluting.

Kip sighed and walked the rest of the way over to Eric's motorcycle. "I'm a gray-eyed Northern girl. Takes a while for my eyes to adjust." She straddled the bike and pulled on the helmet, then let out a big yawn. The watch on her wrist indicated it was half past six, but the sun was still beating down. She yawned again. "I think I need a nap."

"Join the club." Kip watched as the lean woman snapped the helmet strap under her chin and kick-started the cycle. The engine revved loud, and Kip yawned again. *Oh, boy. Too much good food once again.* She looked up and saw Jaime was looking at her, then making a hand gesture that said, *C'mon, let's get a move on.* Kip kick-started the bike, and in short order, they were back out on the road. She wasn't familiar with the area, but Jaime seemed to know where they were going. Inside fifteen minutes, in the distance, she saw the giant white and silver cowboy boot that hung over the Lost Spur and Boot Emporium, and she yawned again. She was happy she had decided to pamper herself. It'd been long enough on the bus, and it was time to spread out a bit, even if only for a couple nights.

When they arrived back at the hotel, the parking lot was void of movement. Jaime wrestled the cycles up the ramp and back into their storage box, and then locked up the semi. The two women strolled over to the door of the hotel and entered to find Wes and Lacey Leigh standing at the front desk, waiting for the desk clerk to get off the phone. The Boot Emporium was closed, and all the racks were wheeled out of the way.

"Hey, girls," the promoter called out. "Been keeping busy?"

Kip nodded. She met Lacey Leigh's eyes, and the diva's face twisted into a frown that caused Kip to look down at her attire. With the exception of the t-shirt, every part of her was dusty. Her legs felt literally dirty, and she could only shudder to think what kind of mess her brown hair was in. In contrast, Lacey wore tiny white canvas shorts, white flat sandals, and a pale pink blouse. An over-sized leather Coach bag was slung over her shoulder, and though it was mostly zipped shut, Kip could see the cap of a bottle poking out one corner. The folksinger noted that Lacey Leigh was neat, clean, and made up, with her blonde hair styled attractively. As they covered the last two steps between the entrance and the front desk, Kip glanced to her right. Jaime was likely every bit as dirty as she herself was, but somehow the tanned tech managed to look tidy and put-together.

"Hello, Jaime," Lacey Leigh said, her chin in the air as she looked up at the taller woman.

Jaime responded in a soft voice. "Hi, Lace. How was the shoot?" She looked down and picked at the adhesive on the bandage on her hand.

"It went well. Real well."

Wes nodded. "It was the best *damn* video this sweet gal's ever done. Gonna go straight to the top of the charts." He patted her on the back and stared down at her proudly. Kip watched her closely and saw that the small woman wore a sad and distant look on her face. She wondered why.

"That's good to hear," Jaime said.

Wes growled, "What the *hell* happened to your hand?"

Jaime examined her palm, then finished pulling away the bandage. "Nothing. Just a scrape. It's fine."

"Damn well better be," he said. "I can't afford for you to get injured."

Jaime gave a curt nod. "So, what's happening with rhythm for the next show?"

Wes grinned. "Got us a live one. Derrick Daniels. Heard of him?"

Jaime frowned. "Didn't he do studio work for Alabama or Brooks & Dunn—somebody like that?"

"Yeah," Lacey said. "He's done a lot of studio work, lead and rhythm. He's good and picks things up fast. Should work out great."

The clerk hung up the phone and turned to the group. "May I help someone?"

Wes held up a hand. "Gimme a minute."

He began giving instructions to Jaime about spending some

time with the new guy, and Kip turned her attention away from them and said to the clerk, "You can help me. I'd like to get a room for tonight and tomorrow night. Something with an oversized tub—or a Jacuzzi would be even better."

"No problem, ma'am." He clacked away at a keyboard and she rested her elbows on the counter and leaned. She could hear much of what Wes was saying, and now he was discussing stage arrangements.

"Oh, by the way, Wes," Jaime said, "we had an impromptu concert here in the lobby last night, and we told the people if they bought anything at the Boot Emporium, they could get a buck off tickets bought the night of the show."

"What? Why in the *hell* did you go and do that?"

"People here have been nice. Kip and I will cover it. I just need you to tell the people at the venue to accept the receipts."

"*Jee*-zus Christ, Esperanza. You don't think I have enough shit to keep track of?"

"We're not sold out. It shouldn't be a problem. With any luck, it'll drum up a little business."

Kip signed the form the clerk put in front of her and accepted the plastic door keycard. "Thanks."

"My pleasure," he said. He raised his voice, "May I assist you now, sir?"

"Damn right." Wes pivoted around and moved toward the counter, brushing Kip's shoulder as she stepped away to stand with Lacey Leigh.

Lacey said, "Derrick is a real professional. But don't expect him to come play for your opening act."

Kip didn't know what to say. She looked at Jaime, then back to the tiny blonde. She opened her mouth to defend herself, but before a sound came out, the front door opened, and a tall, dark-haired man struggled through carrying two heavy suitcases. Lacey let out a tiny gasp, and the folksinger's head swung toward the tiny star. Lacey's attention was riveted upon the man, and Kip watched as a nearly electric transformation invigorated the diva. Her face brightened, a pink flush came to her cheeks, and she smiled wide, showing white, even teeth. Kip wondered if she was imagining the purring sound she heard coming from Lacey, who said, "Well, Derrick, honey. Hello!"

The broad-shouldered man wore a black cowboy hat, black boots, black khaki-style slacks, and a blood-red muscle shirt. As far as Kip could tell, this guy could wear any color he wanted and look like a rock star. *What is it with the color black and country-western performers? And how does he keep from sweating in that outfit?* He was what her mother would call a "fine specimen of a man." The closer he got, the more handsome he looked. She could see the muscles ripple in his lightly tanned shoulders and forearms as he set his bags down near their group.

"Howdy, folks." He tipped his hat, then removed it completely and set it on top of one of the bulging suitcases. "Be right back. I have to pick up my guitars."

He wheeled around and strolled toward the front door, smoothing back his thick black hair as he went. The muscles in the back of his shoulders moved smoothly, and the snug shirt revealed lithe, tight muscles in his upper back. *He's a God—an Adonis. Whew. And look at that nice butt.* She suppressed a grin and sneaked a peek at Lacey Leigh again. *Uh-oh.* The diva's eyes glazed over, and Kip had no doubt what—or who—the blonde star desired. Holding back a smirk, Kip met Jaime's gaze, only to see her face closed and hard. A chill ran through the folksinger, and she was suddenly certain that there was a world of hurt behind Jaime's controlled expression.

As the clerk gestured toward a piece of paper and murmured quietly to Wes, Kip looked over her shoulder and realized that the concert promoter had entirely missed Derrick's entrance.

The new guitarist came up the walkway, carrying two guitars, and Lacey hustled over to the front door to open it for him. Kip rolled her eyes. *Next thing you know, she'll be batting her eyelashes.* Wes finished with the hotel clerk and turned to face Derrick and the three women just as the new rhythm man set down his two guitars. "Derrick!" The promoter stuck out a hand, and Derrick clasped it.

"Nice to see you again, sir."

"No sirs needed around here. Just call me Wes."

He introduced the new man to Jaime and Kip, but before Kip could shake his hand, the hotel clerk called out. "Ms. Galvin. I almost forgot..."

She moved over to the desk. "Yes?"

"Minnie Logan left a note for you."

"Oh, yeah. That's right. I meant to ask you about that. Thanks." She accepted a small envelope and immediately opened it to find a three-inch square scrap of paper.

Dear Kip,
I hope you don't mind, but I do want to take you up on your offer. Would it be too much trouble to ask for a total of 5 tickets? Call me at 555-3420 if that won't work out.
Thank you, friend,
Minnie

When she turned away from the desk, Lacey was picking up the two guitars. "I'll come back for those," Derrick said.

"Oh, no," Lacey said as she rolled a shoulder to make sure her purse was secure. "Not a problem."

"No, really. They're heavy."

"I've got them, Derrick. Don't you worry. They're light as a feather."

He bent and picked up his suitcases and went toward the stairs with her right behind him.

As they disappeared up the steps, Jaime shook her head. "I can't remember the last time she carried a single thing."

"This ain't good," Wes said. "I'm getting too *fuckin'* old for this shit." He took a handkerchief out of his back pocket and wiped his forehead. Kip handed Jaime the note from Minnie and waited for the five seconds it took her to read it.

"Wes, one more detail," Jaime said. "Kip's got some friends coming to the show tomorrow. Five plus Kip—six total. I'll get six comps for her, all right?"

"Yeah, yeah." He put his handkerchief away. "Keep an eye on Lacey, will you?" He was addressing Jaime, but he turned and looked Kip in the eye. "You, too, if you don't mind. I've got a goddamn bad feeling about this. New guy's married, got a baby."

Kip was surprised that Wes had picked up on what had just happened, but then she realized she had no way of knowing what had gone on when Derrick and Lacey Leigh first met. For all she knew, they could have been playing footsie at the first interview. She nodded at Wes.

"All right, then. See you two later." He headed toward the stairs and climbed them slowly.

Jaime handed back the slip of paper, and Kip said, "Thanks. I knew I needed to get that request in, but I wasn't sure if it was the right time. But if I didn't do it now, I wasn't sure when I could."

"Yeah, no problem." Jaime took a deep breath and headed for the entrance. Kip fell in behind her, and when Jaime reached the front door, she seemed surprised. "I thought you got a room."

Kip chuckled. "Well, I did, but without Lacey to carry them, I haven't yet figured out how to magically transport all my clothes and toiletries without going out and actually getting them."

Jaime paused in the doorway. "Oh, yeah. Duh. You want me to help you carry stuff up?"

Kip smiled widely. "No stairs for me. I'm on the main floor." Jaime held the door open for her friend, and they emerged into the warmth. For the first time all day, Kip thought it was cooling down and she said so.

Jaime nodded. "It's finally getting more comfortable out here."

They walked across the parking lot and entered the bus. Kip flicked on the overhead lights and moved toward her stateroom. She stopped just past the booth and turned. The look on the other woman's face was one of weariness and defeat. "Hey, Jaime. You can come over and hang out later, if you like. Or if you want, we could go to the ten p.m. show at that planetarium."

Jaime ran her hand through her dark hair, cupping the side of her head in a distracted manner. "I don't know. You probably need space."

Kip giggled. "Yeah, I ought to have some space tonight. Here I have this postage stamp-sized stateroom, and I just rented what amounts to a suite. I won't know what to do with myself. I'll take a nice long bath, maybe a little nap. If you feel up to it, come over at—" She looked at her watch. "How about nine or so? We can play cards, watch TV, whatever. Room 111. If we want to go to the planetarium, we can—or not."

Jaime let out a sigh and nodded, not raising her eyes, and Kip realized she was blocking the way to her bunk, so she moved down the hall and into her room. She pulled open one of the drawers under her bed and gathered up some of the things she thought she would need. *I don't want to have to make multiple trips, so I had better be thorough.*

WHEN SHE'D ASKED the hotel clerk for a nice big tub, Kip had no idea she would end up with such a luxurious one. *It's practically a swimming pool.* The bathroom was an entire, lavish room of its own with a shower stall in one corner, a double set of sinks, a fancy toilet with a nearly soundless flush, and a sunken whirlpool tub. A marble-top counter sat off to the side with a number of drawers and shelves below it. She unpacked her duffel bag of clothes there, set out her toiletries, and turned on the water for the tub. She got in the shower first, as the giant tub filled, so that she could rinse the dirt and road dust off and wash her hair. Then she stepped out of the shower and crept carefully across the slick floor, dripping water, and stepped down into the steaming tub. It was full enough, so she turned off the tap and before lowering herself, she switched on the whirlpool timer causing jets of water to boil up around her legs. She sat and leaned back against the smooth slanted back, water up to her neck, and sighed. *This feels so good.* She sank further into the water and closed her eyes.

Kip woke with a jerk when the timer for the water jets ran out and they turned off. The water was still hot, and she didn't think she had been asleep for more than a couple minutes, especially because she didn't feel very refreshed. She sat in the tub, not thinking, eyes drooping, for another few minutes. Reluctantly, she felt around with her toe to locate the drain stopper. She could not pull the plug without sitting forward and reaching for it. Rather than waiting for the water to drain, she rose and stood in knee-deep water, letting it all run off her, then reached for the towel on the floor near the tub. Fortunately, there were steps up out of the whirlpool. It was so deep that without them, she figured she would need a block and tackle to get herself out, particularly since all her muscles felt mushy and weak.

She dried off, donned a terry-cloth robe that zipped up the front and went out to the sleeping area. *Should I take the bed near the window and natural light—or the one closer to the door and the bathroom?* Deciding on the latter, as that was closer to her at the moment, she untucked the covers and slid in. Once she pulled the sheet up and curled into a ball on her side, she fell into a deep sleep.

IN THE BUS, Jaime sat facing forward in the brown booth. She looked out the window to watch the sun set. The purple, magenta, and hot pink colors were striking and soothing. Fresh from the shower, she was barefoot and dressed in shorts and t-shirt. With one elbow on the Formica table top, she rested her chin in her left palm. Her right hand had washed up well, but it felt itchy from the scratch. She turned her hand over, palm up and looked at the scrape. Already it was healing, that was clear; but the skin felt too tight to stretch over and cover the wounded area. She thought it was quite amazing that skin healed the way it did, and how fast it happened.

She was entirely out-of-sorts, but she couldn't explain why—except to acknowledge that, as usual, it had something to do with Lacey Leigh. The stiffness between them was familiar. It was the same strain and discomfort she had ended up feeling for most women with whom she had opened up and shared parts of herself. The first time occurred during her sophomore year in high school when she fell head over heels for Benita, a fun-loving, hard-drinking junior with snapping black eyes and a large Mexican family. For the whole school year, after classes were out, they had been inseparable. Over the summer, she and Benita often went to remote areas in Benita's father's pickup and stayed out until midnight. They laughed and talked, drank beer, and fooled around. It seemed like so long ago, almost another lifetime. Jaime didn't remember any specific instance of them making love—just the excitement, the smell of the desert, and the comfort of being held tight in the arms of someone she loved.

But during Benita's senior year, she changed. It happened so gradually that Jaime was not able to pinpoint when, exactly, the girl she loved crossed the line from fun-loving party girl to heavy drinker. The intimacy they shared slowly slipped away. Jaime did everything she could to dissuade Benita from all the drinking, but it did no good. The older girl got some fake ID and started spending time at the bars across the border in Lupton. Jaime was not allowed in. She promised to stick by her friend, and she loved her desperately, but Benita stopped making any effort to maintain their relationship, and finally Jaime had to accept that it was over. After that, whenever she ran into a sober—or even semi-sober—Benita, they were both polite, but cool toward one another.

She hadn't gotten involved with anyone again until she was 22 and halfway through the first year of electrician school. This time, she thought she had picked a woman who was more serious and not a drinker. Cora, an Anglo woman who lived on the outskirts of Gallup, was six years older and on the rebound from a bad relationship with a man. Jaime barely took time for her studies, instead focusing all her energy on her new lover. They dated for two months, and by the third month, Jaime thought Cora was the woman for her. Then the old boyfriend came back into the picture, and Jaime was unceremoniously dumped. She nearly flunked the electrician test. Somehow she managed to pull it together enough to pass, and for a long time after that, she devoted all of her attention to her studies and to her job working as a clerk in the town hardware store.

When she became an apprentice electrician, she went to work for a commercial building company eager to hire women and minorities in order to get government contracts. For four years, she was the only woman on the work crew, but she learned a lot from the men. A few were condescending or, even worse, mildly harassing, but the vast majority treated her with respect once they found out she worked hard and knew her stuff. During that time, the only place to go to meet other lesbians was the bar, and all too often, the women she dated liked partying better than they liked Jaime.

All I ever wanted was a relationship like my grandparents' bond. All those decades of respect and caring, the value of which her grandparents had passed on to her, were what she wanted for herself. Someone she could rely on. Somebody who loved her for

who and how she was. A woman who made her laugh. She had
always thought that one day she would find her special someone,
but lately, she was starting to believe the words of the song Kip
had sung the week before: *It's A Heartache*. Still, she did not want
to believe that there was no such thing as the real deal—but at the
moment, it seemed it might be true.

With a sinking feeling in her chest, she slid out of the booth
and moved slowly through the gradually darkening bus. She
crawled up into her bunk, turned on the light, and sat cross-legged
to scan her long shelf of paperbacks. Nothing struck her fancy. *I
need escape. I don't want to think all these serious thoughts, and I
sure don't want to be blue.* She wished she had stopped at a local
bookstore, but she hadn't. She settled back, nestling her head
against her pillow, then pulled the string for the light and plunged
the bunk into near-darkness. She laced her fingers together over
her belly and crossed her feet at the ankles. If she lay very still and
breathed deeply, perhaps she could drift off to sleep. She stayed
like that for several minutes, but instead of feeling relaxed, she
grew claustrophobic and agitated. She lifted her hand and pressed
the Indiglo button on her watch. *Well, no wonder I don't feel
tired. It's all of 8:30.* She sat up, crawled down to the end of the
bunk, and fished around until she came up with a sweatshirt and
her wallet, which she tucked into the cargo pocket of her shorts.
She put on some socks, exited the bunk, stopped to slip her shoes
on, and made her way out of the bus.

After locking up, she looked over at the hotel, imagining
Lacey Leigh entertaining Derrick Daniels. The big white and silver boot went 'round and 'round. She shook her head and pressed
her eyes tightly shut, then sighed, determined to think of something else. She wondered what Drew was up to, or Kip, or Eric,
and whether anyone was jamming tonight. Maybe she would ask
Kip to go to the Planetarium show at ten. She pulled on the sweatshirt, and as she poked her head through, she realized she didn't
feel like going out to a show after all. *I'm thirsty. What I really
need is something to drink.*

She headed off into the steadily cooling air toward a conve-
nience store sign. It turned out to be further away than it looked,
but stretching her legs felt good. By the time she walked the five
blocks along the busy street and reached the store, she'd decided
to go see Kip. She bought a six-pack of ginger ale because the
folksinger liked it, two bottles of root beer because it was her
favorite, a jar of salsa, and a giant bag of chips.

Holding all those chilled bottles against her chest made her
shiver with cold, and she was relieved to reach the hotel. But it

was much chillier in the lobby than it had been outdoors. She passed the stairwell and went around to the other side to hurry down the hallway toward room 111. The further she moved away from the front desk, the warmer it got. She came to the correct brown door and knocked softly, then stood holding the bag against her, but she didn't hear anything. She knocked again, this time louder, and she thought she heard a noise inside. Suddenly, the door was pulled open, and Kip stood in front of her in a long white robe, blinking sleepy eyes. Her light brown hair was flat on one side and standing on end on the other side, as though she had fallen asleep with it wet.

"Sorry," Jaime said. "I didn't mean to wake you." She shifted the bag and looked at her watch. "I'm ten minutes early."

Kip smiled. "It wouldn't matter if you'd come in ten minutes or two hours. I totally crashed." She held the door open. "C'mon in."

Jaime looked around the room. Two queen-sized beds, a giant TV, one table with four padded chairs, a small kitchenette including a sink, microwave, and mini-fridge, and all with attractive Southwestern décor. "Nice room."

Kip yawned and looked around her. "Seems okay. What have you got there?"

"Oh." She stepped over to the tiny counter in the kitchenette area. "I brought some soda. Chips and salsa, too."

"Great idea. I can't believe I'm hungry after that big meal, but I am." She yawned again. "Let me put on some real clothes, and I'll be right back."

While Kip was in the bathroom, Jaime unpacked the grocery bag and put six of the eight bottles of soda pop in the fridge. She folded up the bag and slid it out of the way partly under the microwave, then picked up the ice bucket. Kip came out of the bathroom barefoot and dressed in a t-shirt and cotton drawstring pants. Jaime asked, "Hey, you want ice and a glass for your ginger ale?"

"You brought ginger ale? Way to go. It's my favorite."

Jaime let out a laugh. "By now I've pretty much figured that out."

"That's nice of you to notice, and yes, I'd like ice."

"Okay, be right back."

She went out and down the hall until she found the alcove with the ice machine, filled up the bucket, and returned to Kip's room. The folksinger was waiting for her, her brown head poking out and partly visible. She opened the door and let Jaime in. "You know, you could have told me when you first got here that I looked like Medusa." She shut the door behind her.

Jaime shrugged. "Everybody looks like that when they first wake up," she said as she moved back into the room and set the ice bucket on the counter.

"I bet Lacey Leigh doesn't."

Jaime stiffened. She tried to hide the alarm she felt, but it was clear that the other woman had noticed.

Kip put her hand on Jaime's forearm and said, "Oh, I'm sorry. I meant that as a compliment to her. I'm sorry, Jaime. It came out sounding catty."

"No problem. I didn't take it that way. It's something else." Kip looked so sympathetic and kind that Jaime felt her face burn with shame and embarrassment. "Look, you know I have—had—a thing for her, so I guess I'm not—well, I haven't figured out, you know, my feelings and all." Hastily she said, "Can I pour you some ginger ale?"

"Sure." Kip turned and walked across the room, then sat at the large, circular table.

Jaime took the other woman's slow stroll across the room as a polite way of letting her recover, and for that she was grateful. She filled two glasses with ice, tucked one ale and one root beer against her body with her left arm, and carried the whole lot over to the table. "Here you go."

"Thanks. You want to play some cards? Or are we just killing time before going to that ten o'clock show?"

Jaime lowered herself into a chair directly across from Kip. "If you don't mind, I'd rather hang out here and not go to the Planetarium."

Kip nodded. "Me, too. I think all that flint and quarry walking wore me out, but I'm not so worn out that I couldn't whip your butt at Phase 10." She reached for her canvas bag, which was on the bed she hadn't slept on.

"Oh, yeah? Bring it on, sister. We'll see who does the ass whupping around here."

FOUR BOTTLES OF pop, half a bag of chips, and most of the salsa later, they finished the tenth hand of the card game, and Kip was crowing. "I do believe we have a winner, ladies and gentlemen! And it isn't the Gentlewoman from Gallup."

"Yeah, yeah," Jaime said, shaking her head and rolling her eyes. "I just had some bad luck. I swear, you must cheat. How in the heck do you get all those deuces?"

"Simply put, it's skill, my friend." She gathered up all the cards into a pile in the middle as Jaime attempted to stick a corn chip into the salsa jar. "Not to be confused with your skill at tapping the last dregs of sauce out of the jar."

"I just want to know how we can have so little salsa left and so many chips."

Kip grinned. "You didn't expect we'd both hit the sauce so heavy, huh? We're drunk on salsa. Next time, buy two." She rose and stepped over to the television stand, picked up the remote, and turned on the TV. "When's the last time you watched something?" She heard the sound of cheering from a sports contest.

"I'm not sure."

"I haven't had access since I left home."

"Well, actually, Kip, you do. There's a TV in the bus."

"What?" She hit the mute button on the remote and turned to face Jaime. "Where?"

"You know where the fridge is built into the back wall?" Kip nodded. "Haven't you ever noticed that line in the middle of the wood about four feet to the right?"

"Not really."

"I'll show you. You press there, and it recesses. Then it can be slid to the right, and there's a TV in there. But it gets horseshit reception. Wes won't pay extra for the satellite system."

"All this time, and I never noticed that." Kip walked between the two beds carrying the remote and hopped backwards onto the bed where she had slept earlier. "Look! It's WNBA. I love basketball. Let's watch a while. Make yourself comfy, why don't you?"

Jaime rose and walked between the two beds carrying her glass of root beer, which she set on the table between the two beds. She pulled the pillows out from under the spread on the tidily made bed, stacked them up against the headboard, then settled onto the hard mattress with her shoe-clad feet hanging off the side of the bed. "I haven't watched any sports for quite a while. I don't think I've seen any of these women's games."

"Oh, this is *great*. It's the Houston Comets playing my Minnesota Lynx. This is way cool—and look! Minnesota is leading!"

"I had no idea you Yankees were so competitive."

Kip looked over with a smirk on her face. "You need to get with the program, girl. Just because you didn't play sports in high school doesn't mean you can't get competitive now in your advanced years."

"How do you know I didn't play sports?"

"You told me, you space cadet."

"I don't remember that."

"Well, it was a few weeks ago. You weren't lying, were you?"

"No. I just don't remember talking about it."

"I asked you in passing one day when you were setting up a stage."

"Oh. My mind was probably preoccupied." She turned onto her side, pushed her elbow into the pillow, and leaned her head into her left hand. "I didn't play any sports after intramurals in middle school. I was too busy working in my grandparents' store."

Kip turned down the sound on the TV until she could only faintly hear cheering and the announcer's comments. "What kind of store?"

"A general store. We sold everything from groceries and hardware to cookware and kites."

Kip turned off the TV and set the remote on the bedside table. She shifted from her seated position and crawled toward the foot of the bed to lie on her side so that she was diagonally across from Jaime and could see her better. "Did you like working there—and is the store still in business?"

Jaime shook her head slowly. "When my grandfather got cancer, he sold the store, and the people who bought it ran it into the ground. We always felt bad about that." She readjusted the pillow, kicked off her shoes and moved her legs to a more comfortable, bent position. "Did you work in high school?"

"Not like in a regular job. In summer school, I tutored young kids in math, and I babysat quite a bit during the school year and made some decent money there. I was very busy with music. My parents, being professors, didn't think it was good for Keith or me to be out working on school nights. I was lucky they could afford to help me through college."

"My grandfather's dying wish was for me to go to school. He left me all his savings for that."

"What about your grandmother?" Jaime looked at her blankly. "Why didn't he leave her the savings?"

"Ah, *comprendo*. She died before he did."

"Oh! I'm sorry. I didn't understand that."

Jaime nodded and let out a sigh. "Here he was the one with cancer, and unexpectedly, she had a stroke and died. He held on for three more months, but then he died, too. So I honored his wishes and went to electrician school."

"How long ago was this?"

Jaime gave her a sad smile. "Long time. Ages ago."

"So you were quite young, then?"

"I was. Twenty-two."

"And your parents? They were both still alive?"

Jaime paused a moment, then decided to speak freely. She

told Kip that she didn't know who her father was and that her mother never recovered from the deaths of her parents. They went back and forth, discussing their respective families—who they'd lost, who was still alive, where they'd lived and gone to school. Before long, Jaime looked over at the clock radio, surprised to see it was eleven p.m. "It's getting late. Should I be heading out?"

Kip made a goofy face. "No. This is early. *Late* seems to be three a.m. around here." Jaime nodded and sighed. They continued to talk for the better part of an hour and through more ginger ale and root beer. After a while, Kip got up to use the restroom, and when she returned, Jaime was asleep. She lay on her back against the pillows, legs crossed at the ankles, thumbs hooked in her front pockets and her hands in fists. In the dim light, her brown skin looked even tanner in contrast with her light-colored shirt. Kip sat on the edge of her bed and studied the sleeping woman. She didn't know what it was about her, but every day Kip liked Jaime more and more. *Like? Hell, I way more than like her.* She suppressed a laugh and went back into the bathroom to brush her teeth and change into sleep shorts and top.

On the way back out, she turned up the A/C, then reached into her canvas bag and found a paperback she had been reading. She pulled back the spread on her bed and got under the sheet and blanket. For the next hour, she read, and then she grew tired. Jaime had hardly stirred the entire time. Putting the bookmark back in the book, she set it on the bedside table, and reached for the light.

The last thing she saw before she turned off the lamp was a relaxed tan face with a wisp of a smile curled up at the edges.

Chapter
Eleven

THE FIRST THING Kip smelled when she woke up many hours later was coffee. It smelled like mint Girl Scout cookies. *Mint coffee?* She opened her eyes and saw her plastic room key and a large paper cup on the bedside table with a post-it note stuck to it that read: *You can reheat this in the microwave if it gets cold before you wake up.*

The folksinger sat up and swung her legs over the side of the bed, yawning all the while. The room was empty, and the bathroom door was open. She had apparently slept through Jaime's departure, return, and second retreat. Rubbing her eyes, she yawned again, then picked up the warm coffee cup. She popped the plastic top off, found the liquid still hot, and took a sip, all the while wondering how Jaime had managed not to wake her.

She carried the coffee with her into the bathroom and got ready to face the day.

WES SLATER, SWEATING in jeans and a short-sleeved cotton shirt, stood smoking at the front of Lacey Leigh's tour bus, which was parked a dozen feet behind the opening act's bus. From across the lot, she saw him squint her way. "Where the *hell* have you been?" he hollered. When she was a couple strides away, he said in a calmer voice, "Jaime, it's not like you to be cattin' around." He took a last deep drag on his Marlboro, then dropped the butt and ground it out with the heel of his cowboy boot.

"I'm not on duty 24 hours a day, boss." She took a sip of coffee from the container she held.

"Yeah, yeah, yeah. I know. It's just—I was lookin' for ya."

She stopped a few feet in front of him. "Well, here I am."

"No. Not now. At about five a.m."

Frowning, she asked, "Why?"

He shook his head and reached in the breast pocket of his light blue shirt to pull out his pack of cigarettes. Tapping one out, he pressed his lips together and fixed her with a baleful stare. Gesturing with the hand holding the cigarette, he said, "She's gone overboard, Jaime. Shelley can't control her. Candy can't control her. *Goddammit*, I can't control her, and I'm the *God*-blessed tour manager!"

Jaime assumed he was talking about Lacey Leigh and nodded. This had happened before. "What happened?"

He pulled a gold lighter from his pants pocket, lit the cigarette, and sucked in. Smoke came out of his nose and mouth as he said, "Buck and Candy went out drinking with her. They took the new asshole with 'em, and Lacey Leigh got stinkin' drunk. Got in an argument with some woman and ended up getting bitch-slapped. Lucky that Buck was there to pull Lacey off the woman. Shit, we're lucky the cops didn't come and arrest her." He gave a toss of his head toward the hotel. "Lacey was sick early this morning, and now she's up there sleeping it off. I have no idea what kind of shape she'll be in for tonight."

Jaime felt a trickle of sweat drip down her back. The sun beat on her, and her teeth felt grimy, as though they were coated with something gluey. She couldn't wait to brush. "I'll see what I can do to help, Wes."

"I'd appreciate that."

"What room is she in?"

"Let her sleep it off until late afternoon, will ya? She's in the suite, 204."

"You got it, boss."

She turned away and went up into the bus to get cleaned up and brush her teeth. She had to be ready by noon when Eric, Tom and Lance were meeting her with the semi trucks to head over to the concert site and load in. She let out a sigh. *Oh, boy. Not again. This doesn't look good at all.*

AROUND SIX P.M., Kip hunted for Drew backstage. "Hey, buddy," she said. "You plan on playing with me again tonight?"

He tipped his black hat back, put a hand on either hip, and gave her an exasperated look. "You think I'd desert you at the last minute? Unless I give y'all some warning, the whole lot of you can expect me, Kip."

"Okay, okay," she said with a smile on her face. "Just checking. I don't want to make assumptions..."

"Don't be silly. I'm enjoying it."

"All right then. I have a totally new song I'm playing." She handed him a page of musical notation. "Starts in my regular key, but I switch up on the last verse."

He pored over it for about a minute and handed it back. "Okay. Got it. Verse, verse, two choruses, verse?"

She nodded. "Actually after the chorus, you can have as many bars as you like for a bridge. Want four? Eight?"

"I'm a humble man. I think four will suffice."

She grinned and handed him the sheet of paper. "Show it to the other guys, will you? I can't wait to hear what you do with this. It's a mellow song, but I can hear a lot of nice lead lines."

Just then, Lacey Leigh came through the side door, flanked by Shelley and Candy, and followed by Jaime who carried a satchel, a makeup bag, and Lacey's black leather Coach purse. The tiny woman wore spandex tights, high heels, and a wrinkled blouse, and she wobbled as she walked. Without her backup singers steadying her, Kip wondered if she would even be able to walk. Though Lacey Leigh wore dark glasses, Kip could see something was wrong with her face. The four women went the opposite direction, away from Kip and Drew, and toward the dressing rooms.

She felt a touch on her elbow, and Eric came up behind her. She met his eyes and he let out a whistle. "Oh, boy," Eric said. "Trouble tonight."

Shaking his head slowly, Drew said. "Damn. She don't look so good."

With concern in her voice, Kip said, "No, that doesn't bode well. She really looks ill."

Drew nodded. "Her hair looks like a cat's been suckin' on it, and even worse, a truck done run over her face."

Kip laughed and rolled her eyes. "Tell me how you really feel, Drew."

"Oh, no, oh no no no. You got me all wrong, Kip. I'm not making fun of her. We all've seen this before. She's hit a bender, and we'll be lucky if Jaime and the girls can patch her up enough to perform."

The folksinger gave him a perplexed look. "You're not kidding, huh?"

"No, ma'am. I am not. She's got herself a little problem, right, Eric?"

"Yeah." He turned to Drew. "If she ever makes it onstage, I'm recording everything tonight. Just wanted you to know. I gotta run now." He wheeled around and went back toward the stage.

Drew said, "I can predict right now, it's goin' to be one helluva night, kiddo."

Kip exhaled, but before she could ask any more questions, the side door slammed open and Wes Slater stomped through it, muttering and cursing. He gave them a quick glance, then turned and stalked off toward the dressing rooms. The two musicians gave one another wide-eyed looks. "Well, I guess you're right," Kip said. "This ought to be an interesting night."

KIP STOOD IN the wings, overly warm in her concert outfit. The concert hall was well ventilated everywhere, it seemed, except behind the maroon curtain where she, Tom, and the loaders stood sweating. She could hear Lance twanging a guitar string somewhere behind her. He had taken her guitar as a favor to her to tune it with his strobe device. For some reason, tonight she was more rattled than usual. She had no idea if Lacey Leigh was going to appear, and for the first time on the tour, Kip actually had a friend in the audience. She hoped her own performance would go well. To add to her nervousness, she heard the clump-clump of cowboy boots behind her and assumed it was Wes. She looked back over her shoulder, and even in the dim light, she saw he was making a beeline for her.

"Kip." He drew near, stepped up next to her, and put one arm across her shoulders. His voice was deep, almost a growl. "Kip, honey, I need a favor tonight. I need you to stretch it out." He spoke quickly and in a low rasp, then coughed. "Can you do that? I'm desperate. I'll make it worth your while."

She shrugged. "Sure, Wes. How long do you want me on?"

He put his free hand to his chin and cupped it. "Well, at least an hour. Uh, maybe more than an hour. C'mon..." He guided her over toward Tom, who was speaking into the comm phone to Eric out on the main soundboard. "Tom. Listen up."

The sound tech said, "I'll get back to you, Eric," cradled the receiver, and gave the tour promoter his full attention.

"We're working on Lacey. Kip here is going to string it out. I'll send word—or come up myself—at T minus about five minutes. You signal Kip when she can do her last song. We'll give the audience a fifteen minute intermission after, and then I'm praying Lacey comes on. Got that?"

"Yes, sir."

Wes squeezed Kip's shoulder and removed his arm. He inclined his head, tipping it to the side a bit. "I appreciate your team spirit, Kip. I'll make it right with you."

She smiled. "Don't worry, Wes. I'll enjoy the extra time onstage, and I've got more than enough material to last a couple hours."

His eyes widened. "Oh, God. I sure hope it doesn't come to that." He turned on his heel and nearly ran out of the wings, leaving her and Tom looking at one another.

"Does this happen often?" she asked.

"Often enough."

"Things have been going so well, though."

Tom nodded. "Yeah, she's fine when she's *with* someone, if you know what I mean. She was on the upswing with Gary when you first arrived." He stepped closer and lowered his voice. "We usually get a good month in, and then she goes wacko and it's two or three weeks of hell. Get ready for a rocky ride. If you thought she was a bitch before, wait'll you see what happens now. My advice? Stay the hell out of her way." He grabbed the earpieces of his headset, one in each hand, pulled them apart, and put the headset on. "You've got about three minutes now." She nodded and turned, her stomach churning.

Lance stood behind her holding the guitar, and beyond him, Drew, Davis, and Buck stood. Jaime was nowhere in sight. Lance handed Isabelle to her. "You're all set, Kip. It sounds great."

"Thanks, my good man. I owe you."

He shook his head. "No, you don't. Just go out there and knock 'em dead."

"For you, that's exactly what I'll do." She put the strap over her head, got it settled around her neck and shoulder, situated the guitar, and took a deep breath. Now she felt better. It was amazing how calming Isabelle was. There was something about being able to hold the guitar in front of her—like a protective shield. She never liked to sing unless she held a guitar. In fact, Kip didn't think she *could* sing without a guitar in her hands. *Now that's an amusing thought: folksinger unable to sing without guitar crutch.* She laughed quietly at herself, and then perked up when Tom snapped his fingers and gave the five count. The house music went off, the stage curtain opened, and Eric's voice introduced her.

Marcus came through the stage door into the darkened wings, and Davis gave him a nod. "Thanks, Marc," Davis whispered. The four band members came toward Kip, and Davis reached out a hand to touch her elbow. "Kip, we don't know if Jaime can join us tonight. I asked Marcus to come up and play keyboards, that is, if you don't mind."

She broke out in a wide grin. "What? Are you kidding? Of course I don't mind. Thanks, Marcus. You're a sweetie."

"Psssssssst."

The noise came from behind her, and she turned. Tom gave

her a frantic high sign, so Kip strolled out onstage. The crowd settled, and she heard scattered applause. At the mic she said, "Hel-
LOH, Amarillo!" She leaned down and plugged in Isabelle, then
returned to the microphone. "Hope you're all staying cool in here.
As my good friend, Drew Michael Donovan here on lead guitar
says, it's so hot the hens are laying hard-boiled eggs." A murmur
of mirth rippled through the audience. "In honor of the Texas
heat, here's a special tune for you."

Drew played the lead-in to the golden oldie, "Heat Wave,"
and Marcus added some honky-tonk piano. The sound of the
band's instruments melded as though they'd played together forever, and she felt that old familiar shiver of excitement as she
opened her mouth to sing. Her eyes searched the front rows until
she located Minnie Logan. The tiny black-haired woman sat, rapt,
her mouth slightly open as though she were drinking in the sound.
With a heart full of joy, Kip smiled down into the fourth row, and
sang to her new friend.

JAIME SAT ON the couch in the dark dressing room stroking
the blonde head in her lap. Lacey Leigh lay on her side, facing
outward, with her head resting on Jaime's right thigh.

"Oh, God, Jaime, it hurts." The petite woman, curled in a
fetal position, brought both hands to her head. She tensed and
shook.

Jaime leaned down and whispered softly, "I know, sweetie. I
know it does. Just relax. It will pass. Try to relax, Lace." She
knew from experience that once Lacey drifted off to sleep, when
she woke she'd feel better.

"I need a little hair-of-the-dog."

"No, you don't. Not quite yet."

"Grrrr..." Lacey's whole body tensed, and she pressed her
feet against the opposite arm of the couch. "Shit, it hurts!"

The seated woman pulled at the stiff form, rearranging limbs
until Lacey sat across her lap with her head lolling over Jaime's
left arm. She cradled her like a small child, and with her right
hand stroked the blonde's forehead. "C'mon, Lacey honey, relax.
The headache will pass." Jaime rocked slightly and crooned a
tuneless lullaby, and after a minute, the figure across her lap suddenly went limp. She continued to rock and hum for a few minutes
until the door to the hall opened a crack. Wes Slater slipped in
and shut the door, plunging the room into darkness once again.

Blindly, he shuffled the three steps to the couch, and Jaime
felt him stop in front of her. He patted around until he smacked

her hand, which stuck out over the end of the couch arm. "How's she doing?" he whispered.

"She's out."

"Kip just went on. We have—at most—maybe ninety minutes. What do you think?"

Jaime's eyes had adjusted to the darkness, and by the faint sliver of light shining in from under and around the door, she could see Wes's outline. "I don't know. Maybe—if she can wake up in the next forty-five minutes or so, then it's do-able. Where are the girls?"

"They're set up next door with all her stuff, ready to go the minute she is. Candy got out extra makeup and changes of clothes so Lacey can pick what she wants. Everything is all lined up."

Jaime didn't say anything for a moment, then in a quiet voice, she whispered, "I can't make any promises, Wes."

He hissed, "I just want to know how the *hell* she keeps getting the hard stuff. She's got bottles of Chivas Regal coming out her ears."

Jaime nodded. "The hands and runners will do anything for her. She just smiles, slips them a hundred dollar bill, and they're ready to marry her."

He sighed. "I suppose what's done is done. I'll sit with her 'til she wakes up."

"That's all right. I can stay." She was protective of her charge, and the yearning she felt right behind her breastbone almost hurt.

"No. You go on up and make sure the act is working," he growled. "Check your watch. In thirty minutes, come back down and see how we're doing."

"All right, Wes." His bare arm slid under hers and lifted up the small form. She scooted out from under and got to her feet. She could just barely make out his light blue shirt as he bent to settle the star back on the couch.

He stood and let out another sigh. "Where the hell is that other chair?" She took his arm and guided him to the left 'til he found the overstuffed seat and sank down into it. "Dammit. I want a smoke."

"There's no ventilation in this hole," she answered. "I could stay, you know."

"No, forget it. Get the hell up there. I can't take the stress right now. I need some quiet, so just get out." He didn't say it with anger. His voice was, instead, tired and resigned.

She opened the door a few inches and slid through the small gap, out into the bright light of the hallway, then quietly pulled the door shut behind her. As her eyes adjusted, she moved down the

cement corridor into the loading area. She passed the security
detail by the exit door and gave him a nod. Every step Jaime took,
the music grew louder. She couldn't hear any vocals and didn't
recognize the song until Kip belted out the next verse. Now she
could tell it was a peppy version of Faith Hill's "If My Heart Had
Wings," and it sounded terrific. Buck was going to town on the
drum part, and she could swear she heard piano.

She arrived in the wings and went to stand by Tom and look
out the opening stage left. He gave her a glance, then returned his
concentration to the levels in front of him. She was surprised to
see Marcus on stage. Her eyes swept across the musicians and
came to rest on Kip. The folksinger was playing the rhythm guitar
part with gusto, singing joyfully, her right foot tapping to the
music. She finished the verse and stepped back to focus on her
strumming. Drew reeled off some mean guitar licks, and she
couldn't help it—the music rushed through her, and the worry she
had been feeling lifted. *I don't care if Lacey Leigh never makes it
out here. I could listen to Kip all night.* The song ended, and
breathlessly Kip introduced Marcus, who had never played with
her before, and gave fairly thorough biographical information. He
looked surprised and gratified, bending in a deep bow to the
cheering audience.

Kip said, "Let's do something a little different now. I know
this is an old song, but a lot of you will remember it." She turned
to Drew and mouthed something, and he gave a toss of his head
and turned to holler something to the band. Buck did a count-off,
and they launched into the beginning of "Piece of My Heart."
Drew had a lot of fun with the guitar lead. Kip's voice wasn't
nearly raspy enough to make the song sound like Janis Joplin's
version, but the deep, rich timbre she brought to it sounded every
bit as good to Jaime's ears. She couldn't help but grin. When she
looked over at Tom, he shook his head and shrugged, also smiling.
Jaime turned her attention back to what was happening out
onstage. *Wow, she's in her element. To have that kind of talent—
asombroso—Amazing!*

Jaime crossed her arms and listened to the tortured chorus,
letting the music run through her as the words hit her in the heart.
She felt like Lacey Leigh had stolen a little piece of her own heart,
and she didn't like it...yet she couldn't stop it from happening. She
wished she could be in love with somebody who loved her back
the way she wanted to be loved, somebody like Kip. But she
couldn't forget about Lacey, couldn't shake her grasp.

She looked out at the brown-haired woman. Kip was no
longer playing guitar. She grasped the microphone in both hands,

her guitar held only by the strap against the front of her, singing the last tormented lines of the song, and then the band was winding down to the end.

The crowd went wild. Kip said, "Thank you! Thanks, all of you," into the microphone, but the crowd kept clapping over it.

"She's a good warm-up act," Tom said. "I don't know how she manages it, but she sure•does a nice job working with the mood of the crowd." Jaime nodded and listened while Kip introduced the next song.

"Folks, I have a special friend in the audience tonight, someone who many of you may happen to know. My friend owns the Boot Emporium up a ways..." She heard a scattering of applause and a loud whistle. "...and not so very long ago, she lost someone dear. When my little brother Spencer died a number of years ago, I wrote this song for him. I'd like to dedicate Spencer's song to Minnie and to her son, Eli, who will be missed always. It's called 'Your Eyes.'" She picked a pattern on the guitar while Drew played a simple lead for the quiet ballad. The bass line was quiet, and neither Buck nor Marcus played at all at the beginning.

> *You were here by my side*
> *It really was too short a time*
> *Now you're gone, I can't go on*
> *Back into a normal routine*
>
> *They say that life just marches on*
> *And time will heal the hurt*
> *But all I find myself thinking of is your eyes*
> *And oh, how it hurts*

At the chorus, Buck played soft percussion, and an entire orchestra of strings swelled, synthesized by Marcus at the keyboards.

> *You don't know how much I would like to see you now*
> *You'll never understand what you have seen me through*
> *Only thing I need you to know is though you're gone*
> *I'll always go around*
> *Remembering times we had together*

Then there was a bridge, and Drew's guitar whined a melody in counterpoint to what Kip was picking. To Jaime's ears, it sounded delicate, almost fragile, as though one wrong note would crack the entire arrangement and it would fall to pieces on the floor. But the musicians were pros. Nobody faltered.

Kip sang the chorus again, and then the song changed key before Kip sang the final verse:

And think of how much life we saw in so short a time
Oh, yes, just how much life I saw through your eyes
Your eyes, your eyes,
They will always haunt me

This time, at the end of the song, a sort of stunned silence engulfed the audience. A good four beats passed before the applause started, and it was long and dignified—not the stamping and cheering that a wild song usually provoked, but a strong roar nevertheless. Kip bowed slightly and spent a moment introducing Drew. No matter what, she always introduced her musicians with such respect that Jaime believed the guys would follow her anywhere.

The band jumped right into the next song, and Jaime watched and listened, wishing she could be out there having fun with them. After a while, she glanced at her watch. Thirty-four minutes had passed, and now it was time to get back and check in with Wes. She could only hope Lacey Leigh was coming around.

Backing away from the stage curtain, she headed out of the wings. With each step, the music receded, and her nervousness rose up all over again. The door to Lacey Leigh's dressing room was open, the lights out, so she passed it and tapped on the next door. It opened a crack, and she saw Shelley's long blonde tresses.

"Oh, hi. Come on in." Shelley nervously opened the door, and Jaime surveyed the room, which was smaller than the headliner's dressing room next door. The makeup table and mirror took up the entire back wall. To the right was a couch and across from it sat three padded wood chairs. With four of them in the room—Shelley, Candy, and Jaime on their feet and Lacey sitting on the sofa—the room was crowded.

She looked first at Candy, then Shelley, both of whom wore worried expressions. "Where's Wes?"

Candy said, "He went out for a cigarette."

Jaime nodded and squatted down in front of the couch. Lacey Leigh's eyes were glassy. A bruise on the left side of her cheek was starting to show, and her face appeared yellow-gray. "Lacey. Lace, honey." She patted the tiny woman's leg. "How're you feeling?"

The diva shut her eyes and opened them again, staring vacantly. After a few seconds, she turned her head slightly.

Jaime asked, "How's your head?"

In a gravelly voice, Lacey said, "Feels like shit."

"Still pounding?"

"Not as bad."

Jaime came up from her squatting position and sat on the couch. She reached over and touched Lacey's cheek. "Can you go on tonight?" The diva closed her eyes and let out a breath of air. "Come on, Lace. I need to know one way or the other."

Blue eyes—without the green contacts—popped open, and for the first time, Lacey Leigh's haggard face was animated. "Fuck off. Just fuck off."

Jaime pulled her hand away and upwards toward her own chin. She studied the small woman as she rubbed her lower lip with her forefinger and thumb. Her eyes went up to the two backup singers. "Who has her bag?"

Shelley nodded. "I do."

"Give it to her."

Shelley looked alarmed, but she bent and picked up the leather bag, passed it to Candy, and Candy handed it to Lacey. The diva set it in her lap and struggled to unzip it. Her hands shook so much that she couldn't do it, so Jaime reached over and unzipped it, then watched as Lacey grabbed the neck of the bottle of Chivas Regal to pull it out of the purse. With a sinking heart, Jaime took hold of the cap, using steady fingers to unscrew it. Lacey tipped her head to the mouth of the bottle, and with shaky hands guided the Scotch out of her bag and upwards until the golden fluid sloshed toward her mouth. Jaime watched her take a sip and swallow. Lacey filled her mouth, pursed her lips, and pulled the bottle away. She closed her eyes and went through a series of swallows, releasing the liquid down her throat. She settled into the couch and tipped her head back to relax against the tall cushion.

Jaime stood and turned toward the door. There was no room to pace, nowhere to go, no way to force down the feelings rising inside her. She realized she felt helpless—totally helpless to deal with Lacey's problem. She put a forearm against the painted door and leaned her forehead against it. Tears stung her eyes, but instead of sorrow, she let a bubble of rage surface, and suddenly she was short of breath. Jaime turned around and looked at the tiny woman on the couch. "Why the hell can't you stop this merry-go-round?" she shouted. "Why?" She looked at the bottle cap in her hand, then threw it across the room, feeling ashamed when she saw the shock and fear on the faces of the backup singers.

Lacey Leigh opened her eyes and, with the tip of her pink

tongue, she licked her lips. She took a deep breath and sighed. "It doesn't matter, Jaime." She lifted the bottle to her mouth and took another pull, which she held in her mouth. Her hands were steadier now. She swallowed three times and licked her lips again. "And don't worry. I'll go on. How much time have I got?"

Jaime stood shaking, her hands balled up into fists. In as calm a voice as she could muster, she said, "Maybe forty-five minutes."

Lacey Leigh nodded. "No problem—right, girls?" She looked up at the two blondes, and they hastened to assent. "Shel—let's get this face of mine fixed up." She struggled to her feet, still holding the bottle tightly. Shelley stepped forward and tucked her arm under Lacey's to guide her over to the makeup table.

"Now where's the cap to this thing?" Lacey asked.

Jaime couldn't stand it any longer. She wrenched open the dressing room door and fled down the hall.

Chapter
Twelve

BY TEN THURSDAY morning, Kip was ready to check out. She took her bags down to the front desk, to the silent lobby, and rang the bell to bring a clerk out from the back office. She paid her bill, and then went toward Minnie's storeroom.

After her set the night before, Kip had gone out into the audience and sat with Minnie and her friends. She hadn't watched one of Lacey Leigh's shows for a couple of dates, and knowing all she did now about the younger woman, it was an interesting experience. She was surprised at how energetic the tiny blonde was. Considering her condition two hours earlier, Kip was amazed at how well she moved and sang. The show was spirited and entertaining, and Minnie's eyes shone with excitement through most of it. At the intermission, Kip signed three dozen autographs from enthusiastic fans. In fact, she'd been practically mobbed. Her new friend watched with stars in her eyes, and when they returned for the second set, Minnie had been so happy that it made the folksinger smile.

Now Kip set her things down near the counter of the closed-up shop and went to tap on the storeroom door on the other side of the sales counter. No sound. She tapped once more and paused before coming out from behind the counter to pick up her bags. Just then, the tiny woman came in the hotel's front door, sandals slapping on the tile as she hurried across the lobby.

"Kip! Sorry I'm late," she called out.

The folksinger smiled at the dark-haired woman as she rushed up. "Hey, Minnie."

"I'm so relieved I didn't miss you." She reached out and squeezed Kip's forearm. "I am still riding high after that wonderful show last night. Do you have time that I could treat you to brunch?"

Kip shrugged. "Yeah, I guess I do. We don't leave until noon."

"Oh, that would be so nice."

"I need to take these bags to the bus, and then we could go."

After Kip dropped off her things, they got in Minnie's car and went to a restaurant about a mile away where they had rich, aromatic coffee, waffles with hot syrup, and fresh fruit. All through breakfast, they talked, and Minnie thanked her for dedicating the song to her. "That made me cry, you know. I do not know how you could sing that song. I would have fallen on the stage in tears."

"You're closer to the pain than I am. I've had a lot more years to grow accustomed to my brother's absence. You aren't yet healed from losing Eli."

"That's certainly the truth."

They talked for a little while longer, and exchanged addresses, and Minnie insisted on buying breakfast. She did make one concession and allowed Kip to leave the tip. They headed back to the hotel, and once they arrived at The Lost Spur, the tiny woman got out of the car and came around to hug the folksinger. "I will never forget you, Kip Galvin."

"I won't forget you either. Every time I look at that beaded purse, I'll remember you with pleasure, Minnie." The tiny woman gave her another fierce hug, then got in the car. Kip looked back as she went up into the bus. Minnie waved and drove out of the parking lot, leaving Kip smiling and waving after her from the first stair.

She pulled the door shut and made her way back to her stateroom. The bus was silent, and Jaime's bunk was unoccupied. Kip passed it and unlocked her stateroom. She opened a bag and dumped the clothes on the bed, sorted through what was clean and what was dirty, and put everything in its proper place. She had enjoyed staying in the hotel room, but everything she had with her was in the stateroom, and in a way, bunking right here made more sense. The only thing that would make a major improvement in the bus accommodations would be the inclusion of the whirlpool bathtub. *Now that's one thing I am going to miss!* Kip closed the closet at the foot of the bed and looked around the room. Everything was tidy and organized.

Checking her watch, she lowered herself to the edge of the bed and sat. Half past eleven—a lot of time to kill. For a moment, she thought she might read, but for some reason, her fingers were itching to get hold of Isabelle. She unlocked the music closet in the hall, removed the guitar, and arranged the pillows at the head of her bed so she could lean back, knees up and feet flat on the mattress, and play the guitar. Closing her eyes, Kip strummed, warming up her fingers and hands, then picked a complicated pat-

tern. After a couple minutes of playing around, she leaned to the
side and opened up her side drawer to fish around for pen and
paper. She felt a song coming on.

FOR KIP, THE next few dates, San Antonio, Dallas, and
Tulsa, were lonely. Nothing more exciting than a run to the laundromat occurred. She didn't even see any side-blotched lizards,
though she did keep a close eye out for them. She washed her own
clothes, alone. Jaime came and went from the bus at odd hours,
always attending to Lacey at a moment's notice. Though Kip and
Drew got together twice to practice and jam, a pall of stress
seemed to settle over everyone, both band and crew, and Kip
missed the lightheartedness she had shared with Jaime.

Kip met Drew's parents and brothers in San Antonio, and she
could see why the guitarist had turned out to be such a nice person. He'd been raised by warm and witty people, and Mr. Donovan had even more colloquial sayings than Drew did. Mrs.
Donovan was so clearly proud of her son, and his brothers were
younger versions of Drew. His parents asked her and the twins to
go out with them after the show, and she had spent a couple hours
at a nice steakhouse with the raucous crew.

Now it was the third week of July. They were scheduled for
concerts in Kansas City and Des Moines, and after that, she'd be
home in Minnesota for three days before they played a double
header—matinee and evening performance—in Minneapolis on
the last Sunday of July. Kip very much looked forward to it.
Everything felt unbalanced—the concerts, the travel, even the
informal jams they tried to get in whenever they could. She could
see how much a headliner could affect crew and musicians. Lacey
continued to drink heavily, but she never missed a show.

After leaving Kansas City, they arrived in Des Moines in the
wee hours of the morning. Kip lay in bed, half-asleep, as the bus
pulled up to yet another hotel. The lights of the hotel shone gold
into the stateroom, and Kip wished she had pulled down the
shades before getting in bed earlier. She opened sleepy eyes and
looked across the bus to see droplets of water running down the
windowpanes. *It's raining* was her only thought, and then she
slipped back into slumber.

When she awoke several hours later, it was still raining. She
lay on her side with the pillow bunched up under her head. A
flash of lightning startled her, and Kip sat up. Three seconds later,
she heard rumbling in the distance. A good old-fashioned thunder-
storm mirrored her mood.

She reached into the side drawer and found her cell phone, then spent the next twenty minutes calling around, trying to find someone to talk to back home. Mary wasn't at home or at work. She got Sam and Rubee's answering machine. The phone rang and rang at her parents' house. She contemplated calling her brother, then decided not to. She put the phone away, slid out of bed, and gathered up her showering gear. The curtain to Jaime's bunk was pulled closed, and Kip wasn't sure whether that meant she was there or not. When she finished in the bathroom, she found Jaime sitting at the booth, facing the rear of the bus.

"Hey, you," Kip said. "How's it going?"

The seated woman's hair glistened with moisture, and she held a container of coffee in both hands. "Okay. I got a cup of crummy coffee at the hotel café—got some for you, too, if you dare." She gestured toward another paper container on the table.

Kip turned toward her stateroom. "Thanks. That was nice of you." She dropped her things on the bed and hung her wet towel over the back of one of the chairs in the room, then reversed course and joined Jaime at the booth. She looked exhausted. Her face was not its natural tanned color, but yellowed and blotchy, and there were dark circles under her eyes. "You look whipped."

"I feel whipped. I think I got all of three hours of sleep."

"Why don't you crawl back into the bunk and catch some more Z's?"

Jaime shook her head wearily and looked at her watch. "Eric and the guys are leaving for the concert venue at noon."

"You've got an hour. I could wake you if you like."

"No. I need to eat. I'll come back later and sleep. You want to go over to the café?"

"Yeah, I'm starving."

Kip rounded up a windbreaker, and the two women trooped over to the hotel through the rain. The air was moist and humid, but it wasn't cold at all. The warm rain came down steadily, though, so Kip hustled around mud puddles and entered the hotel, followed by Jaime. They seated themselves in the cheery restaurant, and the folksinger surveyed all the knick-knacks and painted wood wall hangings. "Somebody really went to town decorating this joint."

Jaime raised tired eyes and glanced around, then yawned. "They sure did. It's a little too busy for me."

Kip laughed. "Exactly what I was thinking."

They ordered breakfast, and Kip sat back to study the face before her. Jaime looked out the window. After a moment, she turned her head and met Kip's eyes. "Do you ever feel like the biggest failure on the planet?"

"Uh—well, not too often." Actually, Kip tried not to define herself as such. "Why? You're feeling like a failure?"

Jaime crossed her arms and nodded. "I cannot seem to get Lacey to understand that the drinking is killing her. I don't understand why she doesn't get it. She'll ruin her career. She's destroying her health—wrecking her life."

Kip examined the tired woman before her. Even her black hair looked dull and lifeless. She wondered if she should tell the truth, that Lacey was a mean drunk with problems bigger than any friend or lover could resolve—or should she instead give support and encouragement to Jaime? She opted for the latter. "You're not getting enough rest yourself, my friend. I find that I feel very bleak and hopeless when I'm tired. Go get the concert hall prepped, and come back and sleep. You'll feel a lot less despairing once you've rested."

Jaime nodded. "You're probably right." The waitress brought over their breakfasts, and they sat silently for a couple minutes, concentrating on the food. Jaime put her fork down on her plate. "Every time this happens with Lacey, I swear I won't take it again..." She let out a sigh. "And every time, I just go through it all over."

"Is she showing any signs of coming out of her funk?"

Jaime shook her head. "To be honest, the only thing that does seem to help is when she gets some new man, but Derrick Daniels isn't budging, and she's run through everyone else she can." She frowned. "'Cept you." She let out a mirthless chuckle. "I'd watch my back if I were you."

"Don't worry about me," Kip said. "I can take care of myself." She just *wished* Lacey would confront her. She was pretty sure she could have a field day trashing the diva, but since their first altercations, Lacey had given her a wide berth.

They finished their meals and split the check. Running through the rain to the bus, Kip wondered what in the world she would do for the rest of the day, and tomorrow, too, before the evening concert. She thought she might get out a book, but that would only hold her a few hours. Jaime disappeared into her bunk, and Kip found the paperback she had been reading. She went to the loveseat in the lounge area and settled there. When Jaime left, she bid her farewell and returned to her book. At least an hour passed before she heard a frantic knock on the side of the bus. She rose, her heart beating fast, and saw Drew and Marcus standing outside in the rain. Dropping her book to the seat below her, she leapt forward to open the door and let them in. The two men stumbled up the stairs and stood dripping, with Drew next to the driver's seat and Marcus on the first stair.

"We're going stir-crazy," Drew said. "You wanna take off to the movies with us?"

"Absolutely."

Drew grinned. "Don't you even want to know what we're fixin' to go see?"

"I don't even care if it's James Bond. I'm going stir-crazy myself."

Marcus laughed. "Maybe we ought to find some good X-rated thing, Drew."

Kip rolled her eyes. "There are so many of those in the early afternoon." She stepped back. "Let me get my wallet and windbreaker, and I'm ready."

The keyboardist said, "We'll meet you in the lobby. I called a taxi, and they'll be here in about ten minutes. There's a sixteen screen cineplex nearby."

"All right," Kip said. "That's great."

Once they were dropped off, Kip found not only theaters, but the cineplex was located in a shopping mall complete with department stores, book, CD, and music stores, an instrument shop, and several restaurants. After the movie, which was an intense action-adventure flick, the three of them ate an early supper at an Italian restaurant. Once they'd eaten, the guys headed to the music shop while Kip went off to the CD store. She spent far too much money on four new disks by artists she loved: Kim Richey, Lucy Kaplansky, Dar Williams, and the quirky Cheryl Wheeler. She debated the wisdom of buying books at the bookstore, but they were still two days from reaching Minneapolis. Once she got home, she could refresh her book collection and leave with new volumes she had not yet read. But to tide her over, she purchased one paperback, the first bounty hunter mystery in a series by Janet Evanovich.

A half-hour passed before she made her way down the wide hallways of the mall to the music store, and what she found there amused her to no end. Drew was nowhere to be seen, but Marcus stood at a huge, portable keyboard. A tiny, silver-haired old lady stood at his side, watching. He'd programmed the piano to play percussion and strings while he played melody and chords. Even from across the store, she could hear that the song flowing from his fingertips was "My Favorite Things" from the movie, *The Sound of Music*. The elderly woman smiled with glee as he finished the final chord and wrapped up the song. He looked down at her with a grin on his face. The woman patted his arm and said something Kip couldn't hear, but then she drew closer and heard his answer.

"That was my mom's favorite movie, too, ma'am. Always reminds me of her to play anything Julie Andrews ever sang."

The old lady looked up at Kip when she arrived. "Is this your young man?" the woman asked. "Because if he is, you're mighty lucky."

Kip smiled. "He's something else, isn't he?"

"He surely is," she warbled. She turned and looked up at Marcus again. "Thanks for making an old lady's day."

Marcus said, "My pleasure, ma'am," and she toddled off toward the exit.

Kip gave him an amused smirk. "I've got good news for you, Marcus. Once your big-time touring career is over, there's a lovely job waiting for you at the Happy Haven Retirement Community." He laughed. "Where's Drew?"

He made a gesture back over his shoulder. "Took some spendy guitar off to one of the soundproof rooms."

Kip wandered around the music store for nearly half an hour. She played a Martin guitar with a price tag of three thousand dollars and a four hundred dollar Washburn. She could tell a difference. She thumbed through several books of music, memorizing chords for two songs she liked. Off in the distance, she could hear Marcus playing piano, and after a while, it faded away. She felt a tap on her shoulder, and he stood by her looking at his watch.

"As far as I can tell, Kip, old Drew would play for hours if we let him. How 'bout you and I go drag him out of whatever room he's hiding in?"

She put down the music book. "Good idea."

WHEN KIP RETURNED to the bus, it had finally stopped raining, and dusk was falling. She didn't think Jaime was there, but as she passed down the narrow corridor to her stateroom, something grabbed her shoulder. She let out a shriek and almost dropped the plastic bag containing her book and CDs, then heard a loud cackle. "Geez, Jaime! Is that a nice thing to do?"

The brown hand disappeared behind the bunk curtain, and a laughing face popped out as the curtain was pulled aside. "That was great. Bet you almost fainted."

"Well, I nearly did," she said with mock indignation. "You should be ashamed of yourself." She leaned back against the doorframe for the bathroom. "Haven't you got anything better to do than attack innocent bystanders?"

"You, *mi amiga*, are anything but innocent."

Kip surveyed the face before her. Jaime looked a lot better than she had eight hours earlier. The folksinger pushed off the wall behind her and moved toward the door to her stateroom, which she unlocked as she said, "So, you get a few hours sleep and you wake up hell-on-wheels."

"Hey! I think I could beat you in Phase 10, too. That's how refreshed I feel."

Kip pushed her door open and laughed. "Don't count on it. I can easily rise to that challenge."

THE DES MOINES concert went without incident, and afterwards, the jam on Kip's bus was spirited. Jaime was missing, though. Lacey had asked her to ride in her bus. Buck and Candy, however, had joined the happy crew, and Kip had a great time singing songs while Candy harmonized.

The music wound down around three a.m., and the folksinger headed back to her stateroom. She was still awake at four a.m., sitting up on her bed, leaning against the wall, when they passed the turn-offs to Burnsville. She felt her heart lift. *I'm home. We're nearly there.* The thought of her own house, her own bed, her own coffee cups and books and roomy home made her smile. She fell asleep and dreamt of gardening in the back yard with Bren's dog, Ozzy, by her side.

KIP HAD THREE days of quiet time, apart from the band and crew, and three nights of fun and laughter with her friends. She woke up alone in her silent house and made elaborate meals whenever she chose. Her tour check for June had arrived in the mail earlier in the month, and she deposited it in the bank. She also laundered every item of clothing, both clean and dirty, and organized all her gear. She watched old videos, changed the oil in her truck, and slept long and late. Friends and family called on the phone and dropped by to visit. By the time Sunday rolled around, she felt much more refreshed.

But all was not well when she arrived at the State Theater for sound checks at eleven a.m. They were scheduled for a two p.m. matinee and a seven p.m. evening show, but the first thing she heard from Tom, was that he didn't know whether the matinee would go on. Lacey had tied one on the night before, and Wes, Jaime, and the girls were struggling to get her out of the hotel and to the concert venue.

Oh, great. Just great. Kip found an employee to guide her down the elevator to her dressing room, and she put her guitar and canvas bag next to the hard sofa and sank down. *I've got everyone I know coming to this concert, and I don't even know if it's going to fly.* The whole thing was particularly vexing because her family members were all coming to the matinee show, while many of her friends planned to attend the evening performance. Both were sold out, so if the matinee didn't occur, her family was out-of-luck.

She sat and thought about how the tour hadn't gone anything like she expected. Since mid-June, she'd played seventeen dates. She was still scheduled to play Madison, Aurora, Indianapolis, Louisville, Knoxville, Memphis, Tupelo, and Birmingham. Eight more concerts. She wondered if she could do it. Her mind wanted to stick by her commitment, but her heart was balking. Lacey's constant threat of unreliability as well as her own mixed emotions about Jaime had been taking a toll on her emotional balance. Being back in her familiar home for the last three days with friends and family around had further hammered that home.

She heard a tap on the door, and a dark head poked in. "Hey, Kip."

The folksinger gave a toss of her head. "What's the story?"

Jaime entered the room and shut the door, then came to sit sideways on the couch, one leg up and her right arm along the back. "I don't know what's going to happen, to tell you the truth. If we start late, and if you stretch it out, that'll help, but even if we limp through the matinee, that just means she has to go on tonight without much break."

Kip shook her head. "This is getting old."

"Tell me about it." Jaime looked down. "I'm real sorry, Kip. It's not supposed to be like this, and, well, I'm especially sorry since this is your hometown and all."

Kip turned to face her and pulled her legs up onto the couch. She put her arm along the back of the couch and gripped Jaime's forearm. "You know what? It's not your fault, Jaime. Lacey is the one with the problem."

Jaime nodded. "I know. I know. I keep trying to talk some sense into her head—"

"Forget it, Jaime." She shook her head vigorously. "She needs help. More help than you or I can give her."

An expression of pain flashed across Jaime's face, and for a moment Kip thought the other woman was going to burst into tears. The folksinger squeezed her forearm and let go, dropping her hand down onto the couch cushion. Jaime took a deep breath and rose. "I'll go check on her," she said in a resigned voice. "I'll try my best to get her ready." With head down, she stepped toward the door, and when she glanced back, Kip thought she looked more defeated than she had ever seen her. The door opened and then clicked shut quietly behind her.

"Well, shit," Kip said aloud. She got up and slid her guitar out of the way. She paced from the makeup table to the door, four steps one way, four steps back. She tried to breathe evenly and to think, wanting as much clarity as was possible. *I have two shows to do today, and that's what I need to concentrate on.* Instead, she couldn't stop worrying about Jaime. The strain of dealing with Lacey Leigh was obviously draining her, and the poor woman was an emotional wreck. An irrational anger boiled up, and her stomach churned in response and suddenly she was angry with Lacey Leigh. *She's a selfish, mean-spirited, stupid, inconsiderate, self-indulgent, egotistical ass! Damn her!* Kip stomped over to the couch and sat on the edge, elbows on her knees and face in hands. *Please, please, please God—don't let me do what I want to do.* She closed her eyes, took a deep breath, and silently counted backward from twenty. When she reached zero, she felt exactly the same way, only out-of-breath.

Okay. Okay, I have no control here. And there's nothing I can do, short of murder. She let out a nervous laugh. *Oh, that would be great. I can see the headlines: Opening Act Chokes Headliner to Death.* Shaking her head, she scooted back and sat against the couch, her arms crossed over her chest. *What's the worst that could happen?* She thought about the question. The worst thing that could happen was that the matinee wouldn't fly, but her experience was that the night show might actually happen. They'd only done two other double performances, way back in the beginning in Mitchell, South Dakota and Provo, Utah. Of course, back then Gary had still been around, and Lacey Leigh hadn't taken on her current drunken persona. It occurred to her that a real team player would offer herself up to Lacey Leigh, and this thought caused her to laugh humorlessly. *Yeah, right. She is* definitely *not my type!*

Now she was filled with nervous energy, so she stood up and opened the dressing room door. She looked back at her guitar and bag, unsure if they were safe. She decided to take no chances and went back for them. She hadn't walked more than twenty paces out of the dressing room before she ran into Buck and Drew and overheard Buck saying, "This is totally fucked, Drew-meister." He stopped speaking abruptly when he caught sight of Kip. "Hey, there," he said. "Have you heard the news?"

Kip shook her head. Drew said, "It's not so bad. Don't listen to Buck. He'd worry the warts off a frog. We're just starting late, 'bout half an hour or so."

She set her guitar down there in the hallway. "I can handle that."

"Y'all want to go get a beer or soda?" Drew asked. "There's a nightclub out on the main drag."

"That's the last thing we need," Kip said, "alcohol. Besides, I've got this guitar to haul around."

Drew said, "Bucky here'll take it up to Lance, won't ya, Buck?" The big man nodded.

Kip said, "The hell with it. We probably won't even go on at two. I may as well hand it over to Lance."

"I don't know," Buck said. "Candy says she thinks we'll go on, so gimme the guitar."

"All right," Kip said. "Let's get away from here for an hour. I know a sweet little café just three blocks down. They've got some micro-brews and really good sandwiches."

"Good girl," Drew said. "I knew you'd see the light." He bent, grabbed her guitar, and handed it to Buck who disappeared for a couple minutes. When he returned, the three of them made their way through the maze of corridors to the side door.

LACEY LEIGH SURPRISED everyone—especially the folk-singer. The diva appeared shortly after Drew, Buck, and Kip returned from the café and stated that "the show must go on." Kip saw her come through the stage door with Candy, Shelley, and Jaime, and it was clear the tiny woman was shaky on her feet. Wes brought up the rear, and as soon as he caught sight of Kip, he hurried over. He smelled of smoke, and his light blue suit pants were rumpled, but the thick white shirt he wore was clean and well pressed. He ran one hand through oily hair and said, "Kip, she's going to give it a run for the money. I'm telling Eric's crew you're going on about ten minutes late. Then I want you to stretch it out fifteen—maybe twenty—minutes. With an intermission after your set, Lacey'll have a good forty-five minutes extra to get her shit together. Does that work for you?"

Wordlessly, she nodded. He stepped past her, heading for the wings, then stopped and turned back. "Thanks, Kip. We'll make it through. Don't worry."

He hurried away, and Kip met Drew's eyes. She didn't say anything. He nodded. "I know, girl, I know. It's maddening."

"I'm going to go see Lance about my guitar, then hide out in the bus. You two are still playing with me, right?"

Drew let out a snort, and Buck laughed. "Of course," the guitarist said. "*We* would never let you down."

Kip had time, on the way down to the dressing room, to pull herself together. She realized she was letting all of it get to her far too much. She thought she should be excited, anticipating performing for all the people she knew, but the fun of it had been leeched away. That made her angry, but she decided to spend some time alone in her dressing room to get into the right frame of mind.

When Lance knocked on her door some time later to give her the five-minute warning, she was much more composed. The matinee went without a hitch, and Lacey Leigh emerged on time after a twenty-minute intermission. They had decided to reverse her sets so that her first songs were ballad heavy. She wore a full-length gown and flats for the first set, and by the time the second set opened, she was capable of wearing high heels, tight pants, and a sexy shirt. Standing in the wings, Kip thought the star shone fairly brightly, considering her physical condition. Later that night, for the second show, Lacey Leigh was her old self, and the celebration in the green room was raucous.

The next morning, the reviews for the concert were complimentary, and the write-up about Kip's performance, at the end, was warm and full of praise.

Chapter
Thirteen

IT HAD BEEN ten days since the Minneapolis performances, and the concert dates in Madison, Aurora, and Indianapolis had gone without a hitch. Lacey Leigh was apparently curtailing her drinking, but Kip took care to avoid the diva whenever possible. She had no desire to be victimized by the star's slashing comments. Jaime was busy keeping close tabs on Lacey Leigh and had spent little time with the folksinger. Kip missed her.

After the night's concert, Kip retired to her stateroom, wanting rest and time alone much more than jam time with the guys. The bus rumbled down the interstate, heading toward Louisville, Kentucky. It wasn't far from the outskirts of Indianapolis to the new hotel, and even with a stop to gas up the buses and semi, it wouldn't be much longer before they arrived. Kip was still awake, sitting on her bed while playing guitar. A melody had stubbornly stayed with her for days, so now she was taking the opportunity to mark down the notes. No words had come to mind—yet—but the melody was insistent.

When the bus exited the highway, Kip put her guitar in its case on the floor, then knelt on the bed and peeped out the window into the darkness of Louisville. With fingertips on the metal edge around the window, she peered into the glittery night. She had come to the conclusion that cities all looked basically the same at night: bright lights, dark streets, fast food signs, and not much more of note. She saw a large sign for Liberty Street and tightened her grip on the window edge as the bus turned. Kip let go and lay back down on the bed, considering whether she should get a room or not. Being at home in St. Paul had spoiled her. More than anything, she missed having a bathtub to soak in. As far as she was concerned, once this tour was over, she was never going to go anywhere again if she had to shower in a stall the size of a casket.

Kip smiled at the thought and wished someone was with her

to share the joke. The bus jerked to a halt, and after a moment, the engine sounds trailed off and the vibrations from it died away. Lying on her back, her body tingled, and even though everything around her was motionless, she had the strange sensation that the bus was still rolling along. She listened to a series of bumps and clicks and the low murmur of voices. In a few minutes, all was silent, and she assumed the band had departed, leaving her alone on the bus. She rose and closed up her guitar case, but left it lying on the floor, then went to open her stateroom door. She was startled to come face-to-face with Jaime, as the taller woman moved soundlessly down the corridor.

"Oh! Hi, Kip." The lean woman grabbed a handle and stuck a foot into the recessed ladder rung and pulled herself up into her bunk. Kip went into the bathroom, and when she came out, Jaime said, "Hey, stranger. How's it going?"

Kip paused in the hallway. "Okay. You?"

"Other than being tired as hell, I'm fine. Actually, better than fine." One leg emerged from the bunk, and her foot found the inset step. Once she cleared the bunk enclosure, she dropped down to the floor. The bus moved ever-so-slightly, and then the two women stood inches apart in the darkened corridor. Kip longed to reach out and touch Jaime. She felt so tired that she would have liked to put her head on the other woman's lean shoulder, but something caused her to hold back.

"Things are looking up, Kip." In the half-light shining in from the windows in the lounge area, she saw Jaime smile, then reach up and run her right hand through her thick hair. "She wants me back, Kip. Lacey's agreed to lay off the heavy drinking, and she wants to try again."

Kip opened her mouth, but no sound emerged. She was glad the corridor was so narrow because she only had to reach a few inches before her hand came in contact with the wall, and she pushed against it to steady herself. She couldn't bring herself to congratulate Jaime. Instead, she choked out a question. "Is this a good thing for you?"

Jaime nodded. She reached up into the bunk and pulled down a stack of clothes. "I think so. I think she's come to her senses—finally."

"Well, if you're happy, how can I help but be happy for you." She said it as a statement, not a question.

"Yes, *mi amiga,* isn't it just great?"

Kip muttered something that, to her own ears, came out as "Oh, yeah," but Jaime didn't seem to notice her befuddlement. She tucked the clothing under one arm against her chest, then reached out with the other hand to pat Kip on the shoulder.

"Thanks, Kip, for being such a good friend. You've been great." She stepped back, out of the corridor and into the area. "Gotta run. Sleep well."

The black-haired woman turned, and Kip watched her amble to the front of the bus, then out the door. As if in a daze, the folksinger turned around and made her way into her stateroom. Her toe hit the edge of the guitar case, and she very nearly fell, but caught herself before going over. Heart beating fast, she stood for a moment, eyes closed, then turned and closed her stateroom door. She pulled all the blinds and stood a moment longer, her mind not registering anything. After a moment, she bent and, with gentle hands, she opened the hasps on the black case and took Isabelle out. She cradled the warm wood to her chest, feeling Isabelle's fragile solidity and the cool strings at her fingertips. Sitting on the edge of the bed, she let a flood of feeling wash over her. She wanted to cry, but she did not. Instead, she closed her eyes and listened for the tune. The notes came to her, and little by little, so did the words.

JAIME WAS JUBILANT as she strode across the well-lit parking lot toward the hotel. The moist night air was very still, but off in the distance she could hear the whoosh of traffic. Despite her well-earned fatigue, she was happy and still had a small measure of energy left. The last time she'd been to Kentucky two years earlier, the band had played in Lexington. The tour had a four-day layover, and she and Lacey had gone to the Kentucky Horse Park. She remembered how impressed she had been with the bronze sculpture of the great racehorse, Man O' War, and how much she had enjoyed the Museum. She loved horses—their sleekness, power, and endurance. Right now she felt like a young colt, herself, as though she could bolt across the parking lot at Kentucky Derby speed. She couldn't help but smile.

She entered the hotel and took the elevator to the top floor. Lacey Leigh was in the finest suite the hotel had to offer, and Jaime looked forward to spending the next few hours with her. She tapped on the door, but got no response. She tapped again. Still nothing. Feeling concern, she knocked loudly, and this time the door was opened. Lacey's face was blotchy, and her eyes filled with tears.

"Hey, what's the matter?" Lacey shook her head, turned away, and walked slowly across the room to the window, leaving Jaime to close the door and hasten after her. She set her change of clothes on the couch, moved across the room, and put her hands gently on the tiny woman's shoulders from behind. Lacey fit exactly under her chin, and fine blonde hair tickled the soft skin of her neck. "It's okay, Lace. You're gonna be okay." She wrapped her arms around the singer, and the figure in her arms relaxed back against her.

"I want a drink." It came out as a soft whisper.

"I know you do. I know."

"I'm trying, Jaime. Really. I am."

Jaime sighed and tightened her grip. She looked out the window, across the dark city dotted with streetlamps and security lights. "It'll be okay, Lace. Really. I'll take care of you. Come with me to bed."

The tiny woman allowed herself to be led away from the window and into the bedroom. She slipped out of her shirt and slacks, and got into bed wearing only her bra and panties. Jaime kicked off her sandals and stripped down to her underwear and t-shirt. She crawled in next to Lacey and lay close to the weeping woman for the rest of the short night, holding her tenderly, until at last they fell asleep.

Chapter
Fourteen

SOME TIME LATER, during what little was left of the night, Kip came to a decision. She finished writing the words to her song and put Isabelle away. She lay on top of the red and gold comforter and considered her choice from every angle. Once she was over the shock of Jaime's announcement, it was easier to see her way clearly. No matter which way she turned it over in her mind, she kept coming to the same conclusion.

The sun was shining brightly into the stateroom when Kip opened her eyes next. She opened the drawer beside the bed and hunted around until she found her wristwatch. 10:33. *I may have gotten four hours of sleep. Big woo.* She swung her legs over the side of the bed, amused to see she still wore socks. She peeled them off to find the elastic had left angry red marks around her ankles.

Holding the socks, she rose and went to stand beside the small table and chairs at the bus window. She looked out across the parking lot and saw they were parked at the Derby-Shire Motel, and wondered if that was an attempt to capitalize on both horse racing and the *Lord of the Rings* hobbit locale. The thought made her smile. *See, you haven't totally lost your sense of humor.* She went over to the closet at the foot of the bed and dropped the socks into the plastic bucket inside, then shut the door. Frowning, she sat on the edge of the bed, pulled her cell phone out of the still-open drawer, and dialed Information. Once she had the number, she called the Derby-Shire Motel and asked for Wes Slater.

She knew she had awakened him when he answered. His voice was thick with sleep, but when she asked to meet him later in the day, he didn't hesitate to assent. They agreed to meet at noon at the restaurant, which, at this hotel, shared a parking lot but was not part of the hotel structure.

She had lots of time to kill, but plenty of tidying and organizing to do, so she set to work.

WES SLATER SCOWLED, shook his head, and crossed his arms. "Fuck-a-duck, Kip! Why you want to do this now?" He sat across from her in the swanky restaurant, and from four feet away she could see how bloodshot his eyes were. "This *fuckin'* tour is going to be the death of me. What do I have to do? Pay you more? Tell me."

She shook her head slowly, then took a sip of her water. This was harder than she expected. "No, Wes. It's not about money. I truly do not feel well. I should have stayed behind in the Twin Cities, but I didn't want to disappoint you."

"Dammit, Kip. You can't just—" He uncrossed his arms, put his elbows on the table, and leaned his head into his hands. After a moment, he looked up. "Do me one favor, please..." Just then, the waitress came with the coffee pot, and he waved her away. He turned his attention back to the folksinger. "Gimme *one* more concert. Please, Kip. If you'll perform tomorrow night, then I have four full days before Knoxville to get someone the hell out here to replace you."

She gave a nod. It was the least she could do, though the thought of staying any longer made her stomach clench up. She felt she owed it to him.

He slid out of the booth and pulled a money clip from his pocket and peeled off two bills. "All right then. One more for the gipper." He gave her a grim smile and dropped the money on the table. "You can go ahead and tell the band."

She didn't look forward to that, but she rationalized by telling herself she would have had only five more concert dates, and they would have needed a new warm-up act then, anyway.

The waitress returned to the table. "Something wrong with the coffee, ma'am?"

"No," Kip said. "He decided not to eat, but I would like to order."

KIP FINISHED BRUNCH and called the airlines to get a reservation for the day after tomorrow. Once that was straightened around, she called for a taxi and asked the cabbie to take her to a nearby mall. She stayed away from the hotel for the rest of the day, keeping busy with shopping for going-away presents. She couldn't bring herself to buy anything for Lacey, and despite the fact that the mall had a lot of different stores, as hard as she tried, nothing seemed right for Jaime. She felt uncomfortable about buying something for her anyway, so she gave up and purchased mementos for the guys in the band, then went to a bookstore and bought herself some magazines.

She ate dinner and read *People* magazine at a place called Spaghetti Warehouse, and then she was tired. The lack of sleep from the night before finally caught up with her, and all she wanted to do was lie down. Dragging a number of packages, she took a cab back to the Derby-Shire parking lot and let herself in to the tour bus. When she entered, she found a note on the table, weighted down with a cool bottle of root beer. The bottle had been chilled earlier, as evidenced by a wet ring around the corner of the paper. She pulled the note out from under the bottle and took it and all her parcels into her stateroom.

The room already looked less lived in. Her bags were mostly packed, and she had dusted, swept, and wiped down the surfaces. She'd stripped the bed, expecting to leave today, but now that she had another day and a half, she wished she hadn't been so thorough.

She put the bags down, mostly on the chairs and under the table, and pulled the shades, then stood in the middle of the claustrophobic stateroom to read the note.

Kip—Wes told me you are done after tomorrow night. He said you aren't feeling well. Please call me at the hotel when you get in. Jaime

Kip let out a long breath. No way did she want to talk to Jaime. And yet, if she didn't call her, would the other woman show up here at the bus to talk in person? That was even less acceptable than a phone conversation, so she dug through her canvas bag, and came up with her cell phone. Since she hadn't written it down, she was forced to call Information again to get the Derby-Shire's number. When they put her through, the phone was answered by Lacey Leigh. Through gritted teeth, Kip asked for Jaime.

"Sure, Kip, just a minute. By the way, sorry to hear you're moving on. I've enjoyed working with you."

"Oh." For a moment she didn't know what to say, but then her manners kicked in. "Thanks, Lacey. I wish you luck on the rest of the tour."

"Um hmm, here's Jaime."

A smooth voice came over the line, and Kip felt a pang of sorrow. "Hey, Kip, you doin' all right?"

"Yeah, I'm okay." She didn't elaborate, and there was a long pause.

"You sure you don't need anything?"

"No, Jaime. I'll be fine. I'm totally whipped, though, so I'm just going to hit the hay and try to rest up for tomorrow's show."

"Okay, good idea. If you need anything, just give a ring up here."

"Thanks. See you tomorrow."

She hung up, feeling lonely and bleak. *She got what she wanted, didn't she? Shouldn't I feel happy for Jaime?* It was hard to feel happy for someone else while feeling so miserable herself. She tossed the cell phone in her bag and got ready for bed.

KIP WAS MUCH better rested in the morning, and she felt stronger. *Resolute. That's what I need to be—a tough, mean bitch.* The thought brought a smile to her face. She might be resolute, but she didn't think she could ever be a mean bitch.

In the early afternoon, she decided to kill time reading another bounty hunter mystery. She was sitting in the loveseat with her feet curled under her, laughing at the character's amusing predicament, when the string of visits began. One by one, the guys from the band appeared. First Drew, then the twins, then Buck and Candy. Lance, Todd, and Eric squeezed in, and even Derrick Daniels poked his head in and wished her well, but he didn't stay. Little time passed before Drew had his guitar out, and Kip went to get hers. Before she knew it, they'd been jamming non-stop for over two hours, and it was now after five p.m.

"People," she said, "is it my imagination, or do we have a show to get ready for?"

Eric looked at his watch. "Damn, you're right." He got up from the leather recliner and stepped around Lance, who was sitting on the floor, leaning against the metal pole behind the driver's seat. "I better get going on the sound checks." He gave a toss of his head, and Tom and Lance got up. "We'll see you over there."

Grinning with contentment, she looked at the relaxed faces around her. She couldn't tell who it was, but someone wore aftershave, and she liked the smell of it. She felt relaxed for the first time in days, and she didn't want that feeling to end. "You know what? You guys are the best—you, too, Candy. How 'bout we go over to the restaurant? I'll buy."

There was universal agreement that dinner was a good idea, but later, when it came time to pay the bill, Buck and Drew fought over it and agreed to split it. In the end, Kip never got the chance to buy at all.

ERIC AND JAIME stood behind the front-of-house sound-board, which was located on a raised platform on the main floor. Earlier, one of the monitors stage right stopped working properly and Jaime had already fixed it, but now they were getting strange feedback from the house PA.

"We've got precious little time to get this fixed, kiddo," he said.

"Probably something weird with the balanced lines to the mics." She slid behind him and traipsed down the stairs to the stage to pull herself up over the edge. It took her awhile to find the cable that was bad, but as soon as she replaced it with a balanced wire that led from a backup microphone, the hum stopped.

"Way to go," Eric shouted. Standing in the middle of the stage, she bent at the waist, executing a full bow. They spent time checking and double-checking everything again, and when they found it all to their satisfaction, Jaime jumped down from the stage and hiked back up to the sound desk. Eric said, "We're set. We're ready."

"And none too soon." She looked over his shoulder, and he turned. The head house usher came toward them to let them know the doors would open in ten minutes, then hurried off.

Eric inserted a tape of music, and Shania Twain's voice started up in mid-song. He adjusted the levels and turned to Jaime. "It's a shame Kip's leaving. She's been a great warm-up act. I've enjoyed having her along, haven't you?"

"Yes. I'm going to miss her."

"I dread finding out who her replacement will be." He smiled. "If the person is nice, Lacey Leigh will run 'em off. If they're not nice, it'll be a pain to work with 'em."

Jaime didn't answer. She brushed some dirt off the top of her hand. "Guess I better wash up and get changed. Back in a bit." She made her way backstage to the corridor leading to the dressing rooms. The opening act's room was open and dark, so Kip hadn't arrived yet. The green door of the headliner's dressing room was closed. A gold star, at eye level, sparkled with glitter, but when Jaime got closer, she saw that much of the glitter had fallen off, and the star looked shabby and old. She tapped on the door, hard pressed to understand why she was feeling so unsettled. Lacey had limited her drinking, and nobody had come to tell Jaime of any problems. She didn't think the diva could have gotten drunk in the two short hours they'd been apart. Still, she felt nervous.

The door opened, and Shelley welcomed her in. Lacey sat at the dressing room table, while Candy rolled her long blonde hair in curlers. Jaime moved across the narrow room and rearranged her tool belt so she could sit on the edge of a hard wooden chair behind and to the right of the makeup table. "It's a big crowd tonight—over four thousand."

Lacey Leigh smiled. She looked sheepish, and it was then Jaime noticed, near the mirror, the stubby glass half-filled with amber-colored liquid. "One hundred or four thousand, it's going to be a terrific concert tonight."

Candy patted the tiny woman on the back. "That's the way to look at it." She grabbed a pink curler and rolled up another lock of hair.

Jaime said, "The hall has good acoustics, and everything is on schedule. Kip will do her regular short set, and you're on right after intermission." She rose and stepped nearer to Lacey, close enough for the tiny woman to reach her hand to the side and pat her on the thigh.

"Don't worry, Jaime. We're way ahead of schedule. I'm going up to listen to Kip, I think, if we have time."

"Okay." Jaime met Lacey Leigh's eyes in the mirror, then turned to go. She would have liked to lean down and kiss her—even just on the forehead—but she knew Lacey would hate it. Jaime made her way through the door and out to the bus, which was parked inside a gated area to the left of the stage door. She showed the guard her backstage pass, and he let her by.

She was two steps into the bus when she heard the sound of a voice singing. For a moment, she thought it was a radio, then realized she heard water running and Kip's voice coming from behind the closed bathroom door. She unhooked her tool belt, set it on the seat of the booth, and moved through the lounge area and down the narrow corridor until she stood in the doorway of the stateroom. Isabelle lay on the red coverlet. The gleaming blonde-colored guitar was beautiful, and suddenly she was itching to play an instrument. It had been days—maybe over a week—since she had jammed with anybody, and other than playing the honky-tonk fiddle solo at the last concert in Indianapolis, she hadn't played her guitar or violin since. She couldn't begin to remember the last time she picked up her mandolin.

The water shut off in the bathroom, and she hastened to hoist herself up into her bunk. Whistling, she sat in the shadows, and when Kip opened the door, she didn't surprise her.

"Jaime?"

"None other than."

"I didn't know you were in here."

"Just arrived." She heard Kip shuffle into the stateroom, and in a louder voice, she said, "Everything's right on schedule, even Lacey."

"That's very good to hear."

"It's a real good crowd tonight."

"As usual."

In short order, Jaime had changed into the ubiquitous black outfit: dark leather boots, jeans, and an open-necked shirt topped off with a cowboy hat. As an afterthought, she crawled back up into the bunk and rooted through her wooden box until she found the necklace Emma had given her. She fumbled with the catch, but managed to get it on, then descended again. The stateroom door was still open. "I'm going over now." She looked at her watch. "You're not due for about ten more minutes. I'll come back, okay?"

"No. I'm ready now."

Jaime watched as Kip picked up the guitar and looked around the room as though afraid of forgetting something, then followed her out and locked up. They made their way through the bus, and Jaime stepped down and out. She turned to watch the folksinger come down the steps and met the pleasant gray eyes. A feeling of regret came to her, and she realized she hadn't been a very good friend to Kip at all. And now it was too late. She wanted to say something, but she didn't know what it would be. Instead, she asked, "Ready?"

"Ready as I'll ever be."

She reached for Kip's arm and escorted her into the hall as she had so many times before.

THE WARM-UP SET started out well, and Kip felt her voice was strong. Of course the performance didn't have the freewheeling abandon she'd experienced earlier while playing with everyone in the bus, but it was still enjoyable.

Tom gave her a high sign at the end of a song, and she knew she had time enough for only one more. She had to make a split second decision, before the applause died down, about what song to go with last—something tried and true? *Aw, hell. Who cares? Nobody cares about my act. They're here to see Lacey, so I'll do whatever I want.* As the applause tapered off, she leaned away from the mic and turned to Drew. "That new one I played earlier today. Okay?"

He gave her a nod and turned to Buck as she spoke into the microphone. "Hey, you've been a great audience. Let me leave you with one final song."

She began a rhythmic pick, and after two bars, Drew's guitar came in with a melodic lead. Davis added a bass line, and Buck played light percussion for the peppy song. She closed her eyes, swallowed, and launched into the first verse.

Sweet, sticky summer day
Something better came along and took you away
And I can hardly hide my happiness for you
Baby, I can hardly believe it's true

Long bitter lonely night
And I'm drinkin' here alone with all my might
Tall Sammy thinks I'm ready for a fall
Good old Rubee's waiting when I lose it all

Go ahead, I know you love her
Go ahead, I'll find another
Rain keeps pouring down
And baby's nowhere to be found

She hadn't expected to feel emotional, but she did, and she fought back a rising feeling of panic as she and Drew worked their way through the bridge. She was grateful for the chance to compose herself, and her voice was still strong when she sang the next verse.

Ain't too far down to low
You're leavin', you just don't know when to go
And maybe long ago sweet Mary she was right
A couple years ago but surely not tonight

Go ahead, I know you love her
Go ahead, I'll find another
The rain keeps pouring down
And baby's nowhere to be found

Go ahead, I know you love her
Go ahead, I'll find another
Go ahead, I'm happy for you
Go ahead, I'll still adore you

Go ahead, I know you love her...

Her voice cracked on the last note, and the bitterness she felt rose up and threatened to make her cry. She was thankful that the guys were backing her up, that they easily covered the fact that her fingers, usually so sure, faltered for a moment. She let them carry the last few bars of the song. As they wound it down, all the air went out of her, and she couldn't have spoken if she'd wanted to. *That's my last song. The last song of the last night of the last tour I ever plan to go on.*

A part of her was glad, even though she knew another part of her was already grieving. The guys brought the song to a close, and the applause was enthusiastic. She bowed and waved, gestured toward her band, and headed for the wings, forcing back the tears flooding her eyes. She caught sight of a dark presence in the shadows to the left of the curtain, but she didn't look that way. She focused on fighting the tears and took a deep breath. Clutching Isabelle in an iron grip, she strode toward the door, with purpose. Just before she reached it, someone grabbed her arm, and pulled her to a stop. Kip glanced back, expecting Jaime—or maybe Tom or Lance—but instead, it was Lacey Leigh.

"I want that song," the blonde star hissed as she leaned in close. Her face was flushed and she smelled strongly of alcohol. She gave Kip a wide smile and raised her eyebrows while rubbing the taller woman's forearm. "C'mon now, hon. Wes'll talk with you. I want that song. What's it called?"

"'Go.'" The word came out flat.

"Now, Kip, I know we've had a difference or two in the past, but—"

"No. That's the name of the song. 'Go.'"

"Ohhh, I see. Well, what do you think? I've *gotta* have that song. Can I?"

Kip tugged her arm away and got a better grip on her guitar. She stared at Lacey for a moment, then said, "You couldn't pay me enough money for that song." She spun around and went through the doorway, ignoring the protests and pleas she heard behind her, and kept walking through the spartan, concrete room, which led to the outer stage door. Though she could hear the house music and a background din from the concert hall, her footsteps echoed. With each step, she felt more and more disconnected from this world she'd been living in for the past two months. She reached the back door, and a security guy asked her if she needed an escort. Kip shook her head and passed through into the waning light outside. She made her way to the two black buses in the gated area. Despite the fact that one bus had red lettering and the other pink, the words *Lacey Leigh Jaxon* scripted on both appeared as though written in blood.

She keyed the combination into the door and opened the bus, locked it behind her, and took the stairs up inside. With tender care, she put Isabelle away. She chose not to cry—not that she didn't want to. It took a lot of energy to hold back the tears, but she didn't want to be a mess for the rest of the evening. Once she had recovered enough to face everyone, she would return to the concert. She had thanks to share and little gifts to give, and she wanted to seem in good spirits on her last night with them. Even if she was not.

JAIME STOOD ONSTAGE, holding the Welling, ready for her part. She closed her eyes and listened to Lacey's sultry voice as she crooned the honky-tonk song. Even after all this time, Jaime still wasn't sure what the song was actually called. When it came out on the next album, she'd probably learn then.

She pulled the bow across the strings and tried to concentrate on the song but instead felt distracted. Her heart beat far faster than was normal, and she wished she weren't onstage at all. She made every effort to focus, and when the fiddle part faded out, she expelled a big breath of relief. Jaime set the Welling on the stand and stood still, waiting for the spotlight to shift so she could slip through the curtain. Her thoughts went to Kip. She knew her well enough now to realize something was seriously wrong, but the folksinger hadn't offered an explanation, and Jaime didn't feel it was her business to pry, however much she wanted to. She hoped she would get a chance to talk with her in the morning, maybe have breakfast with her.

Lacey strutted stage right, and the spot went with her, so Jaime backed up and found the curtain seam. She stepped through and worked her way around to the wings to stand next to Tom. He gave her a thumbs up and turned back to his levels. The air-conditioning was on overdrive, and she shivered as she stood watching the show with her arms crossed.

Lacey wrapped up the honky-tonk song, and the place exploded in applause. Tonight she was completely in her element and seemed to be enjoying the performance more than she had in ages. *Not being totally loaded might have something to do with that.* Jaime felt someone at her elbow, and when she looked to her right, Wes stood there, cross-armed and nodding. He leaned down and whispered, "She's back on track, huh?"

Jaime nodded. "Excellent performance so far. She's really up."

"Thank God."

As the cheering and clapping died down, Lacey said, "Thanks, everyone. What a *great* crowd y'all are. Did I tell you I've always loved Louisville?" This statement was met with more stamping and cheers. She grinned out at the audience, her light-colored pantsuit sparkling in the bright lights. "Isn't it nice when you love something? And don't you think you should admit when you do? Here's a brand new song I just wrote, and guess what? You're the very first crowd ever to hear it. It's called 'It's Always to You.'"

The song was a mellow ballad, and for once, Lacey Leigh wasn't lying. Jaime had never heard this song before. It began with Derrick Daniels' simple strum on the acoustic rhythm guitar, then somewhere in the background, Marcus added synthesized strings and something sounding like wind chimes. Lacey's voice, so vibrant and strong, hummed for a moment, and then she sang:

I go out, spend so much time, with so many other guys
But when I need someone to understand me
It's not to them I run
It's always to you, you know just what to do
You always ease my pain, tell me how to live again

My love for you is sad
You are the best friend that I've had
And when you hold me tight
Love me with all your might
I know you love me, too

Shocked, Jaime stood on the sidelines, trying to figure out to whom Lacey was singing. The diva had never, ever, told her she loved her, and surely she wouldn't do such a thing in front of four thousand strangers. But the more she listened, the more she wondered if Lacey was, indeed, singing to her.

All I really need is you, can't you see and understand
And I don't know what to do
Come touch me and take my hand...
It's always to you, you know just what to do
It's always to you, who I come running to
It's only to you, I give my love to
It's always to you...there's no one else but you.

The song was simple, without much accompaniment, and it highlighted the clear, even tone of the star's voice. Jaime didn't know when the band had had time to work out the orchestration with Lacey Leigh, but knowing Drew's crew, they were winging it with little or no notice. This made her all the more respectful of the band. Eric was probably going crazy trying to keep everything equalized and balanced. First, Kip's unexpected song, and now Lacey's. At least the sound engineer was used to Kip jumping around, but Lacey usually did a pre-arranged set. This was something different, and with a sense of elation, Jaime thought maybe the young woman was finally getting her act together.

The song ended to thunderous applause, and without a break, the band jumped right into the intro for one of Lacey's biggest hits, "Mama Was Right (I Hate to Admit)." Smiling, Jaime turned toward Wes, but instead of the tour manager standing next to her, it was Kip looking rather stunned. Gray eyes met hers, then flicked away, and suddenly, Jaime had the strong urge to take the folksinger into her arms and hug her tight. She cocked her head to the side and tried to figure out what the hell was going on inside her, but the music was loud, her heart was pounding, and everything was too confusing. She turned away, back to the stage, and when she joined the audience in clapping for when "Mama Was Right," Kip was gone.

JAIME ROSE EARLY, leaving Lacey Leigh lying curled up in a ball on the far side of the bed. The singer had been jubilant for at least an hour after the concert, but she crashed hard once they made it back to the room, and she wasn't stirring now.

After a short shower, Jaime dressed. She stopped to drink a few swigs of root beer from a bottle in the fridge, then returned it. Her toothpaste clashed with the soda, and she went off to the elevator with a strange taste in her mouth.

She headed out to the bus and unlocked it. The air-conditioning was off, and it was twenty degrees warmer inside than outside. *Uh-oh. Kip must be roasting.* She cut through the lounge area and headed toward the open stateroom door. "Hey, Kip."

The stateroom door was open with the keys stuck in the lock, and the room itself was completely empty, save for a stack of linens at the foot of the bed. "What the hell?"

She pulled the door shut, locked it, and put the keys in her pocket. With second thoughts, she took the keys out again, found the smallest one, and fitted it into the hall closet lock and opened it to find only her own guitar case, the mandolin, and the violin case. Isabelle was gone.

Sweating in the heat, she shut and locked the cupboard and

hastened to get out of the bus. When she jumped out onto the blacktop, she saw a movement behind the semi, which was parked beyond the tour buses. She stalked over to find Drew watching Eric wheel his cycle down the ramp.

"What are you guys doing?" she asked in an angry voice.

Eric skidded to a stop at the bottom of the ramp. "Drew is borrowing my bike. Don't worry. We didn't touch yours."

"I want to know what happened to Kip."

"She's gone, Jaime," Eric said. "Taxi picked her up a little while ago." He put the kickstand down, and let go of the cycle.

"I thought I was taking her to the airport. Why didn't someone come get me?" Jaime glanced angrily back and forth between Eric and Drew, both of whom looked away, clearly uncomfortable.

Drew stubbed the toe of his tennis shoe into the hard-packed dirt. "Uh...well..."

She put her hands on her hips. "Okay, you guys have really ticked me off. You had to have known I would want to see her before she left. For cripesake!" She gave Eric a particularly sour look.

Eric cleared his throat. "She didn't *want* to say goodbye, Jaime. She wanted to leave the way she did, so we respected her wishes."

Jaime's hands dropped from her sides, and she stepped back, a frown on her face. "I—I don't understand."

Eric shrugged, shaking his head. "That's the way she wanted it."

Her face hard and accusing, she said, "I don't believe either of you. You're just being...being—errrr—assholes!" She turned on her heel and started to walk away.

"Oh, come on," Drew called out. "Wasn't our fault. I don't expect she could face you, Jaime."

She stopped, spun around and came back toward them. "That doesn't make any sense, Drew."

He crossed his arms over his tight t-shirt. "Sure it does. Has it occurred to you that seeing you was hurting her?"

She took two steps forward, hesitantly. "I don't have the slightest idea in hell what you're talking about."

"Jaime," Eric said softly as he reached out to touch her arm, "she was in love with you."

She heard the words, but they didn't sink in properly. "What?" She felt the blood rush to her face, and suddenly didn't know where to put her hands.

Drew scuffed the side of his shoe along the ground, not looking at her. "She cared a lot about you, I think, and the business with Lacey was—well, probably uncomfortable."

"No. You guys are wrong. She said she was happy for me."

The guitarist shook his head and gave her a wan smile. "Jesus H. Christ, Jaime! You're as bad as a man." Eric elbowed the slim man. "Cut it out, Eric. Let me explain it. She may as well hear." He turned his gaze back to Jaime. "Did you pay the tiniest amount of attention to her the last few days?"

"Uh, no...not really. Lacey's needed me."

"Yeah, I'll bet." Drew's voice was mocking. "Did you listen at all to that final song she sang last night?"

She crossed her arms and narrowed her eyes at him. "What's your point? Are you trying to say her early departure is my fault?'

Drew shook his head, and he let out a breath as though he was giving in. "Whatever. But this was what she wanted, and we honored her request. You can figure it out yourself. Eric, I'll be right back. I have to go round up my wallet." He turned to go, then stopped abruptly. With his profile to her, he cocked his head to the side and turned to meet her eyes. "That last song she sang— that was about you, Jaime. I think she does want you to be happy, but—well, anyway, it's none of my business."

She looked accusingly at Eric as Drew walked away. "I suppose you're on his side?"

Eric shrugged. "As far as I can tell, kiddo, there aren't any sides here. We've got a new concert site to leave for tomorrow morning and no opening act until we get to Knoxville. I guess we better all focus on getting adjusted to the new and quit worrying about the old."

Jaime spun on her heel and walked across the parking lot, kicking rocks and fuming. It was true she hadn't paid close attention to anything or anybody this last week or so, but watching Lacey had kept her occupied. That irritated her, but at the same time, she still couldn't believe her good fortune that Lacey Leigh had finally come to her senses. The little star had been sweet and loving for the last several days, and even though Jaime was angry right now, for the first time in a long while, she also felt a glimmer of hope.

KIP WATCHED THROUGH the tiny oval window next to her seat on the plane. All the vegetation below was green and bright in the rays of the late afternoon sun. She gazed down at the Mississippi where the Minnesota River merged with it and thought how odd it was that she could actually see the difference in the two bodies of water. The Mississippi was dark blue—almost black—but where the Minnesota met it, the other river contrasted as dark brown.

The plane seemed to be circling the airport, and sure enough, the captain came over the intercom to report that there was a slight landing delay. She sat back in her seat and thought about whether she was happy the tour was over for her—or not. For a few giddy days earlier in the month, she had actually considered calling the school district and either asking for a leave of absence or out-and-out quitting. *I am so glad I didn't do that! What a disaster that would have been.* She thought about the fact that other than money, she had little to show for any of the fast-paced and crazy events of the last eight weeks. She had written some new songs, that was true. She had undeveloped photos in a disposable camera and a lot of memories, but no tapes of performances and no feeling of triumph or satisfaction. Instead, she felt defeated. *Shit, I'm coming home exactly the same way I left...and I'd had such high hopes.* Tears came to her eyes, so she blinked them away and peered out the window again. Now the plane began descending for real.

As they touched down and the engines raced, she couldn't help but wonder what it was about her that deserved to be abandoned. She had never, not in 37 years, broken up with someone else. Every single girlfriend she'd ever loved had left her, and the two women she had lived with had dumped her, too. Though she struggled not to think this way, it was hard not to feel like a giant failure when she considered the budding relationship with Jaime. *I think I've learned my lesson. I need to be much, much more careful with my heart.*

The airplane taxied along the runway and took a wide, sweeping left turn. Kip turned away from the window and sat thinking, her fists clenched in her lap. The chorus to one of her songs rose up in her mind, melody and all:

Yes, I have had a lot of life
But not enough to quit living
I'm just looking for a fifty-fifty chance t
To do some real taking and giving...

She sat waiting for the plane to come to a stop, and when it did, she realized that she did want someone who would take *and* give—not just take. *Somebody who'll be honest with me. That's what I want. Somebody who'll meet me halfway. Do I believe there's such a thing? I guess that's the million dollar question. If I can't have that, then the hell with it. I can live alone. I've done it for well over a year, and I can keep on doing it.*

It took some time for the plane to clear out. When the man next to her finally rose and moved off down the aisle, she reached up into the overhead bin and took down her two canvas bags, both of which, like her heart, were considerably heavier than when she departed from Minnesota two months earlier.

Chapter
Fifteen

THE SUN BEAT down upon Jaime, the stagehands, and the techs as they loaded in the equipment. Despite the bandshell over the stage, it came in at just the wrong angle, and Jaime actually felt a sunburn on her shoulders. She finished splicing wiring from an amp tower to the electrical box at the outdoor Double T Arena in Marietta, Georgia. The venue seated eight thousand easy, and they had a nearly sold out house for the Labor Day concert, partly due to the success of a video Lacey Leigh had shot two months earlier. Press requests were on the upswing, and *Entertainment Tonight* was supposed to send a crew to film them. Wes Slater was also in negotiations with the hosts of the top talk shows, and Lacey might even get a chance to go on *Oprah*.

Jaime worked swiftly to help Tom get the amp towers set up. The arena contained little more than a bare stage with inadequate PA speakers in the ceiling, so there was a lot of equipment to install. In order to prepare for this concert, it had already taken a full day of labor by Eric, Lance, Tom, and a whole parade of hands. They still had several hours of work left before the stage and sound system were ready. Tomorrow, after the concert, it would take another half day to tear it all down.

Sweat dripped down her back, and she pulled out a pale yellow bandana to mop her forehead and neck. The cloth reminded her of the time Kip borrowed her pale blue bandana. She had forgotten all about the loan, but the day after Kip quit the tour, Jaime left Lacey's hotel room, went out to the bus, and crawled up in her bunk. Sitting on her pillow, she found the beautiful beaded purse that Minnie Logan had given Kip, and inside it was the blue bandana. Jaime turned the purse inside out looking for a note, but there hadn't been one.

Tom, bare-chested and sweating, shook his head. "I gotta go out to the semi—again. We need more wire." She gave him a nod, following him as far as the stage right wings in order to get out of the burning hot sun. She stood under cover wiping her neck and forehead with the bandana, then backed up to a plastic chair off to the side. She sat and let her weariness register. Leaning forward, she put her elbows on her knees and her head in her hands.

The last three nights had been hell. Actually, the last three *weeks* had been hell. She hadn't defined them as such because Lacey Leigh had kept saying how sorry she was. But since Sunday, the diva had ceased to be apologetic about her increased drinking, and now she was defiantly leaving the hotel in a cab whenever she wanted and coming back drunk at all hours of the day and night. She was never without at least one bottle of Chivas Regal, and to say she was imbibing freely was an understatement.

Jaime wasn't sure why they were working so hard to get the arena set up. She did not believe the show would fly this time. Lacey hadn't gotten back to the hotel room until almost eight a.m., and by that point, Jaime was about ready to call the police. She was on the phone with Wes when Lacey Leigh staggered in, stinking of alcohol and smelling of sex and aftershave. She was so disheveled that, for a moment, Jaime thought she might have been raped. But when confronted, Lacey smiled and mumbled, "I met a man—wunnerful man. Coming to the show. Tonight."

Her words had been slurred, but Jaime understood them completely, and they drove a stake into her heart. *She's just drunk*, she thought, fighting back tears. *She doesn't know what she's doing. All I have to do is get her to stop drinking, and nothing like this will happen anymore.*

The drunken diva crawled onto the bed, shoes and all, and fell asleep; as far as Jaime knew, that's exactly where she remained. She looked at her watch. It wasn't quite noon, but four hours had never been enough time for Lacey Leigh Jaxon to sober up. *Dios mio! Twelve hours have never been enough!*

Jaime didn't think she could go on like this. For the past three days, the only thing that had kept her going was the memory of the song Lacey Leigh had sung in Louisville. Lacey never sang it again after that, and the one time Jaime brought it up, the blonde star cut her off without a word of explanation.

Lance came around the corner with two rolls of wire, and she rose and followed him back out into the hot sun. *I need some water soon.*

DRESSED IN HER black outfit, Jaime stood in the wings, stage right, surrounded by Eric, Tom, Lance, and Wes. The guys from the band hovered back against the wall. Keith Urban's latest tune blared over the house speakers, but behind the raucous sound was the pounding of eight thousand hands and feet chanting, LAY—CEY LEIGH! LAY—CEY LEIGH!

Wes attempted to shout over the competing racket. "I don't *give* a great goddamn, Jaime! You drag her fuckin' ass out here, or I'm firing her." He looked at his watch. "I am *sick* to death of this shit. Get...her...out...here!"

Eric held both hands up. "Wes," he shouted, "you're the boss, but what if she *can't* perform?"

Wes's face, which was already red, got even redder, and a huge vein stood out in the middle of his forehead. "She's been playing this game every other date. It's over. Get her ass out here, and let the world see what she's worth."

Edgy with anxiety, Jaime strode backstage as quickly as she could. She made her way to the star's dressing room and entered without knocking. Wearing jeans and a tight t-shirt, Lacey leaned against the arm of the couch, her boot-clad feet up on the cushion, and she cradled an uncapped bottle of Chivas Regal. The expression on her face was surly, and her complexion looked as close to yellow as Jaime had ever seen it.

Across the room, Candy and Shelley sat in chairs in front of the makeup table. Jaime met Candy's eyes, and the worried woman shook her head slowly. She looked back at the diva. "Lacey, you're going on."

"Fuck you." The voice was quiet and raspy.

Jaime squatted down in front of her. "Please. C'mon, Lacey, please. You have to pull yourself together." She reached out. "Give me the liquor."

Lacey tightened her grip on the bottle. Once again, she growled, "Fuck you."

"Listen to me. Wes isn't kidding this time. This is no joke. It's not a game." She stretched out a hand, but before she could reach the bottle, Lacey's heel connected with her brow. Jaime lost her balance and fell back from her squatting position. Before she could clear her head, Candy and Shelley were at her side.

"Oh, Jesus," Candy said. "Are you all right? Jaime!" she said sharply. "Are you all right?

"Oh, no," Shelley said, "she's bleeding bad." The two women hustled her up off the floor and back to a chair across from Lacey. Through one eye, Jaime thought she saw a look of remorse on the diva's face, but the drunken woman made no move to help the backup singers tend to the injury.

Candy held a tissue to the side of Jaime's eyebrow. "Shel, stay with Lacey. I'll take care of Jaime." She helped the wounded woman to her feet, and Jaime let herself be led out the dressing room door and down the hall to the restroom. Once they got in front of the mirror, Jaime could see why Candy was so concerned and why there was so much blood. Lacey's boot had caught her right on the bone at the outside edge of her right brow, and the sharp kick had split the flesh.

Using paper towels, Candy tried to staunch the flow, and she did get it to slow down, but after a bit, she said, "Jaime, this needs stitches."

"No, it'll be all right."

"No, it won't," Candy said firmly. "It's ragged, and it'll heal funny. You'll have a big gaping spot here. Somebody needs to take you to the hospital."

"I don't think that's a good idea. Oh, no! Look. I got blood on your dress."

Candy glanced down at the bosom of the sparkly blue gown. "It doesn't matter. Hell, I can't even believe the show will go on. Come on. Let's get you taken care of."

Jaime went to the Marietta community hospital for sixteen tiny stitches in her brow, so she missed what happened next, but she heard plenty from the crew and band and read about it in the paper the next morning. Lacey went on fifty-five minutes late and fainted onstage before she even made it through the first song. Drew and Marcus got to her first, but Buck carried her offstage. When she came to in the wings, Wes screamed, "If you want to go back to that goddamn trailer park in Florida and live with your drunken, rat-fuckin' father again, fine with me. If not, then you're going to treatment, little girl." Unfortunately, a camera crew had gotten every word of it and ran it over and over on the entertainment news, minus the expletives, of course.

If Jaime had been there to see the "performance," it would have broken her heart—that is, if her heart hadn't already been broken.

Chapter
Sixteen

"JOSH AND ZACH, I am going to tell you this one last time—and then that's it," Kip said from her spot behind her desk. "Stop whispering, or I'm sending you down to the principal's office." Her words were quiet, but everyone in the classroom stopped working on their math problems in order to watch their teacher confront the class clowns. The two boys looked down at their papers, and then from side to side out of the corners of their eyes, just barely restraining their merriment.

Kip didn't blame them. She looked out the window into the September sun, wishing she were hiking or exploring and not stuck inside a stuffy classroom while the last of the summer season passed them by. She felt a little pang, remembering the heat in Amarillo and how she enjoyed wandering around the old flint quarry with Jaime. Even though the sun beat down on her school today, she knew it was nowhere near as warm as it had been in Texas on that day which now seemed so far in the past. She could hardly believe the summer's tour had ended for her over two weeks ago, and she was back at work in Minnesota.

Kip sighed, turned away from the window, and leaned her forearms on her desk. She looked at the bowed heads of her students. After only the first two days of school, she could tell this would be her best class, which was unusual since, in all her years of teaching, the last group of the day had never been anything but squirrelly or downright disobedient. Despite Josh and Zack's antics, these kids were well-behaved.

The bell rang, startling her. She rose. "Leave your worksheets on your desks. Hope you all have a good night."

Before the students had a chance to leave the room, she slipped from behind her desk and over to the first row and began collecting the sheets.

"Bye, Ms. Galvin," one student said, and the others echoed

her farewell.

"See you all tomorrow," Kip replied.

In thirty seconds, the children had cleared out into the busy hallway, and her room became blessedly quiet. She finished picking up the papers and stuck them in her book bag. Tidying up the room and straightening desks, she let fatigue wash over her. Even after a week of workshops and two weeks of teaching, she still wasn't used to the early morning hours. Any day now, she hoped her five a.m. alarm would not leave her feeling bleary-eyed and exhausted.

She looked at her watch to see that she had thirty minutes to get from school to the pizza place where she was meeting Mary, Joyce, Rubee, and Sammy for dinner, so she hustled out to her truck, and headed across town. Kip had a bad feeling about the dinner date, which was confirmed when she walked into the restaurant and found her four friends sitting in the big booth with a woman she didn't know.

"Kip!" Mary called out. Before she was halfway across the restaurant, her friends tumbled out of the booth to hug her and pat her on the back. Though she had seen Mary and Joyce and talked to Mary on the phone nearly every day since returning home, she hadn't seen the other two since the August concert in Minneapolis.

Joyce said, "This is Gayla, Kip. She's joining us for supper tonight."

Kip smiled and reached out. "Nice to meet you, Gayla."

The other woman shook Kip's hand and said, "It's my pleasure. I loved your concert this summer. It was just great." A thin blonde with intense blue eyes, the woman reminded Kip of Lacey Leigh Jaxon. It took all her strength not to shudder as she released the warm grip.

"Thanks," Kip said. She stood awkwardly outside the booth as they slid back into their seats, then squeezed in on the outside just as the waitress came to take drink orders. After a while, they ordered three different kinds of pizza and passed a pleasant hour and a half talking and laughing. Kip tried to ignore the obvious fact that her friends were attempting to set her up. *That's the last thing I need. I don't care if she does seem like a nice woman. I'm not up for this.*

Kip didn't eat much, though nobody seemed to notice. At the end of the evening, Gayla gave her a slip of paper with her phone number on it, but when Kip got in her truck, she crumpled it up and threw it in the trash holder.

Chapter
Seventeen

IF JAIME HAD been a party to the decision, she would have encouraged Lacey Leigh not to worry about who found out she was going to an alcohol treatment center, but the diva was paranoid about it. The tour owners wanted her to go to A Sober Way Home, in Prescott, Arizona, but Lacey Leigh mocked the name. Wes insisted they would send her to the best and most confidential, but that didn't fly with her. The Betty Ford Center was proposed, but the singer stated that too many other famous people would be there, and she didn't want to run into any of them. She had an argument against every place that was suggested, and finally after three days of wrangling, the two men who owned the company laid down the law. She would go to a well-respected foundation in Minnesota or to its branch in Florida, near where she grew up. She refused to go to the Florida unit, but she finally agreed to attend the rehab program in Minnesota.

Shelley and Candy dyed Lacey's blonde hair closer to its original light brown color, and without her green contacts, she wasn't recognizable as the famous pop/country diva. She enrolled in the program using her given name, Eustacia Lynn Jacks, and no one knew who she was. It helped her anonymity that she looked emaciated, and her complexion had gone bad. The shaken woman Wes and Jaime delivered to the center was most certainly not the Lacey Leigh Jaxon who Jaime had known and loved. With great sorrow, she dropped the singer off and left with Wes.

Now, fifteen days later, Jaime was so excited about her first real visit to see Lacey that she had hardly slept the night before. She waited in the center's visiting area with the friends and families of other patients, but Lacey didn't appear. After nearly an hour, Jaime rose from her chair and found someone wearing a nametag. "Ah, excuse me. I'm waiting for Stacia Jacks. Have you got any idea where she is?"

The woman flipped through the papers on a clipboard. "She doesn't have any visitors listed here."

Jaime's brow furrowed. "I dropped her off two weekends ago, and she knew I'd be coming back today. There must be a mix-up. Can you let her know I'm here?"

The woman gave her a skeptical look, but said, "Sure. Have a seat."

Jaime sat on a couch next to a window and watched cars come and go from the parking lot. Nearly another hour passed, and she was ready to give up and go when a man's voice called out her name. She jumped up from the chair and turned. "Lacey!"

The small woman stepped away from the man and stomped over to her, fire blazing in her eyes. In a low voice and through gritted teeth she said, "It's *Stacy*, and don't you forget it." She looked around, as though worried that others had heard, but no one was paying any attention.

Jaime looked at the angry woman, waiting for her face to soften, but the hard lines didn't go away. She wore tennis shoes, jeans, and a pale yellow scoop-necked shirt. She would have looked like a young girl if it weren't for the deep lines around her mouth and eyes. In her right hand, she held an unlit cigarette, which she put between her lips. The muddy blue eyes were clear, but Lacey's face still wore some of the ravages of her drinking. But she looked better than she had two weekends earlier. Jaime wanted to take the other woman in her arms, but she didn't dare do so. She gazed down at her. "You look good," she said softly.

"I'm clean. I'm sober. Are you fuckin' happy now?" Lacey spat the words out with fists clenched at her sides.

Jaime was sure her heart skipped several beats. She had no idea what to say so she stood waiting, her face flushing red. After a moment, Lacey stepped around her and went to the window to look out toward the parking lot. Jaime longed to take two steps, slip her arms around the tiny woman, and whisper into her ear that everything would be all right, but she had the feeling nothing was going to be all right after all. So she stayed where she was, glued to the spot, waiting for the attack she expected to come.

When Lacey finally turned to face her, she looked calmer and had unclenched her fists. She removed the cigarette from between her lips and let out a sigh, then stepped the four paces between the two of them and looked up into Jaime's face. "Why don't you go to the overview program—deal with your own shit. I have a counseling session now."

"But—but—but—"

But Lacey was gone. She moved swiftly across the parquet

floor, up the wide staircase, and disappeared around the corner. Jaime felt like a fool standing on the side of the room with her mouth open, so she closed it, and stepped back to lower herself into a chair. *What does this mean? Overview program? What is she saying to me? It's over? Or not? What the hell!*

She sat for several more minutes until a male employee entered the area and announced that the program was about to begin. She rose, intending to head for the front door, but a gray-haired man walking next to her said, "Isn't this all too much?" She nodded mutely, and he asked, "This your first time?" She nodded again. He said, "I know just how you feel." The group of two dozen people around her slowed at a doorway so they could enter one at a time. The man spoke again, his sad blue eyes matching his sorrowful voice. "Last weekend was the first time I was allowed here to visit my son, and he cussed me out so bad I wanted to leave, but I stayed. Don't know how much good it did, but at least this week, he was civil to me."

They reached the door. The man held it open to let her pass ahead of him, and she was swept down a hall and into a large room filled with rows of chairs. She picked a chair at the back, and the gray-haired man dropped into the seat next to her. He leaned her way and said, "Name's Don Lundquist," and stuck out a callused hand.

She shook it and said, "Jaime Esperanza."

"Glad to meet you. Someone is here from your family?"

She hesitated, then shook her head. "No. A good friend."

"Ah, well. Nice of you to come see 'em."

The man who had led them in walked up the aisle to the front of the room and stood behind a podium. He looked around for a moment, then rapped on it. "Welcome, ladies and gentlemen..." and that was all she heard. Jaime closed her eyes and fought back tears. She crossed her arms tightly against her chest and focused on controlling her feelings, pushing them back. She didn't want to start weeping in front of all these people she didn't know, including this man, Don, who sat next to her looking like he, too, wanted to cry. Several minutes passed before she was able to pay attention to the speaker, and when she did, she couldn't really follow what he was talking about. After a few more minutes, all newcomers were asked to break out from the main group, and she faithfully trooped over to a side room with three other women and two men.

The counselor, a middle-aged woman with a Canadian accent, spent some time describing the program in which their loved ones were enrolled. She answered questions, none of which came from Jaime, then handed out some surveys and inventories. "Feel free to take these home and complete them. You will learn a lot from them. Also, we have books here—new ones for sale, and ones people have left behind that you can take with you. The more you read and learn, the better prepared you will be to deal not only with the new life of sobriety the patient is going to embark upon once he or she is released, but also with its impact on your own life. Now let's take a ten-minute break, and then we'll come back to the large group."

Jaime walked out of the side room and into the main area. "Coffee?" a woman asked. She stood at a small table filling Styrofoam cups and handing them to the participants. Jaime shook her head. "Thanks, but no thanks."

The gray-haired man accepted a cup, turned, and saw Jaime. "Hey, how'd it go in there?"

She shrugged, and he barked out a laugh. "Exactly how I felt last week. People were saying words, and I *knew* they were words, and I even recognized all of them, but I had *no* idea what in God's green earth they were talking about."

For the first time in over two hours, Jaime found herself smiling. Then a little bubble of panicky laughter rose up, and she laughed out loud. "You've nailed it on the head, Don."

"So what do you do—for a living, I mean?"

She looked up into his careworn face. He was dressed in a denim shirt, jeans, and work boots. She thought him to be a handsome man, about fifty, and she bet he had probably been quite a looker in his younger days. "I'm a sound tech."

"A tech? You mean on a movie set?"

Jaime smiled. "No. I work on music tours."

"Tours? Like famous people and all?"

She nodded. "I last worked with Lacey Leigh Jaxon. I've also worked with Nicky Kinnick and several other up-and-coming artists."

"Ah," he said. "I like that guy's music. I hear him on country radio now and again. What exactly do you do on their tours?"

"Production, electrical work, wiring everything, make sure sound runs—stuff like that."

"No kidding?" He looked surprised. "You don't have an electrician's license, though, right?"

"Yeah, I do. Went to school in New Mexico."

"No kidding! Can you get the license transferred to Minnesota?"

She frowned. "I don't know. Why do you ask?"

He ran his hand through his thick gray hair. "Listen, I need electricians bad. Want to come try out with my crew?"

Now Jaime was the one who thought he was kidding. "Listen, Don, I don't know how long I'll even *be* in Minnesota."

"That's okay. You could help me a lot, even if it was only for a few weeks. Are you staying around here while your friend is in the program? I'm working down in St. Paul. If you're camped out anywhere nearby, come work with my crew during the days. I'll pay you a decent wage, and I'll supervise your work. I'm a master electrician." He rubbed his face with the flat of his hand, then took a sip of the hot coffee. "Though I sure as heck don't usually do much wiring any more what with all the headaches of the business."

Jaime couldn't think of any reason to say no. She also couldn't think of any reason to say yes—except that she wasn't doing anything all day anyway, and she'd rather be busy than lying around a hotel room staring at the walls. "All right. I'll give it a try."

Don stuck out his hand, and she shook it. "Thanks," he said as he let go. "We start early. I ask everyone to show up by seven a.m." He set his cup down on the table near the coffee urn, then pulled a small notebook from his breast pocket along with a pen, flipped the pad open, and scrawled an address. He ripped the paper off and handed it to her. "Here's the worksite for Monday. You know where that is?"

Her eyes narrowed as she read the unfamiliar address. "I'll find it."

"West side of the river. Up from Concord and off Annapolis. I've got four houses I'm rehabbing in that neighborhood. You have to bring your driver's license, social security card, and electrician's license for me to show my wife. She's the bookkeeper. All right?"

She gave a curt nod. "Okay, Don. I guess I'll see you tomorrow then."

He put his pad and pen away and picked up his coffee cup. "Meeting an electrician—wow. That was unexpected. Well, maybe today wasn't totally wasted after all." He shook his head and gave a shudder. "I just hate this whole thing."

Jaime nodded. "I keep reminding myself it's for someone I care about."

"Yeah," he mumbled as they wandered over toward the chairs. "And my son better get his act together soon."

JAIME WALKED OUT of the hotel into the cool air and strode across the parking lot, dangling her leather tool belt from one arm. In her hands, she carried a paper lunch sack and a Thermos full of milk which she had purchased the night before, along with a Hudson Street Map guidebook to the Twin Cities area.

The sky to the east was inky blue rather than black, and she could no longer see the stars, but it was still dark outside. It was just after five a.m., and she had left herself plenty of time to get from Center City to the address in West St. Paul that Don Lundquist had given her. She unlocked the rental car and settled into the bucket seat. While the car idled, she looked once again at the address and found it on the map. *Let's see...I have to go Highway 8 to I-35 to I-94.* She tried to memorize as much of the route as possible, then set the guidebook on the passenger seat. As she adjusted the rearview mirror, she caught sight of her eyebrow and examined the healed wound. The stitches had dried up the week before, and she had been able to snip and remove them with manicure scissors. There was still some redness, and she wondered if the scar would be very evident. It was partially disguised by her eyebrow, but she still knew it was there.

At this hour, traffic was light. She pulled out of the parking lot, drove less than a block, and wheeled up to McDonald's drive-through window to get a cup of coffee. She had never been a big fan of the brew, but today, after having two sweet rolls and a banana in the hotel lobby, coffee sounded good. And surprisingly, it was. She set it in the cup holder and pulled out of the lot to head toward the highway entrance.

Along the way, she thought about all that had happened the day before. She knew Lacey Leigh was probably miserable, and she prayed the troubled star would find her way toward permanent sobriety. Lacey was a mean drunk, and based on Sunday's encounter, it appeared she was nearly as mean when she was sober. That wasn't encouraging.

Jaime had been in a contemplative mood in the hours since the visit. For the two weeks before, she'd spent hour upon hour doing nothing more than brooding and not knowing what she wanted or how she felt. At Sunday's meeting she was given a book called *True Selves: Twelve Step Recovery From Codependency,* and she started reading it Sunday afternoon. Codependency, boundaries, making amends, surrendering, recovery—all of these were foreign concepts to her. She could only take in the first step: *We admitted we were powerless over alcohol and that our lives had become unmanageable.* This had been true through her whole life. Her mother and several lovers—including Benita and Lacey

Leigh—had all been addicted to the bottle. Try as she might, she couldn't get a single one of them to give it up. She had no trouble admitting she was utterly and totally powerless over what alcohol did to those she loved. At first, she had a little bit of trouble going along with the second part, that her life had become unmanageable, but the more she considered it, the more she had to admit it was true.

So she was attempting to stay open to the idea that perhaps there was something wrong with her, not just with Lacey Leigh. Could whatever it was be repaired? And how did one go about doing that? Based on what she had read in the new book, she had spent the last twenty-four hours trying to comprehend the thought that she, herself, had a problem that had its roots in a childhood spent with an alcoholic mother. When she completed the inventories she'd received at the meeting, she was struck by the results. She hadn't finished all of the surveys. She found them too painful and scary.

When she and Wes had brought Lacey Leigh to the treatment center, Jaime had believed they were doing it for Lacey—but now she wasn't so sure Lacey Leigh was the only one who needed help. On every page she read in the book she'd been given, she saw a little bit of herself. *What is my true self?* she wondered. *Have I missed something important?*

It was hard to consider, hard to get her mind around, and after a while, she felt frustrated and out of sorts. Switching on the radio, she was relieved to turn away from those thoughts and consider other topics as she examined the scenery on both sides of the highway. The plains were so different from the terrain back home. No sand, no sagebrush, and the trees and vegetation were still lush and green. Clearly, autumn was in full force. Though she wore a t-shirt and sweatshirt with jeans and tennis shoes, there was a chill in the morning air, and she had the car heater running at very low heat.

She was curious whether this job would work out—or not—but she didn't have anything to lose. She had her bank account to fall back on, and Wes Slater still had her on the payroll while she stayed in Center City and kept in contact with Lacey Leigh and the treatment program. If Don Lundquist's job didn't pan out, it wouldn't matter much. She hoped it would keep her occupied for a few weeks, though. She was tired of feeling bored.

Following the Hudson guide, she drove directly to the worksite. By the time she arrived, the sun was up over the horizon, and the sky was a clear white-blue color, totally devoid of clouds. It was going to be a lovely day. She parallel parked the Chevy

Lumina a couple houses down from the address and sat in the car listening to the Top 40 station on the radio. A new artist, Shakira, sang a song with a repeating refrain, "Whenever, Wherever." It was peppy, and Jaime liked it, but she thought, *This girl's got nothing on Kip. Kip's voice is much better. For that matter, so is Lacey's.*

Thinking of Kip brought a wistful smile to her lips. She wondered if she would ever muster up the courage to call her. She didn't think she could face her—not after what had happened.

Just then, she caught movement in her rearview mirror, and a white Ford van came down the street. As it passed, the writing on the side became visible: *Lundquist & Son, A/C, Heating, and Plumbing.* The van moved down the avenue and turned the corner. A minute later it returned and parked across the street and nearly in front of the house. Looking over her shoulder, she saw the driver's door open, and Don got out and went around to the rear to open up the back. She picked up her tool belt, got out of the car and locked it, and strode toward him.

Five-gallon bucket in one hand and holding some wire in the other, he turned and looked surprised. "Hey. You're here already."

She nodded. "Didn't want to be late."

"Wasn't sure if you were serious."

"I try not to make promises I can't keep."

He elbowed the door shut and gave a toss of his head. "C'mon then. I'll show you the Wreck of the Hesperus. It's improving, but it sure was a mess when we started." He walked across the street, and she followed. "I've got three others that are similar, all within a mile of here, but this was the worst of them." They tramped up the walkway and took the stairs to the porch where he handed her the roll of wire, dug in his pocket, and got out keys. They went into the house, which was dim and shadowy. Little light came in through the dirty windows in the entryway, and no overhead lighting was installed yet. She could see wires poking out of the aperture in the hallway ceiling. The linoleum leading to a narrow corridor was stained with dirt and mud, so she didn't bother to remove her tennis shoes.

The typical two-story, stucco house had seen plenty of wear. She followed Don into the kitchen, and surveyed the mess. The kitchen counters were covered with odds and ends: strips of rigid metal conduit, rolls of cable and wire, receptacle boxes, an antiquated fuse box, a roll of electrical tape, and various packages—opened and unopened—of screws, seals, clips, and other items. Here and there on the floor lay bits of paper and plastic as though the workmen opened packages and just dropped the containers where they stood.

Don set down the white bucket he carried and said, "First things first. Let's take a look at your credentials." She set her tool belt up on the counter, took out her wallet, and handed him three cards. He cleared his throat and focused on the first small rectangular plastic card. "New Mexico license." He looked up at her, squinting, and she met his blue eyes. He shook his head. "Picture doesn't do you justice at all." He shuffled past the social security card and studied the electrician's license. "You look younger than this would imply, Jaime. Or else you were about fifteen when you went through your training?"

She smiled. "Yeah, I was an early bloomer."

"So tell me, are splices and taps permitted in cutout boxes?"

She frowned. "Sure. But I try to keep the wiring space at any cross-section well below 75 percent."

"Um hmm. How about if I give you an MC cable—you know, that spiral interlocked metal sheathing? Does it require an internal equipment grounding conductor?"

She nodded once. "Always."

He crossed his arms and leaned back against the kitchen counter with a slight smile on his face. He seemed to be enjoying the interrogation. "How many feet from the HVAC equipment is the max for 125 volt receptacle outlets?"

She looked up to the left and thought a moment. "It seems to me that 25 feet is the max, but I've never installed any receptacles more than a few feet from the appliance, Don. Appliances don't usually come with cords longer than about six or eight feet, and I don't think you can even find extension cords for that kind of appliance."

He nodded. "I know exactly what you mean. Okay, you seem to have some knowledge." He pulled his notebook and a pen out of his breast pocket and took a moment to copy data, then handed over her cards. She put them back in her wallet as she listened to him say, "For an experienced electrician, I've got boring tasks here, but the sooner we get the electrical up and running, the better. I installed a new circuit box last week, and I've run the fish and strung the wire. The old wiring was really awful. I'm surprised the place didn't burn to the ground years ago. Every outlet needs replacing. Every light fixture has to be rewired and installed. You got any furnace repair experience?"

"No. I never focused much on HVAC stuff. I did more outdoor wiring and initial construction type work."

"Well, I can teach you that later." With a frown on his face, he said, "My son usually did a lot of the electrical, not to mention the furnace work." He took a deep breath. "Might be a while before I trust him enough to do electrical work again." He pushed off the counter and bent to pull a tool belt out of the white bucket. "Two other guys will be here by seven. One's working on the upstairs plumbing, and the other will help you and me."

They walked out of the kitchen and into a dining area adjacent to the living room. He spent some time explaining that every spring, he bought houses that he worked on through the fall and winter, then sold for a profit. "I've also got a crew of guys who handle A/C repair in the summer and furnaces in the winter. Unfortunately, since my son Donny has screwed up so badly, I am way behind with these houses. I wanted to sell all of them before the end of the year to avoid the homestead tax loss, but we'll see. Two are on the market. The other two are still a mess."

"When can your son return to work?"

Don shook his head. "This DUI is his first offense. Once he completes treatment and does some time in the workhouse, he's on probation. In the meantime, business has been booming, and I've had to hire lots of extra crew."

"I see."

"Donny will get work release while he's in jail. You'll probably meet him if you stay on for long."

The new guys, Michael and Rici, arrived then, and Don introduced them and gave instructions before going down to the basement to work on the furnace. Heavyset Michael Marz grunted hello and headed right upstairs, leaving her facing the remaining man, a slender Puerto Rican.

Ricardo "Rici" Gutierrez, a handsome man with dark hair and dark eyes, was dressed in black jeans and a gray Twins baseball t-shirt. Jaime guessed his age at twenty-five. He looked at her warily. "So," he said, "you're an electrician?" She nodded. He crossed his arms over his chest and examined her closely. "You have a license to be an electrician?" His voice was suspicious.

She rose to the challenge. Standing up straight, she was at least an inch taller than he was. "Yeah, you want to see it or what?"

"*No, es okay. ¿Hablas Espanol?*"

She grinned. She was intruding on his turf, and she could see he wasn't too comfortable. "*Pero por supuesto. ¿Qué esperó usted?*" To herself she thought, *Of course I speak Spanish—didn't expect that, did you?* She narrowed her eyes, suppressing a smile. "Are you an electrician?"

"No. I am an electrician's helper. And I bet I know how to install, repair, and replace *any* wiring or equipment that you do."

She couldn't hold back a smile. "You got a license for that?"

He gave her a withering look and turned away to pick up his gear. She strapped on her own tool belt and squatted down to take a look at the wires poking out from one of the many holes in the wall. The room appeared to have been originally built with only two receptacles, but Don's crew had cut out holes to add new outlets every six feet per code. Across the room was a cardboard box filled with a mishmash of bright blue electrical boxes, common outlets, and faceplates wrapped in plastic. She grabbed outlets and tucked them in the leather pocket of her tool belt, then gathered up six of the blue boxes and went back to the wall she had examined. Jaime got out a screwdriver and went to work. When she finished installing the first box and wiring the outlet, she left it hanging out so Don could inspect her work.

Rici worked silently behind her. Jaime looked over her shoulder and saw him sitting on the floor cross-legged and hunched over. She turned back to her wiring and thought about all the men she had worked with over the years; how they sometimes thwarted her or were scornful. At first, when she was still in her mid-twenties, she had tried to prove herself and gain their trust. By the time she neared the ripe old age of thirty, she got to the point where she just ignored them, waiting for them to make whatever overtures they wished. Jaime was surprised to find that once she no longer cared what they thought and stopped waiting for their approval, it didn't take long before they sought her out.

Rici was no different. She started her third box as he finished his first. He stood, and when she glanced over her shoulder, he was looking her way. She didn't say anything, thinking he might speak first, but he didn't. He sat down and began work on the second box. She finished up her third and then the fourth one and heard him slide down to work on another. Before long, she had completed work on five receptacles on the two walls, and he was hurrying to finish his third. He looked up at her, a scowl on his face, and tightened a screw, then rose. "You sure you're doing this right?" he asked.

She raised an eyebrow. "Why do you ask?"

"You must be doing a sloppy job."

"Oh, I see. Because I'm faster at it than you, I must not be doing it right." He raised his chin in defiance. "How long you been at this, Rici?"

"I've been going to school for two years," he said, the pride in his voice evident.

She nodded slowly. "Congratulations. That's good. But I've been an electrician seven times longer than you've been in school."

He gave her a hard stare, then turned away and went to the final half-wall left in the living room and dropped to the floor to work on the last receptacle. She got more blue boxes and outlets and moved into the dining area.

AT LUNCH TIME, she was surprised that Don ordered pizza and sodas for the four of them. He said he didn't usually treat, but he was so happy to have a full crew that it warranted celebration. "Besides," he confided sheepishly, "my wife is out of town, and I didn't feel like making my own lunch." Jaime went out to the car and got her Thermos, but left her bag lunch to eat later as a snack.

She and the three men sat on the floor around the pepperoni pizza box in the light of the front room window. Don and Michael turned out to be football fans and spent most of the twenty minutes discussing prospects for the coming season.

"You follow football, Jaime?" Don asked.

"Not lately. I've been on the road so much that I haven't really had the time or opportunity."

Rici's forehead creased in wrinkles. "On the road?"

Don nodded and smiled. "Didn't she tell you she's been working for Lacey Leigh Jaxon?"

Rici looked at him blankly. "Who?"

Michael laughed. "He's way too young."

Rici bristled, but before he could say anything, Don said, "Lacey Leigh Jaxon is a country-western singer, son. You probably listen to that rap music, huh?"

Rici shook his head. "Salsa. Pop. Only a little bit of hip-hop."

"Lacey Leigh has had one crossover hit," Jaime said. "'Wyoming' was the song's name."

"Oh, I know that song," the younger man said. "Came out last summer." She nodded, and he asked, "So you know this singer?"

"I've worked on her last two tours." With that statement, the three men spent a couple minutes asking questions—not about music, not about famous people—but about staging details. She enjoyed explaining all about the sets and rigging. *Men are often so practical. Never ceases to amuse me.*

Michael finished the last piece of pizza, drank a final gulp of Coke, then rose, leaving all the trash on the floor beneath him. Rici got to his feet, and Jaime leapt up, too. She wasn't about to pick up the pizza litter. She'd learned long ago that the men would come to expect housekeeping duties from her, and though it bothered her to leave the mess, she turned her back on the trash and moved across the room to where she'd left her tool belt. When she looked back, Don was gathering up the garbage, and it struck her funny that the boss was bussing the meal. She pushed down her laughter and followed Rici upstairs to work on the second story wiring.

AT THE END of the day, Jaime still felt energetic. She tossed her tool belt into the car and got in, satisfied she had given Don Lundquist a hard day's labor. He had been complimentary about the wiring she and Rici had done, and she resolved to return the next day. In the morning, they would work on hanging the remaining light fixtures. She had yet to see the other houses Don was working on, but it sounded like there was plenty of work to do. She was glad about that.

Rici seemed to have mellowed toward her, and as the afternoon went on, he had asked her some general questions and shared a little information: his mother had died when Rici was a teenager, he had graduated from nearby Sibley High School, and he was single and had recently turned twenty-four. She was surprised to learn that he liked to go dancing on the weekends. He strutted around like such a tough guy that she didn't think he could loosen up enough to dance, but then again, people very often caught her off guard with facts like that.

The traffic grew increasingly worse as she headed north to Center City, and it didn't improve until she got off I-35 and onto Highway 8. By the time she reached the hotel, she'd been gone for nearly thirteen hours. She didn't care. *What else do I have to do?* She rounded up her stuff, got out of the car, and found she was fatigued more than expected. A quick shower revitalized her, and she opened a can of Ravioli to heat up in the tiny microwave. She ate that with some cold carrots and a can of root beer, then gave Emma a call, but her friend was not home. She left a message on the machine and went to lie on the double bed to watch TV. She fell asleep ten minutes into the eight p.m. program.

Chapter
Eighteen

KIP USHERED HER last dawdling student out the door of her classroom and gave a great sigh. She checked her watch and saw she was running twenty minutes behind. She locked up her file cabinet, threw the items littering her desk into a drawer and locked it, then grabbed her jacket from the chair and slipped it on. She shouldered her canvas bag and strode quickly, crossing her fingers that for once she would make it to the car before someone saw her and stopped to chat or ask a question. She was pushing against the metal handle of the school's side door when she heard her name.

"Kip! Kip!" She shifted around and looked back to find the new librarian, Dina Gentry, hustling her way. "The concert—it's tonight, right?"

Kip nodded. She had a hard time believing the librarian was interested in attending. The tiny, mousy woman, new to the school, hadn't seemed interested in anything except books up to this point.

"I saw the flyer in the teachers' break room. I believe I'll attend. I didn't notice an admission fee."

"It's a free will offering benefit for the theater department at Hamline University. Also, we're collecting canned goods for the local food shelf, so if you have anything to bring along, it goes to a good cause."

"All right. That's a nice idea."

"I hope so. You like pop and folk and a bit of country?"

The dark-haired woman nodded, her face serious. "You could probably call me a closet country fan. The kids would laugh, and even some of the other teachers would make fun of me, I think. But I have every Garth album, all of Vince Gill, Tim McGraw, Faith Hill, Trisha Yearwood. I've got records from my father— Johnny Cash, Patsy Cline, George Jones, June Carter, Mel Tillis,

Loretta Lynn—you know, all the old standards, but the new ones, too."

"I'm probably not quite *that* country."

Alarmed, Dina stuttered, "Oh, no, that's okay. I wasn't—I mean..."

Kip reached over and put her hand on the small woman's shoulder. "I know exactly what you meant, and if you come tonight, I think I have a good song to sing that you'll like."

The blushing woman brightened up and smiled. "I'm looking forward to it. I've been so busy learning all the new stuff here, putting in extra hours and all, and really, I need a break."

Kip wondered how old Dina was, and she very nearly asked, but she decided it would be rude. "I've got to run." She looked at her watch. "I need to eat and then get all the gear over to the hall." She leaned back into the metal door opener, and Dina followed her out, pulling keys out of her pocket as she passed through the door.

"Do you play any instruments, Dina?"

"Oh, yeah. Oboe—well, I *used* to play oboe. Haven't done much with it lately. But I also play flute and clarinet."

"Cool. We'll have to get together some time and jam."

"Okay, Kip. I'm looking forward to it." She reached her sedan and gave a wave. "See you later tonight."

Kip got in her Silverado and peeled out of the lot as quickly as she could. She wanted to have time for a good meal, and she still had guitars and gear to load up.

THE FOLKSINGER PLUGGED in the last of the equipment, and gave a sigh of relief. Everything was live and working. Hamline University's Sundin Hall, where she was performing, was part of her alma mater's music and theater complex, and it had wonderful acoustics. Seating 315, the hall was great for chamber music, folk, and choral presentations. Kip had played this stage many times before and loved it because the whole hall was warm and intimate, not to mention well-outfitted. She did not need her own amps or PA system as the hall was more than adequately wired and had side fill and front "wedge" monitors that she thought of as "to die for." Every minute that went by, she was getting more excited. She had a hunch this performance was going to sound excellent, and some of the college kids had agreed to run the state-of-the-art soundboard to tape her performance.

She put up two guitar stands and set out Isabelle and her backup Martin. She was just straightening up when she felt two hands on her waist. "Waaah!" She turned and jumped back, heart beating wildly, then stood with her mouth open. "Drew!"

The slim man grinned as she pitched herself at him and gave him a crushing hug. "Whoa, whoa, honey. Can't kill a fella."

She leaned away, her hands still on his waist. "You look great. How *are* you? And what the hell are you doing here? How in the world did you get in? And did I mention, what the hell are you doing *here?*"

He laughed, and his teeth sparkled in the bright lights of the stage. His blond hair looked lighter and shorter, but his eyes were clear and mischievous. "One question at a time. I'm just fine, and I see that you are, too. I was worried about you when you left, but hey, Kip, you look great, except you're 'bout as thin as a bar of soap after a hard day's washin'."

She blushed as she let go and stepped back. "I'm just fine, too, Drew. But how—what are you doing here?" She pointed toward the stairs leading down into the audience, gave a toss of her head, and clomped down, then gestured for him to sit in the front row. She grabbed one of the security chairs from off to the side and pulled it up close to face him.

He lowered himself into the comfortable audience seat. "You know the show went down in flames."

"I heard about a temporary cancellation of the *Roamin' from Wyoming Tour*. My friend Mary watches the entertainment news a lot more closely than I do. She said the tour was on hiatus."

"Yup. Wes had himself a fit when Lacey Leigh imploded. Everything fell to shit, and it all went under."

"I hadn't heard the details."

"You must not be listening to your country radio at all then. It's been all over the airwaves."

She shook her head. "I've been so busy for the last month with the start of school that I haven't had much time to practice and play, much less pay attention if the tour was making the news."

"Well, that's what happened. Wes is fine, and Lacey's up here somewhere hiding out at some treatment center."

"Hazelden?"

"Something like that. I've been kicking around, taking it easy for the last few weeks. Thought I'd look you up."

"Are you here to watch tonight?"

"Among other things." He got up from his seat. Flashing an impish smile, he jogged up the stairs to the stage and disappeared into the wings, then popped right back out carrying his guitar. "Actually," he said, as he came down the stairs, "I was sort of hoping you'd let me sit in."

"Wow! Are you kidding?"

He set his guitar case down and returned to the plush seat. "Was I ever much of a kidder, Kip?"

"Oh, I would *love* it if you sat in. But Drew..." She reached over and smacked his jean-clad knee. "How did you know I even had this concert?"

"Billy. Billy told me."

"Bill Brett? The sneak who showed my demo to Lacey Leigh's managers?"

"The one and only."

"So you keep in touch with Bill?"

"Oh, upon occasion. I called and asked him what you were up to, and he told me about this, so I traveled up here to see if perhaps a couple of months might have changed your orientation."

She let out a snort. "Oh, yeah. My orientation has changed. It's gone from lesbian to asexual."

With a wistful smile on his face, he asked, "Any chance of you going full circle and coming around my way?"

"I'm sorry, Drew. I'm still waiting for the right woman."

"You and me both." He chuckled.

"I suppose you don't want to sit in now," she said with a playful tone to her voice.

"Oh, yeah. For sure," he said in a mocking tone. "I gotta tell ya, gal, I *need* to play a bit. I need something honky-tonk and bluesy and all complicated-like. It just ain't the same playing all on my lonesome. I need to hitch horses and really plow a field."

"You are more than welcome to do that. And what a great treat for me! Let's get things set up." They hustled onstage and rearranged things a bit, did sound checks, and talked the whole while. He finished telling her about Wes's concerns about Lacey, and then she asked about the guys in the band.

"Everybody went their own way. Buck took over for Nicky Kinnick's drummer, and Candy went with him. Buck and Nicky always got on pretty good, and Nicky's drummer is apparently off the road for a while 'cause his wife just had a baby. Shelley up and disappeared, the twins hauled ass home, and I haven't heard from them since."

"Wonder what ever happened to that first guitarist I met—Gary?"

"Hard to say. Least he didn't make a big ugly scene when he departed."

"What about that other guy, Derrick—the one with the wife and baby he so conveniently kept forgetting?"

Drew shrugged. "No clue, hon. He had zippo personality, worse than a bug on a hot August day."

"Let's go backstage and hang out. There's a nice sofa back there, and I brought a little cooler with some sparkling water if you want one."

"No beer, huh?"

She smiled. "Nah. You know I never could drink anything like that before the performance. But how about after? I'll take you out for all the beer you want afterwards."

"Deal."

They reached the sofa and sank down into it. "How did you get in here, Drew?"

"Showed up with the guitar and told 'em I was your backup player, then showed 'em an old backstage pass from one of the August dates, and they believed me." He shifted on the small divan and leaned his left arm on the back and put his chin in his hand. "You haven't asked about Eric or Jaime."

She nodded. "I was getting there. What's the scoop?"

Just then, the theater manager's assistant came around the corner. He was tall and gawky, with bony wrists sticking out from a plain gray sweatshirt. If she didn't know he was a college student, she would have guessed him to be just a year or two older than some of her seventh grade students. "Miss Galvin, I have been sent to see if everything is to your liking?"

"Sure. Things are fine, and we're all set up."

"Okay. We're opening the doors in about five minutes."

She looked at her watch. "Forty minutes early?"

"Yes. We're hoping to get a ton of canned goods, and we want time to get everyone settled."

"All right."

"Also, there are some people here who say they are family."

"You can send them back."

"What if they aren't family?" he asked.

For a moment she wondered if he was referring to "family," as in other people who were gay or lesbian, but the young man looked far too serious. She wrinkled up her nose and tried to hold back the grin, not quite certain what to say. "Is it an older man and woman and a few others maybe my age?"

He nodded. "Yeah. I guess."

"Don't worry. I think they'll be safe to send back."

When the student disappeared through the door, she said, "I suppose I should be grateful they're staying on top of security—though they did let in a hooligan like *you*—but it's not like we're on Lacey's tour. Now *there* I could see why they were cautious."

They nodded at one another knowingly. "But here...who cares?"

The sound of footsteps and laughter grew louder, so Kip rose, with Drew right behind her, and a whole crowd of people came around the corner: her parents, her brother Keith and his wife, a couple her parents lived next door to, two elderly aunts, and Mary, Joyce, Rubee, and Sammy. She hugged her dad first, then slung an arm around her mother's neck and introduced Drew to everyone. They spent several minutes in animated conversation, laughing and talking until Kip shooed everyone out onto the stage, down the stairs, and into the auditorium. "Pick the seats you each want. When they open the back doors, you all should have your places. Meantime, Drew and I are going backstage."

"Break a leg, Kip," her father said.

"That'd be just my luck, Daddy." She grabbed Drew's arm and dragged him offstage. "I need to get my head together, Drew. What do you need to do to get ready?"

"Same thing as always. Walk out there, close my eyes, and play."

THE CONCERT WENT well. She loved playing with her old buddy and managed to set up some long segues to showcase his fine lead guitar. They'd run the gamut from Wynonna to Dixie Chicks, Cheryl Wheeler to Indigo Girls, Cris Williamson to Kristen Hall and also several of her own compositions. She enjoyed dedicating and playing a Trisha Yearwood song, "I Would Have Loved You Anyway" for Dina who sat in the fifth row looking thrilled. She and Drew ended up doing two encores, and then they slipped offstage into the wings, grinning like silly school kids. He put an arm across her shoulders. "Damn, girl. You're still fun to jam with. Sure you don't want to go back on tour?"

They moved into the corridor while she tried to figure out how to express her feelings. "I liked the stage shows and our informal jam sessions, Drew. I enjoyed some of the people on the tour, but I didn't like living in a bus, driving from one hotel to another, staying up all hours of the night, and having so many people be so cranky and demanding."

He stopped. "You should be on tour with someone who's fun and who doesn't have the problems Lacey does. You know, somebody like Nicky Kinnick. Now *he* was a nice guy. I bet Buck and Candy are really enjoying that."

"Maybe. But strange as it seems, it didn't feel like a real life. I like playing around town, teaching my students, seeing my friends, being with my family for holidays."

He pressed his lips together and looked at the floor. "Those are some good points. I just wish I could play regular—and not have to travel either. But that's the way it is."

They moved around the corner and entered a small reception room complete with two long tables full of cookies and candies and another table with coffee and punch. Kip heard an excited buzz outside the door, and the young man who had talked to her earlier opened the door and poked his head in. "Miss Galvin, are you ready for me to let the fans in?"

"What would I have to pay you to give us three more minutes so we could go use the facilities?"

His face took on a surprised look. "Oh, you need not pay me, Miss Galvin. Just tap on the door when you're back, and we'll open up."

He disappeared, pulling the door shut, and Kip met Drew's eyes. "Is it just me, old buddy, or are kids these days too damn literal?"

Drew shook his head slowly. "I can't speak for all youngsters, but that one—well, he couldn't pour rain out of a boot with a hole in the toe and directions on the heel."

Kip let out a hoot and headed toward the restroom. She called over her shoulder, "You still crack me up, Drew Donovan."

IT WAS NEARLY eleven p.m. before Kip could make good to Drew on her promise of beer and food. Accompanying them to the pizza place were Mary, Joyce, and the librarian, Dina. They parked their various cars and walked through the cool night, along the city sidewalk, talking and laughing. Kip wasn't quite sure how Dina got swept into the group, but the folksinger was in such an excited state that she didn't much care. Drew tucked a lunch-size paper bag under one arm and held the restaurant door open, and the four women marched in.

They had missed the late evening crowd and had no trouble getting seats. The five of them crowded in at a round table more likely meant for four. Drew sat on Kip's left with Mary on her right. The folksinger's friends, Joyce and Dina, filled out the complement and sat across from Kip. She hoped Dina was okay sitting right next to Drew since they didn't know one another at all.

The waiter came and got their drink orders while Drew grinned jubilantly. "Damn fine git-fiddle picking tonight, Kip. That was the most fun I've had since you left the tour."

Kip smiled back and smacked him on the arm with the back of her hand. "You were dynamite yourself."

"Hey, hey! You don't want to injure my arms. These babies are insured for at least a million bucks, you know."

"Like a baseball player's pitching arm, huh?" Dina asked quietly.

He looked her way. "Yeah, exactly. Don't believe I've properly made your acquaintance. I'm Drew Michael Donovan." His right hand crossed in front of him, and she reached over to take it.

"I'm Dina Gentry."

"Pleased to meet you, Dina," he drawled.

Kip picked up the stack of menus and passed one to Mary. "Dina works at my school, Drew. She makes sure all those evil children read and then return their checked-out books."

"That so?" he asked.

Dina nodded shyly. "Yes, I'm a librarian."

The waiter brought out a pitcher of beer, five glasses, and a glass of ginger ale for Kip. He asked if they were ready to order, but nobody had looked over the menu, so he departed. After some discussion, they agreed to disagree. Drew and Dina were the only two who wanted the same thing, so the five of them decided on two large half-'n'-half pizzas.

"This ain't gonna be fair," Drew said. "Me and Dina's got the short end of the stick."

Patting his forearm, Dina said, "Don't worry. I can eat all of about one piece, and you can have the rest."

"Okay, punkin, just so long as you get enough." He picked up the pitcher and filled glasses, all the while keeping up a running commentary about how starved and thirsty he was. He didn't seem to notice the startled look on Dina's face, which quickly turned to a pleased blush. The waiter came back, and they put in their order.

Mary changed the subject, and they discussed the food shelf contributions from the concert. The performance had reaped far more than anyone expected. The conversation ranged here and there, and they all laughed like silly fools. By the time the pizza arrived, Kip had come to the conclusion Drew and Dina were, as her mother used to say, "taken with one another." Over the next hour-and-a-half, she watched the guitarist and her colleague, and unless she had lost her intuition entirely, she could swear they had fallen in love. *Now how could that happen?* She surreptitiously studied the tiny librarian. Unusually dark eyes, hidden behind large glasses, looked tentative, as though any loud noise would cause her to jump out of her skin. But right now those brown eyes sparkled with excitement. Gradually, as the evening went on, Dina became more outgoing than Kip had ever seen her. *Well, I've only known her a few weeks. Maybe she holds back at school.*

The librarian peered past Drew and said, "I just loved what you did to that Kim Richey song, Kip. And Drew, what wonderful accompaniment. You blew me away, both of you."

Smiling, Kip took a sip of the last of the ginger ale, which, by now, had gone flat. "Thanks," she mumbled.

"I'm rather partial to Kim Richey," Drew said.

"You are?" Dina looked thrilled. "I've got every one of her CDs."

"That so? What else you got?"

Dina began to name favorite artists. Kip turned and met Mary's eyes to find her friend sporting an amused expression. She looked at Joyce, and Mary's partner had the same look on her face, as though they were both trying to repress a good laugh. The folksinger looked at her watch. "Gosh, it's getting late. What time does this place close?"

"One," Mary said.

Kip got out her wallet. "I need all the beauty sleep I can get."

"Oh, no," Drew protested. "Everybody stay a little longer."

Mary took that moment to yawn. "I've run out of stamina, Mr. Night Owl."

"Well, y'all wait just *one* minute." He reached down next to his chair and picked up the small brown bag he had carried in. "Kip, this is for you, compliments of me, Eric, Jaime, Candy and the twins."

She set her wallet on the table and accepted the bag. "Do I get to look at it now?"

"By all means!"

She unrolled the top and slid two plastic jewel cases out. Some sheets of paper tucked in the bag tickled her hand. She cocked her head slightly to the side. "What are these?" Neither of the clear CD cases was labeled. She looked up at her friend, and saw a look on his face that, in his vernacular, could only be described as a shit-eatin' grin. She looked him in the eye for a little stare down.

He didn't seem to be able to stop smiling. "I'll just tell you that there ain't no way I can do them justice by explaining. You gotta listen to 'em. But I will say that if I felt any better about how they came out, I'd drop my harp plumb through the clouds."

"Tell me everything," she said. "Come on, Drew."

He shook his head. "Gimme your phone number, girl. I'll call you tomorrow night and see what you think. 'Sides, we gotta get together some more and jam."

Intensely curious, she got out a pen and wrote her number on a napkin. He tucked it into his shirt pocket, still grinning, and looked to the side at Dina. She smiled back as though in on the secret, though how Dina could possibly know what was going on was beyond Kip. She pulled some bills out of her wallet and tossed them on the table. "All right, Drew. You got me dying of curiosity, so now I *really* have to go so I can listen to these in the truck." She rose and bent to place a light kiss on his forehead. "I'm so glad you showed up tonight, my friend. Thanks for making the concert extra special."

Joyce and Mary scooted their chairs back and got up, too. "We'll walk you out, Kip," Joyce said.

"You can't *all* desert me," Drew said. He looked back and forth among the three of them.

Dina said, "I can stay a bit," and Drew's face took on a pleased expression.

He rose and pushed his chair back, setting his napkin on the table. "Now y'all drive careful."

Joyce came around the table and stuck her hand out. "Nice to meet you, Drew." She shook his hand, then Dina's, and Mary did the same.

"Later, Drew," Kip said. "See you at school, Dina," and she and the two other women headed for the door.

Once outside they burst into nervous laughter. Mary said, "I had the impression those two had never met, Kip."

The folksinger let out a puff of air and shrugged her shoulders. "They hadn't, but they sure seemed to hit it off."

"I'll say," Joyce said.

They strolled down the avenue until they reached their cars. Mary said, "I'll call before noon tomorrow to find out what's on those disks." She yawned. "I'm too damn tired to wait around and find out now."

"Okay." Kip gave them each a hug, and got in her truck. She turned the key to start the engine, then opened the paper bag and dumped the contents into her lap. She had no way to know which disk to play first. She randomly selected one jewel case and snapped out the disk to slide it in her CD player, then picked up the papers and the two cases and set them next to her. She put the Silverado in gear, but left her foot on the brake and listened. *Click-click-click-click*, and she heard a familiar lead guitar intro followed by drums with a driving beat. A shiver ran through her body when she heard the strum of a rhythm guitar and the thump of a bass. Her mouth dropped open, but no sound came out—however, her voice, true and strong, soared from the stereo speakers and she heard the first lines of Wynonna's song, "A Little Bit of Love Goes a Long, Long Way."

She put the truck in park, and sat back in disbelief. *This is live? This sounds great! How—how did they do this?* Reaching up with one hand, she clicked on the overhead light and picked up the sheaf of papers on the seat and folded them open. The top sheet was a scrawled note signed by Eric.

Dear Kip,
We hope you get as much enjoyment out of listening to your first tour as we got out of recording, mixing, and mastering these songs. Any questions or problems, let me know. I kept a set of masters just in case—and for my own listening pleasure.

All my best to you—always,
Eric O'Connell

The other sheets of paper were releases from Candy, Buck, Davis, Marcus, and Jaime allowing her to use the music for any purpose she desired.

Kip couldn't believe it. She sat there on the street, listening for another ten minutes and through three more songs before she finally put the truck back in gear, pulled out, and headed for home. Once she got into the house, she put the first disk in the CD changer and the second one after it, hit play, then dimmed the lights and curled up on the couch to listen. The only song she skipped was the first song on the second disk, which was "Go." Before she made it through the whole second disk, she fell asleep.

Chapter
Nineteen

JAIME'S WORK WEEK passed quickly, and she spent Saturday driving around the Twin Cities trying to get the lay of the land. Each day she got more used to going to bed early and rising long before the sun was up. It had been a long time since she'd had that kind of schedule, but already, after just five days of work, she realized once again that she was a morning person.

Sunday morning she sat up in bed and looked at the bedside clock. 6:15. She'd slept in a little, but she felt rested. Even though she wasn't due at the treatment center until early afternoon, she decided to go ahead and get up.

After a quick shower, she dressed and opened the curtains. Her room looked out over a parking lot. Off to the side she could see a kidney-shaped swimming pool. Closed for the season, it was covered over with a turquoise tarp. Beyond the parking lot was a forest of trees still loaded down with leaves, but they were changing color to dull golds and browns. She slid the window open. Sunday had dawned cool and clear, and goosebumps rose on her arms. Jaime stepped back and went to her duffel bag, dug through it, and found a sweatshirt, which she slipped over her head. She went back to the window and stood in the fresh air.

A gust of cool wind blew in, and she closed her eyes and took a deep breath. She thought of her grandfather then, of his kind face. She resembled him more than any of his brother's sons or anyone else on that side of the family. What would he think of her now, if he were still alive? She wondered if he would be disappointed. She tipped her head back, eyes still closed, feeling the brisk air on her neck and face. In times of trouble, he had called to his ancestors for guidance and comfort. She had never done that, and now she wondered if she should. *Grandpa, are you there?*

She listened to the occasional whistle of the wind until the quiet was interrupted by the slamming of a car door. She opened her eyes and watched as a man and woman loaded bags into a station wagon. A small child stood to the side with a thumb in his mouth and a red and blue plaid blanket wrapped around his neck and dragging on the ground. The man closed the tailgate and picked up the child to stow him in the back seat.

She slid the window closed as a feeling of unease washed over her. She didn't understand her trepidation, and then her stomach growled to remind her it had been a long time since she last ate. She took a few minutes to gather up her dirty clothes, locked the room behind her, and went off to get breakfast. After eating, she drove around until she found a laundromat, and for the next two hours, she read a paperback while her clothes washed and dried.

Thoughts of her grandfather continued to come to mind all morning, and when she returned to the hotel room, she sat down at the tiny desk and put a call through to Gallup. Emma's husband, Simon, answered, and she spent some time catching up with him before he put her friend on the phone.

"It's been ages, Jaime. What have you been up to?"

"Oh, this and that. How are you? How are the kids?"

"Everybody's fine. Not all that happy to be back at school, but otherwise, fine. Where's the tour right now?"

"The tour is on hold. I'm up in Minnesota with Lacey Leigh. She's in a 28-day treatment program."

"It's about time! I *knew* she needed help."

Jaime didn't answer. She silently questioned the wisdom of calling Emma and wasn't sure if she was ready for the honest assessment of things her friend was sure to give her.

Emma asked, "What are you going to do?"

Jaime didn't answer for a moment, then took a deep breath. "I don't really know."

"You can always quit the tour and come home."

The same thought had occurred to Jaime, but she wasn't ready to give it serious consideration. "I don't feel I should quit on Wes or Lacey."

Emma let out a sigh. "I will never understand why you are giving up your life—living out of a tour bus, taking care of a spoiled rotten prima donna. Don't you want to have a life of your own?"

"I have a life!"

"Oh, Jaime. I worry about you. Get away from that woman. She's bad for you."

Jaime closed her eyes tightly and fought back the emotional pain Emma's words brought her. "It was different this time. Before this crash of hers, Lacey reconciled with me...she was different."

"Jaime, it sounds the same as before. She sucks you in, then once you're committed to her, she dumps all over you. She's like—like a piranha, or, well, like something with claws. Get away. Now, before she hurts you."

"I can't run out on her now, Emma. She's in treatment. She needs support."

"What about you? Who supports you?"

"That's why I called you, *mi amiga*."

Emma laughed. "And here I am harping at you. I'm sorry. I'm just worried about you. When are you coming home—for a visit, I mean?"

"I don't know. I got a temp job up here, working as an electrician." The conversation turned to the job and soon on to other things, and by the time Jaime rang off, she felt a little better.

She rose from the desk chair, then stood, looking around the cramped room uncertainly. *Is this the way I want to live my life? Hotel room to hotel room? Never having a home? Never putting down roots anywhere? Maybe Emma is right.* Again, something behind her breastbone tightened, and unsettling feelings washed over her. A part of her wanted to cry; another part wanted to push back all the feelings and forget about them. She crossed the room and picked up the hard black violin case that sat on the floor next to a duffel bag. After setting it carefully on the bed, Jaime unbolted the hasps and opened the lid to reveal the battered old Schweitzer. She thought of her grandfather again as the tips of the fingers on her right hand touched the strings. They were cool and smooth. She lifted the instrument out and detached the bow from the clip inside the case.

Kneeling next to the bed, her left hip leaning against the frame and mattress, Jaime put the bow to the strings. A soothing purr, low and tremulous, hummed from the old violin. She fingered the strings and played a soft melody, simple and slow, that reminded her of wind in the desert and the sun on her hair. Tears leaked from her closed eyes, and she ached for the child she once was, back when her grandparents and mother had still been alive, before the alcohol ravaged her mother's life, before the illnesses took her grandparents away. She pulled the bow across the strings. A dissonant note squawked out with the next stroke. She stopped playing and sat back on her heels.

The sound of running water gurgled above her. The violin felt heavy on her shoulder, and suddenly, she just wanted to go home. But where was home? She didn't have one anymore. The instrument slipped from under her chin, and she held it by the neck for a moment before returning it and the bow to the case. Closing the hasps gently, she decided she needed some fresh air. The clock read 11:20, and she wasn't due at the treatment facility until half past one, so she decided to go get something to eat first. She wiped away her tears, collected her wallet and the keys to the rental car, and left.

JAIME SAT IN the busy lobby watching people come and go. Like last week, Lacey Leigh had not yet shown up, and after thirty minutes, Jaime wondered if she would. Part of her wanted to ask that Lacey be notified again, but another side of her was angry at the small woman's inconsiderate actions. She contemplated leaving, but before she could make the decision to go, Lacey Leigh appeared, unexpectedly, at her side.

"Hello, Jaime." The sultry voice startled her, and she turned to meet guarded blue eyes. Lacey wore jeans and a huge, baggy, gray Vikings sweatshirt. Her face was clear, as were her eyes, and there was now plenty of pink color in her cheeks as well as carefully applied makeup. She appeared to have eaten a few decent meals because she no longer looked as emaciated and wan.

"Hey, Lace. Where'd you get the sweatshirt?"

The diva flashed her million-dollar smile. "From a new friend."

Jaime's heart sank. She had seen the sparkly, energized attitude Lacey Leigh was displaying far too many times not to know what it meant. "New friend" could only be translated one way: a new love interest. "What's his name?"

"Mike. You'd like him. He reminds me a lot of you." The cellophane on a brand new package of cigarettes crackled in her hand. "Come on. Let's take a walk."

Mutely, Jaime rose and followed the small woman down a hallway off to the side and out the doorway into an enclosed garden area. The birch and poplar branches had dropped leaves, and someone had raked them into uneven piles under the trees. The walkway wound around stands of trees and shrubs, and every few yards were solid-looking green benches. She fell into step next to Lacey. A breeze blew, rustling through the foliage, and Jaime watched as three tan leaves fluttered to the ground. She heard a snap and smelled sulfur, and when she looked down at Lacey Leigh, the singer was taking a draw on a cigarette. "Since when do you smoke?"

"Since I no longer get to drink."

Jaime stopped. "I can't tell you how bad that is for your voice."

"Yeah? Well, apparently drinking was worse." She took

another puff on the cigarette. "There are a lot of singers who smoke. Billy Joel has for years, and he's still doing fine." She smiled in a dreamy way. "It won't matter if I get a little raspy. I'll just growl better like Shania Twain does. I wonder if Faith Hill smokes?" She stopped and turned to face Jaime. "When I get out of this hole, Wes is taking me to make a new video, and you won't believe how good this one is going to be. It's a crossover, for sure. Finally, I'll be bigger than Faith or Shania or any of those others who don't even write their own songs."

Jaime didn't respond to her claim. She wasn't sure what to say. She didn't know why it was so important for Lacey Leigh to try to best other singers. Why couldn't she just enjoy the music and the applause and acclamation that came her way?

Lacey tapped her on the upper arm. "Listen, Jaime, I need to talk to you about something." She glanced around, then made a beeline over to one of the green benches. When she sat, her toes touched the ground, but just barely. She set the cigarette package next to her on the wooden seat. Jaime followed, feeling uncertain, and lowered herself to the bench. She wished she could sit right next to Lacey Leigh, but instead, she planted herself a couple of feet away. She didn't turn to face her when the other woman began speaking, instead looking across the path at the trees waving in the wind. "We're doing all this paperwork here with this 12 Step business, and one of the things I have to do is make amends. You are one of the people on my list. So, I just wanted to apologize for kicking you in the head. I don't remember it very well." She laughed nervously. "Most of that night is sort of a blur, but I shouldn't have kicked you, and I'm sorry."

Jaime waited, expecting more. She heard another sharp inhalation, and looked out of the corner of her eye at her companion, still waiting.

The diva exhaled blue-gray smoke. "Don't you have anything to say?"

"Not really." Actually, she had scores of things to say and a hundred questions to ask, but something made her hold back, and she chose to remain silent.

Lacey tapped her cigarette against the green seat, and Jaime saw ashes fall to the ground. "So, Jaime, what are you going to do with yourself?"

Jaime was at a loss to answer that question. Did Lacey mean until she was released? Or was she talking about the tour?

Lacey said, "Wes is coming next weekend to check on me." She leaned forward, her hands on her thighs, holding the cigarette between tapered fingers. "You'll have to decide what you want to do. I'll pick up the tour and finish the last seven weeks. I've asked Mike to join us. He can do stagehand work if you want him to. You'll like him a lot."

"What about us, Lacey?" The words came out softly. She turned now and watched as Lacey swallowed. She brought the cigarette to her mouth again and sucked in hard.

"There is no *us*, Jaime. There never was." The diva breathed out acrid smoke, and the wind carried it into Jaime's face. "I've learned a few things since I've been here, and one of them is that you aren't very good for me. I don't mean to hurt you, Jaime, but I'm just not that way. Like you, I mean."

"So, what are you saying? Same whore, different dress?"

Lacey Leigh let out a laugh. "I wouldn't go quite that far. It just wouldn't ever work. I don't feel that—you know—that way about you." For the first time, she turned to face Jaime. "Don't get me wrong. We can be friends, but that's it."

Clenching her fists, Jaime pushed back the emotions threatening to erupt. "I don't understand you."

"Look, let's not kid ourselves. I mean, come on, Jaime. You're Mexican or—or Indian—or whatever, and you're a woman. I'm not interested in—in that." Nervously, she took another drag from the last of the cigarette, then dropped it and leaned forward to stub it out with her toe on the cement path.

Later, Jaime thought that she should have been more shocked, more hurt, but instead, she focused in on Lacey's words: "not interested in that." In "that"—as though she were a thing and not a person. *She doesn't respect that I'm a person with feelings. She has no clue.*

Jaime was very calm then. She got to her feet, surprised that her legs were steady. "Goodbye, Lacey." Without looking back, she walked away. Lacey Leigh did nothing to stop her and didn't say a word to call her back.

With her head pounding, Jaime walked slowly through the building and out to the parking lot. Only then did her legs get shaky. Now she allowed herself the luxury of feeling stunned and shocked. She reached the car, unlocked it, and got in. Several minutes passed as she sat in the driver's seat, the keys in her right hand, waiting to get adjusted to this new situation. She closed her eyes and took a deep breath. *Did she really mean that? Is that it—the end?* A tight, burning sensation settled somewhere around the vicinity of her heart, and her breath came faster. *I've moved here temporarily. Gotten a job to pay expenses. Doesn't she care?*

The disbelief was so strong that it took several minutes before the pulsing in her head abated enough for her to see clearly. She looked through the dirty windshield at the swaying trees lining the south side of the parking lot. The fine branches moved in the wind to the left, returned to center, then leaned left again. She thought that if she were a tree, the wind would blow her over right now.

She closed her eyes again, but hot tears leaked through her closed lids. The face of her grandfather came to her once again, smiling sympathetically, the way he had whenever she was wounded or hurt in any way. The thought of him made her cry harder, and it was another minute before she recovered enough to wipe the tears from her face with her sleeve.

She inserted the key in the ignition and started the car, letting it idle a minute while she watched people enter and leave the building. None of them looked happy, either. Putting the car in gear, she locked her fingers around the steering wheel and made her way to the parking lot exit. Before she'd driven half a mile, her hands hurt, and she realized she held the wheel in a death grip. Relaxing her grasp, she gradually came to recognize she was angry, and it was all she could do to keep from driving like a maniac.

WHEN JAIME ARRIVED at work Monday morning, Don was already inside the house, sweeping in the kitchen. Leaning on the broom, he greeted her and said, "We've got a couple hours of clean-up to do here, and then we're moving operations to another place. The painters were already there, and Michael will work on the plumbing tomorrow."

"Oh, okay."

"I picked up some doughnuts." He gestured toward a bag on the counter. "Help yourself."

She set her tool belt on the floor and opened the white bag to select an apple fritter. "Thanks, Don. This was nice of you." He resumed sweeping, and as she took a bite, she thought about the fact that he was a very nice man. Few of her past bosses had ever participated in the clean-up phase at a job site.

"Missed you at the session Sunday."

The bite she was swallowing stuck in her throat, and she had to force it down. "Yeah, I didn't stay." She held the pastry, realizing that she didn't want to finish it now.

"Donnie gets out in a couple weeks. He was in real good spirits Sunday, and I think things are going to go better now."

"That's good to hear, Don. You still want me to work with you—I mean, for a while, until he gets back on track?"

"What?" He looked at her, surprised. "Jaime, I'd like to keep you on permanent. You do good work, and Rici seems to like you. Wouldn't you like to bone up on furnace repair? I could really use you all fall and winter for tune-ups and repair."

"I'll think about that."

He bent and picked up a dustpan, then guided part of the pile of plastic containers and bits of paper into it. He stood and dumped the contents into a 55-gallon garbage can and went back for more. "I've got a realtor coming to look at this place today. When Rici gets here, I want you two to put bulbs in every fixture and finish sweeping this place. Then I'll give you the keys, and you can head over to the next hovel so we can get to work on it."

She gave him a nod, still wondering what to do with the apple fritter she held. He moved across the kitchen and handed her the broom. "Rici can do the sweeping. I'm going to start taking stuff out to the truck."

She waited until he had left the room, then went to the garbage and dropped the doughnut in. She wiped the sticky glaze on her jeans and hoped he wouldn't bring up the topic of the treatment center again.

JAIME WRESTLED AN eight-foot ladder down two short flights of stairs and stopped at the bottom. She hadn't checked over the new site very closely, and this was the first time they had gone down to the cellar.

Rici glanced around and said, "This place is creepy." They stood at the foot of the stairs in a huge basement area. Precious little light shone through the tiny windows up near the ceiling. Even if they hadn't been so dirt-streaked, the windows were still too small to admit much light.

Jaime smiled and pointed up at the six different sets of fluorescent light fixtures hanging from the ceiling. "I'll bet it would be more than bright enough if the power were on."

"Yeah, what'd they do—grow pot down here?" He held the flashlight out to her. "I'll take down the units. You hold the light." When she didn't reach out for the flash, he asked, "Okay?"

She sighed. "All right. Just make sure you confirm the circuit is dead."

"Yeah, yeah, I know." He gave her the flash, took the metal ladder, and dragged it over under the closest fixture. He got the ladder opened and situated, then climbed up until he was eye level with the hanging light. Putting a hand on the ladder to steady it, Jaime trained the light up on the wiring. Rici fumbled around in his tool belt until he found his Square D wiggy and used it to check the circuit. "It's dead," he said. He dropped the gauge back into his pouch, and she handed him her wirecutters.

He said. "You know what I'm going—"

ZAP!

A flash of bright light blinded her, and a jolt of pain stabbed her hand. She jerked her hand toward her chest. Rici made a strangled sound and fell backwards off the ladder. He landed with a whumping sound, the wire cutters clattering next to him.

"Oh, shit," she said as she dropped the flashlight. "Rici! Rici!" He lay motionless on his right side, facing away from her. She dropped to her knees, rolled him onto his back, and in the dim light, looked at his face. His eyes were closed. "Rici! Can you hear me?" She pressed her fingers into the side of his neck, but didn't feel a pulse. When she put her ear near his mouth, she didn't hear a sound. "Rici! C'mon, kid." She put her left hand under his neck and tipped his head back, then bent to listen again. Nothing. Now she put one hand on the top of his head and the other under his chin and held steady, listening for the slightest sound of breathing. She didn't hear any.

With trembling fingers, she used her right hand to pinch his nose closed while pushing her left palm under his chin. She covered his mouth with hers and breathed tentatively. His chest rose, and she met no airway obstructions, so her second breath was more vigorous. She gave a third breath for good measure, then gently released his head and moved to his chest. She found his sternum and placed her hands where she thought they should go and pressed down with steady force. She backed off, then did it again. Never having performed CPR on an actual person, she wasn't sure if she had it right.

"Come on, Rici. Breathe!" She finished fifteen compressions, then scrambled to his head, tipped it back, and gave two powerful breaths. Back to his chest, she started compressions again. *Don, please. Where are you? Show up. Show up, please.* She returned to Rici's head and placed her mouth over his, but before she could breathe more air into him, she heard a groan from deep in his throat, so she pulled away.

"Rici! Are you breathing, buddy?" She still held his chin with one hand and squeezed the knob of his shoulder with the other.

"Unnnnhhh..."

"Keep breathing. Nice deep breaths." He groaned again. "Good job. Keep taking in air."

"What...the...hell...happened?"

"You got hung up. Something was live."

"Unhhh..."

"Look, I've got to go call 911. Just stay right here." She leaned in close and tried to meet his eyes. "Rici, are you listening?" She shook his shoulder gently. "Don't move. Stay right here."

"Not...going...anywhere."

"Okay, I'm going for help. Just stay put."

She gave him a last pat and turned to fly up the stairs as fast as her feet would carry her. She ran through the house and out the front door.

She ran to the first house she saw. She beat on the door, but no one answered. *Shit! That's it. I'm never going anywhere again without a cell phone.* She turned and headed down the stairs, just in time to see the white van turn the corner. She waved her arm. "Hey, Don!" She ran along the sidewalk. When she was ten yards away, he stopped the van, opened the door, and leaned out. She shouted, "You got a phone?" He nodded. "Call 911! Rici's been hurt."

He didn't ask questions or stop her. She whirled and ran back into the house. As she pelted down the hall, she screeched to a halt and went back into the living room to grab a stack of painting dropcloths lying under the front window near cans of paint. She turned and hustled down the basement stairs.

Relieved to find the young man still breathing, she covered him with the dropcloths. He said, "I'm feeling better now. I could probably get up."

"No. Just wait." She knelt at his side, her heart pounding. Her left hand throbbed, too. She turned it over and gawked at the deep red crease bisecting her palm. *Where did that come from?* She continued to stare at it blankly until she heard a clattering sound on the stairs, and Don burst into the room.

He squatted next to Rici, next to the younger man's knees. "What happened?"

Jaime said, "Electrical shock. He cut the splice in one of the fixtures and we got zapped. Either the circuit wasn't dead or it was a common neutral is all I can think."

"*Hola*, bossman," Rici said, his voice weak.

Don patted him on the knee. "I called for the paramedics. They'll be here any minute, Rici. Just sit tight."

"Jaime won't let me do anything else."

Don rose. "I'll go watch for them."

The next half-hour was a confusing jumble of activity for Jaime. The emergency med techs arrived and took both of them to the hospital: she to have her hand attended to, and Rici to be admitted for observation. The doctors determined that the electrical shock may, indeed, have interrupted the signal to his heart, and one of them said it was lucky she had been there to do immediate CPR. Rici insisted his chest hurt only slightly, and he jokingly blamed the pain on Jaime trying to crush his ribs. However, they also said he might not have had any more troubles than a burn on his hand and a bit of dizziness if he hadn't hit his head when he fell. He had a sizable goose-egg a couple inches above and behind his right ear, and it was that injury they wanted to watch for a few hours.

She was still puzzled about the burn mark on her hand. The doctor asked, "When he cut the wire, what were you doing?"

"Holding the flashlight...looking up...with my left hand on—oh. I was holding onto the metal hinge that joins the two sides of the ladder."

"That's it, then. You got a jolt, too, when Rici did."

He applied burn cream, bandaged the hand, and gave her instructions as she sat on the examining table. She shook her head in amazement, glad that she and Rici had lived through near-electrocution. *That's not the first jolt I've had lately, though, and it probably won't be the last.*

When the doctor finished with her, she left the ER, and moved out into the waiting area where she noticed a Latino man at the check-in desk. He stood holding the hand of a black-haired, gradeschool-aged girl who looked frightened.

Jaime said, "By chance, are you Mr. Gutierrez?" The man turned toward her, and from his face and proud stature, it was clear he was Rici's father. "Hi, I'm Jaime Esperanza. I work with your son." She stuck out her good hand, but he didn't seem to notice it. He let out a torrent of language, half Spanish, half English, and she held up her hand. "Wait, wait! *Señor Gutierrez, va a estar bien.*" In Spanish, she told him, "It's okay. He's fine, with just a bump on his head."

Still panicked, Mr. Gutierrez asked again what had happened to his son. *"¿Qué aconteció a mi chico?"*

Once Jaime had the chance to tell him about the accident, Rici's father settled down, and they stood conversing in Spanish. He had been on the way to drop off his daughter at school and go on to work. He introduced Jaime to ten-year-old Serena, Rici's sister.

Jaime said, "They will come out shortly and let you see him, I'm sure." Just then, Don Lundquist came around the corner, balancing a paper cup of coffee. "Don," she called out.

He looked up, and his face brightened. "Ricardo." He took

the final steps to the counter and set his coffee down, then shook the other man's hand. "Good to see you. I am sorry Rici got zapped."

"The young lady here say he soon be all right."

"Yes. He will," Don said seriously. "Thank God."

Rici's father nodded solemnly. "*Si. Gracias a Dios.*"

HER BOSS ENCOURAGED Jaime to take Tuesday off, but she told him she felt fine and would rather come to work in the morning, though Rici would have some time off.

Don said, "Tomorrow, I'm going to go through that whole damn house and figure out what happened. In fact, I could use your help. Between the two of us, maybe we can make sure nothing like that happens again with that circuit." He drove her back to the work site so she could pick up her car, and she agreed to meet him at the regular time in the morning.

She headed back to the hotel in Center City, and during the ride north, she had plenty of time to go over what had happened. *I shouldn't have let Rici up there. He probably cut some extra wire. Or maybe he didn't test the line correctly.*" Letting out a sigh, Jaime thought about how frightening it had been, but she also felt pride for the way she had handled the accident. She hadn't panicked, and everything was going to be all right.

When she reached the hotel, it was only a few minutes before noon. She opened the door and stepped in, then stood, door still open, looking around at the impersonal, blandly decorated room. *Why am I staying here? What is the point? I'm not going back to see Lacey Leigh again. Like they say in that Al-Anon book, I need to "Let Go and Let God."*

She stepped in, shut the door, and set to work immediately, gathering up and packing her things. Once she had things all organized and stacked up on the bed, she got out a small black book. She looked up a phone number and dialed, taking a deep breath as a man answered the phone. "Wes?" The tour promoter's voice sounded far away. "Where the heck are you, Wes?"

"Driving down the freeway outside Charlotte. Where the hell are you?"

"Same place you left me—but only for a few more minutes. Wes, I quit."

"Quit? You can't quit, goddammit! I'm relying on you to get Lacey Leigh down here in time for a mid-October concert."

"You'll have to rely on someone else. Maybe her new man—some guy named Mike."

"Well, fuck-a-duck! This blows the *shit* outta my day. Why are you quitting?" When she didn't answer right away, he hollered, "Jaime? You still there?"

"Yeah, Wes. I'm sorry, but this just won't work for me anymore. It's time for me to move on."

"What about all your shit?"

"There's not much there. Give me the address, and I'll fly over in a week or two and pick it all up." She grabbed the hotel pen and wrote down the information he gave her, and when she hung up, she felt relieved and nervous, both at the same time.

THE NEXT MORNING when she met Don at the work site, she could tell he was still upset. They set right to work checking the circuit breakers and wiring, but after a time, when he came down from the ladder, she asked what was wrong.

He slipped a screwdriver into a hook on his tool belt. "Things just aren't going well. Donnie's not ready to leave as quick as he wanted. Rici's out for a few days. Michael's kid has chicken pox. Our daughter hasn't had the baby yet, so my wife's still gone." He let out a sigh. "And now, one of the house deals I had fell through. It's just a string of real bad luck, that's all. Want to buy some houses?" He gave her a tired smile.

"I might want to rent one for a month or two. What do you think of that?"

He crossed his arms. "Hmm. I don't know. I was hoping to sell at least two of them. I could let you have a great bargain on one. We can even go contract-for-deed, if you want."

"Sounds like a good deal, but I don't really like this style of house."

"Well, hey, I've got two you haven't even looked at." He looked up at the ceiling and puffed out his cheeks. "How about you and I take a break and run by a house off Smith Avenue?"

They went out to his van, and she rode over with him. The yard was overgrown, but the veranda-style front porch was in good shape, though the porch and entire house could use a new coat of paint. He opened the screen door, which looked new, and unlocked the door. She followed him into an inner porch that she had learned Minnesotans called a mud room. Beyond that was another door into the house. He unlocked it and gestured for her to step in ahead of him.

The floors, starting in the entryway, around the corner into the living room, and back toward the dining room, were hardwood and had seen many years of wear. The living room contained a usable fireplace with a wide mantel and mirror above it, and under one of the two bay windows was a wood window seat crying out for repair and refinishing. The walls throughout the main floor needed paint, but the windows were so new they still sported the manufacturer's stickers. She walked through the house. The kitchen was old-fashioned with a stove, fridge, and dishwasher, all of which Don told her worked. The floor needed new linoleum.

"Check this out," he said. He opened a door off the kitchen to show her a walk-in pantry, complete with a pull-down ironing board in its own cupboard. "This place was built in the 40s, back when they actually put in flour bins." He opened a deep drawer. She nodded and stepped back into the kitchen. In the hallway between the kitchen and dining room, he paused and pulled open another door. The six-by-eight foot room was filled with shelving and must have been used for storage. He said, "If I keep working on this house, this is going to become a bathroom."

He shut the door and opened one on the other side of the hallway. She followed him downstairs to a full basement that had never been finished. The cement floor was clean, the overhead beams looked sturdy, and light shone in from small windows up along the ceiling.

"This is a lot nicer basement than the one where Rici got zapped, Don."

"That's sure true." He strode over to the furnace. "This is brand new, state of the art. It'll be very energy efficient." He pointed to the water heater a few feet away. "Now that's another story. I bet that thing's ten years old, but it works okay for now. So do the washer and dryer. I think they're pretty new."

Along one side of the far wall, someone had built deep wooden shelves from floor to ceiling and there were paint cans, a stack of boards, and a couple of coiled garden hoses on them. Some old boxes sat on the middle shelf, and she moved closer to check them out. "What are these?"

He said, "There's some tile from the upstairs bathroom in one—not enough to re-do it though. I think that's siding in one of those long boxes. Probably a bunch of junk in the others." She nodded, looking around, then followed him upstairs, through the hallway, and to the staircase leading to the second story. She found three decent-sized bedrooms and the bathroom. The carpeting upstairs was new, but the rooms needed lots of work. The walls were dinged up and needed patching and paint, and some of the woodwork needed replacing. Two of the three bedrooms had roomy closets, though. They inspected the bathroom, and she found that the sink had been replaced, but the floor did need new tile, as Don had said.

"There's an insulated attic, and it's a pretty good neighbor-hood with a moderately low tax base. If you want this place—and it's the best of the four—I would swing a deal with you. I can also help you get building materials and supplies at cut rates." His blue eyes sought hers. "Think about it for a couple days, Jaime. No pressure, but it's yours if you want to make a deal. I'll give you all the purchase info and the inspector's sheets." He ran his hand down the wide wood molding in the hallway, then sauntered toward the stairwell, stopping to open a linen closet. She watched him poke his head in and look around.

She didn't know how much he wanted for this house, and to avoid doing anything rash, she wanted to go over every inch of it to check the plumbing, the electrical, the foundation, and all the appliances. But as she stood in the doorway to the bathroom and looked out the window at the maple tree swaying in the wind, it seemed as though the house called to her. She thought that was a very odd feeling, as though she had a kinship with the house. Strangely enough, she could see herself living here, all by herself, even though it was nothing like the ranch-style home in which she had grown up in Gallup and still owned. In fact, Minnesota had an entirely different feeling to it—very different from New Mex-ico. Perhaps this kind man whom she had only known a couple weeks had something to do with the welcoming feeling of the place. She wasn't sure.

Jaime turned from the bathroom doorway. "Don, I am going to give this very serious thought. I just might want to take you up on the deal."

"Ahh, good." He smiled. "But no harm done if you don't. One of the things that's nice about this neighborhood is that there are a lot of Latinos living around here." He hesitated, as though choosing words carefully. "It's very nice to have you working with me, Jaime. I've got so many contracts and projects here on the West side, and to have two Spanish-speaking staff is a godsend."

She nodded. "I'm glad I can help." She took a deep breath and looked up at the hallway ceiling. It needed a new coat of paint, and the light fixture was old and ugly. She made a "hmm" sound in the back of her throat, then met his eyes. "Would you trust me with the keys for a couple days, Don? I'd like to check this place over with a fine-tooth comb."

He dug in his jacket pocket. "Not a problem." He took out a ring of keys and looked through them until he found the right one. "I have duplicates at home, but you go ahead and take this one for now. In fact, if you want to camp out here for a couple of days, feel free to do so."

"I have to make a decision. If I decide to do this, I'll need a few days—maybe a week—to get to North Carolina and New Mexico to pick up my things."

"That could easily be arranged."

"One other thing, would you mind if I put you down as a reference on a loan for a van? I'm going to buy something my equipment will fit in, and since you're employing me..."

"No problem," he said. "I can verify your employment. Just give the bank my number." He handed her a key. "Here's for the house. There's a garage, too."

"A garage?"

"Yup, around back. But I don't have that key with me. Let's go by my house, and we can pick it up."

Chapter
Twenty

KIP COULDN'T BELIEVE how fast time was flying. October had blasted past, punctuated by two coffee shop performances and a Halloween talent show at school for kids and teachers. November had been a little less hectic, but by the time Thanksgiving came and went, she was very much looking forward to the days off at Christmas break. *But first I have to make it through this math section with the kids.* She rolled her eyes and thought about how frustrating it was to teach rational numbers, fractions, and decimals. So many of the students just weren't getting it.

When Dina cornered Kip between classes, the folksinger had other things on her mind so she wasn't listening as closely as she should have been. And then, over the short librarian's shoulder, she saw a laughing, dark-haired boy climbing on top of a locker. Interrupting Dina, she called out, "Hey, you!" The boy scrambled down, looking embarrassed at being caught. "You know the locker tops are off limits. Go see Mr. Morehouse in the office." The kid slunk off, and she turned her attention back to Dina. She didn't know if the kid would do as she had ordered, but she knew him to be a fairly nice 12-year-old, so there was a chance he would follow her instructions. "Dina, can you explain to me why on God's green earth they did something so stupid as to install five-foot-tall lockers?" She let out a sigh and shook her head. "The least they could have done was put a slant at the top."

"Or jagged metal." Dina grinned. "There seem to be a lot of odd things about this school."

"Yeah, tell me about it. Now—you were saying?"

"Drew is having an acoustic jam at my house this weekend. Will you come?"

Kip thought for a moment. She didn't have anything planned, but she was hoping to do some early Christmas shopping. It was Thursday at the end of the first week of December, and there were only two more full weeks until their long-awaited holiday began.

She wanted to make the most of it by getting her shopping done early. "Which day?"

"He was hoping for Sunday afternoon. It all depends on you."

"Me? Why me?"

"He really wants you to come over to sing and play, so whichever day works for you is fine with him."

"Okay, I'm going to do some shopping and Christmas prep on Saturday, so Sunday would work, all right?" Dina nodded, her face alight. "What time?" Kip asked.

"Let's shoot for one p.m., and I'll have mid-afternoon snacks, then some supper around six, if you will stay that long."

Kip nodded. "Sounds good."

"I'll shoot my address and directions over by e-mail." The bell rang and their eyes met. Dina mugged a frantic look, and turned to go. "Hang in there, Kip. See ya later."

The folksinger headed toward her classroom, stopping along the way to pick up a candy wrapper. She dropped it into a trash can, wondering why the kids couldn't take the four extra steps and do that themselves. Kip shook her head and headed into her room, thinking about how much she had grown to like and respect the new librarian. She also wondered about the relationship between Dina and Drew. Though she had talked to Drew by phone only twice, as far as she could tell, he had been spending lots of time with Dina.

The rest of the day went by in a whirl of decimals and confusion. The kids were edgy beyond compare. Kip was sure that a direct correlation existed between attention span and the proximity of Christmas. She saw it every year, and each year she just did her best to keep the students calm and focused. Only ten more days of teaching, and then she had a break. She couldn't help but look forward to it with great longing.

Friday's school day passed quickly, and when Saturday rolled around, she and Mary had a good time shopping. She remembered the previous Christmas as being painful, full of fits and starts, and that she had been prone to crying jags over losing Bren. This year, when she heard the Carpenters singing "Merry Christmas, Darling" over the PA at the department store, she didn't burst into tears. Instead, she just felt wistful.

After several hours of running from one store to the next, she and Mary waited in line at the last shop and paid for their purchases, then hauled them out to the Silverado. "Lucky you have this truck, Kip."

"No kidding. It's very practical at times like these." She

stowed the last of the packages in the back of the truck, shut the hatch, and they both hopped into the vehicle.

"Brrrr," Mary said. "It's definitely getting colder—more snow soon, huh?"

"I think so." She started the truck and let it idle to warm up.

In the meantime, Mary dug around through the CDs in the basket on the floor. "Where is the—oh, here it is." She reached up and pressed eject to remove the CD in the player, then inserted another.

"What are we listening to?" Kip put the truck in reverse and started to back out, but before she even angled out of the parking space, she knew what the song was. She heard the tick-tick-tick-tick of the drumsticks...and then the acoustic guitar. "Geez, you *would* pick this. I gave you a copy, Mar. Why don't you listen to it at home?"

"I do. All the time. I just can't get enough of it."

"Shouldn't we be listening to Christmas music?"

"Nah. I like this better."

Kip rolled her eyes as she heard her own voice rise from the speakers.

Sweet, sticky summer day
Something better came along and took you away
And I can hardly hide my happiness for you
Baby, I can hardly believe it's true...

She wanted to reach over and skip that song, but before she could take her hands off the wheel, Mary said, "Of every song you have ever written, I think this is my favorite."

"Just my luck." Kip hit the gas and pulled out of the parking lot, back tires spinning.

"Oh, Kip. It's such a wonderful song. Listen to it—it's great!"

"I have. Believe me, I have." Truth was, she had listened to the whole CD many times, and this was the one song that troubled her the most. Since the *Roamin' from Wyoming Tour* ended for her, she hadn't played "Go" on her guitar, nor had she sung it at a gig. She tried not to think about it. Still, the feelings from that time, from those jumbled up, emotional two months on tour, still bothered her.

Mary tapped her foot and sang along slightly off-key. Kip listened with a critical ear to what Eric had done to the master. He and Drew, Candy, and Jaime had obviously put some extra time into the recording because there were background vocals on some songs. For a few other musical tracks, various guitar parts, mando-

lin, and a harmonica on one song had been added that had not
been recorded live onstage. All the levels had been balanced out,
and almost every song was mixed well, so much so that it wouldn't
even be fair to use the CD as a demo because she couldn't dupli-
cate any of this in a coffee shop without at least a 5-man band.

"Go" ended, much to Kip's relief, and she heard applause,
and another song began. A few notes into the next song, she found
herself tuning it out and thinking about her tour mates. She wondered how many more guitarists Lacey Leigh had gone through
once she got out of treatment, and how Jaime was doing in the
relationship with her. She questioned whether she would ever see
Jaime again. Kip had no idea how to get hold of her, even if she
did want to get in touch. *I am so thankful that Drew is up here
now. What a neat guy.*

Mary asked, "You want to come in at my place and do some
wrapping? Have a little wine? Play some schmaltzy Christmas
tunes?"

"Yeah, you better get Joyce's presents wrapped before she
gets home. You know how inquisitive she is."

Mary looked at her watch. "Lucky she's not due back 'til
early evening. So you'll help?"

Kip frowned. "Oh, I don't know."

"Oh, geez, don't be a spoilsport. Come on in, why don't
you?"

Kip nodded. "Okay. As long as you lay off *this* CD, I'm
game." She smiled toward her friend, then turned her attention
back to the road.

Soon, they were sitting at Joyce and Mary's dining room table
where they spent a couple of hours wrapping presents, drinking
wine, and eating apple slices dipped in caramel. "This is really
low-cal," Kip said dryly as she licked some sticky caramel off her
thumb.

"Ah, what the hell." Mary snipped the end of a piece of ribbon. "It's Christmas, Kip. Quit being so bah-humbuggy."

"I never said bah-humbug." She put a final piece of tape on a
package and pushed it away from her.

"You're managing to seem completely bah-humbuggy."

"Bah-humbuggy isn't even a word, my dear. How can I be
something that doesn't even exist?"

"It exists now—and you know what I mean." Mary gave her
friend a pointed look, then pushed her last gift away from her.
"Okay, that's it for me."

"I've had it, too," Kip answered. "Time for me to head
home."

"You're not even done with the wrapping."

Kip shrugged. "No big deal. I can finish at home."

They tidied things up, threw away the scraps, and rolled up the last of the Christmas paper, and then Kip gathered things together to leave. She headed out to her vehicle with the first load of wrapped gifts, started up the Silverado's engine to let it warm, then went back for the second of three trips. She said goodbye to Mary and gave her a hug, and by the time she got in the truck, she shivered from the cold. She headed off down the street, slowly, hoping the heat would crank up quickly, but she was very nearly home before she could actually feel it.

She parked the truck, hauled her presents in from the garage, and placed them under her tree. After a sandwich and cup of hot cocoa, she went upstairs to her bedroom and crawled into the king-size bed. She looked around and found the TV remote control on the other side of the bed tucked partly under the pillow next to two math journals. *One nice thing about sleeping alone, I've got a whole half of the bed for storage.* Kip chuckled and shook her head, then flipped on the television and settled down to watch a made-for-TV movie on the Lifetime network, but she fell asleep before it was over.

Chapter
Twenty-One

JAIME LEANED IN front of the window seat, one knee on the edge, and watched as the sun drooped below the horizon, setting behind a pencil-thin line of clouds. The sunsets in Minnesota—sunrises, too—were different from those in New Mexico. The colors were deep and true, but not as neon looking.

She turned, wiping her dusty hands on her work jeans, and surveyed her mostly empty living room. Two sawhorses sat on carpet remnants in the middle of the gleaming hardwood floors. She had sanded down the floors herself, but she hired guys to come in and do the varnishing and sealing. She could still smell the pungent solvent from the lacquer they used on the beautiful red oak. The final result had surpassed her hopes.

Across the sawhorses lay the very last piece of molding for the living room, and once she finished sanding it down, she would stain all the pieces, varnish them, and return them to their proper places around the doors and windows. In her mind's eye, she could already see how stunning the living room would be. This molding was the easy part. The window seat and the mantel over the fireplace had been serious challenges. So much of it had to be done by hand, and she'd worked longer sanding and finishing each of those than she had on all the molding throughout the house.

Jaime picked up the little hand sander, then realized she was thirsty. Bending, she grabbed up a dust rag, set down the sander, and stood to wipe the fine sawdust off her hands. She was trying to confine the dust to one area, but looking around, she saw that it had spread throughout the room and settled in a thin coat everywhere. "Oh, well," she said aloud, accepting the inevitable as she tossed the rag onto the wide piece of molding.

In the kitchen, she opened the refrigerator and debated between milk and root beer, finally opting for the latter. She had no chairs in the kitchen, so she hoisted herself up to sit on the counter, leaning back against a cupboard as she drank the soda and looked around her brightly lit kitchen. Only a couple more days and the table and chairs she'd ordered would arrive. She had also ordered vinyl flooring and was going to lay it herself, which was something she had never done before. The shiny red and gold flooring would complete the room. A vigorous scrubbing of all the grungy-looking cabinet doors had uncovered perfectly acceptable cupboards. She vacuumed them out and relined each shelf with clean Contact paper. For the rest of the room, coats of white paint on the ceiling and ivory linen on the walls plus a new light fixture had brightened things up considerably. Eventually she would replace the stove and dishwasher, but they were fine for now, and the refrigerator was new enough that it looked like she could keep it for years. So far, this was her favorite room. Now all she had to do was tackle that funny little pantry, which only needed cleaning and a coat of paint.

She screwed the top back onto the root beer and returned the half-full bottle to the fridge. *Not much to eat in here. I really ought to make a grocery run.* Shutting the door, she glanced at her watch to see that it was half past five. She moved across the kitchen and closed the blinds on all four casement windows, but just before she had lowered the last one all the way, a diabolical looking face appeared in it, and she jumped back, startled. Then the features rearranged themselves into a grin, and she recognized Rici. She heard the thump-thump of his footfalls as he came up the six stairs, and before he'd tapped on the door, she was opening it.

He said, *"Hola, mi amiga. ¿Como esta?"*

She laughed and let him in. "What are you doing here, *hombre loco!*"

"Hey! I'm not crazy."

"No, just electrified."

He slipped off his jacket and held it, dangling, in one hand. "Thought I'd drop by and help you for a while."

"You don't have a single better thing to do on this fine Saturday?" He shook his head and shrugged. She shook her head slowly and rolled her eyes. "Young guy like you oughta get some friends."

"I know, I know. I'm pathetic, but that's the way it is. They're all busy doing other stuff."

She loved to tease him now. During the last three months, they had gotten to know one another well, and they kept up a constant repartee of bad jokes and pestering. He actually had a whole pack of friends—guys and girls—and she'd met most of them. They were fun-loving kids, and she liked it when they came by. It appeared Rici was never going to stop feeling grateful that she had saved his life. She wasn't so sure she actually had, and every time he mentioned it, she felt embarrassed. But no matter what, that entire event had cemented a bond between the two of them.

"So," he said, "you got anything good in the fridge?"

She shook her head. "I was just mourning the lack of food. I only have one more thing to do, and then I want to go get something. Want to order some Chinese?"

"Sure. What are you working on now?"

"Molding." She turned and headed toward the living room.

"Still? That sucks. You've been stuck on that for weeks." He turned the corner into the living room and took in a fast breath of air. "Well, well. This room is looking great."

"That's what I was thinking, and lucky for you, I'm on the last piece of molding."

"Hot damn. Then can we go on to something good?"

"Like plumbing?"

He dropped his coat on the window seat. "Yeah. That'd be fun. I could come over tomorrow, and we could start the main floor bathroom."

She shook her head. "Not tomorrow. I'm going over to visit an old friend I haven't seen for a while, and I'll be gone most of the afternoon, maybe longer. How about next weekend?"

"Sure, that works, but you know what?" He looked around, nodding, then met her eyes. "You need some furniture. And some Christmas decorations. *Chica,* it's only two weeks 'til Christmas. Maybe I should buy you a wreath or something."

Jaime turned on the sander, and over the buzz of it, she said, "I'm sure that would complete my décor."

"What you really need is a TV."

She shut off the sander. "I'm sick of working. Let's go buy one."

"One what?"

"A television set."

He stepped back and snagged his jacket from the window seat. "I don't need convincing. Sounds good to me. But let's get food first."

She narrowed her eyes. "I swear you always show up hungry, little man."

He smiled, his white teeth sparkling in his handsome face. "What can I say? I'm still growing."

She unplugged the sander, and left it where it lay. "If I had a brother, I'm not sure whether he would be able to manipulate me any better than you do."

Holding one hand up in the air and speaking in an exagger-
ated voice, he said, "Oh, no. That *can't* possibly be so. Besides, I
owe you my life, right?"

"All the more reason why you should buy every once in a
while."

"Okay, you got it. Chinese is cheap, and I know a good
place."

She strode across the smooth floor and headed out into the
hallway toward the stairs. "Let me get cleaned up a little, and then
we'll go."

"My truck or your van?"

She stopped and looked over her shoulder. "Oh, please. I
couldn't bear another ride with you skidding all over and nearly
sideswiping parked cars."

He stuck his tongue out at her. "Your van it is, then. I'll
gladly ride three miles per hour with the old woman."

She took the stairs two at a time, feeling warm inside. If she'd
had a brother—or a son—she would have wanted him to be like
Rici. It was odd how, in such a short time, the kid had grown on
her. She thought about the new friends she had recently made:
Rici, her boss Don, Donnie Junior, new people from her Al-Anon
group, and her sponsor, a woman named Maria. Every day she
was more amazed at how life had opened up to her...ever since she
had let go of Lacey.

Chapter
Twenty-Two

KIP AWOKE SUNDAY morning to find six inches of new snow on her lawn. She got up and cranked the heat, and after she had some cereal and coffee, she sat in the front window and watched the big flakes fall. It looked so peaceful, so lovely. With a pad of paper on her lap and a pen in her hand, she sat and worked on the words to a song she'd started writing over a year earlier. She called it "Bittersweet" back then, and she thought the name would stay the same, though she knew the words would keep getting moved around.

There was a span of time
In my blind love I had it all
Living seemed easy, you were always a thrill
Today it's hard not to cry as I recall

Adventures, excitement, your glowing charm
Full of so much heart and feeling
We were alive and loving
Too late, I watched it slip away

And now wherever, whenever we happen to meet
I feel bitter, but we're both sweet
No one can tell we've been so far before
Bittersweet—as we walk out separate doors

Suddenly, unexpectedly I knew
The bittersweet feeling would win
The memory is poignant, it still makes me sad
To think of how hard it will be, to begin again...

She wanted to write another verse, but no matter how she thought about it, she couldn't get it the way she wanted. Rising from her cozy spot in front of the window, she picked up her coffee and took it into the kitchen, then went downstairs to her music room. She reached for Isabelle and plugged her in, then turned on the amp, the soundboard, and her 4-track recorder. She sat on the wide couch and set to work on chord progressions.

After a while, the words began to make sense in her head, and she murmured along with the chords, not singing, but imagining in her mind how the words would interplay with the guitar. When she originally wrote the song, she remembered quite clearly how just the thought of Bren, of her short, blonde hair and crooked smile, had cut through her like knives. Now when she heard the tune and sang the words, it was as though Bren had receded far into the distance, barely close enough to be seen waving.

Time was a funny thing. The song no longer seemed to apply to Bren at all, and Kip was surprised to find herself thinking of Jaime. This had happened to Kip with a lot of music—and people—over the years. Certain favorite songs had originally marked traumatic or hurtful events. But then, when she heard the tune much later, though she did, indeed, remember the original painful situation, new experiences also got incorporated into her memory of the song. And if the words and melody were stunning enough, she discovered it was no longer associated solely with pain. That had happened with a Cheryl Wheeler song, "But the Days and Nights are Long" and with an entirely different type of song, Sarah Brightman's operatic "Only an Ocean Away." Neither song made her weep anymore, though she remembered the melancholy full well.

She strummed a part of "Bittersweet" and listened to how the strings rang. Three days earlier, when Dina had invited her over to play, she'd come home and changed the strings to give each one time to stretch and settle in. Today they were perfect and held their tune very well. She set Isabelle in her rack and rose to adjust the levels on her soundboard and 4-track, and sat again and reached for the guitar.

Time flew by as she played and recorded the song multiple times, then rewound the tape and listened. She was always so surprised by how her voice sounded. In her head, it was thick and wooly, but on tape it was deep and melodious. Nobody was more critical of any little error, though, and she kept re-doing "Bittersweet" until she couldn't take it anymore. Drew once said she really knew how to kill a song—or as he put it, "You done played that enough to burn a wet dog," whatever that meant. The sound of his voice in her head made her smile.

She paused, holding the warm, smooth guitar in her lap, then glanced at her watch. "Oh, crap." There was just barely enough time to clear the snow off the driveway, eat a lunch, and get ready to go to Dina's. She turned off her equipment, packed up her guitar, and hauled it upstairs. She ran the snowblower and finished in record time. After a quick bowl of soup and some crackers, she donned her boots, heavy coat, and scarf, and took the guitar out to the Silverado. She had one foot in the truck and one still on the garage floor when she remembered she didn't have Dina's address, so she went back in the house and fished through her school bag to find it.

The snowplows had cleared Kip's street, but it continued to snow so heavily that another half-inch had covered the ground since she had finished snow-blowing. She knew it would be a slow trip across town and took her time on the back streets. When she got on the freeway, she never went over twenty miles per hour. Neither did anyone else. She was relieved she only had a couple miles to go before exiting, but then she discovered the side streets in Dina's neighborhood were not yet plowed. Vehicles had already made their way through the drifts of snow, leaving two deep furrows down the middle of the street. She shifted the truck into 4-wheel drive to make it down Laurel Street and drew closer to a white mini-van stuck on the right in a particularly deep drift. With some deft steering, she could make it around the van.

She debated—pull over and help? Drive on? When the driver gave the vehicle a shot of gas, Kip saw the rear tires spin in place, kicking snow out into the wind where it was whisked off to the left in a shower of white crystals. Kip pulled up behind the van and hopped down from the truck. Cautiously she approached the driver's window. In situations like these, she always thought of the movie *Silence of the Lambs* and knew that any kind of sicko could be at the wheel.

She tapped once on the window, and when the person in the bright purple knit cap turned her way, Kip's legs went so weak, she nearly sat down in the snow. Before she could gather her thoughts, the driver's door was pushed open, and a slim figure in black jeans, boots, and a black goosedown jacket slipped out. It wasn't an illusion. Kip stammered, "Jaime? What are you doing here?"

"Trying to get unstuck."

She looked uncomfortable, so Kip kicked into her all-business mode. "How about if I ease up behind the van and push you out?"

Jaime gave her a relieved look, her dark eyes brightening. "Would you? I'd really appreciate it." She shivered and got back in, leaving the driver's door open.

"Just steer forward, and I'll push you out there where the snow is a little more packed down." Kip turned and hiked back to her truck with her mind whirling. *What in the hell is Jaime doing here stuck in the snow?* She shivered as she hauled herself up into the cab, then slammed the door shut. Inching forward through the snow, her thoughts whirred a million miles a minute. *Is she on the way to Dina's? Why else would she be two blocks from Drew's girlfriend's house? What is she doing here?* She came in contact with the back of the van and gently nudged it, but it didn't budge. She rolled down her window and gave a beep of her horn, and leaned her head out. Jaime hung halfway out of the van, looking back. Kip shouted, "When I honk, give it a lot of gas."

The other woman disappeared into the van, and Kip pressed on the accelerator, then tapped the horn. She increased pressure, and the grill of her truck was hit with a spray of snow. Suddenly the van lurched away and skidded forward into the center of the road. Kip slammed on her brakes and watched the van slide as Jaime tried to get control of it and finally stopped the white vehicle in the indented tire tracks running down the middle of the street. The black-haired woman stepped out of the van and waded back toward the truck. Kip felt all the blood in her body race directly up to her face. Fortunately, the window was rolled down and that the twenty-degree air was hitting her cheeks, but with every step Jaime took toward her, the folksinger felt a little more panicky. By the time Jaime reached her window, Kip was entirely tongue-tied.

Jaime said, "Thanks for doing that. I don't know how long it takes spinning wheels to melt snow, but I figure I might've been stuck there for an awful long time. So, are you going to Drew's girlfriend's house?" Kip nodded. "Do you know where it is? I've been driving around for half an hour."

The folksinger nodded again and croaked out, "Follow me."

"How're you going to get around my van?"

This brought a smile to Kip's face. "Watch me." She rolled up her window as she waited for Jaime to get into her vehicle, then, in low gear, Kip backed out of the snow bank. She eased the truck up the street, behind the van, and steered to the right of it. She plowed through a two-foot high pile of snow, like a ship gliding forward through water. When she hit the accelerator extra hard, the truck fishtailed around the van and cut into the track in the middle of the street ahead of it. "Whoo-hoo!" She pressed the accelerator again, and the powerful 4-wheel drive caused the truck to leap forward. In the rearview mirror she watched as the white van followed in her tracks. Turning right off Laurel, she drove up another few blocks until she came to the right street. She hoped there might be parking for two cars, but she was disappointed to see only one spot in front of the home bearing Dina's house number. Kip slowed, rolled down the window and stuck out her hand to point over the top of the cab toward the house. She kept on going down the street another block until she found a spacious spot to park. It occurred to her that she could have stopped in the street, unloaded her guitar, and then parked. Now she would have to drag the heavy case through the snow and ice. *Oh well. I'll live.*

She got out and went around to the passenger side to remove Isabelle. By the time she had the black case out and the door locked, there was a tall, dark presence at her side.

"Here, let me take that."

Kip shook her head. "No way, Jaime. If you walk in snow like you drive in it, I'm not taking any chances."

Jaime's mouth dropped open, and she let out a startled laugh. "You don't trust me with Isabelle? Well, I just can't believe it. Is that all the thanks I get for...for...well, for whatever?"

Kip couldn't help herself, she reached out with her free right arm and wrapped it around the black goosedown jacket to give the other woman a quick hug, then she stepped back. "I've missed your astounding logic."

"I see." Jaime put a hand on the folksinger's forearm. "C'mon. I'm surer footed than you're giving me credit for." They moved onto the sidewalk, which was swathed in at least ten inches of snow, and slogged through the tracks Jaime had made coming from her van to the truck.

Kip brushed her curly bangs out of her eyes. "Just tell me this—why in the heck are you driving a front-wheel drive minivan?"

Jaime shrugged and smiled her way. "It works great for what I need it for."

"Hmm. And that would be what—carpooling small children to daycare?"

"Yeah, right. Me and kids—uh huh."

"It is your van?"

"*Si, señorita.*"

They reached the foot of the stairs leading up to the marooncolored three-story house. Someone had come out and cleared the snow off the cement steps, but they were still slick. The flakes swirling in the air made their way downward, landed, and were sticking. Kip took the first couple steps up, with the other woman following, and suddenly Jaime said, "Oh, wait a minute. Be right back."

She turned and went to the white van to unlock the door. She bent and reached in between the two front seats. When she emerged, she held two instrument cases, which Kip recognized immediately as the battered mandolin case and the newer violin case. Jaime kicked the door shut, then strolled toward her, looking entirely sure-footed. Again, the folksinger found herself tongue-tied, so she turned and mounted the steps quickly, walked up a short sidewalk, and climbed the second set of stairs. Before they reached the porch, the front door opened, and Drew and Dina stood in the doorway, both talking at once.

The lanky guitarist got hold of Kip's free arm and pulled her into the warm hallway. "Y'all look as cold as a witch's tit." Jaime followed them in, and Dina pushed the front door shut.

Jaime bent to set down her instruments, then slipped off her gloves. "I've always wondered what the hell that saying meant. Why would a witch's tit be cold?"

Drew shrugged. "Just a saying is all." He turned to Dina. "This here's Jaime, and Jaime, this is Dina."

The librarian reached out a hand, and Jaime shook it. By then, Kip had her coat off, and Drew took it from her and hung it on a hook along the wall, all the while keeping up a running commentary about how cold it was compared to Texas. As she removed her gloves and scarf, Kip took the opportunity to look around Dina's home, a large, three-story Victorian style house. The entry hall was a good two stories high and was larger than any room in Kip's house. It contained a beautiful dark oak stairwell decorated with garlands and red bows. The hardwood floors were shiny, and everywhere Kip looked, she saw festive Santas and gold Stars of David. She stepped out of her boots, leaving her extra-thick socks on, and zeroed in on Drew as he took Jaime's coat and reached out to playfully sock her in the arm. Kip had never seen him look quite like this before—so animated, so full of life. Granted, when he played guitar, he was often happy, even excited, but the man before her was now lit from within by a glow she had never seen him display before. He looked as though he might break into a jig—or a Texas two-step—any minute.

He turned to her and smiled. "I am so glad you came, Miss Kip. This is gonna be a whale of a good time."

Without thinking, she stepped forward and put her arms around him to hug him tight. He hugged her back. "Thanks for inviting me." She glanced to the left, over his shoulder, and was surprised to see a tight, nervous look on Dina's face. As she released Drew, she realized that she didn't know the librarian all that well, but if she wasn't mistaken, she had just caught sight of a look of jealousy. She glanced back at Drew, then over to Dina, and smiled and nodded. *Uh huh. So that's how it is. Hmm.* "Dina, I have to tell you, this is the coolest house. And wow, have you ever done it up nice for the holidays."

"No, kidding," Jaime said as she looked up from removing her boots. "It's beautiful."

Drew said, "C'mon in to the living room and check this out."

They followed him through the double doors, and Kip stopped short. "Wow!" The ceilings were a good fourteen feet high and were easily tall enough for the enormous, brightly decorated tree. "No wonder it smells so good in here. It's the evergreen."

"Yes," Drew said, with excitement, "and Dina put it up special for little ol' me."

Kip smiled at Dina, whose face was flaming red. "I don't usually put up a big tree," Dina said, "but we went out looking, and he was so excited."

Jaime said, "You're lucky you had enough lights and decorations."

"Well, I didn't." Dina laughed. "But Drew bought a bunch. Have a seat."

"Yeah," Drew said, "y'all have a seat."

Kip ended up on one end of the large maroon sofa, with Jaime at the other end. Drew and Dina sat across from them in a loveseat, and they sat close enough, with his hand resting on her thigh, that all Kip's suspicions were confirmed. Drew was head over heels. As Dina answered questions from Jaime about the tree decorations, Kip met the guitarist's eyes and grinned. She gave a slow nod as she all but smirked at him, and he smiled back with a look of happiness and pride on his face. She winked, and his grin widened as he looked down at Dina with so much love that even someone who didn't know him would recognize it.

The folksinger gazed around the room at the homey furniture—two couches, the loveseat, and two wingbacked chairs. Another set of double doors led into what she thought was usually a dining room, but the table was pushed to the side. The room was taken over by chairs and stools, mics and music stands, amps and soundboards. In the corner, a full drum set was arranged, and she admired the shiny pale blue color. She saw rolled-up electrical cords lying in the middle of the room, appearing ready for use. When there was a break in the conversation, Kip asked who was coming to play.

Drew shook his head. "I got a drummer and a bass, might be a Dobro player, too, but he didn't sound so sure. As usual, musi-

cians are always late. Wait'll you hear Dina's flute and clarinet."
He dropped his arm from the back of the sofa and put it around
her, and she leaned in looking slightly embarrassed. "We oughta
be able to play some damn good stuff. Y'all wanna go get warmed
up?"

Jaime was on her feet before Kip even had a chance to sit forward. Kip watched her walk across the room to the entryway. She
looked lean and lithe in the jeans and a tucked-in long sleeve Henley shirt. Jaime retrieved her two instruments, one under an arm
and the other in her hand, and with her free hand she grabbed
Kip's guitar. As she turned with the three cases in hand, she said,
"Hope you trust me with Isabelle now, Kip. I mean, I've only carried her about a hundred times in the past, and I've never dropped
her yet." With eyebrows arched, her face carried a smiling challenge.

"Just don't fall down now," Kip teased. "People are watching."

Jaime came into the living room and headed through to the
dining room. Before she set the cases down, the doorbell rang, and
Dina and Drew scurried off to answer it, leaving the two women
standing in the middle of the rug in the dining room. "This is truly
some kind of house," Jaime said as she set down the instruments.

"It is. And not a bit like my house."

"I wouldn't want to clean this place. Looks like a lot of
work."

"Yeah. Just my little three bedroom split-level keeps me busy
enough."

"Same with my place, and it is *way* smaller than this."

Kip knelt and popped the clasps on the guitar, then opened
the lid. She touched the guitar with the flat of her hand. "Ooh,
she's pretty cold."

"She'll warm up fast. Same with the Schweitzer." Jaime
squatted down and opened the mandolin and violin cases and left
them sitting on the floor. She rose. "So, Kip, how've you been?"

The question shouldn't have taken the folksinger by surprise,
but it did. She had no idea how to answer. *Fine? Or even better,
fine, but you broke my heart?* The second option brought a smile
to her face. *Ah, melodrama. Just what I need now.* She looked into
Jaime's eyes, and for some reason, she didn't feel afraid or nervous. In fact, she realized she felt brave—even foolhardy. "I've
been up, and I've been down, but I feel great today. You?"

"That's a pretty good way of putting it." The light brown face
relaxed as a smile broke out, and Kip thought Jaime was just as
attractive—if not more so—as ever before.

Kip said, "You look like you've lost weight."

"Hmm. Could be." Jaime looked down at herself. "I never weigh myself, and it's not like I'm wearing any of my summer clothes."

"How are you adjusting to this weather?"

Jaime shrugged. "It's not so bad. It happened gradually enough that I feel somewhat used to it."

"Gradually? What do you mean?"

"Well, it changed so slowly since September. I hardly noticed it, but one day it was cooler, and then cold, and now it's freezing."

"You mean here? In Minnesota?"

"Yeah." She sat on a barstool and put her stocking heel up on one rung.

Kip dropped into a hard wooden chair with a perplexed look on her face. "You've been here since September, and you never once called me?" At that, she could see Jaime's face darken.

"I wasn't so sure you'd want to see me."

This statement took Kip by surprise, but she didn't have a chance to respond to it because just then, Dina and Drew moved through the living room with two men in tow. She knew Bill Brett and rose to cross the room and give him a hug. The other person was a shy young man named Dan who didn't look like he even shaved yet, though already the hair on his head was thinning. He held a drumstick in each hand and looked at her shyly. "Miss Galvin," he said. "You probably don't remember me."

She looked at him closely, trying to place his face. "When did you graduate from high school, Dan?"

"Summer before last."

"And what's your last name?"

"Benson."

"Oh," she said, nodding. "Danny Benson. You were in the seventh grade class with Mike and José and Sam Richter." The kid nodded. "Wow, you've changed a lot in six years, Dan, and you're an adult now, so you should call me Kip." He nodded again, his face red. She thought it was so odd to run into kids she had taught. They truly did not understand how much they changed in just a few short years. "You were a foot shorter then—but you were always a great drummer. I remember a solo you did at the ninth grade pep rally that one year." She turned to the others in the room and said, "He played his socks off, basically. It was awe-inspiring."

Dan went on to tell Kip that he was a sophomore at Augsburg College, majoring in music. Meanwhile, the others hunted for out-lets to plug in cords and moved chairs and equipment around.

She looked at the young man and smiled. "I also remember how you carried your sticks around in your backpack all the time."

"Yeah, I still do."

Drew said, "Never know when you might run into a vacant drum set, huh, kid?" He patted the young man's arm and looked around at the others in the room. "I found him when I went to listen to a choir concert at his school last month."

"So, you're going to do some percussion for us today?" Kip asked.

Dan nodded. "I brought over my drum kit yesterday, so I'm pretty well set up." He stepped toward the drums and slid onto the padded seat.

Kip looked across the room where Bill was playing around with his bass and the amp it was plugged into. Near where she stood, Jaime sat with the fiddle in her hands, tightening one of the tuning pegs. Dina put her clarinet to her lips and sent a smooth, clear note sounding through the room, while Dan underscored it with a roll of thunder on the snare drum.

A surge of excitement coursed through the folksinger, and she could hardly wait to get her hands on Isabelle. She picked up the Gibson and an electronic tuner, closed her case and set it out of the way, and sat in the chair next to Jaime. The strings and wood were warmer now, and the guitar felt so good cradled in her arms. Once she was tuned up, she played some scales and waited for everyone else to get ready. She had no idea what songs they might all know, but it didn't matter. That was the point of a jam—to play a little bit of everything and stretch your abilities beyond what you thought you knew. When a song went badly, you grinned and stuck with it best you could. When one went well, though, Kip sometimes felt euphoric. With great anticipation, she looked around the room, ready to try anything.

TWO HOURS FLEW by before Kip realized she was both hungry and thirsty. Dina had disappeared a short while earlier, and now she poked her head into the dining room doorway and said, "Don't you even think about starting a new song. I'm starved, so you all must be, too. Drop everything, and get in here."

A mixture of grumbling and cheers erupted, and the whole horde trooped toward the doorway. Kip looked around at the huge room they entered. Not only was there a place on one side of the spacious kitchen for a table that seated eight, but there was also a rectangular butcher block work table in the middle of the room, close to the stove, fridge, and sink. "This is great, Dina." She followed the rest of the crew over to the table and sat next to Jaime, while admiring the light-colored oak trim and red and white swirly wallpaper. "Do you live here alone?"

Dina said, "Heck, no. This downstairs is common space. I have the second floor to myself, and I rent out the two big rooms on the third floor."

Kip surveyed the food on the table: a plate of cold cuts, a loaf each of wheat and white bread, two kinds of cheeses, and various condiments. A bowl of corn chips sat near her elbow, so she scooped out a handful and passed the bowl to Jaime who got a funny smirk on her face and quietly said, "I bet you're wishing there was some salsa so you could watch me slop it all over myself."

Kip chuckled. The rest of the table's occupants were laughing and talking. She leaned close, so close that she could smell the light scent of Jaime's cologne. "I'd pay money to watch that again, and I know a great little cantina over in the Midway neighborhood." She raised an eyebrow and winked. "How about it?"

"Now?"

Kip laughed. "Tomorrow would be soon enough, don't you think? Kind of rude to sneak out now."

Drew asked, "What are you two conspiring about over there?"

The folksinger accepted the plate of cold cuts. "Nothing that a little food and drink won't cure. We're starved." She speared some turkey with the fork, put it on her plate, and passed the platter on.

"Well," he said, "white or wheat? And don't be wastin' time pondering. Y'all need to eat quick so we can get back to the music."

Chapter
Twenty-Three

KIP WASN'T SURE how she would make it through this snowy Monday. The drive in to school had been slow and slick, and she'd barely arrived on time, rushed up to her classroom, and never felt caught up since. She felt like hours had passed, but when she looked at her watch, only fifty-six minutes had gone by. *Oh, my Lord, it's going to be a very long day.*

By the time Kip had made it through three classes and the bell rang for lunch, she was wondering what would happen if she choked the life out of the more obnoxious kids. The teenagers shuffled out, and she went to her desk and sat. *Aren't I supposed to be in a great mood—full of energy and happiness? I'm going out with Jaime tonight. Isn't that supposed to lift my spirits and mood above these brats' behavior?*

But she didn't feel lighthearted. By the time they had parted the night before, Kip was filled with a feeling of rising nervousness. Every emotion she'd had for Jaime resurfaced with as much—or more—intensity as she had felt in August, and it scared the hell out of her.

She hadn't wanted to leave the jam at nine, but rising at 4:45 a.m. to get to school on time required it. She had hardly gotten six hours of sleep as it was.

Putting her elbows on the desk and her face in her hands, she let out a sigh, closed her eyes, and thought about how awkward it had been to depart first. When she said goodbye to Jaime in Dina's front hallway, she hadn't been sure what to say, though Jaime seemed more confident than ever. Kip reminded the electrician about meeting the following day at six, and then Kip hugged everyone, even the shy Dan. She picked up her guitar and strode bravely out into the still night air without allowing anyone to accompany her to the truck. Once she got home, she hadn't slept well, and now she felt fuzzy-headed.

She was sitting quietly, face in hands, when she heard a sound in the doorway and jerked her head up. Dina stood leaning against the doorframe, cross-armed, with a moony-looking smile on her face. "Oh, Kip. It was so much fun yesterday. We should have done that sooner. I can't believe how fast ten hours went."

"How long did the five of you play after I left?"

"Until after eleven. I bet all of us are tired today." She grinned. "So, when can we do it again?"

Kip rose and walked toward the doorway. "Maybe after New Year's?"

"That would be great. Let's plan something. Drew is ready to play at any moment."

"Yeah, I bet. When it comes to music, he's insatiable."

Dina rolled her eyes and laughed. "He's like a little kid in a candy store. You want to come over for dinner and play some more in the next few days—just you, I mean?"

"It's a tough week. In fact, I'd better not commit to anything until after Christmas."

Dina nodded. "Okay. If you don't mind, I'll keep checking with you."

"Sounds good. You going to the teachers' lounge now?" When Dina nodded, she said, "Let me get my lunch and join you, okay?

AT THE END of the work day, Jaime parked her mini-van in front of Rici's apartment. They lived only eight blocks apart, and since she had a lot of useful equipment in her van, they usually rode together to the job sites. Lately, they had been working on St. Paul's Eastside at a three-story office building that was being remodeled.

The young man opened the door and stuck one leg out. He paused, letting in cold air. "You sure you're okay?"

Surprised, Jaime nodded. "Yeah. Why?"

"You've been so quiet all day."

"You think so, huh?"

He nodded. "See you tomorrow, then. Same time."

"*Si, señor*, same bat time, same bat channel."

He slammed the door shut and hustled through a pile of snow and up the walk. She watched him go, feeling real affection for him. It was funny that he had noticed her mood. She certainly had been quiet—pensive and reflective—all day. The honest truth was that she was nervous. Yesterday Kip had seemed so self-assured, so happy, and there was only one time when the other woman had faltered in the least. When Kip was leaving, she seemed nervous and strained, and Jaime didn't know what to attribute that to. It bothered her. At the table, Kip had agreed to go out for dinner, but what if she'd had second thoughts as the evening went on? They had exchanged phone numbers. *Am I going to go in the house and find a cancellation message on the machine?*

Jaime pulled away from the curb and headed for her place. She skidded down her alley, plowing along through a couple inches of new snow. As she drew close to her garage, she pressed the remote door opener and watched with satisfaction as the big door rolled up. It had been near freezing when she installed the new opener, and she'd made short work of it, getting it right the first time. Every time it worked, she felt proud of herself all over again. She pulled into the middle of the two-car garage, pressed the button, and was out of the van and through the back door before the garage door finished closing. She made a dash across the yard to the kitchen entrance, let herself in, and slipped out of her boots on the throw rug just inside. After hanging up her coat and dropping her gloves on the floor, she hustled across the cracked and chilly linoleum, stopping in the hallway to crank up the thermostat, then went into the living room to check whether Kip had called. The only message was from the plumbing supply store to inform her that the parts she had ordered were in.

She headed up the stairwell, feeling the plush carpet under her feet, and went straight into the bathroom where she turned on the faucet to let the water warm. She stripped out of her work outfit, dropping every stitch of clothes into the laundry chute. *Thank God for the washer and dryer in the basement. I dirty up a ton of clothes every day—that's for sure.* She checked the temperature of the running water as she stood shivering, waiting for the hot water to make its way up from the water heater in the basement. Despite having a thirty-gallon heater, she never got much more than ten minutes of hot water. She knew that a lot of sediment had probably built up in the unit, which was at least ten years old, and it was next on her list for replacement. She bent, ran her hand through the water again, and frowned as a sinking feeling came over her. *Oh, shit.* The water was only lukewarm and not getting any warmer.

Quickly, she stepped into the tub and got down on her knees to splash the tepid water over herself. She didn't bother with the shower switch, figuring it would deplete what little warm water there was. Instead, she turned off the tap, grabbed the soap, and lathered up the best she could, then turned the faucet back on. The furnace chose that moment to start pumping air up through the vents, and a blast of cool air hit her, causing her to shiver.

Dammit! This is not how I planned getting ready to meet Kip.

She finished rinsing and stood, shuddering from the cold. The water grew icier by the second, so she turned off the tap and reached for the towel to dry off as fast as she could. When she stepped out of the tub, she could see herself in the mirror over the sink. Her hair was sticking out all over. She ran one hand through it, willing it to lie down, then shook her head and looked up at the ceiling. *Oh, boy, I look like hell.*

She dressed in a hurry, glad to get warm clothes against her chilled skin. Then when she looked at her watch, she realized she had more than an hour before she had to go. *So much for leisurely and relaxing preparations. Maybe I should go down in the basement and shoot the hell out of that blasted hot water heater!* Instead, she went downstairs and checked the answering machine again to see if anyone had called while she was in the shower. There were no messages. She picked up the phone from the window seat, and dialed her boss's phone number to tell him about her predicament.

Don said, "It's not five yet. I'll order you a nice forty-gallon tank right now, and you and Rici can put it in tomorrow."

"We're going to need some real bruisers to help haul the old one out. Bet this thing is going to weigh a ton."

"Yeah, I kind of had a hunch about that, Jaime. Probably got a lot of sediment built up."

"My thoughts exactly. I'll drain it as best as I can tonight."

"Roger. See you tomorrow."

She hung up the cordless phone, went down to the basement, and hooked a garden hose to the spigot on the hot water heater, then strung the other end over to the floor drain. When she opened the drainage tap, it was a good twenty seconds before a trickle of water drizzled out and into the floor drain. She rolled her eyes. *Great! All sediment, no water. The damn thing is really going to be a mess.*

She stomped upstairs. In the living room she checked to make sure she hadn't gotten her jeans and sweater dirty or wet. Even her hiking boots had come away unscathed, which was a relief. Jaime went to the window seat, and put a knee on it to look out. Two young kids on cross-country skis were playing in the front yard across the street. One boy, in a red snowsuit, kept falling over and getting up, then slipping and falling again when he tried to glide on the skis. His friend picked up a glob of snow and hit him when he was down, and the boy on the ground got out of his ski bindings and chased after his buddy who couldn't get out of his bindings fast enough. The red-clad kid tackled him, and they rolled in the snow, shrieking and laughing so loudly that she could hear it faintly all the way across the street.

The two kids disappeared around the side of the house, and Jaime watched, feeling a wistful pull from her own childhood. She'd been so lonely until freshman year in high school, and then Emma and Luz came along. They'd never rolled in the snow, but she remembered how much fun it was to horse around, tickling, teasing, telling jokes. Luz was much smaller than she or Emma, and occasionally Jaime just picked her up, threw her over her shoulder, and spun around. Just thinking of how Luz screamed made her smile. She'd loved spending time with those two friends. They made her school life worth living as much as her grandfather had made her home life happy.

She didn't know what had happened. Somewhere along the way, life had gotten so serious, first with her grandparents' deaths, and then her mother's worsening alcoholic condition. It seemed like one day Jaime woke up, and she'd been out of high school for fifteen years. Magdalena, her mother, was on a downhill slide, and though Emma was around, Jaime was lonely again. And then Magdalena died, and Jaime was truly alone. Getting the tour job had been a real blessing—and a curse. The blessing of it was in making friends again, like Eric and Drew. The curse was the confusion and agony of her relationship with Lacey Leigh.

Thinking of the blonde diva gave Jaime the usual heavy sensation around her heart, and she sank down onto the window seat. She leaned against the wall where the molding would be—when she finally replaced it. With one long arm along the windowsill and the side of her head against the edge of the window frame, she closed her eyes. She wondered if there was something lacking in her, some essential quality that made her unlikable to all but a few. All of her life she had felt alone so much of the time, and today was no exception. And now she was going to meet with someone who had treated her like a friend and who had always been kind, and, put quite simply, she was afraid. *I'm afraid to lose something I don't even have yet. Is that dumb or what?*

When beset with negative thoughts, some of the people in her Al-Anon group had suggested taking stock of the good things in her life. She mentally ticked them off: a decent job, and friends in Don, Rici, and Donnie Junior; a sturdy, solid house, though it currently lacked for a hot water heater; one new friend, Colleen, and her reliable old friend, Emma; and then there was Maria, her Al-Anon sponsor who had already been tremendously supportive. *I also have my health. That's a real plus. But I don't have that special someone, the "real deal," that I've always wanted. What if*

Kip is the "real deal" and I screw it up? She wanted to smack her-self in the middle of the forehead when she considered this. *I thought Lacey was the real thing, too, and look how that turned out.*

The thought made her more nervous than she cared to feel, and she wanted to get up and run. Or throw things. Or hide.

When she remembered the summer tour, especially the events surrounding the last month or so, she felt ashamed at how dense she had been. She was still embarrassed that Eric and Drew had to tell her about Kip's feelings. *I wasn't the slightest bit aware. I had a good friendship going with Kip, and I threw it all away to be with Lacey. I should have known better. And now it seems that the friendship is restored, but what if I blow that, too?* She looked out the window again. *I don't want to think about this anymore.*

She shifted on the hard wooden seat, feeling uncomfortable. Looking down at the window seat, it occurred to her that a cush-ion would vastly improve it. She wondered if she could get one made to fit? She was also going to have to do something soon about furniture. *Once I get the molding up and the sawhorses out of here, I'll go buy some.*

The boys across the street came back around the side of the house carrying some long, flat boards, and she watched a moment to see what they were doing. They hoisted one end of an eight-inch-wide plank up onto the porch railing, and lugged the other one up next to it, forming a long ramp out into the yard. The kid in the red snowsuit took his skis up on the porch and bent to put them on. Just then, the front door opened and a dark-haired woman poked her head out. She seemed to take stock of the situa-tion and, coat-less, stepped out onto the porch. She gestured toward the ramps and shook her head, pointing one finger at the boy in the universal language of all mothers, which Jaime figured said, *No way, José!* Jaime could see shoulders slump on both boys, and they slogged through the snow to pull the boards down and drag them back around the side of the house. She shook her head and smiled.

A look at her watch revealed she still had half an hour before she was due at the restaurant, and she decided she could use a pep talk. She picked up the phone and punched in numbers she had memorized. The phone rang, and her Al-Anon sponsor picked up. "Hey, Maria? You have a minute? Good. I need some advice..."

THE END OF the school day hardly came soon enough. Kip headed home in her truck, giving a wide berth to all the impatient drivers on the road. It had stopped snowing earlier in the day, and the roads were mostly clear, but there were still patches of packed-down snow and ice to avoid.

She got home and had a snack-size container of yogurt to tide her over until six when she was to meet Jaime at a Mexican restaurant over in the Midway neighborhood. She had no idea what to wear. Her hair was giving her fits. She was grumpy and crabby, and she didn't know why. She thought she should feel excited, and actually, she was impatient to get on with the meeting, but at the same time, she was out-of-sorts.

Sitting down on the couch in her living room, she looked around at the Christmas decorations. After a moment, she pulled her feet up under her and took the afghan from the back of the sofa and snuggled up in it. *Time for a reality check. It's only a dinner date. I can do this.*

SHORTLY BEFORE SIX p.m., two nervous women drove to the restaurant thirty seconds apart and ended up parking on opposite sides of the poorly plowed lot. When Jaime hopped out of the van, she stepped into eight inches of snow. She carefully made her way toward the restaurant and wasn't paying attention to anything at all but her foot placement when someone came up behind her and tugged on the waistband of her black down coat.

She jumped and turned. "Hey! What are you doing sneaking up on me?"

Kip grinned. "I'm slopping along behind you like a herd of elephants. Can't imagine how come you didn't hear me."

"Maybe I was concentrating."

"Mm hmm." She fell in step next to Jaime. "Must seem a lot different hiking through snow as compared to sand in the desert."

"It sure is." They reached the front door of the Mexican restaurant, and Kip pulled it open. Her light brown hair stuck out from under a stocking cap, and her gray eyes were merry, though Jaime thought she looked tired.

They seated themselves at the far right of three open areas. On the far left was a smoking area, the middle section was full of larger tables for families or big parties, and the third area was up two stone stairs and ran along the side wall of the restaurant. The booths were small and intimate, and Kip had selected one toward the back. Before they'd even gotten their coats off, the waiter delivered chips and salsa and asked if they wanted something to drink. Once they ordered, he sped off, and Jaime finished removing her coat, which she set next to her on the bench.

Kip took off her stocking cap and ran her hands through her hair, which was electrified. "Good grief. I hate it when I get static electricity in my hair. I bet *you* never have that problem."

Jaime shook her head. "Not all that much, though when it comes to bad hair days, you don't even want to go there." She smoothed her short hair back, glad that it seemed to be lying down for once. "How was your day?"

Kip got a serious look on her face, as though she was debating, and then she said, "Kind of shitty. Yours?"

Jaime sighed. "Mine went well until I got home from work and took a shower. My hot water heater is out."

Repressing a grin, Kip asked, "You took a cold shower?"

"Not by choice, and actually, it was sort of lukewarm."

Kip opened her menu. "Must have taken you back to the days on the bus."

"Believe me, the bus shower was never *that* cold. Why was your day shitty?"

"It was long. The kids were brats, and I was tired. I just didn't want to be there."

Jaime nodded. She put her forearms on the table in front of her and leaned over them. "What's good here?"

Kip tipped her head to the side and looked up. "Pretty much everything. It's probably not quite as authentic as some of the stuff we ate down in your stomping grounds, but I still like it."

"Once I get my kitchen organized, you'll have to come over for my hot-hot chili."

"Not just hot, but it's hot-hot?" Kip laughed.

"You're laughing now, but you'll be crying when you have this hot-hot stuff."

"And this would be fun, how?"

Jaime paused, then met gray eyes. "You always use lots of salsa and hot sauce. I just thought you liked spice."

Kip reached over and squeezed her forearm. "I'm teasing you, you fool. I *do* like spice—but not so much that it burns the tastebuds off your tongue." She picked up a chip and dipped it into the salsa. "These guys have perfect salsa. Try it."

The waiter came and took their orders, and for the next several minutes, they munched on chips and talked about their jobs. Then the meals came, and they made small talk. They were halfway through their food, and Jaime was starting to feel fairly relaxed when Kip hit her with a tough question.

"I've been meaning to ask you about what happened in Tennessee, Jaime, but I don't want to bring up anything that makes you uncomfortable."

Jaime paused, a bite of burrito at her lips, then pulled it away and set the fork down on her plate. "What do you want to know?" She watched Kip take a deep breath.

"Well, actually, I don't understand what happened—with you and Lacey, I mean."

Jaime nodded. "She turned out to be a selfish, spoiled rotten user, just like you probably thought all along."

"What?" With a surprised look on her face, Kip touched her linen napkin to her mouth. "I never said that!"

"You didn't have to say it, Kip. You've got so much more class than she does—it just isn't even funny." She knew her voice came out sounding bitter, but she couldn't help it. The subject of Lacey Leigh still hurt, and even worse, it made her feel stupid. "Let's not talk about her."

"Wait, Jaime. Wait a second. I want to understand. I felt so badly for you, from the first time we talked about Lacey in that café in Albuquerque. I knew you cared about her, but I wasn't sure why. I could never figure out *why.*"

Jaime pressed her lips together tightly and raised her gaze to meet the concerned eyes across the table from her. She teetered on the edge of indecision. To tell or not to tell, that was the question. If she let down her guard, what would happen? If she shared her feelings with Kip, would it prove the death-knell to their friendship? She opened her mouth, and everything poured out: how Lacey had been charming and sweet at first. How the younger woman had led her to believe they could be a forever thing. And then how it gradually soured as Lacey Leigh increased her drinking and carousing. "I thought it was over and done with when I signed on for that second tour, Kip. I thought she'd treat me like she did all her other conquests—you know, ignore me, or if she couldn't do that, berate me. But she didn't." She crossed her arms over her chest and sat back against the cushioned booth. "I can't say that I understand at all. It would have been so much easier if she had just been a bitch toward me, but she wasn't."

"It's different between women," Kip said. "Maybe it was harder for her to really let go. I'd have to say your relationship was probably a lot more complicated than the mindless sex she probably had with the men. Plus, Jaime, you're essentially a good person, and you took care of her a lot. Maybe she felt like a real asshole for working you over that way."

Jaime felt a rush of hot liquid stinging in her eyes, but she blinked and forced it back. "She *is* a real asshole." Kip's face was more than a little concerned when Jaime recounted the last meeting at the rehab center and the diva's racist and ignorant remarks.

"You are totally correct, Jaime," Kip said, her eyes flashing angrily. "She is an asshole. I'd love to get my hands on her drunken neck and just squeeze."

The ferociousness in Kip's voice startled Jaime. "Hey, she's gone now. She's gone forever, and I'm working on letting all of that go. Some of it is embarrassing to me. I think I fell in love with who her best self might have been—that is, if she hadn't grown up with an abusive, alcoholic father, and if she wasn't drinking herself into oblivion, and if she wasn't self-centered and egotistical. But you know what? There are just so many things wrong with her, and it wasn't like I could fix any of them." A ghost of a smile came to her lips. "I'm learning a lot now about what happens when you spend time with alcoholics, and I have to say—I'd rather not."

Kip nodded and slowly, a smile came to her face, too. "So, you're saying if I start drinking, you're heading for the hills?"

Jaime gave one nod and grinned. "I have a hunch you're not the drinking type, Kip. You're solid in a way Lacey Leigh never was."

"You think so, huh?"

"Yes, I do."

The waiter chose that moment to ask if they wanted dessert, and when they both declined, he left for a moment, then came back with a plastic tray containing the check and two peppermints, which he set on the table. "No hurry, ladies. Whenever you're ready."

He cleared a few dishes and departed, and Jaime turned her attention back to the kind, gray eyes in front of her. Despite feeling sheepish about all the admissions and confessions she had just made, she met the other woman's gaze, and for several seconds neither said anything. "I guess you probably think I have pretty bad judgment."

Kip let out a laugh. "Maybe your biggest flaw is not in judgment, but in caring too much and too long. That's not the worst flaw to have, Jaime."

Jaime looked down, blushing. She reached and pulled the check out from under the mints, leaving them on the tray. "I'll get this."

"Oh, no you don't. I was going to treat *you*."

Jaime smiled. In a teasing voice, she said, "Guess you'll just have to get the next meal." She pulled out her wallet and removed some bills, which she put on the plastic tray, then picked up one mint and offered the other to Kip.

The folksinger took the mint and unwrapped it. "I picked this place, so you can pick the next."

"I know a good Chinese restaurant—want to go there tomorrow night?"

Kip shook her head. "I've got the school board meeting tomorrow, and then math curriculum committee Thursday. It'll have to be Wednesday or Friday."

"I have my Al-Anon group Wednesday, and I told a few of them I'd go out for a bite to eat afterwards, but I could cancel."

"No, don't do that. Friday would work just fine."

Kip smiled, and for a moment, Jaime thought the other woman looked a little shy. She asked, "Kip, what are you doing this weekend?"

The folksinger shrugged. "Christmas prep. Running errands. Shopping. Why? You have something in mind?"

"Got any interest in driving around and looking at all the displays of Christmas lights?"

Kip laughed out loud. "I know where there are some absolutely appallingly extravagant ones."

"Good. How about we do that Friday night?"

"Sure. That'd be fun. I'll bring my canned goods along."

"What?"

"Oh, don't they do that down in New Mexico? Lots of these places take donations for charity and the food shelves. For a small fee, some will take a Polaroid of you with Santa or Mrs. Claus, and they've got Santa's helpers and elves running up and down the street collecting money from cars and answering questions. There was one block last year where they had a contest to see who had the most lights, and I guess the winner had, like, 10,000 or some gawd-awful amount that was just ridiculous. I know of a house in St. Paul that even rented a pair of live reindeer, but they escaped and it took the cops all night to round them up, so I don't think that's allowed anymore." By this time, Jaime was roaring with laughter. "I'm not lying," Kip said.

"Oh, I believe you. I believe. It's just—just so funny." But actually, her laughter had less to do with the comical way Kip related the story, and more to do with the fact that she had actually arranged a date with the woman, not to mention that she felt like she was back on her old footing with the folksinger. The relief coursed through her like electricity, and the proper response—short of kissing the other woman—was laughter.

When they stepped out of the restaurant a few minutes later, Kip turned to Jaime and said, "Let me know if you need to borrow a shower."

Jaime looked at her blankly for a moment. "Oh, thanks, but

that's not necessary. I'll have a new hot water heater in the morning."

"Well! You must have a hotline to the service company."

"No, I'll just put it in myself. A guy on the crew, Rici, and my boss are coming over and we'll install it."

"Jaime Esperanza, you must be a real handy gal to have around."

The black-haired woman grinned and nodded. *Yes, I am. I am handy to have around. How nice of you to notice.*

Chapter
Twenty-Four

THE TWO WOMEN sat laughing in the corner booth at Yang's Chinese restaurant. The red booth and its décor were classic Chinese, with dimly lit, orange lanterns hanging from the ceiling. The walls displayed traditional folk art and calligraphy. The place felt cozy to Jaime, and she had been there so often lately that the waitress knew her on sight and had ushered them to the most comfortable booth in the place.

Kip took a sip of her hot tea. She set the thick porcelain cup down. "I still can't get over that one house with the live Santa and his family perched on the roof." On one street in Mendota Heights, obviously the neighbors were trying to outdo one another. This homeowner had built a sled and attached it securely to his roof. He and his wife and children, all dressed in little red suits, were attached to the sled by leather cords, and they stood on top of the house, waving bravely, surrounded by scores of brightly wrapped presents and piles of fake snow.

Jaime said, "It's cold out there, too. I think the kid elves looked like they were freezing."

Kip laughed. "It's just so ridiculous what people will do. I should've brought a camera for that one."

Jaime watched as Kip scooped up another spoonful of spicy Chinese soup, and then the waitress arrived with their meals. She set their plates on the table and hastened off, returning with a bowl of steaming, sticky rice. "This place makes great entrees, Kip. I love their *Moo Goo Gai Pan*. Try some of mine."

"Only if you eat some of this sesame chicken. I'll never make it through this huge portion."

"That's another good thing. I always have enough to take home for breakfast."

"Oooh," Kip said, laughing. "Cold Chinese for breakfast?"

"No. I heat it up."

"Thank God for microwaves."

"Actually, I don't have one yet. I'm going to buy one soon, though. I just stick the leftovers in the oven."

Kip swallowed her first bite of the chicken. "This is heavenly. You're right. Great food."

"I'm glad you like it. Rici introduced me to this place."

"Rici, huh? You work with him, right?"

"Yeah. He's a nice kid. I don't know why, but we get along great. I've worked with lots of men over the years, and he is one of the more respectful—while at the same time, he's your typical male. I don't know—I've grown to like him a lot. He must have had some good parenting."

"You know what? You have a real way with men, Jaime."

Jaime was taken aback by that. "What? What do you mean?"

"Men can't help but like you. You get along well with them."

"You should talk! You're the same way."

Kip laughed. "No, I'm not."

"Ki—ip." She drew the name into two syllables, then grinned. "You had all the tour musicians eating out of your hand."

"Oh, that was nothing," Kip said, raising her hand and making a single dismissive wave. "I think a lot of straight men are comfortable with lesbians because we don't put any pressure on them and just sort of accept them as they are."

"I haven't even broached the subject yet about me being gay," Jaime said. "Coming from a strict Catholic and Latino background, I wonder how he'll take it." She sat quietly for a moment. "He's a good kid, and ever since he got shocked, I've felt protective of him."

Kip asked her for the details about that, and they discussed it for a while, then moved on to other aspects of Jaime's job. Kip asked, "Once you get these houses all wired and set up, is the job over?"

"Oh, no. We've been working on some apartment units in Cottage Grove, and Don has a whole bunch of contracts for furnace repair all over St. Paul. People call him out of the Yellow Pages, too. It's a booming business. His wife does the scheduling, billing, and office work. He now has a crew of seven working with him. He'd like me to stay on permanently."

"Are you going to?"

"I don't know. I just might."

They continued to eat, sharing their meals, and laughing about a variety of things. The waitress took good care of them and refilled their teapot regularly. After a while, Jaime sat back and sighed. "I can't eat another bite. Looks like you'll have plenty of leftovers."

"No, *you* take the leftovers for breakfast. I won't eat 'em. And hey, it's my turn to pick up the tab." Kip took her wallet out of her pocket and caught the waitress's eye. "Ma'am, could you box this up?" The waitress smiled and nodded, then departed with their plates.

Jaime felt a pang of disappointment. She glanced at her watch to find it was only a quarter to nine, and she didn't want the evening to be over. She watched Kip count out bills. The other woman's light brown hair shone in the low light, and her cheeks were pink. She wore a royal blue turtleneck under a dark blue waffle-weave shirt, and Jaime thought the colors suited her. Kip had always looked good in blue. She also looked good in green—and black or purple or red or several shades of brown. Jaime frowned. Kip looked good in any color, and right now, Jaime didn't want her to leave.

The check arrived at the table along with two white take-out containers. Kip checked the tab, and then left a stack of bills on the little black tray. Jaime pointed and in a teasing voice said, "You only carry ones?"

Kip giggled and shrugged. "There's a ten in there, too, but yeah, I had a lot of ones that I'm glad to get rid of." She looked at her watch. "The night's still young. So, what's next?"

Jaime felt a surge of relief. "We could see a late show."

"Oh. That's a good idea. What did you have in mind?"

"In mind? I just now thought of it."

"Let's hustle over to the multiplex and see what's on. I haven't been to the movies in ages." She picked up her coat from the seat next to her. "If we get going now, we're sure to catch something that starts shortly after nine."

"Okay. Let's go then." They slid out of the booth. Jaime stood and reached over to help Kip into her coat. When the parka was settled across the other woman's shoulders, Jaime let her hands rest on Kip's upper arms, which she squeezed.

Kip turned and smiled. "Thanks." She picked up the two white containers.

"No problem." Jaime put her own coat on as she headed toward the exit with Kip at her heels. She got to the door and held it open. Kip stepped through, juggling the leftovers as she slipped on a pair of thermal gloves. Jaime realized she had left her gloves in the van.

"Good Lord, aren't you cold?" Kip asked as the door shut behind them.

"I'm sure I will be, but no, not yet." Actually, she felt toasty. The light wind brushed her face, but its chill served only to highlight how warm she actually did feel. She was pleasantly full from the meal and happy that the evening with Kip was not yet over. As far as she was concerned, nothing was going to make her feel cold.

Chapter
Twenty-Five

IN A CRAWL space under a stairwell, Jaime lay on the floor on her back, both knees up, and her work boots flat on the cement floor. Rici was squeezed in next to her, attempting to train a flashlight on the junction box she was dismantling. She coughed from the dust. "Who the hell in their right mind would have stuck a junction box under here?"

Rici must have shaken his head because the flashlight wobbled. "I bet they ran out of conduit or wiring or something."

"Maybe. Or maybe they wired first, then decided to put stairs in. Let's get the damn thing out fast so we can go for some lunch." A lot of the wiring she ran across was not up to code, or even if it was legal, some senseless idiot had to have designed the installation. "There. Got it." Sweating and feeling claustrophobic, she waited a second as Rici shifted away and scooted toward the triangular opening.

They both crawled out into the dark basement and clomped up the stairs into the early morning light. They reached the kitchen where it was cool and bright. With a smirk on his face, Rici said, "Lucky you're way too old for me, Jaime. All this work in close quarters could be hard on a guy."

She looked at him in amazement, and then her eyes narrowed. "Should I whap you upside the head for your blatant ageism or for your sexist assumptions?"

"No, no—that's not exactly what I meant—I mean, you know, we're like in cramped spaces and I—I—"

She held up a hand. "You should quit while you're behind, Rici, and I hate to wound your manly pride, but you're not my type—even if you were my age."

They moved out of the kitchen and toward the front room where they gathered up coats and gloves. He didn't say anything until they had locked up the house and headed out to her van. "So, out of curiosity, what kind of guy is your type?" he asked.

She unlocked the van and got in to start it up. When his door slammed shut, she pulled away from the curb. "The kind of guy who's my type is female."

"Oh. I see." Jaime felt his eyes upon her and turned her head to meet his eyes briefly. He didn't look away. In a quiet voice, he said, "I don't think I've ever talked to a gay person."

She laughed. "Of course you have. We've talked to several just since I've worked with you."

"We have? I never noticed."

"Yeah? That's because everyone assumes a person is straight until proven otherwise." She turned onto Rice Street. "Want to go down to that hamburger place?"

"Okay." He was quiet for a minute. "Can I ask you a question?"

"Go ahead."

"Why—I mean, how come you like women more than men?"

She slowed down for an upcoming yellow light and came to a stop at the intersection. "What is it about women that *you* like better?"

He shrugged and let out a breath. "I don't know. I like the way they make me feel. I like the smell of their perfume and how they laugh. Also, they cry and let you know if you hurt 'em. And I like how they're actually a lot tougher than you think they are, but at the same time, a really cool girl doesn't make a big deal out of that."

The light changed and she stepped on the gas. "Do you feel that way about men?"

"No! Not at all. I have some guys for friends—you know that—but I don't, like, want to get close to them or get physical or anything like that."

"Right on. And that's exactly how I feel, Rici. Guys make great friends, but I feel the same way about women that you do. I've always felt that way." She turned into the entrance of the restaurant parking lot. "Does that make any sense to you at all?"

He didn't answer. She parked the car and they got out. The electrician could see the top half of Rici's head across the roof of the van. He met her eyes, and she waited to see if he had anything to say. Instead, he turned and headed toward the restaurant. She didn't see him duck down by the tire, scoop up some snow, and make a quick snowball, but she did see the sudden rapid movement as he tossed it. "Hey!" She stepped aside, but it still clipped her on the right shoulder.

"Ha ha!" he shouted, then took off toward the front door.

She followed him at a fast walk, and when she got to the front door, she saw him standing inside grinning like a fool. *I guess I'll take that as something positive. And later on, that boy is going to get it!*

Over lunch, Jaime's cell phone rang, and she pulled it out of her pocket. As soon as she discovered it was Kip, she rose from the table and stepped over to the doorway to have a brief conversation. She was picking up Kip at seven to go to a party, and the folksinger just wanted to verify that they were still on. A warm feeling coursed through her as she heard the rich tones of the other woman's voice. Kip couldn't talk long, so they hung up quickly, and Jaime returned to the table.

Rici grinned at her. "I'm finding out all kinds of stuff about you today. You got a date or something?"

Jaime couldn't keep from blushing, but before she said anything, the phone rang again, and she dug it out of her pocket expecting it to be Kip. Instead, her boss came on the line and asked them to abandon the work at the house and head over to Cottage Grove to help install 32 sets of washer hookups. She got off the phone and relayed the information to Rici.

"Sounds good to me. I just hope I don't get cramped up in another crawl space with my lesbian partner."

She wadded up her napkin and threw it at him.

KIP SAT AT her desk in a classroom that was mostly quiet, except for the sound of students shifting in their chairs, pencils scratching on paper, and an occasional sigh. She knew the last Friday before Christmas vacation was hard for all of them, but this class had been so squirrely and rude that she'd given them a pop quiz to quiet them down. Once they were sufficiently calmed, she planned to let them play math games like the other classes had.

In front of her was a stack of papers to correct, but she couldn't focus on them and was instead looking out the window at the light, fluffy snow falling steadily. She found it hard to believe that it was finally Friday and that Christmas was next Wednesday. The entire month had blown by, and she felt like she had sleep-walked through most of it with only one dream—about Jaime—running constantly in her mind. They had been meeting as often as possible, but between Kip's after-school meetings and Jaime working late on two projects, they hadn't seen each other nearly as much as she would like. Kip had the number for the electrician's new cell phone, and all week they had been talking on the phone or leaving one another messages whenever either of them had a few spare minutes. She looked longingly at her bag, which sat on the floor next to her desk. She had talked to Jaime briefly over lunch, but she had a hunch that if she could just call and check her messages, there might be another one from Jaime since then.

She turned and looked at the clock over the door, and ten minutes had passed, so she rose. "All right, kids. Take one more minute to finish up the problem you are working on, and then pass your papers to the front." Some students whispered, and the classroom noise went up several decibels. "I want to remind you to keep your voices down. If you behave, you can play games until the period is over. And remember, let's all cooperate."

The next twenty-five minutes seemed an eternity, but finally the bell rang, and the whole crew of rambunctious 13-year-olds gathered up their things and went whooping out into the hall. She knew exactly how they felt. *Hallelujah. I'm free until after New Year's. Thank God!*

She gathered up her own things and stuck all the students' tests in her bag to correct sometime over the holiday. She had plenty of time to kill before Jaime picked her up to go to the party, but all she wanted to do was flee the school and forget all about geometry and algebra for the next two weeks.

IN THE DAYS since Jaime and Kip had met on the way to Dina's house, the whole tenor of Jaime's life had changed. It was hard for her to believe a mere twelve days had passed. She woke up every day excited about what would happen next. She conscientiously charged her cell phone and checked its messages regularly. When she worked on her house, it was with an energy that didn't burn out quickly. She finished all the molding and remounted it piece by piece and was more than satisfied with the outcome. Touching up the paint on the living room walls had gone well, and they were as near to perfect as she could manage. She found a comfortable and wide cushion at Pier 1 Imports. It made her especially happy that the print on the window seat cushion was gold, red, and black. It reminded her of the Aztec patterns that had graced her grandparents' house.

She stood in the living room admiring the glossy floors, clean walls, and beautiful molding and trim. *Now all I need is more furniture than just a window seat.* She turned and headed up the stairs to clean up. Once the water heater was replaced, she had what seemed like an unlimited supply of hot water, and she luxuriated in it. When she finished her shower and stepped out onto the rug, which lay on the newly tiled floor, she felt a surge of satisfaction. She had every single thing she needed in the bathroom. Fully outfitted with towels and necessities, it was the only room she had nothing further to work on. The living room was done, but it still needed furniture to be complete. She now had a kitchen table and chairs, but she hadn't replaced the cracked linoleum floor yet. And she hadn't finished installing the fixtures in the new bathroom downstairs. For that, she was going to have to ask Donnie and Rici for help.

She finished in the bathroom and went to the room in which she had been sleeping. Jaime still wasn't sure if she wanted this room as the master bedroom, but the queen-sized bed was set up there. No chest of drawers, so she dug around in one of many duffel bags for socks and underclothes. All of her pants, sweaters, and shirts—even t-shirts and sweatshirts—hung neatly in the closet on hangers. She selected an outfit and dressed in a pair of gray, light wool slacks, black ankle boots, and a black turtleneck. Over the latter, she slipped a blood-red fatigue sweater, looked in the mirror, and was satisfied. As an afterthought, she squatted down and opened a suitcase. She pulled out the shiny wooden box with the piñon tree on it and opened it. Rolled up inside it she found the purse Kip had left for her and took it out. The beads felt smooth and cool against her thumbs, and she wondered what was happening with that tiny Minnie Logan, the boot-maker. She opened the purse and removed the only item in it, the necklace Emma had given her. The amethyst pendant looked nice in the V of the sweater, nestled against the black of her turtleneck. With one last look at the beaded purse, she returned it to the wood box, stuck it back in the suitcase, and stood. *I'm ready.*

THIS WAS THE first time Jaime had been to Kip's house. She pulled into the driveway and walked up to the front porch. Before she could knock, the door was opened and Kip welcomed her in and shut the door behind her. Jaime stood just inside, on a thick mat, kicking the snow off her feet and feeling awkward. The living room was decked out with holiday decorations, the sofa and two chairs looked comfortable, and the Christmas tree lights blinked, reflecting from various tree ornaments in twinkling colors.

"Come on in," Kip said.

Jaime gestured at her feet. "I'll get snow all over everything." She bent to unlace her boots, but Kip strode back toward her and put a hand on her back.

"That's okay, Jaime. I'm ready, so you don't have to take your boots off." She stepped around the other woman and opened a closet door to get her coat.

Jaime straightened up, still feeling the pressure of Kip's touch in the middle of her back. She reached out to help Kip with her coat, and when the other woman turned to face her, they stood face to face and eye to eye. Jaime tipped her head to the side. "Are we the same height?"

Kip nodded. "Right now we are—as long as I've got these tall, clod-hopper boots on." She grinned and pulled a wool cap over her hair. "Aren't you cold without a hat?"

"Not really. This thick hair of mine keeps my head warm. My ears get cold though."

Kip turned and reopened the closet door and ducked halfway in.

Jaime heard a muffled statement. "What? I didn't hear that."

The folksinger emerged from the closet with a pair of gray earmuffs. "Here. Try these insulated muffs. Your ears will never get cold again." She adjusted them in her strong hands, reached up, and settled them on Jaime's head, then stood looking at Jaime with a smile on her face. "How's that?"

In slow motion, Jaime brought her hands up and moved the earmuffs until they settled comfortably. "Good." Kip stood close enough that Jaime could smell her perfume, and her earlier conversation with Rici about why he liked women popped into her head. It hit her that Kip was just the sort of person who met Rici's description and that his wish list, though vague, held true. Kip was a woman worthy of attraction, and with sudden clarity, Jaime realized that the woman who stood before her was close enough to kiss. She wished she could lean right over and kiss her.

Kip looked down as she pulled on her gloves. "Now remember, Jaime, we don't have to stay all that long. I don't know half the women who'll come to this party, so if it gets overwhelming for either of us, we can split."

Unable to say a word, Jaime nodded and stepped aside so Kip could open the front door and insert her key in the deadbolt. As they walked single file toward the van through the chilly night air, she felt more than a little star-struck.

EVEN THOUGH IT was still early in the evening, the party was in full swing when they arrived. They entered to find the huge home packed full of women. Lila Peterson, a teacher friend from another school district, co-owned the house with her affluent stockbroker partner, and every Christmas they threw The Party To End All Parties. This year was no exception. They'd gone all out with the decorations, hors d'oeuvres, and drinks. Kip and Jaime had no sooner gotten in the door and hung up their coats than Lila caught sight of them.

"Oh, Kip! I am *so* glad you're here. We were just talking music, and Mickie Shelton is itching to play piano. Come sing in a bit, why don't you? And who do we have here?" The short woman looked up at Jaime, appraisingly, and back to Kip, so Kip introduced them. "Nice to meet you, Jaime," Lila said.

And then Kip was mobbed by several other women, and she stood for the next twenty minutes introducing Jaime, answering questions, and chatting. After a while, she caught Jaime's eye, leaned in close, and quietly asked, "You doing okay?"

Jaime smiled sheepishly. "Sure."

"Should we go get something to snack on?" At Jaime's nod, Kip threaded her arm through the other woman's and excused them from the group. "You are going to tell me when you can't take it anymore, right?"

"Sure."

Kip laughed and met her eyes. "Earth to Jaime. Is that all you can say—'Sure'?"

Jaime smiled back. "Surely?" She laughed. "Is that better?" Kip elbowed her and pulled her onward.

They wound their way through clusters of people, across a Persian carpet, through wide double doors, and into a spacious dining area with three buffet tables. In an alcove to the right, a crush of people was waiting to put in drink orders with the two bartenders.

Looking all around, Jaime said, "This is quite the place."

"No kidding." Kip leaned in and quietly said, "It's way too ostentatious for me, but I love coming here for a party. Wait'll you see the music room."

They filled their plates with olives, pasta salad, and meat pastries, and then before they could move, Kip was approached by several more women who started up a spirited conversation with her. Jaime stood listening as she munched on the hors d'oeuvres. When she finished, a server came by and took her plate and utensils. A waiter passed through with a tray full of empty glasses, and she stopped him to ask for soda. A few moments later he came back and gave Jaime a glass of something fizzy with lemon, and she drank it gratefully.

Kip gave her plenty of opportunities to join the conversation, but Jaime was content to listen and comment little. It gave her the chance to watch the folksinger and how she interacted with acquaintances. Jaime liked how warm Kip was toward people. She thought she was gracious and generous, remembering personal details about women she apparently did not know all that well. It was very clear to her that people were drawn to Kip.

After a while, Lila tracked them down and dragged Kip off toward the music room. Jaime followed, amused, as the chatty little woman literally pulled the folksinger by the sleeve of her green and white Christmas sweater. Kip had been right about the music room. It had great acoustics, and from what Jaime could see, the Steinway grand piano sitting in the middle of it was breathtakingly gorgeous. A pack of people stood around the piano singing Christmas carols with a second ring of women sitting in chairs behind them, talking and downing mixed drinks. The pianist finished off the final flourishes of "God Rest Ye, Merry Gentlemen," and a cheer went up.

Lila pulled Kip through the crowd. "Mickie! She's here now."

The woman behind the piano was dressed in a full tuxedo. She rose and gave a nod of her head. "Nice to see you, Miss Galvin."

"And you, as well, Miss Shelton. I trust all is in order?"

With a nod of her head, Mickie gave an amused laugh. "Spectacularly." She settled back on the piano bench, and Kip went over and gave her a hug. It wasn't until later that Jaime learned Mickie and Kip had been butler and housekeeper, respectively, in a high school play set in England. Even without that information, their quaint greeting reminded her of English drawing room mysteries.

In an entirely different voice, Mickie growled out, "You ready to rock'n'roll?" Kip gave her a nod, and the musician launched into a wild piano intro, which Jaime soon recognized as "Boogie Woogie Bugle Boy." In short order, Kip belted out the lyrics. Even without any vocal warm-up, she sounded great.

Jaime stood at the end of the piano behind a shorter woman directly across from the pianist. Kip was off to the side, on Mickie's left, with her hands on the edge of the top of the shiny black surface. The electrician looked down at Kip's hands and realized she was gripping the piano tightly. She watched the folksinger and wondered why she was so nervous. Others joined in on the chorus of the song, and Kip seemed to relax. Jaime had never heard Kip sing in public without her guitar, and she wondered if she was nervous without Isabelle. She raised her eyes and found Kip looking her way, so she winked and smiled, and that seemed to further relax the other woman.

Jaime stepped back and surveyed the room. Mickie finished off that song and segued into another, and Jaime decided Mickie Shelton was one hell of a pianist.

Across the room sat two ceiling-high bookcases. She wandered over to find that someone in the household was a real music
buff. Not only were there shelves of books of sheet music, but also
an entire bookcase devoted to the history of jazz, the blues, rag-
time, swing, rock, African drumming, calypso, and more. She pondered whether Lila was a music teacher or just an overly enthused
lover of song. As she leisurely examined the books, she listened to
Kip's smooth voice and the intricate piano. The next song trailed
off, and before Mickie segued into a new one, there was a commotion at the door. Jaime turned to watch a group of five women
enter. One called out, "Kip! Hey girl, how ya doing?"

Jaime focused on the short, stocky blonde who swaggered in,
weaving her way through and around people until she stood on
Mickie's right. The look on Kip's face was hard to decipher, but
for no good reason at all, Jaime felt a stab of alarm. She stepped
away from the bookcases and eased her way toward the piano.

"Why don't you play my fave song?" the woman asked. "You
know, the one you always used to sing for me."

Now Kip looked positively stricken. Jaime stepped around
the short blonde and sidled past Mickie. She met Kip's eyes and
frowned. Taking a deep breath, she reached out a long arm. Kip
placed her cold hand into Jaime's warm one. Quietly Jaime said,
"We've got to run now," as she pulled Kip toward her and gripped
her hand tightly.

"Hey," the blonde woman protested. "Who are you?"

Jaime didn't reply. She wasn't sure how to answer that question, so she acted like she hadn't heard it. Instead, she smiled and
kept her eyes on Kip as the folksinger leaned down and placed a
kiss on Mickie's cheek. Jaime heard her tell the pianist, "I'll call
you sometime soon to jam." Mickie reached back and patted Kip's
leg, and then a torrent of piano erupted. Kip slid past Mickie,
guiding Jaime ahead of her, then stepped around the frowning
blonde woman, still clutching Jaime's hand in a death grip.

They stumbled out of the music room and moved quickly
down a long hallway leading out toward the dining area and
beyond. Before passing through the door into the foyer, Kip
stopped short, tugging on Jaime's hand. Brought to a halt, Jaime
turned to face the blushing woman. "How did you know?" Kip
asked.

Jaime shook her head and shrugged. "I'm not sure what was
going on. I only know that you didn't like that woman."

Kip stepped forward and wrapped her arms around Jaime's
waist. In the other woman's ear, she whispered, "Thank you for
getting me out of there," then leaned back and smiled. In a normal

tone of voice, she said, "Let's blow this pop stand, and I'll tell you more."

"Shouldn't we say goodbye to the hostess?"

Kip shook her head. "I'll call her tomorrow and chat. She isn't going to notice us leaving. There's got to be over a hundred people here. Come on."

Jaime felt Kip's hand slide down her sleeve until fingers, now a little warmer, threaded through hers. Electrified and shivering with excitement, she let herself be pulled forward to the foyer area where they found their coats and fled into the cold night. As she got into the van, she could still feel the warm pressure of Kip's arms around her and the grip of the other woman's warm hand. She had liked that. She wished she could reach out and take Kip in her arms, but she didn't.

KIP SAT IN Jaime's van shaking as much from nerves as from the cold. She was surprised to find it was only a quarter after nine. She felt so unsettled, and it seemed so much had happened that, for all she knew, it could have been midnight. They hadn't driven far when Jaime asked, "You want to go home? Get a cup of coffee? Drive around?"

Kip wasn't ready to go home yet, but she didn't want to sit in a busy restaurant or anywhere she might run into people she knew. "Can't we go to your place?"

The lights from the oncoming traffic were just enough to illuminate the amused look on Jaime's face. "Sure, we can go there, but be forewarned. I haven't got any furniture to speak of. However, I do have a table and chairs in the kitchen, so if you want a snack and some coffee or cocoa, I can be a good hostess."

"That would be great." Kip gradually stopped shivering as the van warmed up, and by the time Jaime came to a stop, she was feeling halfway human again. She wasn't sure how to explain what had just happened, and the thought of the entire event embarrassed her terribly. She got out of the van and trudged up the walk, hardly paying attention to anything other than her footing. So it was with great surprise that she entered the foyer of the house and Jaime clicked on the lights to reveal gleaming hardwood floors and a newly painted entryway that led into a large open living room. "Wow! This is beautiful." They stood on a large square of carpeting, which she wiped her feet on.

Jaime smiled. "Here, let me have your coat." Kip slipped out of it, tucked her cap and gloves into the sleeve, and watched the other woman hang it up in a closet to the left of the front door.

Kip looked up at the immaculately white ceiling. "Smells like paint. You must have done a lot of work on this place, huh?" She wiped her feet some more.

"Yes, I guess I have. Don't worry about your shoes. The floors clean up great. Come on."

Kip followed Jaime straight ahead, down a hallway, and into a kitchen. "What a great room. Wish mine was large like this."

"I've got work to do on it still. Needs paint, and I have to install some kind of new floor covering."

Kip looked down at the faded gray and pinkish red colored pattern on the floor. "Yeah, I have to admit that this sucks. Must be circa 1950."

"Maybe even older. Have a chair." She pointed toward an oak table and chairs, and Kip strode over, sank down in one, and found it to be comfortable.

"This is a nice chair."

"Thanks. I liked those a lot. I always want a kitchen chair that doesn't put my legs to sleep. I can't believe how awful so many of them are. Now, do you want coffee? Cocoa? Root beer? A shot of Scotch?"

"You don't really have Scotch?"

Jaime shook her head. "Would you have wanted it?"

"Hell, no. I want something that's not artificially warm— cocoa would be my first choice."

"Coming right up, then."

She watched Jaime open a cupboard and get out a big pan, then reach for the handle of the fridge. A contented sigh escaped her, and she was glad Jaime didn't seem to notice. The black-haired woman moved fluidly, her red sweater in sharp contrast to the light brown counters and faded yellow walls. Kip let herself take in all of the other woman, from the tip of her dark hair to the black boots, and everything in between, finally deciding that Jaime looked terrific in red. *I think I may have to buy her something red to wear. Maybe some earmuffs.* She smiled to herself. She had not yet bought Jaime a gift, but now she thought she would do some shopping in the morning. She cleared her throat. "So, Jaime, you probably think I was nuts tonight at the party, huh?"

Shaking her head, Jaime turned from the stove. She continued to stir the liquid in the pan. "Who was that woman?"

"My ex."

"Oh."

"My sentiments exactly."

"I don't mean to be insensitive or nasty, Kip, but even if she's your ex, I just have to tell you she was a rude bitch."

Kip laughed aloud. "Isn't that the truth. As far as I can tell, both you and I have been burned big time by blondes."

Nodding, Jaime turned back to the stove. Over her shoulder, she said, "So do you miss her an awful lot?"

"What! No, I don't. I don't miss her at all anymore." She said it with vigor and conviction, but the force of her words couldn't disguise the fact that she still felt bitter. She put her forearms on the table and watched as Jaime poured cocoa from the pan straight into two mugs, then set the pan in the sink and ran water for a few seconds. She turned off the tap and picked up the two mugs to carry them over to the table. Kip leaned over the mug placed in front of her. "This smells great." She wrapped her hands around the hot cup and smiled. "Thanks for making this."

"You're welcome." Jaime settled into the chair across from her. She took a tiny sip from the mug. "Whew. Got pretty hot. Sorry I don't have any marshmallows."

"I don't need 'em. This is fine." She took a small sip herself and set the mug down. "So I suppose you want to know why I freaked in the music room."

Jaime shrugged. "It's okay. If that had been Lacey Leigh, I would have wanted to split as fast as I could, too. I understand."

"No, listen." Kip's grip on the handle of the mug tightened. "If she had just come in and said 'Hi,' I probably could have taken that. But she asked for me to sing a song—our song—and that was so damn callous and insensitive of her."

"What was the song—if you don't mind me asking?"

Kip smiled bitterly and shook her head slowly. "'Every Breath You Take'—you know—that old Police song." Jaime bit her lip. Kip could see two white teeth as Jaime obviously fought back a grin. "Go ahead, Esperanza. Laugh." She said it in a mocking tone, but Kip couldn't hold back her own smile. "No flippin' way was I going to give her the satisfaction of ever hearing me sing for her again." She reached across the wood table and placed her warm hand on Jaime's forearm. "Thank you so much for rescuing me. Every woman at the party is wondering who the hot-looking chick is that Kip Galvin took off with." Jaime sat back, and her face flushed dark with embarrassment. "C'mon, Jaime. You don't know how good-looking you are?"

"Uh—uh—"

"You didn't seem to have any problem earlier tonight saying 'Sure.' That would be a good word to use now." She gave Jaime's arm a squeeze. "I shouldn't tease you." She let go of the electrician's forearm and picked up her mug. A tapping sounded behind her, and she looked at Jaime, then glanced over her shoulder. Jaime rose and went to the back door to look out, and Kip turned sideways in her chair, curious about who would be knocking at this time of night. The door opened, letting in a gust of cold air.

Jaime asked, "What are you two doing here?"

"Hi, Jaime," the man said. "I didn't know you had company."

A black-haired man, a little shorter than Jaime, backed into the kitchen dragging what Kip quickly identified as a Christmas tree. The tree was followed by a young girl wearing jeans, white Sorel boots, and a pink coat and hat. She carried a large box.

Jaime grinned. "I know it's hard for you to believe, Rici, but I do have a friend or two. This is Kip Galvin. Kip, this is the work partner I've mentioned, Rici Gutierrez, and his sister, Serena."

"We've got something for you!" the girl said in an excited voice. She was vibrating with excitement, and Kip wondered how much longer the young girl would be able to hang on to the awkward box. She rose from her chair as Jaime took the box from Serena's hands so that the girl could remove her coat and hat. Kip said, "Nice to meet you both. What have you got there?"

Serena said, "It's a tree. For Jaime. Rici says she needs to get in the Christmas spirit, so we went and got her a tree. We came over earlier, but she wasn't home, so now I get to stay up extra late."

Rici said, "I have to run back out to the truck and get the stand. Be right back."

He slipped out the back door and disappeared into the night. Kip looked over and met Jaime's amused eyes as the other woman set the big box on the table, then took the hot pink coat and hung it over the back of one of the kitchen chairs. She set the pink knit cap on the seat, and said, "So, where should we put this tree, Serena?"

Serena said, "In the living room, silly. Kind of by the fireplace." She stepped out of her boots, and strolled across the linoleum and through the doorway leading into the far end of the living room. Kip watched her push off with one foot and slide along the glossy wood floor. When she looked at Jaime, both women grinned. "Cute kid."

Jaime nodded. "The whole Gutierrez clan is made up of nice people. Serena's the youngest, Rici's the oldest, and there are four other kids in between."

The back door opened, and Rici entered carrying a red and green old-fashioned metal tree stand, which he handed to Jaime. He smacked the door shut. "My dad dug this up. It's no great shakes, but it can hold up this little tree." He stepped out of his heavy-duty boots and reached a hand toward Kip. "Glad to meet you, Kip. Hope you don't mind us barging in."

She shook his hand, which was surprisingly warm considering how cold it was outside and that he wasn't wearing gloves. "Nice to meet you, too. Here, let me take your coat." He slipped out of the down coat, and she put it over Serena's on the chair.

From the living room, where Serena was still skating in her stocking feet, Kip heard a plaintive whine. "Hurreeeeeee..."

The three adults chuckled. Kip reached for the box on the table, and Rici picked up the tree. Jaime still held the tree stand. She set it down, saying, "I'll get a piece of carpet from the basement to set this on. Be right back."

Twenty minutes later, the four of them stood looking at the five-foot-high tree stuck securely in its stand. It was adorned with a double string of twinkling lights and twelve shiny red ornamental balls. Serena said, "Looks pretty good!"

Kip nodded. "Do you think Jaime will get in the Christmas spirit now?"

The dark-eyed girl nodded. "But she does need some presents for underneath."

Jaime asked, "One for you would be a good idea, huh, Serena?" The girl grinned and squinted up at her happily. Jaime looked over at Rici. "You want a snack or something to drink?"

Rici shook his head. "Raincheck." He looked at his watch. "We better get going. It's way past Serena's bedtime."

"Rici," Serena whined.

"No, *mi hermana*, I promised not to keep you out too late. You have to get up early in the morning. C'mon, let's go."

After Jaime shut the door behind them, she smiled at Kip and said, "They're both balls of fire." She leaned back against the door, and Kip stood a couple feet away.

"I can see that," Kip said. "He seems very nice."

"Yeah, he is. I had no idea they were going to do that." She looked over at the table. "You want me to warm up the cocoa?"

Kip shook her head. "Not yet. Would you give me the grand tour first?"

"Sure."

"Seems to be the word for the night from you."

"Sure?" Kip nodded. Jaime straightened up as Kip reached out and touched the pendant she wore around her neck.

"I've always liked this necklace. Where did you get it?"

"Emma bought it for me in Gallup."

"It's quite beautiful."

Kip released the necklace and Jaime nervously pointed

toward the foyer. "Want to see the upstairs or downstairs first?"

AT MIDNIGHT, THE two women still sat at the kitchen table. Kip yawned. "I should probably go home. You have to get up early tomorrow?"

Jaime shook her head. "I'd rather sleep in on a Saturday."

"I'm supposed to go to a brunch at my cousin's at ten."

"Well, let's get you home, then." She rose and cleared away their mugs.

"I was wondering—are you doing anything Tuesday night?"

Jaime shook her head as she set the cups in the sink. "That's Christmas Eve. I work all day." She turned on the water.

"You have plans after work?" When Jaime shook her head again, Kip went on. "Want to come with me to my parents' house for the evening?"

Jaime turned the water off, picked up a terry cloth towel from the counter, and dried her hands. "What happens at your parents' house?" She set the towel down and turned to face Kip.

"Christmas cookies and snacks for a while. Dinner. My nephew opens presents for himself and his baby brother. We adults have stopped passing presents around amongst ourselves, but we lavish them on Christopher and little Spence."

"Oh, I don't know, Kip. I'd be intruding."

Kip smiled and shook her head. "Not really. The older fellow from across the street always comes over. My great-uncle the bachelor and his widowed sister-in-law usually come bearing terribly bad fruitcake. The pastor from my parents' church drops in. Keith and his wife almost always bring a pack of people from Cathy's family. It's usually a free-for-all. Believe me, you'll fit right in."

"Okay. If you're sure I won't get in the way."

Kip smiled warmly. "You never get in the way, Jaime."

Chapter
Twenty-Six

JAIME WENT DIRECTLY from work to a brick church near the *Mercado de Mexico* in her neighborhood. Alcoholics Anonymous and Al-Anon meetings were held in the basement at St. Cecilia's. Ordinarily she went to a seven p.m. Al-Anon group on Wednesdays, but because Christmas fell on Wednesday, and since she had plans for Christmas Eve, she'd chosen to attend her weekly meeting on Monday at five p.m. She was fifteen minutes early and sat alone for a good ten minutes in the large conference room near the monsignor's office before another woman came in, followed shortly by two other women. She didn't know any of these people, and that made her feel shy, but over time she had come to understand it didn't matter. Regardless of what meeting she attended, they all had nearly identical formats, and without exception, people treated one another with respect.

Right on time, at five, the week's group leader called the meeting to order. After some quick announcements, the eleven people in the room joined hands. Jaime always liked to recite the Serenity Prayer: *God grant me the serenity to accept the things I cannot change, the courage to change the things I can, and the wisdom to know the difference*. This was some of the wisest advice she had ever heard. She released the hands she held and sat quietly as they went around the room, each saying their first name and receiving a "Hi" from all the others. Then each person read one of the 12 Steps. It was a comfort to go over the same material each week. Jaime thought it made it easier for her to remember during the rest of the days.

A different step was focused upon at each meeting. Her regular group was scheduled to talk about Step 7, but this group was on Step 1: *Admitted that we were powerless over others and that our lives had become unmanageable*. Back in September when she attended her first meeting, Step 1 had not been difficult for her. By the time Lacey Leigh was done with her, Jaime had no trouble admitting that she was powerless and that her life was unmanageable. Every so often lately, she stopped and marveled at how much more peaceful her life was without the blonde diva in it. Sometimes she still wondered about Lacey, but she was working hard at letting go of all that had happened. It was over. Though she still felt angry or hurt when she thought about it, those feelings were gradually becoming less intense.

Each week a participant came prepared to talk for a few minutes about how a particular step was affecting him or her, and the woman who shared today had many good things to say about Step 1. When she was done, they went around the room, and everyone had a chance to talk for a couple of minutes. When it was her turn, Jaime thanked the woman for her comments and passed. Today she didn't have anything special to add and was content to sit through the rest of the meeting listening to the others. The three men and seven women who sat around her were ordinary people. Two were Latino like herself, and the other eight were also folks from the neighborhood. They all had similar problems— but also remarkable differences. The bottom line was that each person had been touched in some way by the terrors of alcoholism, and each came humbly to the meeting, looking for support, information, and an occasional dose of comforting. It didn't seem to matter what walk of life people were from, where they lived, who they loved. All of them struggled with similar issues. Jaime felt accepted here, regardless of her age, race, gender, or sexual preference. Nobody seemed to care about any of that.

The meeting ended at six, and Jaime made her way out to the van. She was hungry, but rather than driving immediately to the store or a take-out place, she picked up her cell phone from the passenger seat and checked her voicemail messages. One message. It had come just fifteen minutes earlier. She pressed the recall code and heard Kip's voice. "Hey, you. How was your afternoon? Just got done helping Mom make chocolate truffles. Wait'll you taste these. They're sinfully delicious. I'm on the road to Mary and Joyce's and I'll be there for a bit, then I'll be back home about eight or so. Give me a call when you can."

The message ended, and Jaime sat back with a goofy smile on her face. She dialed Kip's house, knowing she wasn't home, and left a message on the answering machine. She couldn't wait for eight o'clock to come.

JAIME HAD CHOSEN to work on Christmas Eve day, but after that, all their jobs were on hold for Wednesday through Friday of Christmas week, and she didn't have to be back to work until Monday. She had agreed to be on call if Don needed her, but he didn't think anything would come up. She had been touched when he gave each of his workers a fresh turkey and a Christmas card containing a fifty-dollar bill. She was with Michael and Rici when he told them with a big grin on his face, "Wish I could give you all a thousand dollar bonus. Here's a down payment. More to come next Christmas."

She got home from work, put the turkey in the freezer, and rushed around to get cleaned up. An edge of nervous anticipation crept over her, so that by the time she was ready to go to Kip's, she was in a high state of agitation, her stomach roiling. She had met Kip's parents, in passing, back when the tour had come through the Twin Cities near the end of July but she remembered little about them. She'd had no time to pay attention to anyone then because of Lacey's condition. Now she regretted not focusing on them. She only vaguely remembered two middle-aged people who looked like Kip and had seemed pleasant.

Kip had told her to dress comfortably and casually. She wasn't sure what that meant, exactly, so she opted for a pair of dark blue corduroy pants, a black and blue flannel shirt, and a lightweight sweater that was electric blue. She hoped her ensemble was appropriate.

She thought about all that had happened since Friday. Kip called her after the brunch on Saturday, and they met for a late afternoon supper at an Italian restaurant. Because they monopolized the table for so long, Jaime left a tip equivalent to half the check. She didn't care. She would have been happy to pay double because suddenly, all she wanted was to be close to Kip.

They went off to the movies, and before the trailers even rolled, Jaime found herself distracted. She wanted to reach out, to touch Kip. They shared a small bucket of popcorn, which Kip held, so Jaime had every occasion to lean close, but she wasn't able to bring herself to take the folksinger's hand, and she was mad at herself for being a coward. She felt like she could have stayed up all night, just to be with Kip, but the other woman had to head home after the movie so as to get enough rest to rise in time to sing at a friend's church service the next day. Jaime asked if she could come along to listen, and Kip had been surprised, but fine with the idea.

The church service was nothing exciting, but the folksinger's version of "Ave Maria" was remarkable. She knew exactly how Kip's voice had sounded on stage, but truly, she had no idea Kip could sing like she did in church. Accompanied only by piano,

Kip sang the start of the hymn in a restrained fashion and ended the verse with such power that it gave Jaime the shivers. *Wow* was the only word that came to Jaime. She heard it over and over in her head: *Wow! She's incredible. Wow!*

She was sitting on the hard pew in the old-fashioned Episcopal church when she realized she felt more than friendship for Kip. Every day that had gone by lately, she was drawn more to the other woman, but it wasn't until Kip returned to the pew and sat next to her among so many strangers that Jaime understood she had fallen in love. It seemed to have occurred so gradually, though, that she wasn't sure when it had happened. She glanced to the left to find Kip looking at her out of the corner of her eye. "Good job," Jaime whispered. She lifted her left hand from her lap and patted Kip on the thigh, then pulled her hand away, conscious of all the people around them. Kip blushed and whispered back, "Thanks," and the church service had gone on.

They spent the rest of Sunday driving around town, shopping, and stopping when they needed to for snacks or coffee. The day blew by so quickly that Jaime was dismayed when Kip reminded her she had to get up early for work the next morning. "You don't want to miss out on all that electricity," Kip had said with a smirk on her face.

Despite going to bed at ten p.m., Jaime hadn't slept well. Instead, she spent time trying to make sense of the tumultuous feelings coursing through her. She now knew how she felt about Kip, but were her feelings returned? Although she still remembered what Drew and Eric had said back in August, Kip hadn't given her any indication of the depth of her feelings, if she had any for Jaime at all. Were they just friends? Or was it possible to have more?

Though Jaime was grateful for the work to keep her mind occupied, the two workdays hadn't passed quickly enough. She hadn't seen Kip since Sunday night, but had spent as much time as she could on the phone with her. Now she was eager to talk with her, to see her in person and decide if she could manage to share her emotions. She hoped Kip would understand what she felt, but since she wasn't sure, she felt troubled and edgy.

It was still light out, but just barely, when she got in her van and pulled out of her garage. The streets were clear of snow, for the moment, but the weather forecasters predicted a near blizzard on its way. She had to laugh at how obsessed Minnesotans were with the weather. Every local news program on radio or TV opened with dire weather updates. She wasn't complaining, but it was so different from New Mexico where the weather was only periodically a factor.

She took the turn to Kip's house and pulled into the driveway and sat for a moment with the van idling. The automatic garage door began rolling upward, and by the time it had opened all the way, she saw Kip standing next to the blue truck, beckoning to her. With a gloved hand, Jaime turned off the ignition and looked at the item on the floor next to her seat. She had a small package for Kip, but she decided to leave it in the van and not take it with them to Mr. and Mrs. Galvin's house. She thought she would rather give it to Kip later.

Feeling more than a little trepidation, she got out of her vehicle and walked along the icy driveway toward the garage. Kip reached into the passenger side of the truck, then emerged, shut the door, and turned toward her as she entered the shelter of the garage. Jaime met Kip's eyes, and she felt something fill up somewhere in the vicinity of her heart. She wasn't sure if it was the expression on Kip's face or the electricity crackling between them, but she suddenly knew that what Eric and Drew had told her all those months ago was true. *Kip more than likes me. She does love me. I don't know why, but I can tell. The guys were right.*

"Hey, you," Kip said.

A foolish grin came to Jaime's face, and she couldn't hold it back. "Hi yourself, Kip. Merry Christmas." As she stepped closer, she opened her arms, and Kip leaned right into her. Jaime enfolded her in a tight hug. They stood swaying for far longer than good friends ordinarily would, and when their grips loosened, neither released the other right away. Jaime was flooded with warmth and heat. All the nervousness and unease she had been feeling fled from her. She felt her heart beating at a rapid clip, and she wished she could scoop Kip up and take her into the house. Into the other woman's ear, she whispered, "You sure we have to go now?"

Kip's body shook, and Jaime realized she was laughing. "If I don't show up, my parents will send out a posse."

"Can't have that now, can we?" Jaime stepped back and sought out Kip's eyes, which she found twinkling with merriment.

"Come on, Esperanza. Gut it out for a few hours."

Jaime smiled back. "Okay. Let's go."

KIP'S PARENTS' HOUSE was packed with people. The folksinger, holding a glass of white wine, stood in a doorway and looked out upon one very full living room. She counted eighteen people. Her mother and aunt were in the kitchen, and if she counted the baby sleeping in the bedroom, that made twenty-one.

To her right, Jaime sat in the middle of the couch with four-year-old Christopher sitting on her left. Great-aunt Maggie, the only relative who insisted on calling Kip by her given name, sat on the other side, and the three of them were making their way through the second of three family photo albums. Aunt Maggie patiently pointed out and named various relatives, including her own now dead husband, while Christopher kept asking to see the pictures of him and baby Spence. Kip peered closely at Jaime, concerned that she might be bored, but she seemed to be enjoying herself.

"And that," Aunt Maggie said, "is a nice shot of Elizabeth the year she decided to sleep with her Halloween candy."

Jaime turned her head and met Kip's eyes. She pointed down at the photo album. "This is the pink hair you told me about." Kip nodded. "It's not so bad." The folksinger rolled her eyes and shook her head slightly.

Aunt Maggie turned the page. "It's not so bad from the front. You need to see the side, Jaime. It's *really* pink from this angle."

Jaime examined the photo and broke out laughing, her face lighting up with pleasure. She looked back up at Kip and laughed harder.

Christopher giggled, too. "Auntie Kip has pink hair. Auntie Kip's in pink hair!"

All three of the photo viewers, three generations of people Kip loved, laughed uproariously. She took a sip of her wine, glad that they were having so much fun, and listened as they continued to work their way through the photo album. In a way, she wished she were sitting right next to Jaime, going over each picture, telling her the context and the stories, but she had a hunch there would be time for that in the future. She had the distinct impression that what had happened in the garage earlier was the beginning of much more. If she'd doubted Jaime's feelings before, she did so no longer. Something had changed. She was hard-pressed to identify when it had happened, but she was sure Jaime was on the verge of declaring her feelings, and Kip was certain they were much stronger than friendship.

She looked around the room. Her father stood by the fireplace, his arm leaning on the mantel, as he and Dickie Nelson from across the street talked with the pastor. Her sister-in-law, Cathy, and Cathy's sister played the Candyland board game on the floor near the tree with three squirrelly grade-school-aged girls. Her brother stood in the doorway to the kitchen talking to his wife's brother. The room buzzed with laughter and conversation.

She looked back toward the couch to find Jaime gazing at her. If a look were translatable, then the expression on the other woman's face translated to "I long for you." Kip felt her face grow warm, and she knew that if anyone were to notice her, she'd feel like a fool. But everyone in the room was busy, oblivious to the fact that two nearly black eyes met hers hungrily.

Aunt Maggie interrupted the moment. "Here's a shot of that nice fellow who used to live behind Elizabeth's parents' old house."

Jaime looked away. Kip took a deep breath and tried to still her heart.

"Look," Christopher said. "He has skin like yours, Jaime."

Aunt Maggie said, "Nonsense, Christopher. That man was African. He's a Black man. Jaime, you're Spanish, right?"

"Nuh-uh, Auntie Mags," Christopher insisted. "He's the same. The same color as Jaime."

There was a lull in the conversation in the room, a moment of tense expectation. Aunt Maggie said, "But it's *not* the same, honey."

Christopher was indignant with his forehead wrinkled up. "I know my colors, Auntie." He looked up at Jaime. "Why is your skin brown?"

Jaime said, "I grew up where it was sunny and warm almost all year, and we never had snow the way you do. All of my people have skin that's been baked by the sun."

"Oh," Christopher said as though he understood completely. "My momma makes me wear sunblock or I get burnt. When I'm five pretty soon, then I don't have to anymore."

"Nice try, sport," the boy's father said. "Your mother even makes *me* wear sunblock."

Several people in the room snickered at that, including Aunt Maggie. Jaime raised her eyes and grinned at Kip again, and the rest of the room's occupants returned to their conversations. Kip smiled back. She hoped that the love she was feeling for the other woman showed as much to Jaime as Jaime's expression revealed to her.

THE EVENING PASSED quickly, and before Jaime knew it, it was nearly eleven. Kip wished everyone a very Merry Christmas, and there were hugs all around, including for Jaime. The two women said their farewells and exited into a windy night which was made slightly less frigid by the new earmuffs Jaime wore. Kip's Christmas gift, insulated and scarlet in color, pleased Jaime immensely. She adjusted her jacket collar and the earmuffs as she followed Kip to the truck.

Snow fell steadily, accumulating at a rapid rate as well as
blowing all over avenues that had been clear when they'd arrived.
After a slow and dangerous drive across town, Kip finally rounded
the corner to her street, cut past Jaime's white van in the driveway, and waited for the garage door to rise.

Out of the corner of her eye, Jaime watched the other woman
steer into the garage, then reach up and press the remote to close
the door. "Whew. That was some drive, Kip."

"No kidding. If the snow keeps up like this, we'll have more
than a foot or two by morning." They each opened a truck door,
and Kip went around the rear to open up the back.

Jaime said, "Here, let me get one of those bags." She took the
heavier one, which contained a crockpot.

Kip pulled the lighter one out and shut the canopy. "You're
coming in for a while, right?"

Jaime nodded and followed her, feeling nervous, but excited,
too. Kip had been silent the whole way home from her parents'
house with Christmas music on the radio being the only sound for
company in the truck. She knew the folksinger had been concentrating on driving, but she also wondered if maybe Kip was as nervous as she was. She stepped up into the house and slipped off her
gloves. "Brr...it's damn cold."

"I must be a total space cadet," Kip said. She sighed and set
the bag just inside the door. "I thought I left the heat up, but I
must have turned it down."

They spent a minute taking off coats and scarves and gloves.
Jaime hung her coat over the back of the dining room chair. She
shaped her lips into an 'O' and blew out, surprised at the misty
cloud her moist breath made. "You must have turned it way down,
'cause you're right—it's damn cold in here." She stood awkwardly
on the rug, wiping her boots.

Kip stepped out of her Sorels and headed across the room to
the thermostat on the wall. A frown creased her forehead with
wrinkles. "I *did* leave it up. It should be at least 65 in here. Instead
it's—ah—geez, it's 46."

"Not good." Jaime bent and untied the laces of her snow-
packed hiking boots and stepped out of them. She grabbed her
coat and put it back on. "Where's the furnace?"

"It can't be the furnace."

Jaime laughed. "Unless you left a door or window wide open,
I pretty much guarantee it's the furnace. You've got power, so I'm
assuming you have a gas or oil furnace?"

"Gas."

"Show me to it."

"Hand me my coat. I'm freezing."

Jaime took the coat from the coat tree next to the door, crossed the room, and handed it to her. She followed Kip into the utility room under the stairs, which contained the washer and dryer and ample storage space. A door there led down to a dark basement. Kip hit the light switch and descended.

The basement was small and under only the main floor of the house, not under the split-level side. They reached the bottom of the stairs, with a few steps across the cement floor, Jaime found an older furnace. "When was this put in?"

Kip shrugged. "I've owned the house eleven years. It was here when I bought it."

"Hmm." She looked at the stickers and labels still affixed to the metal contraption, but there wasn't much to tell her the age of the furnace, and she didn't recognize the brand. "When was this house built?"

"1946."

She didn't think the unit was that old. "The basement is certainly insulated well. It's a lot warmer down here than it is upstairs."

"So maybe the furnace is working after all."

Jaime went down on her knees and opened a metal door. "Nope. Pilot light's out, and this isn't an electronically ignited one. Let me see if I can get it lit. You have some matches? And what have you got for tools if I should need 'em?"

Kip brought her a dented red toolbox and a container of wooden matches. Jaime spent some time trying to get the pilot light re-ignited, but it wouldn't stay lit. She dug around in the red box, but didn't find anything useful. "I should go out and get my own tools. I could probably figure this out."

Kip rose. "I'm going to call Excel Energy. I pay a bunch of money every month for them to fix stuff like this. Let's let them do it."

Jaime rolled back from her knees and into a squat. "It's Christmas Eve, Kip. Don't be surprised if they're short-handed." She rose, pulling her unzipped jacket tighter around her, and followed the folksinger up the stairs. Her stocking feet were freezing.

Kip went to the phone in the kitchen, and Jaime sat around the corner, cross-legged on the couch, listening to the conversation as she rubbed her cold feet. She looked around the tidy living room. A four-foot-long Santa stocking hung on one wall, and three two-foot-long socks labeled Elizabeth, Spencer, and Keith hung on the mantel over the fireplace. Everywhere she looked, she saw garlands and mistletoe and reindeer statuettes. Two cross-stitched Christmas scenes hung on the wall above the television. All through the room were kitschy touches of the holiday season, including a family of snowmen—*snow-people*, she corrected herself—and a manger scene on the coffee table in front of the couch. The Christmas tree, next to the couch, was decorated with strings of lights, a variety of ornaments, and silver tinsel. Jaime scooted down to the end of the sofa and surveyed the tree until she found a switch attached to a light cord. She flipped the switch and the tree lit up, green and gold, red and blue. The shiny colors made her smile. She got up and went to the gas fireplace, squatted down in front of it, and opened a tiny metal door at the base. She monkeyed with the buttons, and with a whoosh, the pilot light flamed to life. *Well, since this works, now we know it's not the gas line to the furnace.* She turned a knob and a fan started up, then she turned it another notch and the fan shifted to high. In seconds she could feel heat rolling out, and with a sense of satisfaction, she closed the little metal door just in time to hear Kip raise her voice in exasperation.

"What do you mean *tomorrow!* We could freeze to death tonight."

Jaime nodded slowly, thinking there was no way any repairman wanted to come out on Christmas Eve, especially in a snowstorm. For some reason, at times like this, mechanical devices seemed to take on a life of their own, almost like they wanted to enjoy the holidays and not work, just like their owners. She figured it would be a while before anyone arrived, and without taking the whole thing apart, she couldn't help. She lowered herself to the edge of the couch again and pondered whether she should go out to the van, get her tools, and start the work of tearing apart the broken furnace. At least the expense for Kip would be decreased if the repairman had less to disassemble. And who could tell—maybe she could fix it.

Kip hung up the phone and came around the corner from the kitchen. She looked like she wanted to yell. She stood under the arch between the rooms, pulling her coat close. "Those damn fools said it would be twelve to eighteen hours."

"Yeah, I figured. Christmas is always a big jinx." She gestured toward the fireplace. "Well, I got that to light. You could always sleep here in front of it." She rose and stepped around the coffee table.

"I'm thirty-seven years old, Jaime," she snapped. "Way too old to enjoy sleeping on the hard floor in front of the goddamn fireplace."

Jaime took three easy steps until she stood in front of Kip.

Without hesitation, she reached out and took the folksinger's chilled face in her hands. Leaning in close, she locked eyes and stepped closer. Kip's eyes had gone wide, but she didn't pull away when Jaime pressed her mouth against the cool lips. When Kip responded, Jaime closed her eyes and turned her head slightly, then pressed tighter, the tip of her tongue exploring. Her heart was beating so fast, she thought she might faint.

She pulled back and opened her eyes to find Kip looking at her with surprise on her face. The folksinger said, "I—I didn't expect that."

Jaime dropped her hands from Kip's face. She swallowed and looked up. "You *are* standing directly under the mistletoe."

Kip looked up and let out a startled laugh. "So I am. And hey, I *was* needing a warm-up."

"Actually, you were beginning to look like you needed a cool-down. I thought you were going to throw a fit."

"I'd like to! Those damn people can't get out here until tomorrow."

"Uh oh, there you go again." She reached out her right hand and took Kip's cold hand into her own.

"You're warm," Kip said breathlessly. "Your hands are warm."

"My feet sure aren't. Don't you have some sort of heater—a space heater or something?"

Kip nodded. "There's one in the garage. I hope it still works."

"Okay, if you get that, I'll get my tools from the van, and let's see if I can work some magic on your furnace."

IT TOOK JAIME only a few minutes to find the problem. A burned out thermocouple was preventing the furnace from firing up. She showed the part to Kip. "No wonder the pilot light went out. It's under this little rod, which goes to fuel control. Without this, the whole system shuts down."

"Oh, crap. Tomorrow's Christmas." She looked at her watch. "Actually, it's Christmas Day in half an hour. I suppose I'll have to wait another day to get the part."

Jaime looked up, surprised. "The part? I've got a million of these in the van."

"You're kidding?"

"No. I'll be right back."

Jaime put on her boots and gloves and exited out the garage's back door, braving the cold again. The wind had picked up, and it cut through her, causing her to shiver. She opened the sliding door to her van and pushed aside the full-length, insulated work suit that lay there. She wished she was wearing it, but it was stiff as a board and would probably take longer to thaw than it was going to take to install the part. She knelt on the doorway's edge and fished around through boxes and plastic bags until she found a compatible part. She checked it closely under the overhead light, thinking she did not want to have to come back out. That thought made her laugh. If Kip sent her home, she would have to come back out in the cold anyway, but she realized that she wanted very much to spend the night. She hoped Kip would ask.

She shut the sliding door, opened the driver's door, and reached in to pick up the small package between the seats, then slammed that door shut and hiked back along the icy sidewalk. The lips that had kissed Kip a short time before were stiff and quivering from the cold. She moved quickly around the back and into the garage and rushed into the cool house. After the ten-degree-below-zero windchill outside, the house actually felt warm, though she knew it wasn't more than fifty degrees.

Kip stood in the kitchen. "Oh, dear, you look totally frozen."

Jaime set the part on the table and nodded. She shivered as she took off her gloves. "All I can say is that I sure hope this works."

"Should I heat up some soup?"

"I'm still stuffed from dinner. How about some tea or cocoa?"

"Which?"

"I think tea." She stepped out of her boots. "Wish me luck."

Kip came across the room and took hold of Jaime's arm, squeezing it through the black down jacket. "I feel bad about you having to do this."

Jaime looked into the gray eyes and smiled. "I'll only charge the basic house call rate. If you're lucky, it'll run you a mere two hundred dollars for the thermocouple."

The folksinger looked alarmed. "Whoa—that's a very spendy part."

Jaime couldn't hold the laugh in. "I'm kidding. It's—let's see—about six bucks, give or take a dollar." Kip smacked her playfully on the front of her jacket with the flat of her hand, and Jaime grinned. "You can just count it as an extra Christmas present."

"Extra? I haven't seen *a* Christmas present yet so how can it be *extra*?"

Jaime grinned. "You'll see."

"I only hope it works."

"I think it will. Let me go give it a try."

"You want some slippers? Or wait, why don't you just go

ahead and put your boots back on?"

"Nah, don't worry. It's not too bad down there with the space heater going. I don't want to get your carpet all wet and snowy. I'll be right back." She turned and strode into the living room and headed toward the steps. Kip watched her disappear down the stairwell, all the while feeling a sense of disbelief. Now that she was alone once more, she reached up and touched her lips with the tips of her fingers. *She kissed me. I still can't believe she kissed me.*

She returned to the kitchen and pulled down two mugs, filled them with water, and put them in the microwave to heat, then rooted around in the cupboard until she found some Good Earth tea. She considered turning the oven on for warmth, but everything she had ever read advised against it. Besides, she hoped maybe Jaime would succeed in fixing the furnace and the house would soon be warming.

And then what? Then what happens? Despite the chill air, warmth spread from her knees upward to the middle of her abdomen. Her heart rate quickened as she thought of Jaime's laughing eyes, of her gentle hands, soft lips, lean hips. *Oh my. Get hold of yourself.* The microwave dinged, and she opened it, removed the mugs, and dropped the tea bags in. She stuck a spoon in each and stood dunking the bags for another minute. When the tea had steeped enough, she tossed the tea bags in the garbage and carried the cups through the living room and down the stairs to the basement. The space heater was hooked up on the far side of the room, and the heat from it actually made the room cozy. She found Jaime on her knees with one hand stuck inside the furnace. "This thing's not going to blow up or anything, is it?" Kip's voice came out worried.

Jaime grinned. "I cut the gas. I suppose there's a little in the lines, but no, you're perfectly safe."

Kip offered the electrician the mug, but Jaime shook her head. "Give me a minute." So Kip placed it on the stair and sat on the second step from the bottom. She pulled her coat tight and took a sip of the hot tea, welcoming the feeling of it burning its way down her throat. For the first time in nearly an hour, she was finally starting to thaw.

"Okay," Jaime mumbled, "let's give it a try." Kip watched the other woman monkey with a pipe on the side of the furnace, and then she was back on her knees lighting a match. A whoosh sound came to her ears, and Kip heard a quiet tick-tick like metal expanding. Jaime looked at her, expectantly, and they both waited until a soft humming noise started up, and she heard air moving.

Kip said, "Is it actually working?"

"Yup." From her kneeling position, Jaime grinned happily and sat back on her heels. "Cross your fingers that will do it. You can have those Excel people double-check it tomorrow, but hey, I'm pretty sure it'll do for tonight." She brushed her hands together and got to her feet, moving slowly toward the stairs. "I think I'm a bit dirty."

Kip set her mug on the stairs and rose. She took one step, met the other woman halfway, and worked her arms under the black jacket and around the slim waist.

"Kip, I'm going to get you dirty."

"I don't care." She tightened her grip and leaned her chin on Jaime's shoulder. They were so close that the sides of their heads touched, and Jaime's ear was considerably warmer than Kip's.

Jaime leaned away and looked at her in the dim basement light. "Your ear is cold."

"A lot of me is cold." She looked shyly at her companion. "Will you warm me up?"

"Gladly." Jaime drew her closer and covered chilled lips with her own, then pulled away and buried her face against Kip's neck, kissing it softly. Her hands found their way inside the folksinger's coat and caressed her back from neck to waist, which was the same thing Kip's hands were doing to her. "You are all I want, Kip," she whispered in one chilled ear. "Could we—could we have—a life together?"

Kip leaned back slightly. "You would want that?"

"Yes."

The folksinger found Jaime's hand and took it in her own. She led her to the foot of the stairs and bent to pick up one mug. Jaime bent and grabbed the other, then stopped before they took a step. She said, "Uh oh. Better turn off the space heater. Wait a sec." She let go of Kip's hand, set the mug on a step, and went to the far corner to unplug the cord. "Hey, you know what? This is a pretty good heater. If the furnace fails, you could always put it in your room."

Kip laughed. "You seem like a better heater to me."

"It's possible." She picked her way around a tall box and returned to the foot of the stairs, where she picked up the mug again. She took a sip. "Mmm. I never much cared for tea until I moved here."

"C'mon."

Jaime followed Kip up the stairs, her heart pumping with excitement. She hit the basement light switch when she got to the top, and then in the utility room she looked at her free hand. It was streaked with grease, as was her wrist. "I definitely need to wash up."

The folksinger nodded. "Use the upstairs bathroom." She moved out into the hall. "The furnace *is* working. Feel that. It's actually getting warmer in here." She climbed the stairs to the living room with Jaime following.

"Just think—it might save you three hundred bucks."

"Nah, I already told you I pay big bucks on the bill every month for them to come and fix the furnace when it breaks."

"Well, then, you just got ripped off because they'll get here in the morning and have nothing to do."

"Like I care? I'm just so happy to have heat. There isn't anything more depressing than huddling for warmth alone on Christmas Eve."

They reached the top of the stairs leading to the living room, and Jaime grabbed her arm. "You wouldn't have to huddle for warmth alone. I would've stayed with you."

"Would have? You're not staying now?"

"If you'll let me, hell, yes, I'm staying!" She looked at Kip hopefully.

The folksinger pointed up the stairs. "First door on the left is the bathroom. The room down the hall to the right of it is mine. I'll lock everything up, turn out the lights, and meet you up there in two minutes." Jaime handed her the nearly full mug and headed up the flight of stairs. Kip called out, "Hey, hot stuff." Startled, the other woman wheeled around, and Kip chuckled. "There are a couple of brand new toothbrushes in the second drawer on the right, next to the sink."

Jaime didn't say anything, but she took the last four stairs two at a time and disappeared into the bathroom. Kip stood for a moment in the living room, clutching the mugs while her heart thudded in her chest. She cut through the living room, took the tea to the sink, and dumped the liquid out of both mugs. She knew she should rinse the cups, but she just left them sitting on the sideboard. She flipped off the kitchen light and moved through the dining area to the door leading to the garage and turned the deadbolt. She took off her coat and hung it on the coat tree and shivered. Despite the heat pouring from the registers, it was still cold, so she hustled across the room and saw the thermostat now read 53 degrees. *It's going to take a while to get back to normal.* She adjusted it to 65 degrees and flicked off the living room light switch, then she pivoted around and looked at the brightly lit Christmas tree. The tinsel glittered and twinkled, and she couldn't help it. She stood there grinning as she took it in, thinking that it looked positively magical. She was shaken from her reverie by a shiver. Crossing over to the front door, she checked to see that it was locked, then clicked off the tree lights and hurried up the stairs to the now vacant bathroom.

WHEN JAIME FINISHED washing up, she went down the hall to the next room. Uncertain, she stepped through the doorway, leaving only the hallway light on behind her. The king-size bed wasn't made, though the covers on one side were folded back diagonally as though Kip had left it that way to be inviting. Otherwise, the room was tidy. The closet's bi-fold doors were both open and displaying neatly organized shelves and hanging racks. Two oak dressers sat close together on one wall, and across from the foot of the bed, an entertainment center held a large TV and a VCR. Struggling with an attack of the jitters, Jaime looked at the huge bed and felt her knees go weak. With no chair in the room, she stepped over and sat gingerly on the edge of the bed while her heart beat like a piston.

She pulled her coat tightly around her, then became aware of water running in the next room. As quickly as she identified the noise, it ceased, and she heard a door open. Before she had time to prepare, the hallway light went off. The bedroom was plunged in darkness with only a fine beam from a streetlight shining through a gap at the bottom of the window shade. She could see a dark form and hear footsteps coming closer, and then Kip's voice asked, "You still have those matches in your pocket?"

"Yeah." Jaime fumbled in her jacket, and by the time she pulled them out, Kip had stepped between her legs and put a hand on her shoulder.

"I'll take those," Kip said.

She let go of the matches and Kip moved away. To Jaime's right, light flared and the match hissed as it took flame. The sulphur tickled her nose, and she watched the eerie glow as Kip lit a candle perched on one of the dressers, then blew out the match and set it and the matchbox on the dresser, too.

The folksinger, silhouetted by pink and orange and gold light, turned to face her. "What kind of candle is that?" Jaime asked.

"I don't know, but it's pretty, don't you think?"

She nodded—and then Kip was standing close to her again, raising her hands to either side of the seated woman's face. Jaime put her hands on the folksinger's hips and pressed her face into her shirt.

"You're not wearing that coat to bed, are you?"

In a muffled voice, Jaime answered, "I wasn't planning on it."
She felt Kip pulling it down and off her shoulders, and she shivered.

Kip said, "I'm cold, too. Can't seem to stop shaking."

Jaime pulled her closer. "It's not just the cold."

"Ah, I see." Kip's hands moved to her shoulders, massaging softly. "Crawl under the covers, why don't you?" Jaime pulled her sweater over her head and dropped it on the floor, then reached for the top button on her shirt, but Kip said, "No, just get in—let me do that."

The shivering woman scrambled toward the head of the bed. She fumbled for the covers, tucked her feet and legs under, and squirmed until she lay on her back in the center of the huge bed with her head on the middle pillow.

Kip joined her, pulling the covers up and shifting until she came to rest on her right side with one elbow next to Jaime's head and her other arm across her chest. She unbuttoned all the buttons on the flannel shirt, and then leaned down and found Jaime's lips. The kiss was long and deep, a slow, luxurious kiss, leaving them both breathless. Jaime turned a little, onto her left side but still below Kip. She pulled the folksinger closer and found the turtleneck underneath Kip's sweater. She untucked the front, and rested her hands against soft skin. A warm voice breathed in her ear.

"Will we regret this in the morning?"

Jaime pressed her palms against Kip's ribs. "Only if you throw me out and I never get to see you anymore."

"I wouldn't do that."

"Good." She untucked the back of the turtleneck and helped pull the tight neck up and over Kip's head, then got her arms out of the shirt and rearranged the covers around them. Jaime pulled the folksinger close and pressed a kiss to a very warm collarbone.

"I want this to last and last," Kip whispered.

Jaime tightened her grip, and the two women lay facing one another, legs entangled, with the blanket up to their necks. "I might be a little out of practice, but I'll try to make it last."

"No, I mean *us*. Not making love. Us."

"Oh. Well, I'll try for both," she said in a husky voice. "But..." She let out a sigh. "I'm not sure I'm all that great at either, but I'll do my best."

"You think *you're* out of practice! Seems like years. It's been ages for me." Kip tucked her face into the dark hair, her face flaming red.

Jaime chuckled. "Same with me."

Kip froze. "But—but, what about Lacey?"

She made a huffing sound and loosened her hold on Kip's shoulder. Now it was her turn to blush. "Get real." Just the thought of Lacey made her feel a sinking sensation, as though she were falling through a hole and down to a painful crash. She rolled onto her back and let out a sigh. "She led me on the first time, on the first tour. We were intimate, but—well, anything she did happened while she was drunk. She always—I mean—oh, geez! Let's just say our physical relationship was never fulfilling for me. There." She shook her head slowly. "This is embarrassing to admit." She shut her eyes and swallowed hard. "I kept hoping, kept trying to believe in her. She's not gay, Kip. She's not straight. She's—I don't know what she is, or if she even knows."

"She was a drunk. That's what she was. Alcohol was running her life." *And yours*, Kip thought. She didn't feel comfortable saying it out loud, but she hoped Jaime understood that. She shifted and scooted down until she could rest her head against the shoulder below her. Jaime wrapped an arm tightly around her, and Kip laid her hand on the lean woman's stomach. "You went back to her after all that?"

"Yeah, yeah. Rub it in. I thought she'd changed. She led me on the first time. She led me on the second time, too, and both times I was too stupid to see it."

"I'm sorry. Very, very sorry, Jaime."

"Hmph—not your fault. I wish someone had told me." She thought about that for a moment, and realized that Emma had tried to tell her. And in his own way, so had Drew. She hadn't listened. She didn't think she could have heard it anyway.

In a quiet voice, Kip said, "You win some, lose some."

"As far as I'm concerned, that loss is one that isn't worth worrying about any longer. We were a bad match, and I should have had enough sense to know it." She brought her hand up and ran it through Kip's hair. "Your hair is soft."

"My hair is too *fine*. I can't do a damn thing with it."

"I like it." She turned her face to place a kiss on the folksinger's forehead. With her free hand, she stroked from Kip's shoulder, down her arm, then to her side and on to her hip. "I don't want to think about the past," she whispered. "I only want to think about the future. I want to make love with you...and...I want to make it last and last." She slid her hand upward, found ribs under her palm, and moved her thumb across a breast until she felt the center of the bra's cup.

Kip's breath caught, but she managed to choke out, "Making love? Or a relationship?"

"Both." Jaime pulled up and away and propped herself up on

her left elbow, until Kip lay on her back, looking up at her. In the
candle-dappled glow, Jaime sought assent, watching as the pale
gold light flickered and made the gray eyes below her look dark
blue.

"Yes," Kip whispered. "I want that. I want you."

"Good." Jaime kissed her. She closed her eyes and put all the
love she felt into the kiss. Without breaking contact, she slid
across the body below her until one knee slipped in the V of Kip's
legs. She felt strong hands caress her back and sides as her own
hands stroked the face and neck below her. And then she needed
air. She broke away, panting, and nuzzled into the very warm
neck. She moved to the side until her hands could reach behind
Kip to unclasp the hooks there. "Sit up." Still straddling one of
Kip's legs, she pushed away from the bed and up on to her knees,
pulling the folksinger up with her. Off went Kip's bra, and then
Jaime felt quick, sure hands unzipping her pants. Her bra disappeared next. The air was cold on her upper body, and before she
had the chance to get out of her pants and bare her legs, Kip
pressed against her. Jaime was not prepared for the jolt of electricity when the seated woman covered her breast with a warm, moist
mouth.

"Ohhhhh..." Her legs went weak, and if Kip hadn't had her
arms around her waist, she would have fallen over. Her hands
found the other woman's shoulders, and she held on for dear life,
letting the pleasure flow through her like a current. "Yes, yes..." It
was the one word she could think to say. She let Kip guide her
down to the bed and slip away the rest of her clothes. She had
thought she was in control, but for the next few minutes, she relin-
quished all semblance of power, letting Kip's hands and mouth
touch her at will. Never once did she say no; the only words out of
her mouth were, "Yes, yes..." and every touch, every breath was
electrifying. The climax she finally felt came in powerful jolts, and
when she cried out, it was still "Yes. Yes, Kip! Oh, yes."

She lay there, trying to catch her breath, stunned by what had
happened. Kip pulled her close, and then Jaime couldn't restrain
the laughter that gurgled out.

"Was that all right?" Kip's voice came out hesitant, almost
fearful.

"Are you kidding? *¡Dios mio!* Nothing like that's happened
to me since I was about twenty." She wrapped her arms around
the worried woman above her and squeezed tight. "That was, like,
unbelievable. Hey," she said, concern in her voice, "you aren't
even undressed yet."

"I'll have you know I'm halfway decent."

"If you don't mind, I'd like you entirely *in*decent." When she rolled onto her side, Kip slid away from her and onto her back in the middle of the mattress. Jaime's hand caressed the soft stomach. "Oooh, you feel cold." Jaime pulled the blankets up and covered them both. "Now, off with the pants."

"You should talk, you don't even have your socks off."

"Good point." Jaime reached down and slipped off each of the thick socks and looked to the left, then the right. "This bed is huge." With a flick of the wrist, she lobbed the socks overhand, and they disappeared, to be followed shortly by the bundle of clothes Kip dropped over the side. Jaime snuggled up close to the folksinger, letting her hands have free rein to touch and stroke, then found Kip's mouth and kissed her with passion.

The folksinger's mind was racing, and she was feeling anything but relaxed. The searing kiss didn't help matters. Her body's physical excitement increased, but at the same time, her panic level rose. "Wait," she gasped. "Wait."

Jaime froze. "What? Did I hurt you?"

"No, that's not it." She wrapped her arms around Jaime and rolled on her side so that they lay looking one another in the eye. "It's just going too fast."

"Believe me, I know the feeling." Even in the dim candlelight, Kip could see her roll her eyes. "So much for the 'let's make it last and last' idea."

Kip smiled. "We'll get back to that. I've never been that good at letting go, and—well, I—I—"

"You're saying you're nervous?"

"Yeah, you could say that. You're beautiful and thin and uninhibited..."

"Hey, wait a minute. You're beautiful, and you are shaped exactly like my favorite instrument and—"

"What? Favorite instrument? What are you talking about?"

"You remind me of my violin. In fact, I am now going to start calling her Elizabeth, after you. Elizabeth and Isabelle—sound good to you?"

Kip let her hand slide down to Jaime's hip where she tightened her grip and tickled her.

"Aaaarrgghh! No, don't do that!" Jaime backed up in the bed, scrabbling away and pursued by the crawling woman.

Kip giggled. "Thought you weren't ticklish."

"I'm not—not too much." Jaime straightened up, on her knees, and fended off the folksinger with her hands, all the while laughing maniacally. Suddenly, she stopped pushing Kip away and put her arms out to the sides. "All right. Go ahead. Torture me."

She pinched her eyes shut. Kip stopped laughing. On her knees she eased over until she was knee to knee, middle to middle, breast to breast, with the black-haired woman. Jaime opened her eyes and, with her arms still out, tipped her head back slightly. "Do with me what you will. As you command."

Kip reached out and put a hand on each of Jaime's hips, then wrapped her arms around her and tucked her face against the slim woman's neck. In a raspy voice, she said, "I think it's me who should be saying that, not you." Long arms encircled her, and they held one another tightly. "You can do with me what *you* will."

"How about you tell me what you like, what you want. You know—as you command."

Kip looked up into the black eyes and decided to trust. "I love you, Jaime. I have since last summer."

Jaime swallowed. "Wish I hadn't been so stupid then." Her tone was bitter. She sat back on her heels and leaned to the side, and Kip did the same. They scooted down onto their sides and lay down. "I'm sorry."

"I had no claim on you."

"That doesn't matter. I hurt you, and I didn't mean to. I didn't even realize. I was stupid." She stuck her legs under the covers, and they took a few moments to rearrange the blankets and themselves until they lay face to face again, skin on skin. "I felt so bad when I didn't get to say goodbye, and as the days went by I felt worse and worse. And then I began to understand..."

Kip waited, but Jaime didn't go on. She leaned forward and put a soft kiss on the red lips before her. "Did you hear me? I love you, and I don't care what happened before. That's the past now."

"But I don't want to repeat the past. I don't think I ever knew what love was, Kip. I've slept with a few people in the last twenty-plus years, but I guess they weren't people I really loved. Lacey Leigh always said, 'Same whore, different dress,' like everyone who loved her was just a variation of the same rotten greedy asshole she so often ended up with. I want a different dress, but no whore. Emma says I've been confusing need with love." She paused, waiting for some negative response from Kip, and when none came, she went on. "Kip, right now, I have to admit being a little confused because I know I've grown to need you."

"I need you, too. There's nothing wrong with that. I think what Emma means is I'm not needy. I can take care of myself, Jaime. I'm not like Lacey Leigh."

In a quiet voice, Jaime said, "No, you're not. Not at all."

Kip whispered the next words. "Just living with you in the

bus for those few weeks, I grew to need you, to want you."

"I'm sorry I didn't understand that."

Kip grinned and raised her hand to stroke Jaime's tanned cheek. "Better late than never," she whispered. Their lips met, and Kip let herself get lost in the feelings washing over her. Now she felt warm and comfortable. Two words popped into her head. *Safe. I feel safe.* And the second word was *Irritating.* Something was interrupting her slide into reckless abandon, and over their breathless eagerness, the sound came clear. *Beep-beep. Beep-beep.* It sounded muffled and distant. She froze. "What is that?"

"Nothing. Ignore it."

But there it was again. *Beep-beep. Beep-beep.* "You got a pacemaker or what?"

Jaime exhaled. "It's my pager. They can wait."

"They? Who's they?"

"Whoever's on call—somebody wants to reach me. They can wait." The pager went off again. *Beep-beep. Beep-beep.*

"I'm not neurotic. I need you to believe that."

Jaime laughed. "I don't think you're neurotic."

"Good. I hope you understand that I can't make love with that thing going off every ten seconds."

"I'll find it and turn it off." She scrambled out from under the covers, slipped out of the bed, and searched around on the floor for her jacket. When she found it, she got the pager out of her pocket and went over closer to the candle to check it. "Yeah, it's the work cell."

"Are you on call tonight?"

Jaime turned, the outline of her physique highlighted from behind by the candlelight. "Yeah, I'm probably getting called in." She took the four steps over to the bed and crawled back in. "I don't *want* to call back. They can wait." She curled around the warm figure next to her, reveling in the feel of velvety skin and plush limbs, but the mood was broken.

"I'm not going anywhere, Jaime."

She let out a sigh. "But I'll have to leave if I call in."

"You can always come back."

"Dammit, this makes me mad. I can't believe it, but...all right, I better call. Where's the phone?"

Kip rolled to the far side of the bed and picked up a cordless phone from the bedside table. "Brrrrr," she said as she scooted back toward the middle. "Baby, it's *cold* over there."

Jaime accepted the receiver from her. "We have to get us a smaller bed, Kip. This thing's way too big."

Kip shook her head in mock disbelief. "Hasn't even been a

day, and you're already buying new furniture. Next thing you'll tell me this page is from the U-Haul company, and they have your stuff outside already in the driveway."

Jaime laughed. "Very funny. You've seen my place. I wouldn't need a U-Haul. More like a large car trunk." She leaned over and kissed Kip soundly, then ran her free hand along the side of Kip's cheek and down to her warm neck. Pulling away, she sat up and juggled the phone. "I hate these things. Can't ever find the right button to turn them on." Kip reached over and pressed something, and the phone lit up. "Thanks." She punched in the numbers and waited.

Someone picked up on the third ring and a male voice said, "Hello?"

"Rici? Is that you?"

"Yeah. Thank God, Jaime. I need help."

Hearing the urgency in his voice, she sat up. "What's the matter?"

"I've been here on the West side working on a furnace for a couple hours. I can't figure out what's wrong."

"I just fixed a thermocouple tonight. Did you check that?"

"You think I'm *estupido*? I checked that first. I don't know what it could be. Can you come help me?"

"Rici," she protested, "it's Christmas Eve."

In the background, Kip quietly said, "Actually, it's now Christmas Day."

"The lady here, she is very nice. She's got three very little kids, Jaime. They gotta have some heat soon. Right now, only the oven is working. *La casa es muy fría.*"

The house is very cold. Jaime groaned and closed her eyes. She didn't want to leave Kip, and the thought of it made her feel sick to her stomach. She covered the mouthpiece. "It's a furnace that's gone out in a house across the river. I'm sorry, Kip. I have to go. This woman has kids—"

"I'll go with you."

"Don't be crazy. You stay here and keep the home fires burning." She smiled. "I'll come back as quick as I can."

"At least take my truck. It's probably snowing again."

"No, that's okay. I may need all the parts and equipment in the van." She uncovered the mouthpiece of the phone and said, "All right, Rici. What's the address?"

Before she was off the phone, Kip was out of bed and had the overhead light on. Jaime watched her slip into a robe and slippers and then bend and gather up clothes to place them on the bed. Humming, she tossed a bra and the blue and white shirt Jaime's way, and the electrician dressed.

"I'm sorry, Kip."

The folksinger paused in her sorting. "I'm not upset. This is how real life is. Furnaces go out, stuff breaks down, people have problems." She shrugged. "That's life." She handed over one balled up sock and squatted down to look under the bed where she retrieved the other sock. Jaime reached for her corduroy pants and slid to the edge of the bed to put them on. Kip stepped between the V of her legs and put warm hands on either side of her face. Grinning, she said, "It's only in romance novels that people's lives turn out perfect, and they have tons of money and mutual orgasms, and every lovemaking session turns out to be rockets, bells, and poetry—in the words of a long dead singer." Leaning down, she placed a light kiss on Jaime's lips. "I'm going downstairs to microwave hot water for instant coffee. I'll fill you a Thermos."

In amazement, Jaime watched her slip out the door and into the darkened hallway, and then the light out there went on. By the time she finished dressing and left the bedroom, it seemed like every lamp in the place was illuminated. She descended the stairs and went down to the basement to gather up her tools. She carried the kit upstairs, set it on a dining room chair, and stepped around the corner into the kitchen. Kip was leaning against the counter, her arms crossed over her chest, as the microwave hummed. She lifted her gaze, and when Jaime saw the tired gray eyes crinkle in a smile, she was filled with a warm buoyancy the likes of which she couldn't remember ever feeling. Desire. Longing. Hope. All of these emotions ran through her, and she crossed the kitchen and wrapped the other woman in her arms.

"I love you, Kip," she whispered into a warm ear, and the folksinger hugged her back more tightly.

The microwave dinged, and they parted so Kip could take out the steaming, quart-size measuring cup. Jaime zipped up her coat and pulled her gloves out of her pockets, while Kip carried the boiling water across the kitchen and set it by the sink. She picked up a Thermos filled with hot tap water and dumped that water out. She spooned some instant coffee in and poured the boiling water over it, then screwed the lid on and shook it. "I know this is going to taste semi-crappy, but it's better than nothing. I hope you're not there a long time, but if you are, at least you can have a little warmth and caffeine."

Jaime accepted the silver Thermos. She felt lightheaded as she leaned in for a kiss. The metal container was in the way between them, but she pressed forward anyhow. "Thank you, Kip.

For everything. Thank you."

Kip smiled. "Go. And be careful." Jaime turned and picked
up the tool kit from the chair and headed toward the garage door,
but Kip smacked her on the butt and pointed toward the front
door. "It's quickest that way—less time in the wind."

They kissed again at the front door, and Kip pressed a set of
keys into her hands, which Jaime put in her pocket. "I'll be back
as quick as I can."

"I know you will."

And then she was out the front door and into the shock of the
blowing wind and swirling snow. *I ought to have a photo of me
walking in this and call it "Below Zero With Windchill."* She shivered as she reached the van, and she shook even more when she
had to set down the tool kit and take one glove off to find her
keys.

Once in the mini-van, she started it up and sat for a good
minute waiting for the engine to warm, then backed out and into
the icy street. It was slow-going, across town, over the bridge, and
down to the West side. Luckily, the address was easy to remember—just off Concord and not quite a mile from her own house.
By the time she pulled up, the heater was finally emitting tepid
heat. She considered leaving the van running, but she thought it
might be hours before they fixed the furnace, and that wouldn't be
good for the engine or the low gas tank. She reluctantly switched
it off and got out to gather up her tools, the Thermos, and her
insulated work suit. She slammed the door, and leaned into the
wind on the way up the walk to the front door.

Before she could knock, the door opened, and Rici pulled her
into the house. He said, "Thank God you're here." She had a
chance to nod toward a dark-haired young woman dressed in an
over-sized snowsuit, mittens, and cap, and then Rici was dragging
her through the kitchen. She paused long enough to set her Thermos on the counter and drop her half-frozen work suit on the
kitchen floor, and then he led her down some stairs and across the
dank and musty-smelling basement. A few minutes later, the
young woman followed and perched on the second to the last step
to watch, reminding Jaime of Kip's pose earlier in the evening.
The thought of the folksinger made her heart beat faster, and she
knew she was sporting a stupid grin. Luckily, Rici didn't notice.

He dropped to his knees. "Okay," he said, "I've checked the
thermocouple and the heating element and even the gas lines.
Nothing seems to work."

In less than ten minutes, she gave him the bad news. "It's
electronic," she told him quietly. "We can't fix this. It probably

needs a new board, and we can't get it until at least tomorrow, maybe even the day after Christmas."

"Oh, shit," he said quietly. He pursed his lips and winced, whispering, "What's this lady going to do? She's got three tiny ones up in bed together trying to stay warm."

She sat back on her haunches. "Take them to your place."

His eyes widened. "Oh, no. No, no, no. I live in a one-room studio apartment. No room for four more people, Jaime."

"Hotel?"

"She's just moved here from Mexico City, sponsored by her kids' uncle on the father's side. The children's father is dead. She's in school, on welfare, and no way does she have the money for a hotel."

"Seems like you've gotten to know a lot about her."

"I've been here two hours, Jaime. What can we do to help her?"

The electrician considered for a moment. "Well, you guys could use my house—but it's going to be tough for the kids. I have one bed, a TV, a kitchen table and chairs, and a five-foot tall Christmas tree. We'll have to haul their Christmas stuff over to my place, and you'll have to keep an eye on them."

"Me? Why me? Why not you?"

A wide smile split her face. "Don't you think I would have been here a lot sooner if I had been home?"

Understanding dawned and he let out a laugh. "Oh. I see." He rose, and so did she. "*Señorita*," he said. "*Es muy mal...*"

Jaime squatted back down and collected her tools, all the while listening as the young man explained the situation in Spanish to the woman whose name she now learned was Rosita. She stood and looked at the small woman who was really not much more than a girl. The bundled up girl shivered, and her eyes brimmed with tears. Rici patted her arm and bent over her, trying to console her.

In Spanish, Jaime said, "Please, don't worry. We can help you." The woman looked up at her with dark eyes spilling tears. Jaime smiled. "My house is your house, at least for the night."

Rosita looked skeptical, and the electrician wondered if she would trust them enough to pack up her three kids and come with them. Jaime turned to Rici and the two carried on a spirited conversation, which the young woman listened to, contributing a comment here and there. They finally decided that Jaime would warm up her van as much as possible, and Rosita would dress the three kids in many layers for the eight-block journey to her house.

The three of them went upstairs. Jaime's zip-up suit had been spread out on the floor in the kitchen in front of the stove, and she was happy to find it now mostly thawed. She gestured at the tan suit and smiled. *"Gracias, Rosita."* She was rewarded with a wide smile from the younger woman. She took a moment to slip the suit on over her clothes.

All three children fit in the front seat of the van, two on the floor between their mother's legs, and the baby on Rosita's lap. Ordinarily Jaime wouldn't have allowed the kids in without seatbelts, but she didn't think the mother would let them drive over one at a time without her. It was only eight blocks, and Rici was right behind her in the truck, so they made the risky pilgrimage.

When they arrived at her house, the baby was awake and fussing, but the other two kids were asleep again. Rici carried the little boy, and Jaime took the girl as Rosita sheltered the infant in her arms. They made it into the house, and Rici handed the boy to Jaime who gave a toss of her head toward the stairwell. *"Esta manera,* Rosita. Come this way."

Rici took the baby from Rosita. *"Es okay."* He held the fussy little girl against his shoulder, and she calmed down and settled against him. After a moment of hesitation, Rosita seemed to relax.

Jaime headed up the stairs, carrying both kids, one on each shoulder. The young woman followed her, and with Jaime's help, they stripped the two children of their layers down to their pajamas and put them both in the queen-size bed. Jaime marveled at how the tiny children could sleep through it all. She covered them and told Rosita they would be warm now.

"Gracias, Señorita," Rosita said.

"No problema."

They hustled back downstairs. Rici had the TV on in the living room and paced as he held the baby and watched it. The little one made quiet cooing noises. Jaime looked at her watch and thought about Kip back at the house, waiting for her. All she wanted to do was leap back in the van and peel out. "Rici, I'll go out and get the bags and stuff from your truck. Where are your keys?"

"It's unlocked."

"Okay." She went out into the howling wind. A blast hit her and snow went down the neck of her work suit, so she pulled up its hood. Even the thought of Kip waiting for her in bed wasn't enough to keep her warm, and she shivered violently. She managed to grab every sack and two sleeping bags and haul them toward the house in one load. When she got inside the front door, Rosita hastened to help her.

"Okay, kids," Jaime said. "You're on your own. Rici, you

guys can eat anything you want, but there's not much to be had. In the morning you'll have to run to the 7-11 for milk." She looked at each of them. Rosita shook her head, and gave a wave with her hand. She looked nervous again. *"Rosita, necessitas leche para los niños."* Jaime knew she didn't have many groceries in the cupboard, and certainly no milk. She also knew Rosita would be reluctant to take anything from her, since she was a stranger, but she thought she could figure out a way to work things out with her. She told her not to worry, that she would be back in the afternoon, and she bid them farewell and trudged back out to the van.

Chapter
Twenty-Seven

KIP LAY IN the big bed, swathed comfortably in blankets, and wondered how the furnace repair was going. She looked at the bedside clock and calculated that Jaime had been gone for an hour and a half.

The TV was on, but she wasn't watching anything. Using the remote, she made a slow pass through the cable channels, yawning all the while. *It's a Wonderful Life* played simultaneously on a local channel and on WGN out of Chicago. She skipped back and forth between George Bailey walking alone and Clarence the friendly angel doing a little speech. The local channel had obviously started playing the movie before WGN had.

She yawned again. After all the excitement of the last few hours, she was finally winding down, but she didn't want to fall asleep before Jaime returned. *Oh, wow. I still can't believe this is happening.* She marveled at all that had occurred in one short night.

Still clicking through the channels, she paused at the music video station and nearly went on—but she recognized a physique and paused to stare. She pressed the volume control until the strings and piano were loud. Lacey Leigh Jaxon, dressed in a diaphanous, gauzy dress, walked barefoot through what looked like a giant Victorian-style home. The house was empty of all furniture, though each room did contain curtains and drapes. The woodwork was dark, as were the walls and wallpaper. The tiny woman held a bottle of Chivas Regal in one hand as she danced slowly through the house looking out windows and singing a slow, contemplative song Kip had never heard before.

> *It must be very late at night*
> *When I am so tired that I kick out*
> *All the misconceptions*
> *And oddities of reality*
> *By which I survive day to day...*

Her hair was long and wavy, and she swept it back with one hand as she took a draw from the bottle of golden liquid. Kip watched, fascinated. Lacey seemed oblivious to the presence of the camera, as though she were singing privately to herself in the dark mansion. She leaned and swayed, balletic in her movements.

Then I peek around the room
And slowly drop my guard
My life appears in strange hues
Of brightness and black
Contrasted together...

Kip wondered who had written the song and arranged the shoot. The words were nothing like what she expected from Lacey Leigh, and the video was beautiful, in a gothic sort of way. So far, she thought it was brilliantly done. The blonde woman floated across the wood floor and ascended the stairwell while humming along with the music. She moved down a long hallway to another set of stairs and paused, her profile to the camera.

I think of places and people
I have known
All along wondering what was behind their colors
So many minds and so much color
The world can't see...you just can't see...

The diva took another swallow of liquor, then mounted the next set of stairs as the bridge to the song played. Kip was entranced by the melodic piano and strings. It made her think of Sara McLachlan and Tori Amos. *Whoever wrote this song has written a winner,* she thought. *Maybe Lacey finally has her really big-time crossover hit.* The little star reached the top of the stairs and walked to the side of a room that, as Kip's eyes adjusted to the dim light, appeared to be no larger than an over-sized closet. It was so dark and dim that Kip couldn't see well, but the video angle changed as the camera focused on a large window and burst through the glass and outside into dusk. The next view showed Lacey Leigh in the window of a cupola that jutted up from a mysterious looking manor. She stood framed in the enormous window from mid-calf upward. The low window looked dangerous, as though the singer could easily fall forward and plunge down three stories. She held the bottle against the center of her chest as she swayed in the window, jagged glass around the frame. Her hair shone white-blonde, and the gauzy white dress sparkled like a thousand tiny gems were attached to it.

> *I know I must shield me, protect myself*
> *I am fragile behind my guard*
> *It is only when I am very tired*
> *Late at night*
> *That maybe...just maybe*
> *You might catch a glimpse of me*

Lacey Leigh took one last drink from the bottle in her right hand. The camera receded as the piano faded out, and then she disappeared from the window. She didn't step back; she didn't fall. She disappeared, and the jagged edges of the window knit back together and became whole. The song faded out as the camera retreated, lifting up and away, until the house was a speck below, and slowly, the picture faded to black.

"Well, that was something."

Kip jumped and nearly let out a scream. "Geez, Jaime! How long have you been standing there?" She sat up in bed and glared.

"Long enough to see Lacey has a hit on her hands." She came into the room and sat on the edge of the bed as Kip hit the mute button on the remote control.

"I didn't hear you come in." Kip reached out a hand, tentatively, and rubbed Jaime's forearm. The light from the television cast a bluish tint, then changed to orange, highlighting Jaime's black hair.

"Thought you might be asleep, so I tried to be quiet."

"Are you cold?"

"No, it wasn't too bad. I wore my lined jumpsuit."

"What was wrong?"

Jaime shook her head. "Couldn't fix it. Too much for Rici and me to repair."

"You tired?"

"No. Well, only a little." She let out a sigh. "I just couldn't wait to get back, and it seemed to take forever."

Kip smiled. "Get in here, why don't you."

"Let me go wash up." Jaime rose. "Be right back."

Kip snuggled down into the covers. She stuck out a hand to pick up the remote control and turn off the TV. The room plunged into darkness, and she realized the candle had guttered out sometime earlier. Not knowing whether Jaime would be able to see her way into the room, Kip turned on the bedside lamp. A thrill of anticipation ran through her, and she shivered even though she felt perfectly warm. Water ran in the distance and then stopped.

She heard the bathroom door open, and Jaime was back in the room, bare-legged, and carrying her shoes in one hand and her pants over her arm.

"I think this time I'll be a little tidier about disrobing," Jaime said, as she set her shoes on the floor and the pants on top of the chair.

"What? You don't want to explode your clothes all around the room?"

"Nope." Jaime pulled her sweater over her head, folded it, placed it on the pants, and unbuttoned her flannel shirt.

When she slid the shirt off, Kip could see her ribs. Kip watched the other woman remove a necklace and set it on the bedside table, and then she noticed the odd expression on Jaime's face and frowned. "Hey, what's wrong?"

"Nothing, why?" She laid the shirt on the chair with her other clothes and, still wearing her bra and panties, bent and turned off the bedside lamp.

Kip folded open the covers for her, and she crawled into bed. Jaime's comment aside, Kip knew something was wrong, but she didn't know whether she should press the issue or not. She turned on her side, facing Jaime, and touched the warm skin around her middle. "You're right. You don't feel too cold."

"And if I am, you're plenty warm enough."

Kip put her right arm over Jaime's hip and shifted until they were forehead to forehead. Voice breathless, she said, "You sure you're okay?"

Jaime let out a sigh. "Yes, I really am." She paused and reached out. Kip felt herself pulled closer so that there was no space between the two of them. They lay pressed together with arms tight around one another. Jaime said, "I have to admit that it threw me to see that video."

"Oh," Kip said. "It must bring up old feelings."

"No, that's not it." She let out a sound like strangled laughter. "I just realized I'm still angry at her, so much so that I guess I don't want her to have any success."

"Success?"

"Yeah. That's a great video, and a very strange and striking song. She'll hit the big time now, and it totally pisses me off."

"Especially after all she put you through, huh?"

Jaime didn't answer. After a moment Kip felt the touch of smooth skin against the middle of her back, and she shivered. "Kip, here's what I think. Happiness is the best revenge, and I choose to be happy. I'd like to be happy with you, if that's all right."

Kip smiled. "Works for me." She let her hands explore the body in front of her and stopped with the flat of her palm on Jaime's hip. "Could you answer me a question?"

"Hmm?"

"Why did you come to bed wearing these?" She tugged at the elastic waistband of Jaime's underwear. "And this?" She reached up and unhooked the back of Jaime's bra and ran her hands along the soft skin.

"I don't know. Shy, I guess."

Kip whispered. "You don't have to be shy with me."

Jaime answered in her ear. "You can be shy with me, but I can't be with you?"

"There's no reason to be shy." Kip leaned in and kissed her and suddenly found herself wrapped in a tight hug. The kiss was long and searching, and when Jaime broke it off, Kip wanted more. Jaime shifted up onto her elbow and slipped out of her bra. Breathlessly Kip asked, "Need help with anything else?"

Jaime chuckled as she reached down and removed her last article of clothing. "I think I can handle this. Handling *you*, though—that's another story." She rolled toward Kip and covered the folksinger's body with her own.

"I beg to differ," Kip whispered. "You can handle me any way you want." With hands on either side of the cool face, she gently guided Jaime to her own lips and kissed her on the mouth, the neck, and the ear. Bodies entwined, they moved against one another, stroking, massaging, and murmuring softly as their excitement grew.

Kip shifted as though to change places. "Ah ah ah," Jaime teased. "You relax and let me just touch you." She angled to the side so that her body was only partly covering Kip's. "You're beautiful, Kip. Just beautiful. Tell me what you like...tell me..." She dipped her mouth to Kip's neck and nuzzled there.

"I like that...yes, I like that..." Kip closed her eyes and let the feelings wash over her like the sound of wind chimes on the prairie as Jaime stroked her shoulders, across the top of her chest, down to her breasts to cover her torso with kisses. When warm lips and hands found her sensitive breasts, Kip lost herself in the sensations. She held Jaime's head gently and voiced her delight with a soft moan. Warm and wet, breathless and elated by the rhythm of each touch, she gave herself over to Jaime, allowing her free access to every part of her body and soul. When the surges of pleasure climbed to a crescendo, Kip let go of all thought, all reason, as her whole being begged for release. One more touch triggered a powerful tempo that pulsed through her, rocking her body of its own accord. The cadence slowed but didn't stop, as a strong rhythmic flow continued to throb through her body. She cried out and pulled in one ragged breath, and only then did the pulsation weaken and gradually abate.

"Whoa," Kip said, still breathing fast.

Jaime moved up next to her. She arranged covers over them and laid her head in the crook of Kip's shoulder. With one hand on Kip's breastbone, she snuggled close. "Are you okay?"

Kip giggled. "More than okay. Whoa!"

Jaime laughed. "Translation, please?"

"Whoa. That's all I can say. Whoa." She grinned and kissed the side of Jaime's head, luxuriating in the physical warmth they shared. Finally when she felt she had gotten her breath back, she said, "You are wonderful, Miss Esperanza. Do you know that?" She knew Jaime wouldn't know what to say in response, so she went on. "That was like hearing the 'Hallelujah Chorus' or some other incredible musical work."

"I see. Feel free to sing anytime you want."

"That wouldn't be possible."

"Why not?" Jaime asked, a teasing tone in her voice.

"Who can remember words at a time like that?"

"Hallelujah...how hard is that?"

Kip raised her hand up and stroked the side of Jaime's face. "Believe me, it was impossible with what you were doing to me."

"I'll take that as a compliment."

"You should." Jaime's shoulders tensed, and she loosened her grip on Kip. In one smooth motion, she rolled away to get out of bed. "Hey, I forgot something," she called over her shoulder.

"What?"

"Be right back."

Kip clicked on the lamp on the bedside table and lay in bed for half a minute, wondering what Jaime could have forgotten, and then the electrician returned and slid under the covers.

"I wanted you to have this."

Jaime slid back under the covers, and something cool and smooth was placed in Kip's hands. "Hey, it's a Christmas present."

"*Si, mi amada.* It is. Open it."

Before she got the paper peeled away, Kip knew what it was. She could feel the beads through the thin paper. "Hey, it's that purse!" She ripped off the rest of the wrapping and found the soft beaded purse Minnie Logan had given her. The blue sky across the top looked dark in the low light, but the orange sun in the middle reflected brightly. As she tilted the bag to the side, the field of wheat below appeared to ripple, as though blowing in the wind. "Oh, I *really* like this purse."

Jaime turned on her side and adjusted the pillow below her head. "Then why did you leave it for me?"

Kip took a deep breath. She didn't answer for a moment. "I'm not sure, Jaime. It was a spur-of-the-moment thing. I just felt like—I don't know—leaving you with something to remember me by." She scooted over next to Jaime, still holding the purse against her chest. "I also thought that every time I saw this, it would give me a pang of remorse, and to be honest, I didn't want to feel that. I just wanted to get out of the tour intact, without any more pain or confusion than I was already feeling."

"I wish you had told me."

"I couldn't," Kip said. "I'm sorry. If you had a chance with Lacey, I wasn't going to come between you."

Jaime shook her head slowly. "I can only wish you had." She let out a snort of laughter.

Kip reached up and brushed a lock of black hair from Jaime's eyes. "Do you know how long I've loved you?"

Jaime paused for a moment before answering, "No."

"All the way back to Albuquerque. I started to figure it out there the day you tortured me with that botched up lizard in the laundromat."

Jaime let out a laugh. "It was a simple little side-blotched lizard, and I didn't do one bit of torturing."

Kip let out a long sigh. "Oh, yes, you did. Oh, you did. That was the start of it, Jaime. By the next morning, I knew I was in trouble." She stroked Jaime's hip, feeling where the hipbone and the soft flesh met. "I pretty much can't believe things are turning out this way between us."

"Probably should have turned out this way much sooner. Look at all the chances we had to consummate our relationship in a moving bus."

Kip laughed. "That's all I needed—a bunch of horny guy musicians gossiping about us as we rock 'n' rolled down the road."

"Yeah, well, I'm just glad I got things right now."

"Me, too." She reached over Jaime's shoulder, put the beaded bag on the nightstand, and snuggled in close. Jaime shifted and pulled her tight, and they lay in one another's arms.

"I can't believe how tired I am," Jaime said in a grouchy tone of voice.

Kip turned her head and looked at the bedside clock. "It is four a.m. When's the last time you were up 'til practically dawn?"

"Not since the tour." She yawned. "I'm definitely not used to it."

"I take it you're not going to let me ravage you."

"Hmph...can I have a raincheck for tomorrow?"

Kip nodded. "Sure. Can I have a raincheck good for every night for the rest of our lives?"

"Yes," Jaime said without hesitation.

"Jaime?"

"Hmm?"

Kip knew Jaime was fading fast. In a quiet voice, she said, "I love you."

Sounding sleepy, Jaime said, "Love you more."

Kip smiled. "We'll see about that." She adjusted the pillow behind her head, then tightened her grip on the sleepy woman in her arms. She lay there for several minutes after Jaime fell asleep and thought about how incredibly lucky she felt. "Merry Christmas, sweetie," she whispered. Before long, she closed her eyes and drifted off, too.

Chapter
Twenty-Eight

JUNE WEATHER IN Minnesota is unpredictable, but the forecast for the day was promising. The rising sun peeked up over the St. Paul skyline long after Jaime had gotten out of bed and moved around the house to get things in order. She put coffee on to perk, then settled in at the kitchen table to eat a muffin and drink a glass of milk while skimming some of the articles in the newspaper. She read part of a confusing article about school financing, then gave up on making any sense of it. She turned the page, and a crumb from the muffin dropped into her lap and bounced off onto the floor. She rose and dampened a paper towel, cleaned up the bits from the gold and red floor, and tossed them in the garbage. She was still pleased with how bright and sunshiny the kitchen floor was. Everything about it had turned out classy. She and Kip had redone the cabinets and decorated in bright Aztec colors, and it was her favorite room in the house—during the day, anyway. At night, it was their bedroom she liked best. A smile came to her face, and she felt a thrill of happiness. *Five-and-a-half months, and she's still in love with me. Wow. That has to be a new world record.* She had gotten to the point where she was truly starting to believe that she had found the real deal.

She returned to her chair and checked her watch. In a couple of hours they were scheduled to pack their remaining bags into the van and head for Iowa. They'd kicked off the *Kip Galvin's Summer Breeze Tour* the night before at a coffee shop in Hastings, and she still couldn't get her head around what had happened. First off, the place had been packed, so much so that the owner of Professor Java's Coffee Shop had been forced to cycle people in and out. Jaime was so glad she'd brought extra amps and lines. She set up an additional PA system outside the shop so that even people waiting on the sidewalk could hear the music. Neither she nor Kip had expected such a big crowd. They hadn't expected musicians to come to just "sit in" either. Drew and a six-month pregnant Dina

arrived an hour early, and shortly after, Dan Benson showed up
with his basic drum kit. They barely got everything set up in time
to start at eight p.m., but with Dina on flute for one song, Drew
playing lead guitar, and Dan providing percussion, Jaime was able
to focus on keeping the sound system running at top efficiency.
She played fiddle on two songs, mandolin on one, and she did a
bass line for Kip's favorite Wynonna song, but other than that, she
got to watch and listen a lot. It had sounded wonderful.

But that wasn't the amazing part. Halfway through the night,
for the last song of the first set, Kip said, "Well, folks, I have a
song to sing now that no one here has ever heard before. I'm going
to play it on my own and give Danny and Drew a break. Go
ahead, guys. Go get some refreshments. They're on me. Let's have
a big hand for Dan Benson and Drew Michael Donovan!" The
audience exploded into applause, made all the louder by the close
quarters of the small coffee shop. When the cheering and clapping
trailed off, Kip went on. "All right. This is the first time to sing
this song in public before we leave on the *Summer Breeze Tour.* It
debuts here at Professor Java's, and I'm dedicating this one specially to my sweetie who I love with all my heart."

Jaime's head jerked up from the soundboard, and a hot blush
suffused her face. She looked around, but no one seemed to
notice. Kip played an acoustic intro, and then she started singing,
her voice low and smoky-sounding.

> *Lying here in the summer breeze*
> *The sunlight glows upon your hair*
> *I can't believe that this is me*
> *Lying here, you right there*
> *I can't remember where we've been*
> *Together we've been so many places*
> *I lay and dream beside you in the sun*
> *All I think as I look at your face is...*

Kip's voice went up, and she sang strong and true:

> *I never had a love like this*
> *It just turns my head around*
> *It's really strange how love can be*
> *I can't believe that this is me*

It very nearly took Jaime's breath away. Her heart pounded in
her ears, and she willed it to stop because she didn't want to miss
one note of the performance. She sat, electrified, loving every dip,

every tremor in Kip's voice.

I think we found each other late
But that you're exactly right for me
Through it all, we ended up right
And I know you're all I need
I watch the hawks and lie and think
I wonder what's on your mind
Though I don't ask, just take your hand
I know I'll never find
A heart feeling love like this
It just turns my head around
It's really strange how love can be
I can't believe that this is me...

Kip stopped singing and looked down at the guitar as she played the bridge. Jaime watched her pick an intricate and melodic pattern. The folksinger's brow creased in concentration, and when she finished the two bars, she glanced up at the audience and found Jaime's eyes.

A special love like this
It just turns my head around
It's really strange how love can be
I still can't believe that this is me...
I can't believe that this is me

She finished off the pick pattern and gave one final, slow strum. The audience reacted with solid approval. "You guys are a great folkie crowd," she said into the mic. "If I have half as good a crowd in Iowa tomorrow, I'll be blessed." They cheered some more, and over the whistles and clapping, she hollered. "Take a break, everybody. Have some treats and coffee. Best coffee in town, you know!"

She set Isabelle in the rack, and when she turned around, she grinned mischievously at Jaime who still sat rooted to her seat. Jaime wasn't quite ready to get up for fear her legs would be shaky. She couldn't believe Kip had kept that song from her. When had she practiced it? When had she written it? They'd been together every single night for five-plus months. *That little rat.* A laugh bubbled up, and she grinned at Kip. *I'll get her for that,* she thought as she rose and stretched out her shaky legs. *Just wait until I get her under the covers tonight.* She crossed her arms and hugged herself, then grinned back at her mate.

Jaime sat in the kitchen of the house she owned with Kip and looked out into the yard at the flowerbeds they had planted just the day before. Mary had been enlisted to come over for the next four weeks and make sure the flowers were watered. After that, they'd be back to care for them for the rest of the summer. The house was theirs—and St. Paul National Bank's. They'd closed on it with Don's blessing two months earlier. Kip's house had been listed in mid-January and sold in a heartbeat, but it didn't matter that the timeline was short. The folksinger had already moved ninety percent of her things into Jaime's place by New Year's Day.

Jaime watched the sun come up over the horizon and cast weak rays through the stand of trees in the neighbors' yard. The weather forecasters were right; it was going to be a lovely day. A creak sounded in the little hallway between the foyer and the kitchen, and she shifted in her chair to see Kip wander in, barefoot, and dressed in shorts and a t-shirt. Her hair was tousled, but the gray eyes that met hers were merry.

"'Morning, sweetie," Kip said. "You're up early."

"And you're up late."

Kip went to the cupboard, took down a mug, and poured herself a cup of coffee. She picked it up from the counter and moved across the kitchen, placed it on the table, and sat sideways on Jaime's lap with her arms around her neck. "Have I told you that I love you?"

Jaime grinned. "Repeatedly, last night. But not since then." She tightened her arms around Kip's waist and tucked her head under her chin. With her left ear against Kip's chest, she could hear her heartbeat.

"I'm sure I must have called it out in my sleep."

"Nope, but you certainly called out enough other things before you went to sleep." Jaime said slyly, then laughed.

Kip smacked her on the shoulder. "You were *such* a tease last night!"

"Ha!" she chortled. "That's what you get for sneaking songs into the act without telling me."

"I wanted to surprise you."

"You did. Believe me, you did. Now I know why you insisted on calling this the *Summer Breeze Tour.* Until last night I didn't understand."

"Yeah, I know it was sneaky of me."

In a soft voice, Jaime asked, "Did I thank you?"

Kip nodded. She hugged Jaime tighter and said, "Every word of the song was true. I love you, Jaime."

"Me, too. I'm so lucky. What was your line? 'It's really

strange how love can be, I can't believe that this is me'?"

"Yup, that's it, dead on." She rose and placed a kiss on top of Jaime's head, then tugged her t-shirt down a bit. She sat in the chair to Jaime's right and reached for her mug.

"It's true, Kip. I've never been this happy before—well, not since I was a really small child anyway."

Kip swallowed a sip of coffee. "That's good." She paused. "Isn't it?" She peered at her partner closely, and Jaime pushed the newspaper aside and put her elbows on the table.

"Yes, it is good. But I was just thinking this morning... When I first woke up, I looked at you, and I realized, you are all the family I have." Kip nodded, so she went on. "I wish there was some way to seal that permanently."

"Like marriage—something like that?"

Jaime nodded, and the corners of her lips turned up a little. "Something like that." She reached out her right hand and put it over Kip's. "I love you lots, you know. I never want to lose you."

Kip nodded. "I'd love to have a commitment ceremony on our anniversary. You got anything planned for Christmas Eve?"

"Is our anniversary Christmas Eve or Christmas Day?"

"Hmm. Good question." Kip looked up at the ceiling, and gradually a smile crossed her face. "We consummated our relationship—fully, that is—on Christmas not on the Eve." She laughed out loud. "It *could* have been Christmas Eve, but you and your pager ruined it."

Jaime squeezed her hand. "Either way, nobody wants to come to a commitment ceremony or an anniversary party on Christmas."

"My family will. Mary and Joyce will. Bet Rici and Rosita and those cute kids would come. And you know Drew and Dina would pop in. Hey, we'd even have their baby there. Let's do it! What do you say?"

"I say this gives us a lot of busy work to puzzle over as we drive cross-country on this little tour of yours." Kip smiled, and as Jaime looked into her gray eyes, she felt the strong pull of love and saw the strength and integrity there.

"Until then, I only have one question." Jaime looked at her, with an expectant look on her face. "We leave in less than two hours. Didn't you eat the last muffin?"

"Huh?"

"There's nothing to eat in the house, Jaime. We've eaten, tossed, or given everything away."

"True. Get yourself pulled together, and we'll leave a bit early and go out for breakfast. I've got the van all set, and we're mostly packed, so I'd say we can go whenever you're ready."

Kip patted her hand. "That's my girl. Good idea." She rose, holding the mug in her hand. "I'll go shower now." As she turned Jaime patted her on the behind. "Hey, you'll make me spill my coffee."

"Yeah, yeah, I seriously doubt it. How much can be left in there after all the slurping you've done?"

"I do not slurp," Kip said. She stopped at the coffeepot and helped herself to a refill. "I'll be back shortly."

Jaime sat back in her chair with a goofy grin on her face. She wasn't sure how she had gotten so lucky—but then again, she'd had so much bad luck for so long that maybe she had been due. *Yes, that's how I'll look at it. I was due to finally find somebody like Kip.* She picked up her own coffee mug and took a drink, then looked out the window again at the flowerbeds, now clearly visible in the slant of the sun's rays. She imagined she could see the tiny shoots emerging, curling outward, and growing into hardy plants. When they returned from their eleven-date tour, she hoped the flowers would be all grown up and blooming so she and Kip could sit on the back porch swing and enjoy them. Until then, they had places to go and things to do. She rose, scooped up her mug, and went to the sink to rinse it out. The shower water went on upstairs, and she paused. She set the mug down in the sink and looked at her watch, calculating how much time they had. She grinned to herself.

I'll teach her to surprise me. Let's just see what she says when I catch her off guard in the shower. She laughed out loud, then ran up the stairs, shedding clothes as she went. *Oh yeah. This is going to be fun.*

Available from
Quest Books

Gun Shy

While on patrol, Minnesota police officer Dez Reilly saves two women from a brutal attack. One of them, Jaylynn Savage, is immediately attracted to the taciturn cop—so much so that she joins the St. Paul Police Academy. As fate would have it, Dez is eventually assigned as Jaylynn's Field Training Officer. Having been burned in the past by getting romantically involved with another cop, Dez has a steadfast rule she has abided by for nine years: Cops are off limits. But as Jaylynn and Dez get to know one another, a strong friendship forms. Will Dez break her cardinal rule and take a chance on love with Jaylynn, or will she remain forever gun shy?

Gun Shy is an exciting glimpse into the day-to-day work world of police officers as Jaylynn learns the ins and outs of the job and Dez learns the ins and outs of her own heart.

Second Edition
ISBN: 1-930928-43-2
Available at booksellers everywhere.

Under the Gun

Under the Gun is the long-awaited sequel to the bestselling novel, *Gun Shy*, continuing the story of St. Paul Police Officers Dez Reilly and Jaylynn Savage. Picking up just a couple weeks after *Gun Shy* ended, the sequel finds the two officers continuing to adjust to their relationship, but things start to go downhill when they get dispatched to a double homicide—Jaylynn's first murder scene. Dez is supportive and protective toward Jay, and things seem to be going all right until Dez's nemesis reports their personal relationship, and their commanding officer restricts them from riding together on patrol. This sets off a chain of events that result in Jaylynn getting wounded, Dez being suspended, and both of them having to face the possibility of life without the other. They face struggles—separately and together—that they must work through while truly feeling "under the gun."

ISBN: 1-930928-44-0
Available at booksellers everywhere.

Another Lori L. Lake title
available from
Yellow Rose Books

Ricochet In Time

Hatred is ugly and does bad things to good people, even in the land of "Minnesota Nice" where no one wants to believe discrimination exists. Danielle "Dani" Corbett knows firsthand what hatred can cost. After they suffer a vicious and intentional attack, Dani's girlfriend, Meg O'Donnell, is dead. Dani is left emotionally scarred, and her injuries prevent her from fleeing on her motorcycle. But as one door has closed for her, another opens when she is befriended by Grace Beaumont, a young woman who works as a physical therapist at the hospital. With Grace's friendship and the help of Grace's aunts, Estelline and Ruth, Dani gets through the ordeal of bringing Meg's killer to justice.

Filled with memorable characters, *Ricochet In Time* is the story of one lonely woman's fight for justice—and her struggle to resolve the troubles of her past and find a place in a world where she belongs.

ISBN: 1-930928-64-5
Available at booksellers everywhere.

Coming in November 2003

Stepping Out

Something a little different from novelist Lori L. Lake. Here is a book of short stories written about ordinary people with uncommon—and also universal—problems.

A mother and daughter having an age-old fight. Small children bullied on the playground taking back their power. A father trying to understand his lesbian daughter's retreat from him. A frightened woman attempting to deal with an abusive partner. An athlete who misses her chance—or does she? An elderly couple stalked by an old woman. These stories and more are told in Stepping Out: Stories by Lori Lake.

The collection has been described as a series of mini-novels, with each story being odd and quirky, as though slightly off-kilter at the beginning and regaining stability by the end.

Lori L. Lake lives in the Twin Cities area with her partner of twenty-two years. She worked in government for almost two decades and recently resigned in order to work full-time at writing, teaching, and reviewing. She is an avid reader, loves to sing, play guitar and banjo, and enjoys movies, weightlifting, and all the kids in her life. Lori worked at writing short stories for over a decade, only discovering her knack for writing novels in her 30s. It took her several years to find a publisher, and she continually advises other writers never to give up.

Different Dress is Lori's fourth novel. *Ricochet in Time* came first, then *Gun Shy*, which was the first book in the "Gun" series, and *Under The Gun,* the sequel to *Gun Shy.* Her fifth book, *Stepping Out: Stories by Lori L. Lake* (formerly titled *Jumping Over My Head*) will be published in late 2003. She is at work on her next three novels, a WWII story called *Snow Moon Rising*, a post-apocalyptic action adventure tentatively entitled *Isolation 2020,* and *Missing Link,* which is a coming out story about an 18-year-old high school basketball player. She hopes to start the third "Gun" book before too long as well as a mainstream mystery.

Lori very much likes to hear from her readers. You may write her at Lori@LoriLLake.com. Further information about her can be found at her website: http://www.LoriLLake.com.